The GREAT PURSUIT

The GREAT PURSUIT

BOOK TWO OF THE
EURONA DUOLOGY

Wendy Higgins

An Imprint of HarperCollinsPublishers

HarperTeen is an imprint of HarperCollins Publishers.

The Great Pursuit

www.epicreads.com

Library of Congress Control Number: 2016949971
ISBN 978-0-06-238136-1

Typography by Carla Weise
17 18 19 20 21 PC/LSCH 10 9 8 7 6 5 4 3 2 1
❖
First Edition

To Danny and Jeff

You're bigger than me, but you'll always be my baby brothers

KINGDOMS OF EURONA AND THEIR RULERS

LOCHLANACH, THE WATERLANDS,
King Charles and Queen Leighlane Lochson

ASCOMANNI, THE COLDLANDS,
King Dagur and Queen Agnetha Vikani

TORESTA, THE RIDGELANDS,
King Gavriil and Queen Lavrenty Cliftonia

ZORFINA, THE DRYLANDS,
King Addar and Queen Meira Zandbur

KALOR, THE HOTLANDS,
Prince Vito Kalieno

LOCHLANACH ROYAL FAMILY

KING CHARLES AND QUEEN LEIGHLANE LOCHSON

Princess Aerity (17)

Princess Vixie (15)

Prince Donubhan (10)

LORD PRESTON AND LADY ASHLEY WAVECREST (YOUNGER SISTER TO THE KING)

Lady Wyneth (18)

Master Bowen (14)

Master Brixton (12)

Master Wyatt (9)

LORD JAMES AND LADY FAITH BAYCREEK (YOUNGEST SISTER TO THE KING)

Master Leo (12)

Lady Caileen (8)

Lady Merity (6)

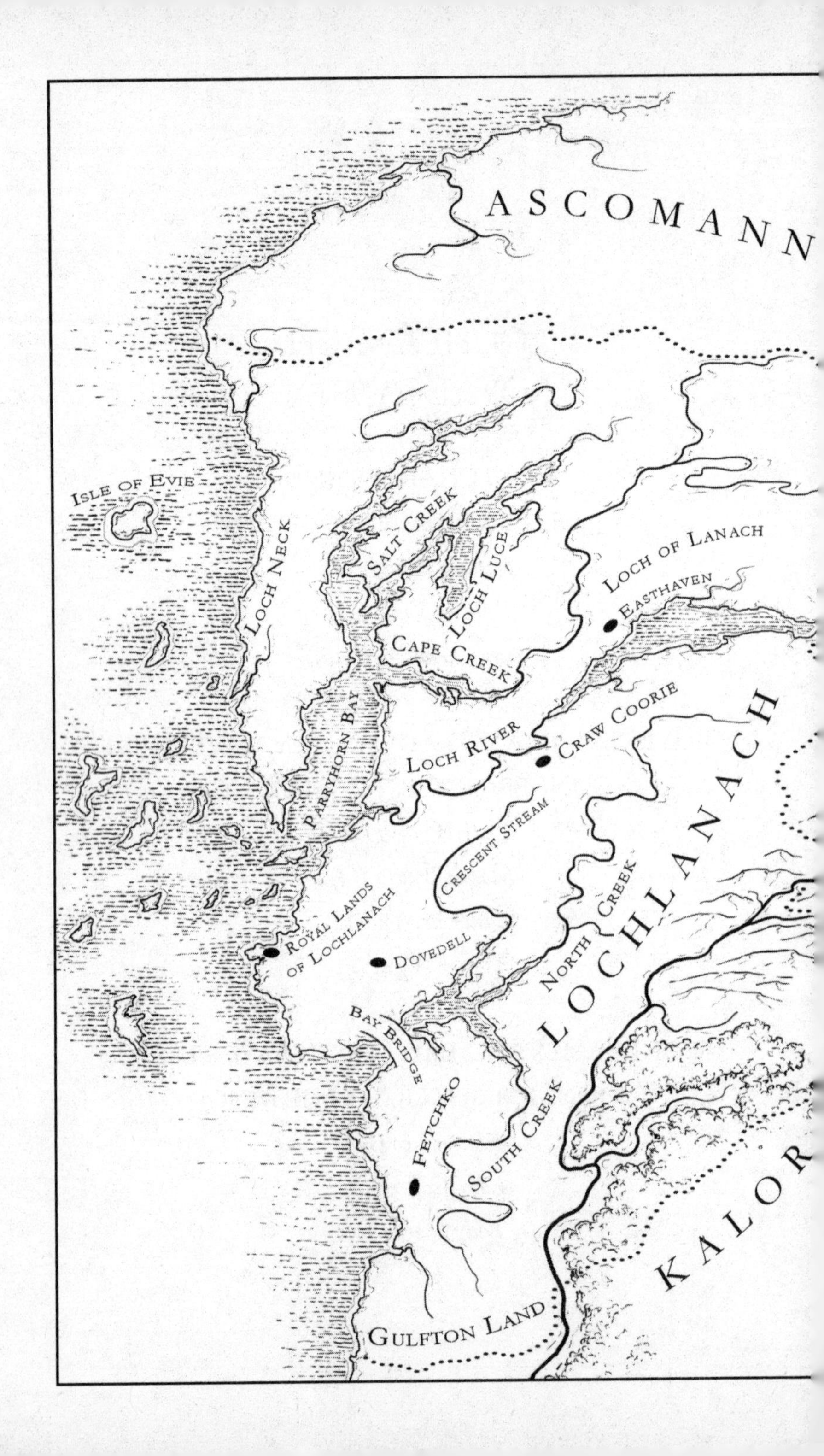
ASCOMANN
Isle of Evie
Loch Neck
Salt Creek
Loch Luce
Loch of Lanach
Easthaven
Cape Creek
Parryhorn Bay
Loch River
Craw Coorie
Crescent Stream
Royal Lands of Lochlanach
Dovedell
North Creek
LOCHLANACH
Bay Bridge
Fetchko
South Creek
KALOR
Gulfton Land

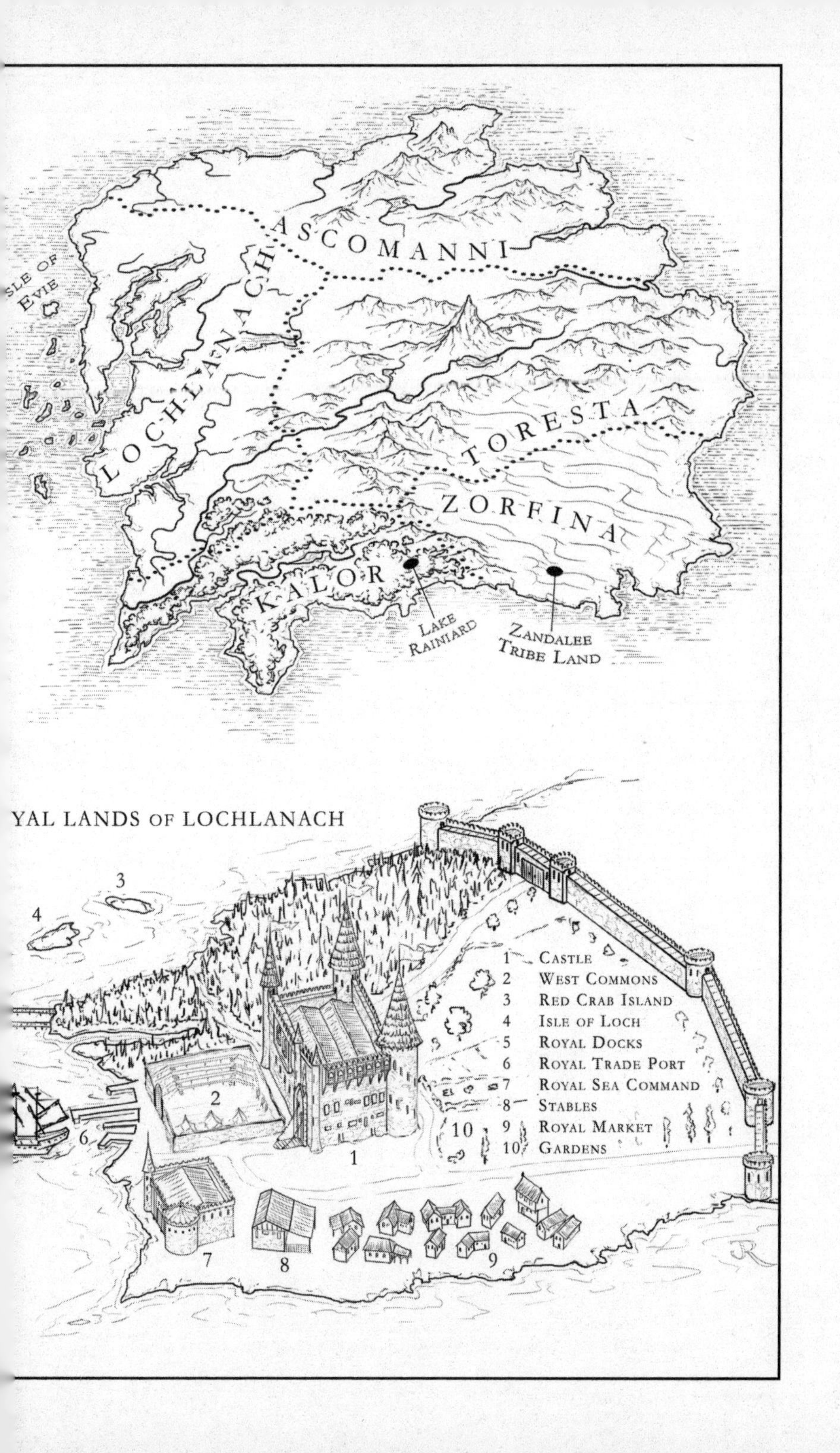
SLE OF
EVIE
ASCOMANNI
LOCHLANACH
TORESTA
ZORFINA
KALOR
LAKE
RAINIARD
ZANDALEE
TRIBE LAND
YAL LANDS OF LOCHLANACH
1 CASTLE
2 WEST COMMONS
3 RED CRAB ISLAND
4 ISLE OF LOCH
5 ROYAL DOCKS
6 ROYAL TRADE PORT
7 ROYAL SEA COMMAND
8 STABLES
9 ROYAL MARKET
10 GARDENS

Chapter 1

A new beast roamed the kingdom of Lochlanach, killing at will. A second unnatural monster created by the hands of Rozaria Rocato, granddaughter of the most infamous and hated Lashed One of all time.

Princess Aerity Lochson's mind was a blur of piled-up worries as she rushed from High Hall of the castle, away from the frightened commoners and guests who'd come for her betrothal ceremony, and toward the office of her father, King Charles. She turned at the sound of heavy footsteps behind her and found both her childhood friend Lieutenant Harrison Gillfin and her betrothed, Lord Lief Alvi, following. Lord Alvi looked every bit the hero—his broad stature striking, with elk furs about his shoulders and a black kilt to his knees above leather boots. His blue eyes were filled with bright passion and hunger, but those emotions were not for her. They were for the beast. The new hunt.

He had killed the first creature, thereby earning her hand in marriage. The thought twisted Aerity's stomach with discomfort and turned her mind to the man who'd disappeared weeks before when the beast was killed—the Lashed man who'd taken her heart with him and would likely never return. She clenched her jaw. This was no time to think of Paxton Seabolt or her drowned desires. The kingdom was suffering again—rendering everything she'd sacrificed to have been in vain.

Her eyes shifted from Lord Alvi's to Harrison's and found a fierce, protective comfort there. Harrison stood tall, lean, and capable. Never faltering. The thought of her noble friend fighting yet another beast filled her with sharp fear. So many lives had already been lost, including Harrison's cousin Breckon, who'd been the true love of Aerity's cousin Wyneth. Half a year was all it had taken to trample the dreams and futures of so many.

Aerity gave the men a nod to follow her. She lifted her long white skirts and moved quickly down the tapestry-lined hallway to her father's office. Guards and soldiers ran past, shouting orders, fully armed with bows, swords, and lines of throwing daggers strapped across their uniformed tunics.

She opened the door without knocking. No fewer than twenty faces shot toward her. She recognized the burgundy red hair of her mother, along with her aunts and uncles, military elite, and royal advisers. Her father invited them in with a quick flick of his fingers.

When the door closed he asked her, "What is the state of things in High Hall?"

"The people seemed to have calmed for the moment, Father," Aerity said. "And supper is being served."

"Your daughter gave a rousing speech," Lord Alvi proclaimed in his rumbling voice. "She is to thank for the calm."

Aerity's face flushed with heat at the unexpected compliment. Then he put a heavy hand on her shoulder and pulled her close. Aerity fought the urge to shrug away. For the sake of the kingdom, she had made a commitment to become his bride, and she would follow through regardless of what her heart wanted, and regardless of the fact that she was certain feelings had grown between Lief and Wyneth.

"Did she?" The king's eyes softened with pride, and her mother, Queen Leighlane, smiled at Aerity and Lief, no doubt thinking what a lovely couple they were. If she only knew.

Behind them Harrison cleared his throat. "Are we to begin hunting the creature, Your Majesty?"

King Charles nodded, his face lined with anxiety. "Aye. But most of the hunters have dispersed." *Or been killed*, Aerity thought with sorrow, remembering the men who'd come from all over Eurona and even a huntress who'd lost her life.

"I can have a message sent to Tiern Seabolt," Harrison said. "I'm certain he would return with haste."

Aerity's abdomen tightened. Tiern was Paxton's younger brother. He'd nearly been killed by the first beast and had been saved by Paxton's Lashed magic. It was the very reason Pax had fled the kingdom—using magic was illegal, even to heal. Aerity didn't want Tiern to hunt again. She didn't want Paxton's sacrifice to have been a waste.

"And his older brother?" the king asked.

"Nay." Harrison paused. "He disappeared after the hunt. We don't know his whereabouts."

"Must you call Tiern back?" Aerity asked. When her father's eyebrows drew together she emended, "He's . . . so young."

"He's the same age as you, Daughter," the king reminded her. "Seventeen. A man who's already proven himself in the hunt." Aerity pressed her lips together and nodded. She could not keep Tiern safe any more than she could force Harrison to stay out of harm's reach. Their heroic hearts would urge them forward.

"Can we send word to the Zandalee?" Aerity's uncle Lord Wavecrest asked.

The king shook his head. "I'm afraid not this time. The letter from the Rocato woman stated that her creatures have now been released in all the lands of Eurona. The Zandalee will be needed to fight in their own drylands of Zorfina."

A fearful silence fell over the room. Each kingdom was on its own with its own beasts to battle now. Lochlanach was a quaint kingdom of fishermen and crop villagers, farmers, that had enjoyed many years of peace. The people had risen together to fight the first beast, but how much more could the king expect from them? It was too much. To imagine this kind of horror inflicted on innocent people all over Eurona sickened Aerity.

"Perhaps another proclamation?" Lord Wavecrest suggested carefully. At this proposal from Aerity's uncle, the men in the room glanced around at one another, and the hairs rose on the princess's arms. The queen caught her daughter's eyes, and they both went still.

The last proclamation had offered Aerity's hand in marriage to whoever killed the beast. The only thing left to give was the second princess, Aerity's fifteen-year-old sister, Vixie. Her father stared down at his desk.

"No." Aerity stepped forward, out of Lord Alvi's embrace, her body trembling. "You cannot offer Vixie's hand."

The king's hazel eyes, filled with regret, rose to hers. "I have nothing left to give." With Vixie's hand would come her dowry of lands. Using Vixie as a prize would surely smother her soul. Aerity wouldn't stand for it.

"And why should you oppose it?" her uncle Preston asked haughtily. "The first proclamation provided you with a fine match. It can do the same for Vixie."

Aerity stilled, forcing back the torrent of words that flooded her mind: *unfair, poor match, confinement, no joy, no love.* She was to endure those things for her kingdom, but the thought of Vixie losing her freedom to choose her future . . .

it gutted Aerity. She knew how it appeared to the world—that she'd landed a handsome, noble, brave lord—but the heart didn't care about appearances. It wanted who it wanted.

"And then what?" Aerity asked. "Who shall we offer for the next beast, and the one after that? Your own Wyneth? Or perhaps six-year-old Merity?"

Lord Wavecrest scowled.

"Enough, Aerity," Queen Leighlane said quietly. Aerity met her mother's eyes and felt an understanding there. No one knew better than the two of them how this would crush Vixie's spirit. These men couldn't possibly understand.

"Vixie's nearly sixteen," Lord Wavecrest pressed. Aerity wanted to claw out his eyes and force him to stop speaking.

"A proclamation offering Vixie's hand will be my very last resort," King Charles said, standing taller. "It is my hope that the people will rise of their own free will to protect their families and lands as they did in the last hunt. I will not hinder them with further curfews."

Lord Wavecrest shook his head and crossed his arms. Aerity breathed a temporary sigh of relief.

"Sire, we should address the *other* part of the Rocato woman's letter." This was from the king's oldest adviser, Duke Gulfton. This duke had been the closest adviser to Aerity's grandfather King Leon. His views on the Lashed were legendarily conservative and strict, and he was a proponent of keeping the Lashed lists up to date. All persons with Lashed capabilities and their families were notated in the records and checked regularly for markings.

The stooped man wore a sea-green robe around his shoulders and a perpetual serious frown on his face. He leaned on his cane. "We cannot do as the Rocato woman demands. We cannot burn our records of Lashed Ones in these lands, or give them rein to take over our kingdom."

A few of the other older men murmured their agreement.

Harrison stepped forward. "What if we made a copy of the list? Then it wouldn't matter if one was destroyed."

"I've got scribes copying pages as we speak," the king responded. "But the Rocato woman has called for the records to be burned by sundown. The copy won't be complete. There are thousands of names."

Thousands of persons with Lashed blood in Lochlanach. *Amazing*, Aerity thought. Only a small percentage of those on the list actually had magic, though. Paxton's family was not on the list. Aerity wondered how many others of magical blood had been able to elude the system.

"How will the madwoman know the difference?" Duke Gulfton asked. "Burn papers to appease her, then kill her and her monsters once and for all. End of story."

"Here, here!" a few men shouted, as if it were that simple. As if they wouldn't have done it by now if they could.

The king's jaw was set. "I have a terrible feeling this woman has eyes and ears everywhere."

The room quieted and a sense of unease spread as heads turned and everyone eyed the others present. Her father's council was a small group of family and a mere handful of wise advisers, all landowners, who'd been loyal to the kingdom since her grandfather ruled. She couldn't imagine this group being compromised.

"With all due respect, gentlemen," Lord Alvi said to the room, "we will find every beast and even Rocato herself, but we cannot guarantee immediate success. The last hunt took two months."

"Aye," Harrison added. "And she's threatening to kill seven men each week."

"You'll have to work faster this time," Duke Gulfton told them.

The room tensed. During the last hunt they'd had a hundred men. They'd sought the monster nearly ten hours a night and spent the days scouting and preparing. The lands of Lochlanach stretched far and wide. Yet people like Duke Gulfton were expecting a miracle of the sea.

Queen Leighlane cleared her throat. "The fact of the matter is that we're going to have to at least put on a show of honoring her wishes. We need to buy time as we plan."

Another elder, Duke Streamson, asked, "What are you proposing, Your Highness? Rocato is demanding that all Lashed be allowed to freely work magic."

Magic that wasn't all *bad*, Aerity thought. Magic that had saved Tiern and could save others. If only she could get them to embrace that.

"I have an idea." Aerity's brain whirred as all eyes turned

to her. "What if we set up a public area just outside the royal lands and invited Lashed from throughout the kingdom to come, and any Unlashed who wishes to seek their healing can receive it?"

Duke Streamson made a choking sound. "Round up the people of Rocato to turn against us in one place? That's precisely what she wants!"

Aerity rushed on. "I don't believe all Lashed are 'her people.' The entire area would be heavily guarded so that if any Lashed got out of line, they could be dealt with immediately." The old dukes scoffed at her.

One of the military advisers stepped forward. "Our numbers are not as large as they once were. Our troop sizes have been modest in the past fifty years. I've got to keep men patrolling the seas and borders, and we've lost many in the past months. I worry that a large-scale showing of the Lashed will bring crowds."

The room broke out into fervent debate. Those who were against Aerity's idea were adamant, passionate in their fears. Those in favor seemed on weak, shaky ground.

"Given permission to put their hands on innocent people, it could be a massacre!"

"What if the Lashed overwhelm our guards?"

"They'll rise up throughout the lands!"

". . . commoner revolts . . . war . . ."

Aerity felt a hand on her shoulder and turned to see Harrison, his light brown eyes showing the never-faltering respect he seemed to hold for her. She gave his hand a quick squeeze of gratitude before he released her. Aerity caught Lord Alvi watching the exchange with curiosity, so she turned her gaze forward again—she would let him think what he wanted.

"Enough!" King Charles's voice silenced the room. "I will think on it. I must put safety first. I'm not ready to overturn our laws—" Aerity opened her mouth to argue that she wasn't suggesting a complete overturn, but a one-time, enclosed, secure circumstance. Her father held up a hand to stop her. "This blasted parchment from Rozaria Rocato is bound to have our people in terror. If I take the stability of our rules away, it will cause chaos. Tonight on the lawn we will burn whatever pages my scribes have managed to copy, to keep Rozaria satisfied, but the original lists remain with us. I pray to the sea this works."

He looked at the hunters. "Lord Alvi. Lieutenant Gillfin. Gather as many hunters as you can and begin hunting this new beast immediately." They nodded and took their leave. Aerity watched them go, swallowing a dry lump in her throat. The king looked to his military advisers. "I want every soldier on duty, and round-the-clock patrolling of royal lands. I want Rozaria Rocato, dead or alive." He turned to his top castle guard. "Send messengers to the other four lands to let them know of our new foe and to find out their circumstances."

Without another word, the king swept from the room with Queen Leighlane and a line of advisers close behind.

Aerity felt the brush of velvet on her arm and peered

down at the old man beside her. It was Duke Gulfton, his eyes glistening. "I mean no disrespect, Princess, only a piece of advice. In times of fear and upheaval, absolute routine and stability in the law are called for. Any slight change can set the people off."

"As I recall," Aerity said steadily, "Mrs. Rathbrook healed your ailing heart last year." Mrs. Rathbrook was the royal healer—the only Lashed allowed to work magic.

He grasped the top of his cane with both hands. "Aye."

"Should we not allow the people of this land to benefit from magic as you have?"

He looked down at his hands, nodding solemnly. "Not all Lashed are as trustworthy as Mrs. Rathbrook. You saw the Rocato woman face-to-face. You know the evil of which she is capable."

"I suppose everyone is capable of evil, Duke Gulfton. None of us is immune, Lashed or not. But I choose to believe the best in people until they show me otherwise."

Duke Streamson, waiting in the doorway, cleared his throat. Duke Gulfton peered up at Aerity and patted her hand. "Once they show you otherwise, it is often too late. As a rule it is not safe to take such chances. Seas help Lochlanach in our time of need."

As Duke Gulfton shuffled away, Aerity whispered in return. "Seas help us, indeed."

Chapter 2

Lady Wyneth waited outside the king's office with a bow across her back. Something inside her had changed, had grown and hardened like a grain of sand into a stony pearl. Perhaps it was being face-to-face with Rozaria Rocato and her beast on the Isle of Loch, certain she would not survive. Or perhaps it was her wreck of a life. In the past season she had lost her beloved betrothed, and soon after gained the affections of another. And now that man was to marry her cousin. Wyneth looked down at her gray gown, the mourning color she still wore for Breckon, and she experienced yet another stab of guilt.

She'd watched in High Hall as Aerity and Lord Alvi held hands, a striking couple, and addressed the frightened people.

The very strength of their partnership had seemed to calm the masses. A strong, handsome warrior from the coldlands and Lochlanach's own cherished princess. Though it twisted Wyneth's insides with unwarranted jealousy and sadness, she knew that what was done was done. It was good for the kingdom in many ways, and she would not stand in the way. Her hope was that the two would come to love each other and that her own feelings would fade into a distant memory, so far away that they couldn't hurt her anymore.

The heavy door swung open, startling Wyneth, and two men rushed out, on a mission. Wyneth's heart dropped into her stomach at the sight of Lord Alvi's and Lieutenant Gillfin's serious faces. They both stopped in their tracks when they saw her, their fierce eyes softening a fraction. Wyneth dragged her gaze from Lief's to Harrison's, and a familiar ease filled her. Harrison—so like his cousin Breckon and yet so different.

"Another hunt is to begin," Harrison told her.

A wild urge overcame Wyneth. She bent and grasped her skirts. "I am coming."

Harrison's brow furrowed, and Lief stepped closer. Wyneth kept her eyes on Harrison. It was easier that way.

"Don't be absurd, Wyn," Harrison said gently. "Stay in the castle where you're safe."

Wyneth knew she was being stupid. She was soft and frail in every way, and could barely hit a target with an arrow. Yet she also knew her cousin Aerity had played a hand in killing the first beast, while she herself had swum for help. "They listen to a woman's command. Don't you recall?"

"That was the first beast," Lord Alvi said. Wyneth still could not look at him. "We don't know if this new creature will be the same."

True. But she had nothing to lose. If there was even a slight chance she could be of help, she would. Harrison tilted his head and studied her. She tipped up her chin, not backing down, and he gave a small grin and shake of his head.

"She's got her mind set," he told Lief.

"I will ready my horse," Wyneth told them. She walked swiftly past the men and heard Lief make sounds of exasperation as they rushed to catch up. She couldn't explain the fire of recklessness awakened in her heart. She'd felt so helpless and terrified when Breckon was killed, and again when trapped on the island between the first beast and Rozaria Rocato. She was tired of feeling weak. "Do your jobs and pay me no mind."

When Lord Alvi appeared ready to argue, Harrison said, "Perhaps we should see if she's right about being able to command the beast." Harrison turned a warm gaze her way, making Wyneth's chest bloom with pride at his confidence in her. "But you cannot make any sudden moves, my lady. Remain with us at all times."

"Lady Wyneth." Lord Alvi grasped Wyneth's hand and she yanked it away.

"Don't touch me!" she shouted. "Please . . ."

Lord Alvi's arm fell to his side. She finally looked at him, and as they locked eyes, she felt that heaviness inside her transferring to him. Her heart beat erratically and her breaths were short. Beside them, Harrison's jaw clenched. She knew he wanted to say something more but held back.

Wyneth spun and moved forward again, her eyes stinging, a sickening lump in her throat. The men said nothing else and did not try to stop her again. When they got to the doors, one of the guards eyed her and opened his mouth as if to protest, but Harrison spoke up. "Lady Wyneth is with us."

A blustering sea wind blew Wyneth's red curls and made her squint as she bounded down the steps and onto the cobblestoned path. Clusters of armed guards and soldiers stood poring over maps, discussing, pointing. Wyneth looked toward the eerily desolate market and shivered. At this time of day it was usually bustling.

Harrison stopped to talk to the soldiers and she heard him mention Tiern Seabolt. Was the lad to return? That should make Princess Vixie happy. She'd been quiet and forlorn since he'd returned home to Cape Creek after the hunt.

Wyneth headed left toward the market. The path turned from smooth stones to pebbles and crushed shells, then to dust and hay as they reached the stables. Her legs burned from walking so fast.

Happiness filled Wyneth at the sight of her bay, Mosby. She cooed softly as she opened his stall, and took a moment to pat his brown coat and run a hand down his black mane. "Don't be afraid today, boy," Wyneth whispered. She didn't know what was in store for them, but it sounded as if the new beast was land dwelling. How that madwoman Rozaria was able to get it onto royal lands was a mystery. She most likely had people working for her, villagers who she'd bribed or threatened.

Wyneth became very aware of Lord Alvi several stalls down; he was too loud to be missed. She had no idea how he could be stealthy on a hunt when his very masculinity rang out every time he came near: grunts as he worked, his hulking footsteps on the beaten soil, his deep humming voice as he spoke to his horse. Wyneth swallowed hard.

They led their horses out at the same time, and found Harrison waiting for them on his military steed. Wyneth and Lord Alvi mounted, Wyneth hiking her skirts up to her knees.

Harrison stared at her with his serious dark eyes before quietly sighing. "The beast disappeared into the north forests. It'll be blocked by the royal walls and the seas, so unless the bloody thing can fly, it'll still be in there."

Lord Alvi gave an ill-humored laugh. "Are any of your men to accompany us?"

"Aye. A dozen will flank us, in an arc, with bows and swords at the ready. I've ordered them not to advance unless you or I are wounded."

Both men looked at Wyneth, who sat up taller, jutting out her chin to ward off any last-minute orders for her to stay behind. "Let's go, then."

"Your father will have my hide for this," Harrison told her.

"I'm of age. Even he cannot stop me."

"You don't have to do this, Lady Wyneth," Lord Alvi said.

Wyneth dug her heels into her horse and he jumped forward. "Neither do you," she called over her shoulder.

"You have nothing to prove!" he hollered from behind her.

"Neither do you!" she yelled back.

Harrison caught up, and they galloped side by side in silence. A dozen soldiers on horseback crested a hill and followed. As they passed the west commons and neared the forest, Lord Alvi sped up to Wyneth's other side. The three slowed their pace and eyed the trees, then the men scanned the ground.

"There." Harrison pointed to a spot of slightly uprooted dry grass where it looked as if hooves had dug in.

Their horses moved at a slow pace, the hunters easily following a path made by the creature. The farther they got into the woods, the quieter and more shaded it became. Wyneth's heart thumped too loudly and she found herself holding her breath. Her senses became keenly sensitive to each snapping twig and rustling leaf. Her eyes swiveled from side to side. A wild bush to the left looked funny to her, lopsided as if it'd been trampled. She pointed to it and the men nodded, changing their direction.

"Good eye," Harrison whispered. Wyneth felt a small bubble of pride.

They traveled on, led by barely discernible clues, until Wyneth could see the high stone walls signaling the border of royal lands. Where was the creature?

All at once the three of them stopped as they sighted movement near the wall. Wyneth's ears buzzed as she heard a far-off shuffle of hooves, followed by a low, gurgling growl. Her eyes focused and pinpointed through the trees a large, reddish-brown body with a greenish head.

Deep seas . . .

Slowly, Harrison moved his arms behind his back, opened his hands wide, and pulled them apart. It must have been some sort of "spread out" command for his soldiers because she heard shifting behind her and in her peripheral vision she saw horsemen closing in on the beast.

Wyneth's heart was in her throat. Harrison and Lord Alvi moved ahead slowly. No sudden movements. As they neared, the creature made a hissing-growl sound and began to stamp the ground in agitation with a front hoof. Wyneth suddenly wished she had a more substantial weapon than a bow, a sword perhaps, but only the most well-trained soldiers carried swords.

The closer they got, the more detail Wyneth could make out. The head was that of a marsh reptile—an elongated jaw with rows of gleaming sharp teeth. The neck was strong, like a horse's, but scales traveled down to its forequarters, where it became a mash-up of smooth fur and patches of scales. Wyneth stared in horror at what Rozaria Rocato had constructed with her magic. How could a person's mind work in such a way? She tried to imagine what these poor animals had been through, to be kept alive as they were cut into parts and pieced back together, then forced to grow and expand unnaturally.

At twenty paces away, Wyneth's horse's nostrils flared and his head whipped from side to side. She'd only seen him behave this way once before, when they happened upon a coiled snake. She should have anticipated her horse's fear. Before things could get any worse, Wyneth gently slid from his back and gave him a pat on the rump, sending him lumbering back toward the stables.

This had been a mistake. The beast did not wait to see what would happen next. It charged.

Lord Alvi's arrow was pointed before Wyneth could take a breath, but the beast wove behind a stand of trees.

"*Stop!*" Wyneth yelled in Kalorian as the beast burst out from behind the trees. It reared up, obeying her with reluctance, and Lord Alvi let his arrow fly. The arrowhead shallowly pricked the thick skin at the beast's chest and fell out as the animal came back down hard on its front hooves.

Harrison and Lord Alvi jumped from their horses. Harrison, quick and agile, got to it first and dodged to the side as the beast snapped its reptilian teeth, just missing him. Wyneth gasped.

"No!" She searched her Kalorian vocabulary, wishing she were as adept as Aerity.

While Harrison distracted it, Lord Alvi shot another

arrow. Wyneth was certain his arrows were flying with great strength, but the beast's skin was extremely thick, allowing only minor flesh wounds. Lord Alvi swore.

Wyneth fumbled for her own bow and an arrow from over her shoulder, nocking the arrow and pulling the bowstring tight. The beast heaved forward and flung its long head upward, catching Lord Alvi by surprise and knocking his bow away, before turning back to Harrison, who slashed with his sword, slicing upward against a line of scales at the creature's chest. It reared and let out a shrieking whinny of pain. Wyneth finally recalled a Kalorian phrase. "*Be still!*"

The monster stopped, leaning back on its haunches, but stretched its mouth wide in a growl of pain and frustration. It appeared torn between its obligation of obedience and its instinct to kill. With a yell, Wyneth released her hold on the taut bowstring and watched in shock as her arrow lodged itself in the roof of the creature's mouth. It came down hard on its front legs, thrashing.

Lord Alvi leaped on its back to hold it down and Harrison used all his power to thrust his sword deep into the soft spot where its chest met its front leg. Wyneth saw blood and felt an uprising of pity and remorse as the beast let out a high whine, kicking out as it fell. It seemed to convulse forever before going still.

Wyneth went to her knees, shaking, and dropped her bow. All around her she saw soldiers on their feet. They'd circled close during the fight and she hadn't noticed. The men surrounded the monster, tying it with ropes, led by Lord Alvi.

She felt capable arms gathering her close, lifting her to her feet. "Come, Wyn," Harrison said softly. "Take my horse." She was in a daze as Harrison helped her mount. All she could see was blood. So much blood and death.

As he was about to send her on her way, she grasped his hand and looked into his forlorn eyes.

"Don't leave me," she whispered.

Harrison's entire body seemed to shiver with surprise as he stared up at her. He glanced back at the busy soldiers and called out. "I'm taking Lady Wyneth back to the castle. I will let them know the grounds are safe for now."

Lord Alvi narrowed his eyes at Harrison from where he tied the end of the rope to his steed. Before he could say anything, the lieutenant pulled himself up behind Wyneth and pressed his heels into the horse's sides. His free hand went around Wyneth's waist. She was shaking uncontrollably. Her hands took his wrist and pulled his arm tighter around her. He felt so safe.

"Must they drag the creature?" Wyneth asked. "It's shameful."

"It is too large to carry. And it killed people, Wyn," he reminded her.

"It's a victim in all of this. It can't help being made." She recalled its suffering as they killed it—the role she had played in bringing it pain—and a sob rose up in her throat.

Harrison pulled her closer, pressing her back to his chest.

She could feel his breath at her ear. "Some things cannot be reformed or redeemed, sweet Wyn. That creature . . . it could not be tamed into a pet or kept alive for pity's sake. It *had* to be killed. It's out of its misery now."

She leaned her head back onto his shoulder and shut her eyes. "I won't try to accompany you on any more hunts." She was useless. She couldn't even help kill a foe without feeling sorry for it.

Harrison's voice was as steady as always. "You were brave. And I'm glad your heart is still so tender after all you've been through. I'm proud of you . . . and Breckon would be too."

With those words, Wyneth allowed her tears to run freely.

Chapter 3

In order to get to the drylands where the Zandalee tribe lived, they had to pass through hotlands jungles. Paxton wasn't a fearful man, but being in the jungle did not put him at ease—he wasn't particularly fond of the giant bugs that insisted on taking chunks out of his skin while he slept, or the rattling of overgrown snakes that he knew were near. It did, however, help his frame of mind to be surrounded by warrior women who seemed to fear nothing and never complained.

It was early morning, and though the temperature was not necessarily hot yet, a layer of moisture permeated the air at all times, stagnant and humid. Oversized birds cawed their loud screeches in the overhanging branches as the Zandalee fed their sleek black stallions. Paxton packed the last of their things and then stood, pushing his hair off his damp forehead.

He'd lost track of time. How long had they been traveling? A week? Two? Time no longer mattered to him. Days ago he'd asked the Zandalee leader, Zandora, how they'd made it to Lochlanach so quickly for the hunt when the trip back to their home seemed to be taking so long. She'd wryly responded, "We did not have a man to haul along with us."

Aye, he'd become accustomed to their humor and the jabs at his gender. And he thought perhaps they were taking him on the scenic route, attempting to ease his dark mood before dumping him on their tribe.

By now they must have realized his temperament was here to stay, because in the last day or so they'd picked up the pace. The jungle seemed to be thinning. Fewer roots to step over and vines to wade through amid sinking mud spots. The only ones who seemed to dislike the jungle more than Paxton were the horses.

He opted to walk today rather than share a saddle with the younger of the sisters, who wasn't at all shy and enjoyed the nearness of a man very much. Zandora had said, "She tells us she prefers your brother, Tiern, but you'll do in a pinch."

"Isn't she newly married?" Paxton had asked.

"Oh, *jes*. And she would slice off your fingers if you tried to return her advances. Zaleek only likes to play." Zandora had winked.

Seas almighty, these Zandalee women. In truth, though,

he appreciated them. And he was glad for the distraction of their company. The last thing he needed was to be left alone with his thoughts.

By midday the sun was glaring, and the moisture of the air was overpowering. He sorely missed the cool breezes of Lochlanach. It was early winter there. He'd be able to see his breath in the morning air while hunting. . . .

Paxton shook the thought away.

They trudged for hours, chewing venison jerky from Paxton's stores, the only respite coming when the three Zandalee would raise their voices in a tribal song, harmonizing and keeping the beat with one hand smacking their thighs. Their voices rang like jewels, vibrant and clear. Paxton let it soothe him as the sun lowered, another day gone.

As they pushed through a mass of leaves as large as two hand spans, Paxton heard a distant noise and stopped, holding up a fist. The Zandalee halted their horses, and the four of them surveyed the area.

Muted voices sounded from ahead. The youngest Zandalee pointed upward at a thin plume of smoke rising in the hazy sky above the trees.

"We are not far from the Zorfina border now," Zandora whispered, her brow furrowed in suspicion. "I do not know of any Kalorian tribes near Rainiard after the slaughters."

"This is Lake Rainiard?" Paxton asked. His grandmother's words about the rumors of safety for Lashed at Lake Rainiard came rushing back to him. A place of freedom that may or may not have been a myth. "What slaughters?"

"It is said that the last act of King Kalieno before he became ill was to have all the inhabitants surrounding Rainiard killed. He wished to silence the rumors of Lashed safe havens in his kingdom once and for all."

"Deep seas," Paxton muttered, his chest tight.

The middle sister, Zula, whispered something in Zorfinan and Zandora nodded. "Tribes always have scouts placed along the borders of their territories, but there are none here." Her eyes grazed the trees.

"Perhaps these are only travelers," Paxton guessed. "Gypsies. We can go around them."

Zandora shook her head. "I am bored. Let us approach. Perhaps we can find someone to fight."

A breath of laughter huffed quietly out of Paxton's nose as he shouldered his pack and bow. In truth, a fight with strangers didn't sound like a bad idea to him either.

They approached the clearing and watched from behind the trees. Paxton counted seven people milling about, ranging from a young girl to two middle-aged men. They were doing everything from cooking and scrubbing laundry to playing cards of some sort. Two of the men had the smooth, shaved heads of Torestans and olive skin. Their garments were threadbare. Three horses were tied under a thatched stall of sorts. Definitely travelers from afar.

A structure stood nearby, two stories high with a watchtower of sorts on a third level. The rock and mud masonry appeared beaten, chunks missing and broken, as if the building had been through a war. Beyond the structure was a wide lake, so still the surface reflected the grayish sky. Near the people were three tents propped open.

"I'll approach first," Paxton offered. He touched his bow and felt for the arrows in his quiver before stepping out of the trees. The moment he entered the clearing all eyes snapped to him. All three men and two lads jumped to their feet. A sudden zap of something in the air buzzed warmly across Paxton's skin.

They were Lashed, like him. He could feel their energy. He slowly raised the palms of his hands to show peace and began walking forward again. One of the men grabbed a wooden club and the other reached for a bow. Paxton turned his hands around to show his nails. His heart was pounding as he got close enough for the people to see the purple lines that ran through the middle and bottoms of his nails—lashed marks from when he'd started fires for warmth and to cook food, and to heal his brother. The people seemed to relax a fraction, but they didn't move.

"My name is Paxton Seabolt, and I'm traveling through with my three companions to the drylands of Zorfina. We mean no harm." He couldn't help but look toward the hands of the men, thrilling to see purple lines on two of them as well.

"You sound Lochlan," the older of the men said with distrust. His Euronan was choppy. Torestans were known for not speaking Euronan, just as most Lochlans did not speak Torestan.

"I am . . . formerly Lochlan," Paxton said, "but no longer."

"Because you are Lashed?" The shorter man ran a hand over his smooth head.

Paxton nodded, feeling that pit of loss stir deep within him.

The travelers had all come forward now, and their eyes grew wide as they looked past Paxton. The Zandalee had entered the clearing on their horses.

"They are friends of the Lashed," Paxton explained. "Women of the Zandalee tribe."

The travelers all gasped and stared, whispering. The warrior women were a sight in their fitted black leathers with black head scarves, their blue eyes bright against dark skin. As the Zandalee approached and dismounted, Paxton introduced them.

"This is their leader, Zandora; her middle sister, Zula; and the youngest sister, Zaleek. The younger two only speak Zorfinan."

The huntresses eyed the people and their camp in full before nodding. Zandora seemed disappointed that nobody wanted to fight.

"We are three families," the Torestan man said. "Two from Toresta and one from Eastern Lochlanach near our borders." He pointed to a man with a mop of stringy brown hair and gaunt cheeks. "My name is Chun Aval. I worked as King Gavriil's chef until I did magic to save my daughter from a severe burn in the kitchens. It was then, as we packed to flee, that my brother also admitted one of his sons is Lashed. We left in the night without a word and found this Lochlan on the path, facedown and near starvation. He had been beaten. We could not leave him when we saw his lash marks."

The Lochlan man put his hands behind his back, as if on instinct, and stared down at the ground.

So, this man Chun had worked for the royalty—that explained he and his family's language education.

Chun introduced them to everyone in their group: his wife, daughter, brother, and two nephews. Only Chun, his nephew, and the Lochlan man were Lashed. Paxton set down his pack and joined the men sitting on fallen logs while the Zandalee went to explore the lake.

"What brought you to Kalor?" Paxton asked.

"Rumor of Prince Vito's Lashed sympathies," Chun said. "Our king and leaders in Toresta do not trust the prince, so I wondered. And it has been true. Twice on our journey we encountered Kalorian tribes who let us be when they saw our markings. Some even traded goods to have their tribesmen healed of various ailments. Each time they pointed south and told us, Lake Rainiard. So we have come. We have been here three days and seen no one."

"But there were signs that others were here just before us," the Lochlan man said quietly from the other end of the log.

"What is your name?" Paxton asked him.

"Konor. Konor Shoal."

"What signs did they leave, Konor?"

"They'd buried their scraps and covered their fire, and the dirt looked fresh."

Paxton was riveted. Was Prince Vito truly breaking the Eurona Pact by allowing magic and giving refuge to Lashed from other lands?

"We are not sure who to trust," said Chun. "While we are glad for our safety, we fear the Rocato woman who has created these creatures in all the lands. If Prince Vito is in partnership with her—"

"What did you say?" Paxton's heart was a hammer inside his ribs. "They're in partnership?"

"It is rumored among the Torestan nobles," Chun answered. "I heard a great many things while serving meals."

This was not good news. "And what do you mean *creatures in all the lands*?"

"Haven't you heard, man?" asked Chun. "There were notices on all the paths. . . ."

"We kept off the paths," he explained.

Paxton's head began to split. The beast was dead—all was supposed to be safe. He wouldn't have left Lochlanach if he had thought otherwise. What was happening there?

The other Torestan man, Chun's brother, pulled a worn, folded paper from his pocket and handed it warily to Paxton, who flipped it open and ran his eyes over the words in disbelief. They were written in all languages.

Granddaughter of Rocato . . . created the beasts with Lashed powers . . . burn Lashed lists . . . terrorize all the lands until the laws are changed . . .

"One group of travelers said they think this is where she

comes to—what is the word?" Chun thought and snapped his fingers. "Ah, *recruit*. I do not know what to think of this woman. Some speak of her as evil, while other Lashed revere her as a savior. She is building an army of Lashed from those like us who want to fight for our freedom to do magic."

"Extraordinary." Paxton handed the paper back to the man, careful not to let his panic show. "Excuse me a moment. I need to inform my companions." He moved swiftly toward the water, where the Zandalee had taken off their head scarves and looked ready to brazenly strip down. The women turned at his quick approach, their eyes widening when they caught sight of his pale face.

"There are more." He sucked in a deep breath to steady himself. "More beasts, and they're in *all* the lands now. Rozaria Rocato—she has an army of Lashed, and they're threatening to kill innocents until the laws are changed. It seems that she and Prince Vito are possibly working together, which would mean she has more backing and power than anyone knew."

Zandora cursed harshly in Zorfinan and translated for her sisters, whose nostrils flared with anger.

"If Zorfina is under attack, we must go there," Zandora said. Paxton nodded. He understood. But he could not go with them now.

Aye, he wanted freedom for the Lashed, but not by Rozaria's extreme means. He'd seen innocents killed first-hand. That was *not* the way. He had to be smart. Where would he have the most advantage over the enemy? If there was a chance that Rozaria Rocato would come here, he knew he needed to stay, though it took every ounce of his willpower not to return to Lochlanach that very second to check on his family and Aerity.

A scorch of envy and loss filled his chest. Aerity had Lief to look after her. And she was smart. Resourceful. Paxton needed to remain in Kalor and attempt to find the Rocato woman on her own turf.

Zandora reached out her arm and took Paxton's shoulder. He did the same, blocking the two of them in. Her hair was long and wild outside its wrap, black as night. She had a smudge of mud along her jaw, and Paxton's heart swelled. He realized he would miss her. He held tight a moment longer before releasing her. At Zandora's side, Zula kissed her fingers and touched them to her shoulder, a gesture of love and respect. Paxton nodded.

Zaleek grasped the side of Paxton's head and pulled him down to kiss the corner of his mouth. Zandora punched her youngest sister in the arm and shoved her away, but the girl only laughed and rushed off, pulling her head scarf around her hair as she went to her horse. Zandora gave Paxton one last roll of her eyes before putting on her own head scarf and swinging herself onto her horse's back.

"I hope you get all you deserve in this life, dear Pax, which is far more than you think."

And with those last words from the huntress leader, the women dug their heels into the horses and were gone.

Chapter 4

Princess Aerity stared out from her chamber window that evening at the darkened skies above the royal port. Princess Vixie and Lady Wyneth watched at her side. A massive bonfire had been built outside the west commons and was open to the public. All persons' hands had been thoroughly checked for lash marks as they entered royal lands, and guards patrolled as far as the eye could see.

Tonight's spectacle was twofold. People could see the body of the latest creature for themselves and know that their king was capable of keeping them safe. But at the same time the people were watching as their king burned the lists of those who were Lashed, an extreme act that struck fear in traditionalists. The king wanted his people to know that he was trying to appease this madwoman in order to keep his people safe, but Aerity was not expecting peace that night. Her entire being was on high alert.

"We should be down there," Vixie said. Aerity and Wyneth both shook their heads.

"This is for the people," Wyneth told her. "And to keep Rozaria from killing again. It is not safe."

"Since when do you care about your safety, huntress?" A smile of admiration grazed Vixie's teasing lips. "We heard about how you faced down that monster and made a perfect shot."

"What I did today . . . I wish I hadn't been a part of it. And I wish Lord Alvi would not have glamorized my role." Her voice was so serious that the sisters shared a sad glance and went back to staring out the window in silence.

The princess felt as trapped as she had several months ago when the first beast was on the loose and the royals were ordered to remain in the castle. She'd come to loathe feeling helpless, especially after she'd helped kill the first creature. It didn't matter that today's monster had been so swiftly slain, because there were more. Until Rozaria and her like-minded followers were captured, there would always be more.

Hundreds of people gathered around the bonfire, the unnatural creature lifted high on a scaffold beside it. Aerity's parents watched from the balcony below her window. A line of royal soldiers marched up the cobbled path. Harrison led the way, in uniform, carrying several parchment scrolls. The people moved to make way for them. Harrison and the other soldiers climbed the scaffold and stood before the creature's body. Harrison appeared to be addressing the crowd, holding up the scrolls.

"He was so kind today," Wyneth whispered. She leaned her forehead against the glass.

"He's always such a gentleman, isn't he?" Vixie asked.

"Always," Aerity agreed.

They watched as Harrison threw the scrolls one by one into the roaring fire. And then the men set to lifting the beast. Before they had a chance to fully stand, the girls heard a muffled scream through the thick windows. All three pressed their faces closer. A small opening in the crowd revealed a woman laid out on the ground, completely still. Another woman leaned over her, screaming, shaking her head. All around her people began to push and run in different directions.

"Deep seas, what's happening down there?" Aerity asked.

"Is she dead?" Vixie stared down.

Voices rose and the crowd became a frantic mob. As people fell, others trampled.

"No!" Wyneth covered her face.

Aerity watched in horror. The king and queen were ushered from the balcony back inside the castle as guards and soldiers flooded the grounds below. She couldn't make sense of anything happening below, so she clambered from the window seat and grabbed her skirts, rushing from her chambers with her sister and cousin close behind.

They ran straight to the king's office, where she knew her parents would be brought. Moments later they shuffled in with a feeling of high expectancy in the air.

"What in Eurona happened out there?" King Charles asked.

Royals, advisers, and guards all peered around at one another, wearing matching faces of confusion and disappointment. Nobody knew. The king began to pace behind his long desk.

"They will get things under control," Queen Leighlane tried to assure him, but her lips pursed with worry. The king rubbed his face.

"This is what happens when we take away the people's stability," whispered Duke Gulfton, his eyes fervent.

It took only five minutes of waiting, but it felt like the longest five minutes of Aerity's life before Harrison burst through the door with a paper in his hand. Behind him was another soldier with a young, ragged boy. All three were breathing hard. The boy's eyes were rimmed in red.

Harrison and the other soldier gave short bows to the king.

"What news?" he asked.

Harrison spoke. "A villager woman was killed, Your Majesty. No signs of a weapon mark, so we can only assume . . ."

"A Lashed One," the king hissed. "Was he captured?"

Harrison's face fell. "Not yet, Your Majesty. People began

to shout about a Lashed attack and chaos ensued. But the men are searching. And this lad gave this paper to my soldier." He motioned to the boy and the soldier behind him. "The child says a woman with brown hair and a blue cloak paid him a copper outside the gates to the royal lands to give this paper to a soldier during the burnings. We believe the boy knows nothing else. He claims he can't read." Aerity believed it. The boy sniffled and rubbed his eyes. Harrison handed the paper to King Charles. Aerity and the others watched.

He read it through once, and his face grew grave. "Great seas alive." He motioned to the soldier and said, "Take the boy and find his parents. Question them. See if anyone else saw this woman or knows her whereabouts."

The soldier saluted and left with the boy.

King Charles wiped his face again. "The letter says, 'He who attempts to fool is a fool himself. For burning a fake list you shall lose a member of your kingdom. Do not underestimate my reach. Tomorrow morning your complete Lashed lists and the copies you have made will burn or more shall die.'" The king looked up with wide eyes, the room heavy with dread. "There is a traitor among us."

Aerity stood with water lapping at her legs, the edges of the scene blurred in her mind. She was alone with the great beast. The creature stared eye to eye with her, giving a snuffle against her outreached hand. She was not afraid. She knew it would not harm her. In its own way the monster seemed to smile around its massive tusks, its eyes drifting closed as it took comfort from Aerity's caress of its wiry jaw. Her stomach lurched, knowing what she must do. Slowly, like a cruel punisher, Aerity dug the sharp blade into the beast's throat. Its eyes flew open, striking her with a brokenhearted look of disbelief. She twisted the knife and it howled.

Aerity shot upward, awaking in semi-darkness. She blinked to adjust her eyes. *Only a dream, only a dream*, she reminded herself. Still, she pressed a hand to her clenched abdomen, breathing away the feelings of sadness and guilt that the dream always brought. Her emotions were a snarled mess.

Only the slightest hint of moonlight entered the arched windows as she felt for her slippers with her toes, pushing her feet into them. She peered out over the silent, dark grounds, thinking it all seemed spooky despite its innocuousness.

She needed fresh air but didn't dare swing open her windows. No flying beasts had been discovered, but they'd been ordered to keep the castle windows closed just in case. Nothing seemed impossible at this point.

Aerity grabbed her robe from the bedpost hook and shrugged her arms into it. She would take a walk to clear her mind of her dream of the monster's eyes. She passed a guard at the entrance of her chambers, who straightened at the sight of her.

"I'm fine," she said before he could speak. "I need a walk. I'll return shortly."

He gave a nod, but sent a wary look up and down the silent halls, as if danger were lurking around every corner.

Surprise flitted inside her when she became aware where her feet were taking her. Lord Alvi's quarters. She'd never visited him before. Never had reason. Aerity hadn't thought of him as a confidant, but she found herself wondering if his kingdom had ever dealt with treason. If he was to be her husband, she would need to learn to turn to him. There were some aspects of the coldlander she respected, such as his leadership and political outlook.

Her feet stopped halfway down Lief's hall as she realized the ridiculousness of waking him in the middle of the night, though he likely wouldn't mind. He was open to her in many ways. It'd been she who kept a wall between them. She stood there deliberating when she heard his door click open. Oh. Well, then, that settled it. Perhaps he couldn't sleep either. She took a step forward as a hushed, breathy, feminine bout of laughter issued from his doorway.

Aerity halted and stared in shock as a young woman came out, a beaming smile on her pretty face, her hair a wavy brown mess of a braid undone. A shock of recognition jabbed Aerity in the stomach. Caitrin! Her maid . . . Lord Alvi reached out from his doorway and grasped the girl around the waist, a dashing grin on his face as he pulled her to him. He wore a towel loosely tied around his hips and nothing else. The shock of it made Aerity gasp. She covered her mouth to muffle the sound, but it was too late.

Both heads turned toward her. Caitrin leaped away from Lord Alvi with a cry and Lord Alvi's eyes bulged. One hand held the towel while the other went to his blond hair, as if grasping for something, anything. "Princess, what are you . . ." His question trailed off.

A full-force gale began at Aerity's feet and circled its way upward, turning her insides around and around, straight up to her head where she thought her mind might explode.

"Oh seas." Caitrin crumpled to the floor, her hands pressed to the stone as her body heaved with uncontrollable breaths. "Your Highness! Princess, please. Please, I'm so sorry."

Part of Aerity wanted to lift the girl to her feet, this girl who she thought of as a friend, and the other part of her felt utterly betrayed. Of all the men she could have had.

Lord Alvi finally dropped his hand and stood taller, staring from Caitrin to Aerity.

"Why have you come?" His tone was tinged with uneasiness. "Is there danger?"

She could not yet speak, only able to shake her head slowly. Caitrin had quieted, but kept her face down, nose to the floor, sucking in loud breaths as she fought for air, shaking.

Aerity licked her dry lips. "I needed to walk. I thought we might talk."

Lord Alvi's eyes searched her. "I was not expecting to see you."

"Obviously."

Caitrin let out a low moan and curled in on herself like an animal in fear.

Aerity was so tired, so numb, that she felt she'd rather turn and walk away than deal with this. But as she stared at her betrothed, still flushed from his time with her maid, a darker part of herself—a part she'd worked so hard to confine—began to rise from deep within her. It was the part of her that was angry about being a pawn, a prize, a victim of these tumultuous circumstances. It was the shameful part of her that did not want to sacrifice her love and happiness for the kingdom. Aye, that piece of her that wanted to be selfish, to rebel and run away from it all. To take something for herself, just as Lief was doing, no matter the consequences.

She took a shaking breath and allowed that sunken part of herself to surface, like a raging fire in the pit of her despair, kindled by the scene before her and her bleak future ahead.

This is my life, Aerity thought. *This will always be my life.* And then a simple decision arose within her. Lord Alvi actually appeared frightened of her.

Caitrin wailed, her nails scratching the stone.

"Enough," Aerity said. She trembled on the inside with the power of her unleashed emotions. She moved forward. Caitrin's forehead touched the floor as she pressed a hand tightly over her mouth, her body shuddering. The girl knew what could be done to her. If Aerity had a mind to punish her, she could be beaten, sent to the dungeon, even killed. But her anger was not for her maid. "Stand up, Cait."

Lord Alvi stared, as if unsure what to do, but Aerity did not acknowledge him.

Caitrin, a year older than Aerity, was someone she'd cared

for since she became her maid three years ago. She knew she had every right to be angry with the girl, but the fact was that she did not love Lord Alvi, and Caitrin was quite aware of that. She also understood the allure of the handsome, powerful lord from the coldlands.

Caitrin shuffled to her feet, her face still down, wiping at her cheeks and then fumbling with her skirts.

"Look at me," Aerity said.

Caitrin lifted her face and looked at the princess through watery, guilt-lined eyes.

"You will fetch me dye, something dark like mahogany. And shears. Bring them to my chambers tomorrow at sunset."

"Sh-shears, Your Highness?" Caitrin croaked and reached up to grasp her flowing locks, aghast.

"We're not cutting your hair, Caitrin," Aerity said impatiently. "I'll also need a commoner's dress and boots. Be discreet about this, do you understand? Not a word."

"My lady . . ." Lord Alvi said with concern, but Aerity kept her eyes on her maid.

"*Go.*"

Caitrin nodded, grasping her brown skirts and rushing away.

Only when the maid was out of sight did Aerity turn her fearsome gaze on Lord Alvi.

"I can see you're angry," he said with care. "But to be fair nobody was ever to know—"

"In the future you will keep your dalliances outside these

castle walls." It was bound to get out eventually that there was no love between the two of them, and that her future husband would take other women. Aerity was not looking forward to the pity she would no doubt receive from people.

Lord Alvi nodded. "That is fair."

A huff of unamused air blew from Aerity's nose. "None of this is *fair*," she said.

His eyebrows came together, and he stepped closer. "What do you expect from me, Princess? I am a man. You, my bride-to-be, are busy dreaming of a lawbreaking man who's run afar, and your lovely cousin will not so much as glance at me."

"You poor, dear thing." Aerity moved closer, too, practically hissing. "I'm so very sorry my cousin and I are not meeting your *needs*—"

Footsteps echoed down the hall and they looked to see a guard checking out the noise.

"Leave us!" Aerity yelled.

The guard gave a stiff nod and turned on his heel.

"I am trying to learn your ways the best that I can, Princess, but my blood will always run cold—I am Ascomannian. Your Lochlan ways are not instinctive to me. I cannot understand why your society hinders its people in so many ways."

In his voice was something akin to homesickness. Aerity could almost hear the mirrored sense of entrapment that she felt.

"What are you planning?" Lord Alvi asked. His eyes held distress. Always, this man confused her with his brutish instincts and untimely kindnesses.

"It's none of your concern."

"I disagree. You are my concern whether you want to be or not. If you are planning to put yourself into danger—"

"Do not fret about my well-being. I will seek Lieutenant Gillfin for help and companionship."

"Ah, a Lochlan man you can trust," he said as if hurt.

"Aye, that's right," Aerity said back. "A man who's loyal and won't make a fool of me someday."

Lord Alvi grasped Aerity by her shoulders, his hands large and hot. His face was close to hers, and then, *oh seas*, she heard the towel fall to the floor. Her eyes stayed glued to his, and he seemed unaffected by the fact that he was now stark-naked. She closed her eyes.

"Kindly retrieve your towel." She kept her eyes closed until she heard him shift the cloth back into place.

"It doesn't have to be this way between us, Aerity."

Her eyes burned when she opened them. She knew that she could try to make things work with this man. She could attempt to be affectionate. Perhaps over time her feelings for Paxton would lessen, if only she could put it from her mind that he was out there somewhere feeling the same way as she. But she didn't think she could let Pax go without closure. And there was one other person whose feelings she couldn't forget.

"What of Wyneth?" Aerity whispered.

His hold on her loosened and he dropped his arms. "I admit . . . she pervades many of my thoughts. But I swear,

I will leave her be. I'm trying to respect your ways, though you Lochlans make everything more complicated than necessary with your unspoken rules." He said this last bit with wry humor that Aerity could not bring herself to feel.

She swallowed hard. The whole situation would be simpler if she'd been raised to view marriage as Lord Alvi and his people did. Perhaps if her parents hadn't instilled in her the value of love and monogamy, only to rip it away. But they each were who they were, and beliefs were not so easily changed.

Lief's deep voice softened. He loomed before her, his body seeming confident while his eyes gave off nervousness.

"Could we at least try to make this work? I do care for your happiness, Princess." His sincerity made her suck in her breath, only to catch the scent of honeysuckle.

"You still smell of my maid."

He broke away, looking to the side with a regretful shake of his head.

"There is something I must do," Aerity said. "Afterward . . ." She took another breath and looked into his disappointed eyes. "When I return, we shall see."

"You're going searching for him, aren't you? The Lashed One."

Aerity said nothing.

"It's not safe," he said. "And I don't wish to seem cruel, but if he had wanted you, then—"

She gritted her teeth. "I don't expect you to understand.

But I cannot move forward until I see him one last time. I beg you to let me leave and not say a word to anyone. You of all people know the need to have something for yourself."

Lord Alvi's eyebrows suddenly knit sharply. "If you find him, what do you mean to do?"

Aerity smiled wickedly. "You're not the only one with *needs*, Lord Alvi."

Though Princess Aerity's motives in finding Paxton were more about her heart than her body, the look of offense on Lord Alvi's face as she walked away was something she'd forever cherish.

Chapter 5

Lady Wyneth disobeyed her father's orders to stay inside the castle during the Lashed list burnings. Her urge to make herself useful had fled, but the feeling of reckless abandon was still there. She stood inside a patch of trees, watching in the gray morning light as soldiers rekindled the still-smoking flames of the night before. Her face was cold, but she felt numb to the elements.

The other royals stood watching from the balcony, wrapped in shawls and cloaks against the chill.

The castle grounds were emptied of villagers now. Many had been trampled and injured during the night's chaos. People had flooded out of royal lands, too many at once, and their hands could not all be checked upon their mad exit.

Only one died, a maiden, engaged to be married. And her killer was not yet found.

A gust of wind blew, lifting leaves from the cobbled path and spinning them away, only to be replaced by others. She watched as Harrison, atop the scaffold above the fire, threw the giant scrolls onto the flames, one by one, as his soldiers handed them to him. His jaw was set. His eyes squinted when the wind turned the smoke toward him. The last scroll hit the top and tumbled down, charring before their eyes.

Harrison stood tall and peered around at the vacant royal lands. His eyes skimmed the rows of soldiers standing nearby, and rose to the castle's balcony. *He's a fine man. So handsome.* Wyneth jolted at the thought and blinked it away. *It's just that he is so like Breckon was*, she told herself.

"It is done!" Harrison shouted. His voice reverberated through her, the finality of his words sinking deep. They had succumbed to the madwoman's first demand. They no longer knew who the Lashed were throughout Lochlanach. But did it really matter? How many had kept their abilities hidden, like Paxton Seabolt? Wyneth didn't believe the people on those lists were ones they needed to worry about. The true foes were hidden. Lurking.

All was quiet but for the crackle of flames and rustle of leaves. When nothing happened, the royals slowly made their way back into the castle, and the soldiers dispersed. Harrison stopped and stared in her direction. She lifted a hand to signal she was fine, but she quite liked the idea of his companionship. He caught her eye a moment longer, then made a move as if to go to her, until one of his soldiers said something, and he nodded, turning to follow. He spared one glance back at her and a small smile of acknowledgment.

Wyneth's hope for his company sank. He had work to do. She didn't want to be alone, and with Harrison there was no pressure to feign happiness. He understood her pain in a way few others could.

Something hot touched her arm, and Wyneth jumped.

"My lady, you're freezing," Lord Alvi said.

She wrapped her arms around herself and realized how right he was. His eyes narrowed at her in worry, the close attention giving her a heady rush. His own arms were barer than hers, but he radiated heat. A sudden urge to lean into that heat overtook her and she cleared her throat, shaking out her arms. She needed to get a grip on herself.

"I'm fine. I was just about to return to my chambers." She turned and sensed him following in silence.

As they reached the hall leading to her chambers, Lord Alvi called out. "Lady Wyneth, may I have a moment?"

As always, his voice and attention created a maelstrom in her, causing her body to feel oversensitive. She turned and slowly lifted her eyes from his boots up his muscular legs to the kilt that fell to his knees and then to his strong, wide torso. His face was so masculine and dashing that her breath halted. Soon, soon, this man would be marrying and bedding her cousin and she hoped to the deep seas that she would not always react this way to him.

"What is it?" she breathed out.

Surprisingly, he kept his distance. She felt both disappointment and relief.

"It's your cousin."

Wyneth's senses cleared, and she stood taller. "Aerity? What of her?"

"I fear I've . . . failed her. I fear I might always fail her." He kept his eyes on his hands, turning them over in a nervous gesture, searching them. Wyneth cocked her head as she watched him, floored by his openness. "I'm trying, you see. I'm trying to learn what is expected of me, though I don't quite agree with the restrictions. Right now . . . I'm trying not to touch you."

His voice had lowered, and Wyneth hugged her arms around herself again, though she was no longer the least bit cold. When he looked from his hands to her eyes, she dropped her gaze. "Good on you for your efforts." It came out embarrassingly scratchy. Shame filled her. She shouldn't feel disappointed by his self-control. This is what was best. She should fully *want* him to keep his hands to himself.

"Aye, well, for what it's worth, if you truly wish me to leave you alone, my lady . . . I will."

Now she let herself look into his sincere eyes. She believed he was trying. It made her sad and proud. Her eyes burned, and she nodded.

"Yes, Lord Alvi. That is my wish." Her words were thick, as if she had to shove each one from her throat.

"So be it." Lord Alvi swallowed. "And I might reap your

cousin's wrath for telling you this, but she's planning something this evening. I think she is going after the Lashed One, Paxton." Lord Alvi nodded when she gasped. "I don't agree with her decision, but I will not try to stop her. Perhaps you can try, but I will not."

Why that little sneak. Would she really leave without a word?

"Thank you," Wyneth told him. She reached for his hand and squeezed quickly, releasing before his warmth could envelop her. "Thank you for everything."

He bent at the waist in a shallow bow and turned to leave her. She watched him unabashedly. For all his faults and outlandish behavior, he had unknowingly helped her through the most difficult time of her life. Though she wished she'd never fallen for the man who would become her cousin's husband, she would always be grateful for the distraction he had provided during those initial weeks and months after Breckon's death, wrong though it might have been.

She smiled sadly while he disappeared from sight. Things were changing. Everyone around her seemed to be moving on, moving forward, and yet she felt . . . stuck. Wyneth looked down at the drab mourning garb she'd been wearing for nearly half a year. Breckon wasn't coming back. The thought hit her with enough force to make her grab the doorframe. Once she'd taken several steadying breaths, she reached for her heavy cloak, pulling it around her shoulders.

And then her feet were moving.

She didn't let herself think about where she was going

until she was through the castle doors and halfway down the path. Inside, she trembled. She did not want to do this. She'd vowed to herself never to return to that place of her nightmares, yet her feet continued to take her forward. She clutched her cloak tighter against a gust of wind.

She took a fork in the path to the left. It was a less trodden path that had become overgrown over the fall when there were so many other areas of importance to tend. She crunched through piles of leaves and pine needles, past trees with brittle branches. Wyneth's feet halted at the sight of the long wooden dock. Her eyes trailed down the planks of wood until landing at the end.

The last time she'd seen it, it had glistened with dark blood, which she braced herself to see again. But it was only wood. Nature had washed all traces of Breckon's death away. She knew instinctively that seeing it from afar was not enough. If she was to move forward, she needed to be at that spot one last time, to confront the fear and loss that held her captive. *You must do this*, she told herself.

Wyneth moved like an old woman, slowly, as if her bones protested. Her body fought against each step, remembering the horrors. She pressed through the last of the trees, over the brush, closing her eyes against the chilling breeze from the creek as she pushed into the open space.

She was cold and alone, so alone, walking down that dock—a complete turnaround from the last time she'd walked it, when she'd been on Breckon's arm, her heart full, her body warm and at ease. As bouts of panic threatened to rise, she repeated the mantra to herself over and over: *You're fine, you're safe, you're strong.*

When she made it to the edge, she fell to her knees and hesitantly pressed her hands against the wood, moving her fingers over the grooves. Not a single trace of him. Her tears hit the dock, leaving small, dark droplets like rain. Wyneth raised her head, staring out at the spot where he'd pushed her in, and the line of the creek where she'd swum to the dock at the other side. All the while, she pushed down her panic, her instinct to run from that place.

"I miss you, Breck. I'll always miss you." She stared down at the wood where he'd laid her back and kissed her. Wyneth wiped her eyes. "Please forgive me for what happened with Lord Alvi. Forgive me for my need to move on. My heart . . ." She sucked in a breath and wiped her eyes again. "I want to hold on to you forever, but it hurts to mourn you still."

She could almost feel Breckon's warm embrace, his confident smile, telling her he could not be angry. That she needn't grieve forever. That it was all right to live.

A light snap echoed over the water from the woods, and Wyneth stopped breathing. She peered up, heart pounding, and saw the shaded form of a man leaning against a tree, watching her. *Breckon!* An involuntary sound of disbelief rose from her throat. And then the figure moved, stepping out.

Harrison. Oh, seas. She pressed a hand to her chest. He was so very like Breckon in his physique and stature. Her pulse was still racing as he made his way down the length of the dock, squatting to face her with concern in his eyes.

"Wyn?"

"I'm all right," she whispered. "From afar you appeared to be . . . Never mind." She shook her head, then looked at him. His eyes gleamed. "Did you follow me?"

Now he appeared sheepish, moving his gaze to the water. "I hope you don't mind. You seemed upset when you came out of the castle. I waved, but you didn't notice."

"This is my first time coming back to this dock." She forced herself to stand, and Harrison stood too.

"I came every day after . . ." He looked all around, as if searching for signs of Breckon. Finally, his eyes landed on hers. "And every day I thanked the seas that you were spared."

Heat spread through Wyneth at the intensity behind those words. She searched his gaze until he dropped it, amending. "That's what he would have wanted. For you to be spared, even at his expense. His love for you was like no other."

Wyneth nodded, cooling. "Aye. That it was."

A long breeze whipped small waves in the creek, gusting straight up Wyneth's gray skirts. She held them down and shivered.

"Let me escort you back to the castle, if you're ready," Harrison said.

Wyneth nodded. Harrison held out his elbow, and she took it. He kept her hand warm in his strong embrace. Together, they walked the forsaken dock, and Wyneth felt a small piece of herself being left behind, allowing her to begin the healing process. Her gaze remained forward until the dock was out of sight.

Aerity was exhausted as she stood in her father's office. The lists had been burned, and, thank the seas, all had gone well, though her father was troubled about having destroyed the compilations of their magical families. She knew he was worried about having no records of the kingdom's Lashed Ones and their bloodlines. But in Aerity's mind, having lists made no difference. A compilation of names simply gave the people a false sense of control over the people on that list.

"We'll do a new census after this madness is over," he had whispered on the balcony, and Aerity's heart had contracted with sadness. As much as she hated Rozaria Rocato and her fanatic ways, she had felt like burning the lists was a way to move forward. The kingdom needed change.

Rebellious excitement writhed inside her at the thought of what she would do that night. She could barely take in the grave faces of her parents, aunts, and uncles. All she could think about was that she would soon escape these walls, seas willing, and have one final adventure—one final moment for herself—before she sacrificed it all to her arranged marriage with Lord Alvi.

Would her parents be furious? Aye, without a doubt. But she was confident that she would return and finally have the strength to move forward with her obligations to the kingdom. No harm would be done. They would eventually see.

"Have you any clue who the traitor might be?" Lord Wavecrest asked her father.

King Charles shook his head. "Nobody in my council has behaved out of character."

"But it has to be one of them," Lord Wavecrest said.

"Funny . . ." The king sat back in his chair. "They pled their innocence and said it had to be one of you, the family."

Her aunts and uncles gasped, posturing with outrage.

"That's preposterous!" Lady Baycreek said. "What reason would we have to betray our people?"

The king held up a hand. "I know. I know it's none of you, and I told them as much. I've got several military officials questioning them. They've been trained to retrieve information."

"Do you mean torture?" Lady Wavecrest pressed a hand to her chest. "Several of the council are elderly."

The king raised an eye to his sister. "Just intimidation tactics."

"They won't go overboard," Queen Leighlane assured her. "These are councilmen we've always trusted. But if there's a chance any of them are consorting with the Rocato woman or being used by her, we must take measures to weed them out."

Lady Wavecrest's hand slowly dropped as she nodded.

"We should have the royal Lashed questioned," Lord Wavecrest said.

Aerity's spine went rigid. "Mrs. Rathbrook? She would never!"

"She is Lashed," her uncle said. "I know she's always seemed loyal, but in these times you never know."

"She is not part of the council," the king stated. "She is not privy to information, so she has been ruled out."

"Any news from other kingdoms?" Lord Baycreek asked as Aerity stewed in anger.

King Charles shook his head. "I'm hoping for messengers to arrive today. In the meantime we need to discuss what to do to appease this madwoman and keep her from killing again."

Just as Aerity opened her mouth, a knock sounded on the door.

"Enter," the king called.

A guard opened the door and ushered in a page boy of Aerity's age. He was sweating and panting. The king stood.

"Do you bring news from afar?"

"Nay, Your Majesty," he said, holding his side. "I have news from two villages, Craw Coorie and Dovedell."

"Yes?"

Aerity's abdomen tightened. The lad looked distressed. What could be happening?

"Townsmen have burned the homes of their known Lashed. It's said that people in towns all over the lands are spreading word to try to drive out Lashed Ones."

"No!" Aerity flew to her father's side. "We have to stop this!"

"What did we expect?" Lord Wavecrest asked. "They surely feel that the Lashed are waging war after a woman was killed by one of them in the people's midst."

"They're trying to drive out the Lashed before the Lashed

have a chance to rise against them," Lady Ashley agreed.

"Well, we can't sit by idly and let our Lashed be killed!" Aerity shouted. This was personal to her. All she could imagine was Paxton and his family, trying to live a quiet life, being rooted out with violence.

The king motioned to the door guard. "Send word to Lieutenant Gillfin. Disperse troops to Craw Coorie and Dovedell to stop any rioting. Find the primary culprits who set the fires and slap fines on them. Arrest any who don't cooperate." The guard nodded and jogged away. Another guard was there to take his place, and the king motioned for the door to be closed.

"Fines?" demanded Aerity. "That's all? For destroying homes and possibly killing people?"

The king's hands clenched at his sides as he turned to his daughter. She surged on before he could speak.

"We have to offer refuge to the uprooted Lashed."

"Surely you are not suggesting bringing hordes of Lashed onto royal lands," Lord Wavecrest said to her. "We cannot discern who is good and who is against us."

"The good ones will be mark free," Lady Ashley pointed out.

"Any with markings need to be killed," Lord Wavecrest said.

Aerity shook her head, anger simmering. "They're most likely only using magic to defend themselves."

"The laws must stand!" Lord Wavecrest shouted.

The princess faced him, her blood buzzing with passion. "And in the meantime the real, actual evil ones, who are hidden, will kill our townspeople one by one. Because it is apparent we are too stubborn to compromise our outdated laws. Too fearful of retaliation to protect our people who are under attack!"

"Look at me, Aerity," the king told her. She brought her hazel eyes up to his stern ones. "You need to realize that what you are suggesting will bring as much death, destruction, and heartache as any other path of action at this time. Our people are scared of the unknown. They don't know what to believe. These are uncharted waters, and we must weigh each decision with care. You are being led by your emotions, not your mind. I think it is best if you let us discuss this without you until you can learn to work with us calmly."

Aerity gaped at her father's open dismissal, as if she were the only one in the room driven by emotion. Here she was, the one who'd sacrificed her future and her happiness for the sake of the kingdom—their future queen. Dismissed. She blinked twice, her gut twisting into a gnarled mess, before swallowing hard and grasping her skirts to leave. It would be the last she'd see of them for a while.

Good riddance, she thought.

Chapter 6

The first thing Aerity noticed when she sat down across from Wyneth in the library that afternoon was her cousin's sea-green gown, the way it brought out the green in her hazel eyes. Aerity sat down and spoke carefully, seeing how Wyneth fidgeted nervously with her skirts.

"You look beautiful in that color, Wyn."

Wyneth shook her head. "I fear it is too soon."

"I don't believe so," Aerity said. "It is right to mourn, but there is no shame when it's time to move on. It doesn't mean you won't always love him and remember him."

Wyneth ran a hand down her skirts, calming.

Caitrin came into the room and bumped into the

doorframe, spilling hot tea across her tray. She'd been jumpy that morning as well, dropping a stack of linens when she passed Aerity in the hallway.

"Seas alive," Caitrin breathed. "I'm very sorry, Your Highness and Lady Wyneth. I'll be back with more."

"Caitrin!" Wyneth said with a funny look. "It was only a small spill. I'm sure there's still plenty more in the pot."

Caitrin hesitated before bustling forward and setting down the tray. Her hands shook as she wiped the spilled tea and poured cups for both girls. Once she'd served them and rushed away, Wyneth gave Aerity an amused look.

"What do you suppose has come over her?"

Aerity gave a stiff shrug. If Wyn knew, it would upset her.

They sipped their steaming tea in silence. It had been ages since Wyneth asked Aerity to the library. The princess used to accompany her cousin weekly to watch her draw. Those had been peaceful days.

Wyneth set down her cup and watched Aerity closely. The princess ran her fingers down her long braid before asking, "What is it? You've something on your mind?"

Wyneth slowly shook her head. "Nay. Do you?"

"Nay."

At the same time they picked up their cups and sipped, eyeing each other over the rims. Of course Wyneth would be able to tell something was happening with her—they never could keep secrets. Aerity didn't want her cousin to worry, but she also knew Wyneth could be trusted and wouldn't try to stop her. And as much as it pained her to think of leaving without telling her sister, Vixie, she knew the younger princess would want to accompany her, and that simply was not happening.

Aerity set down her cup. She glanced toward the doorway, but the guard was too far down the hall to hear. Still, she lowered her voice. "You know my parents are pushing up the wedding date to winter?"

Wyneth touched her fingers to her throat, swallowing the hot tea before she nodded.

"Well, I plan to have one last adventure before I do their bidding. I will leave a letter so they know I'm safe." Aerity twisted her braid tightly in her hands.

Wyneth set down her cup and watched her closely. "But will you truly be safe, Cousin?"

"I plan to be, of course. I don't aim to be reckless. And I won't be alone. I'm seeking a favor from Harrison."

"Harrison?" Wyneth's brow scrunched with worry. "What about his work? Won't he be reprimanded for abandoning his post?"

"Not if I can make it seem that he gave chase to find me and bring me back."

Wyneth's fingers drummed the sides of her cup, seeming lost in thought. "Where will you go?"

Ah, there was the question. Aerity didn't fully know.

"South," she said. "Before Tiern left, he told me he believed Paxton had set off to supposed safe lands in southern

Kalor, or perhaps to Zorfina to the Zandalee tribe."

"That could take you weeks to find him, even on horseback. How long will you search before you return? You must give yourself a limit, Aer, or we'll all be worried sick."

Aerity felt her insides trembling at the unknown. "I will search for two weeks, and if I don't find him, I will return straightaway. One month. That is how long I plan to be gone. No longer."

"That will hardly give you any time with him."

Aerity knew this. It was one of the plan's many possible flaws. Would a day or two be enough to tie up their loose ends and allow her to move on?

"I don't know if I'll find him at all," Aerity whispered. "Or if he'll be glad to see me, for that matter. I'm trying to prepare myself for any outcome."

Wyneth brought the cup to her lips but didn't drink. Her eyes were distant and lost.

"Please don't worry, Wyn," Aerity whispered.

"Is it strange that I'm jealous?" Wyneth asked softly.

Aerity's chest tightened. "Would you like to join me?"

"Nay." She shook her head. "It's just the thought of being out there, free, with you and Harrison . . ." She smiled to herself. "But I fear I would slow you down. And I think I'll be needed here to help calm your parents and sister."

Relief rushed through Aerity. She had been counting on Wyneth to keep things running as smoothly as possible in her absence. "I don't imagine I'll be missed. My ideals are bothersome to them. They kicked me out of the office today! I am afraid of what is happening in this kingdom." She eyed her cousin. "Am I completely horrid to leave when things are the way they are?"

Duty warred with her heartfelt desires.

Wyneth took Aerity's hand tightly. "You have the rest of your life to sacrifice all for this kingdom. Lochlanach will rule you as much as you rule it. A single month, in the scheme of things, is nothing. If the most wayward time of your life happens before you're even of age, then I'd say you will succeed."

Aerity's eyes burned. Nobody understood her quite like Wyneth. "I have a favor to ask. Are you willing to deliver messages to Harrison and Miss Rathbrook asking for their help? And will you see me off from my chamber tonight?"

"Aye. I will be there."

An hour after sundown Caitrin knocked quietly on the princess's chamber door before opening it slightly. Aerity waved her in.

"Quickly. Shut the door."

Caitrin bustled in, her cheeks pink. She held a brown cloth bag.

"Do you have everything?" Aerity asked.

"Aye, Your Highness."

"Did you tell anyone at all?"

"Nay, Your Highness." Caitrin appeared tight with

discomfort, as she had each time Aerity saw her since catching the girl with Lord Alvi.

Aerity stood and took the bag from Caitrin. The maid dashed past her and set to work making a fire. She then filled a pot and hung it in the fireplace to warm. Once she finished, she stood awkwardly, like a beaten dog awaiting its next command.

Aerity approached her. "Have you not thought of me as somewhat of a friend, dearest Caitrin? Have I given you reason to fear me?"

Caitrin's eyes squeezed shut, pressing out beads of moisture. "Nay, my princess, you have always been kind."

"Then why fear me now?"

"Because I deserve your punishment, Your Highness. I am s-so ashamed."

Aerity had to calm her if they were going to make any progress that night. And it was breaking her heart to see her in this state.

"Be honest. Did you seek Lord Alvi?" Aerity asked. Caitrin's eyes flew open, and she shook her head. "Did you set out to seduce him?"

"Nay, my lady! That is, I do not wish to speak ill of him—"

"My betrothed is a scoundrel," Aerity said flatly. "He saw a pretty girl who blushed at his flirtations, and he advanced. I'm sure he was quite flattering. In Ascomanni, men have no qualms about such things. Married, single, engaged—men do as they please and women live to make them happy. He is handsome and charming. You never thought anyone would find out. And I'm certain it will never happen again."

"Never, Your Highness. *Never!*" Caitrin began to kneel, but Aerity made her stand.

"Then let us put this in the past, aye?"

Caitrin's lips tightened as she appeared to suppress another surge of emotion.

"Here is what I need from you tonight, without question." Aerity walked to the chair and took off her robe. She wore only a thin shift underneath. "You will cut my hair from my waist to my midback, and then dye it dark brown. I will be leaving the castle for one month's time and then returning to my duties. I will leave a letter for my parents. You will not be named as an accomplice. I plan to find Paxton Seabolt and give him the proper good-bye that was robbed from us. Do you have any questions?"

Her maid gawked at her, speechless.

"Well, then. Start cutting."

Caitrin hesitated for a moment longer before dropping to her knees and fumbling for the shears in her bag. She came to Aerity's side, her breathing ragged. "You're certain?"

"It will grow back, and the dye will fade. I am absolutely certain."

Caitrin paused . . . and then the crisp sound of shears cutting and a soft *thwap* of hair hit the floor. A chill of excitement and trepidation ran up Aerity's spine.

"Seas, Princess!" Caitrin hissed. "What have I done?"

"Keep going."

So, she did. It seemed like forever before Caitrin stepped back, surveying the mass of strawberry-golden hair, as pink as the sunset, lying at their feet. Aerity's chest rose and fell with speed. This was really happening. No turning back.

"Now, the color," she said.

Caitrin applied oil to the skin surrounding Aerity's hairline to prevent the dye from staining. Her efforts to do a clean job were painstaking and slow. Aerity calmed, enjoying the feel of fingers in her hair. Her mind wandered to Paxton, and what would happen when she saw him. She thought of their kiss, and what she'd give to feel that again . . . and more. The "more" part filled her with a burning curiosity that made her quiver with nervous excitement. Was she willing?

Aerity thought about Lord Alvi, and while she felt a reluctant respect for him, she felt no obligation to retain her innocence for a man who didn't love her. That left one question. Did Paxton love her? He'd never said as much. They'd scarcely scratched the surface of the feelings between them before he left without a good-bye. But if she saw him, and if he felt the same as her . . . aye, Aerity wanted everything with him. Even if only for a day.

But she had no idea what to expect from "everything." This wasn't exactly something her mother spoke of. She could ask her maid, but the thought of it made her stomach flip with nervousness. It took many minutes of working up the nerve before the question croaked out of her.

"What is it like, Caitrin?"

The maid stilled, and the princess's face flamed.

"That is," Aerity amended, "not Lord Alvi in particular, just . . . what is it like?" She fidgeted with her fingers in her lap.

After a moment, Caitrin slowly began working again. "May I tell you a story?"

"Please." She listened, trying to relax.

"Do you recall last spring when I told you about a lad who had come calling for me?"

"Aye." Come to think of it, Aerity had wondered what happened with that. All spring Caitrin had been full of smiles and joy. And then, Aerity realized with shame, she'd never thought to inquire further. She'd been wrapped up in her own world.

"He was an older boy I'd grown up with who'd left to become a sailor and returned from sea. I'd fancied him for years and you can believe he knew it! Well, I was quite certain he was going to ask for my hand when he returned from his next stint at sea. My parents believed so, as well. Even his siblings were sure of it. So before he left . . . I stopped halting his advances. I figured if I was going to marry him anyway, you know."

Aerity listened attentively, not moving a muscle.

"It wasn't anything ground shattering, I regret to say. In fact it wasn't comfortable or as enjoyable as I expected, but it felt special to me. It was only once, and I had hopes that it would get better over time."

Aerity was getting a horrible feeling and didn't dare speak.

"When he returned from sea midsummer, he was not alone. He'd brought a girl from the south. A girl he had married in port because her father had caught them together and insisted upon her honor being salvaged." Caitrin stopped and sniffed, wiping her nose against her shoulder. "He tried to see me, but I refused. My older brother blackened his eye. By then it was known throughout town that I was not an innocent anymore. And while there are plenty of men who don't care about that, it's usually the older widowers and what have you. So I suppose you can say I haven't been in a good frame of mind when it comes to men, or my own self for that matter." She sniffed again.

Indignation fired through the princess. "I'm so sorry you went through that, Caitrin."

"Nay, Your Highness, don't pity me. I made a choice."

Aerity stared down at her hands and let a few beats of time pass. "So . . . it's not enjoyable, then?" If that was the case, she couldn't understand why such a fuss was made about it.

"Well, I mean, it certainly can be." Aerity couldn't see Caitrin's face, but it sounded as if she were embarrassed. Her maid rushed on. "I think it is different for every person and every couple. With my sailor, I believed we were in love. I can't say being together did much for me physically, but in my mind it made me feel closer to him."

Aerity felt tired of being in the dark about all things. Preparing her mind was the only thing she felt she had power over anymore. She took a deep breath and asked a question that was likely inappropriate, but she didn't care about propriety at the moment.

"And Lord Alvi?" Caitrin's hands stiffened in her hair, and Aerity continued. "Let's just pretend he was a passing traveler and not my betrothed. . . ." Her stomach swooped. She didn't know why she was pressing this except that inquisitiveness seared her from the inside. She heard Caitrin swallow before the girl spoke in a dry, low tone.

"He will make you a very, *very* happy bride if you let him."

More chills zapped the column of her spine. And then Aerity giggled. Perhaps it was the nervous tension finally cracking, she didn't know, but the giggle turned to pure laughter, and she bent at the waist, cackling.

"Oh, Princess!" Caitrin scolded. The girl tried to cover her smile, but she broke into a reluctant giggle too. "Shame on you. There's dye on your neck now. Be still."

Aerity sat up again, gasping for air and covering her mouth as Caitrin dabbed her neck and applied the last bit of dye.

"Let it sit as long as you can stand it, and then I'll bring in a basin to rinse it."

A barely discernible tap came from the door, and it opened a sliver. Aerity's heart leaped into her throat until she spied the shock of red curls. Seeing her cousin sent a bout of guilt through her, thinking of the conversation she'd just been having. She hoped Wyneth never found out about Lord Alvi and Caitrin.

"Come in," Aerity hissed. "Hurry!"

Wyneth slipped in and closed the heavy door behind her, leaning against it. "Look at you. You're really doing it!"

Aerity grinned. "Did you deliver my message to Miss Rathbrook?"

"Of course," Wyneth said. "And Harrison, too. Though he says you will owe him. He expects to be made high captain with no further effort from himself. He had to rearrange the schedule to put himself on night watch."

Aerity was elated that the people she cared about were willing to help her, even under the circumstances. She only felt bad about not telling Vixie, but Aerity needed to focus on herself.

They chatted quietly about nothing in particular, both nervous talkers, until Caitrin carried in a basin and began filling it with water warmed in the chamber's fireplace.

When her hair had been rinsed, Aerity stared down at the dark brown water.

"Deep seas almighty, Aer." Wyneth stared at her in wonder.

Caitrin began drying her hair with a cloth, then twisting strands from the sides and pinning them in the back, as was common among village girls.

"I could only get my hands on temporary dye, Highness. It should stay up to a few weeks if you don't wash it vigorously or often. Water and brushing will fade it. I've put the last of the jar in your bag." Aerity nodded, though she was not looking forward to having unwashed hair for any length of time.

The princess stepped into a drab, tan dress. and Caitrin buttoned it, tying a sash around her waist. The fabric felt thinner and itchier than she was used to. Next Caitrin pulled out a wad of cotton and a small jar of shimmering dirt . . . or so it looked to be.

"We need to cover some of your freckles," Caitrin explained. She ran the cotton over Aerity's face and neck, focusing on her cheeks and nose. When she finished, Aerity made her way to the mirror.

Wyneth stood over her shoulder, eyes widened, as they both stared at the unrecognizable maiden in the looking glass. The only thing that looked the same were her hazel eyes, but even they looked different with her changed appearance, lighter against her dark hair and darkened cheeks.

"Well done, Cait," Aerity breathed.

"Oh, Princess. Do be safe. The kingdom would be lost without you."

Aerity turned and pulled her maid into an embrace. Caitrin hesitated before hugging her back. The maid then handed the princess a pack and a worn cloak.

"I've filled it with extra clothes, extra dye, and food."

Aerity donned the cloak. When she looked at Wyneth, her cousin's eyes were wet, but she stood with her shoulders back, poised. "Paxton had better appreciate this or he's a fool." She reached for Aerity's hand and they pulled each other close.

"I will leave letters for my parents and sister." Aerity pulled away, startling at the sight of dark strands across her shoulder before remembering they were hers. "Don't let Vixie hate me too much."

Wyneth sighed. "I make no promises about that one."

The three of them jumped at a tap, tap sound. The door. Caitrin rushed forward and opened it a crack, then farther to reveal Miss Rathbrook, the royal Lashed healer. The older woman eyed Aerity with admiration.

"Your guard is resting, Your Highness, but not for long. His mind is sharp and his instinct to protect you will not let him sleep heavily."

"Thank you so much," Aerity said, grasping her frail hand. "How did you do it? You won't be in trouble, will you?"

"My guard and I were out for a stroll and the two men began to talk. I touched a soft finger to his neck from the side and put him into a sleep. My guard lowered him to the ground. He'll think he's fainted. My guard and I will be there when he awakens, to make him believe it was a momentary blackout. You must go."

"Aye, thank you." Aerity took one last look around her room, at her cousin and maid, at the letters lying on her window seat. Then with a final nod she straightened. "Let's go."

Wyneth kissed her cheek and left first to be sure the hall was clear. When she didn't return with warning, Aerity and Caitrin picked up large baskets of clothing and headed out, their heads down.

The princess followed Caitrin to a part of the castle where she'd never been: the laundry chambers. Scents of soap and wet fabric wafted down the damp-feeling halls. Behind her, Aerity heard the voice of her younger brother, Donubhan, and her heart stopped.

"I'm not even tired," her brother whined.

"Back to your chambers, young prince," called a nursemaid as she ran to catch him. "You don't want your father finding out you're roaming the halls after dark."

"But I'm nearly eleven!"

Aerity bit her tongue and rushed away as the maid chased Donny down a different hall and their voices faded. It took all her might not to turn and tell her rascal brother to be obedient for once. Caitrin's eyes were big as she waved the princess to a squat cellar door and took the basket from her.

She helped Aerity into a brown hooded cloak that cinched at the waist, and put a strap over her shoulder, across her chest. "Here is your bag. I've wrapped enough food for ten days. More than that would go bad, so Harrison will have to hunt."

Aerity nodded as she adjusted the bag. Her heart beat so loud she could scarcely think.

"I'll lead you out the servants' door, but try not to let the other maids see you. Wait here while I check." The two of them froze at the sound of footsteps passing and hushed female voices. She could have sworn she heard one of them mention Lord Alvi. Caitrin shook her head as if to tell her to pay no mind.

When all was quiet again, Caitrin peeked out and grasped Aerity by the hand, pulling her out to the very end of the hallway, beyond the bustling laundry room where she could hear voices. Aerity had no idea the staff worked well into the night on laundry. These were details she promised herself she would learn when she returned. Caitrin stopped at the servant cloakroom and grabbed her own cloak.

"Just keep your head down," Caitrin whispered. She led Aerity through the door where two guards stood outside in the crisp air. The coolness went straight through her thin clothing, and Aerity grasped her cloak tighter.

"Evening," Caitrin said to the men as she pulled her cloak over her head. Aerity heard their muttered polite replies as the girls made their way down the stone steps. Delight rushed through the princess as she realized they would not be followed—that they wouldn't even have to explain where they were going! For the first time in her life she was free of a guard's presence. She stifled an exhilarated laugh.

Caitrin accompanied Aerity until the stables were in sight. A lantern was lit within.

"This is where I shall leave you," Caitrin whispered. "I will enter the castle at the west doors and finish my night's work. I wish you all the blessings of the seas."

Aerity hugged her hard and quick. "The seas be with you as well." Her heart never slowed, and she began to wonder how long she could go at this pace of excitement. She made her way into the guests' stable and found a capable mare ready, as planned. She was to leave royal lands first, heading east then south, and Harrison would join her on the other side of the bay bridge.

She blew out the lantern at the stable entrance and made her way in the dark. Aerity led the horse from the stable, cooing at it in a tone she hoped it found comforting. It was a cloudy night, which made it darker than normal. A chilly breeze forced her breath to catch as she pulled herself onto the thin saddle. Her nerves shot up an extra notch. Being on horseback always made her uneasy. She hitched her heels into the horse's side and they began moving down the cobbled path.

In ten minutes' time she could see the gate of the royal lands, and for the first time Aerity wondered if this was a dire mistake. She rarely left royal lands and had never done so without protection. She breathed through the fear, slowing as she neared the guard. Surely he would recognize her! A mustached man came forward with a lantern so bright she lifted a hand to shield her eyes.

"Name?" he asked.

"Callie Hazlett, sir." She hoped he didn't detect the tremor in her voice.

"Hands," he said.

She held out a hand and he inspected each finger before releasing her and holding the lantern higher. "You don't look familiar, Miss Hazlett."

"I am a new maid in the soldiers' quarters."

"Where are you headed?"

"To the south village of Port Lorn where I'm from."

He tilted his head to stare up at her, and Aerity looked down at the reins.

"Why are you leaving so late?"

"I received message today that my gran is ill, but I couldn't leave until my work was done."

He gave a gruff nod and lowered the lantern. "Hope she heals. Be aware of your surroundings. It's not safe these days. Seas be with you."

"And also with you." As her horse trotted forward she let out a heaving sigh.

"Keep an eye out for foreigners and strange folk!" The guard called. Aerity raised a hand to acknowledge him. She could hardly make out the worn path as the lantern light faded. Her horse could apparently see as badly as she could in the dark, and she kept having to steer it back to what she believed was the center of the path. Thankfully they were surrounded by fields of low vegetation where it would be hard for people to hide.

It felt like forever before Aerity made it to the outskirts of the town of Dovedell, where the path intersected. She took the southern route and immediately began to question herself as she entered the forest. Thankfully the path was plenty wide, but it was even darker amid the trees. Her ears were perked for sounds of people or creatures. Her head swiveled from side to side, and she tried to remain calm so as not to startle the horse. She pulled her cloak tight to ward against the chill.

Aerity rode for a long while until the tree canopy gave way to a cloudy night sky and she heard the sounds of water. She spotted the bay bridge to the southern lands and made her way across, feeling as if the horse's hooves echoed on the wood for all of Lochlanach to hear. Her heart did not slow until she got to the other side of South Bay. Thankfully it was a narrow waterway.

She moved into the tree line, patting her horse's head and caressing its neck to keep both herself and the horse calm. Her eyes darted around to every leaf rustled by the breeze, every frog croaking by the water's edge. A cool wind shook the trees. Above her, the clouds crept out toward the sea, revealing the moon and stars in all their glory.

Finally, *finally*, a single horse crested the hill, coming toward the bridge. Aerity could make out the form of her old friend, even from afar. A smile stretched across her face, and a sense of adventure hummed through her blood once again.

"Oh, you will be in such trouble with your parents in the morning, young lady," Harrison said when he reached her.

"As long as I'm back to make good on their deal with the coldlands, that's all that matters," she responded drily.

"Aer." She looked at him, her eyes adjusting to the

moonlight. "You're more to the people than just the bride of Lord Alvi. Remember that."

"Thank you, Harrison. For everything. For coming with me."

"As if I had a choice, Your Highness." But he grinned. "I am at your service to a fault. But I hope you will let me be in charge on this journey?"

Aerity spread a hand to the path in front of them. "All yours, Lieutenant. For the next month I am your subject. And if anyone asks I am Callie Hazlett."

"That is what I like to hear. I've mapped out a journey to Zandalee tribe land in Zorfina. It is best to stay in Lochlanach as long as possible. We will cross south creek and journey along Eurona River down to the border of Kalor. We'll follow the border until we come to the junction of Toresta. The ridgelands are not lenient with foreign travelers. As you know, they require papers. So at that point we will go south into Kalor, following the Kalorian border until we nearly reach the sea. Kalor is known for its lax borders. Only then will it be safe to pass into Zorfina. They are even less trusting than Toresta, but since the Zandalee control that portion of the country I'm hoping we won't run into any issues."

Aerity swallowed hard and nodded. Oh, seas. What had she gotten them into?

"Good. Now follow me, Miss Callie, and have no fear."

Chapter 7

Dearest Mother and Father,

I am in need of time to myself before my marriage takes place. I am leaving of my own accord and I swear to return. There is no need to alarm the kingdom. Perhaps it is best if no one knows of my absence outside the family. It is not my intention to cause you to panic or worry, though both are likely imminent. It is my sincere hope that you will someday forgive me. Please do not use your army to search for me. They are of more use searching for the enemy and keeping our people safe. I have a solid plan in place for myself.

In respect and love,

Your first daughter, Aerity

Dearest Vixie,

As far as adventures go, I can think of no one I'd rather have at my side than you. Please don't think I'm on a grand journey without you. This time will clear my head and put a lid on the things of my past that I cannot afford to take with me into my marriage and future. I promise to regale you with anything of interest that may happen during my time away from you, but in all honesty I'm hoping for an uneventful quest to embrace the woman I need to be. I will return to you very soon.

In the meantime, you are the princess of the castle. Enjoy.

With all my heart,

Your sister, Aerity

Vixie must have read the letter a hundred times. Blast that Aerity! How could she leave like that? Without telling her? Without a good-bye? Uneventful adventure or not, Vixie could have helped. She would have been willing to act as her maid if that's what it would have taken to get herself out of this confining castle and into the wild lands beyond.

Ugh! Vixie crumpled the paper and threw it at her bed. It hit far too softly. Jealousy and hurt and absolute boredom fought against her better nature.

She'd been left to deal with a mother driven mad by worry and a father who wanted to tear Eurona apart to find his oldest daughter. Vixie had squeezed her way into the family meeting that morning next to Wyneth. Her cousin could feign doe-eyed innocence all she wanted, but Vixie was no fool. Wyneth knew—Aerity would have told her everything. She'd stared hard at Wyneth during the meeting until Wyn gave her a sharp elbow in the ribs when no one was looking. Aye, so guilty, that one.

The final verdict from her father was to wait until they heard back from Lieutenant Gillfin, who had been on night watch the prior evening. His men said he left to check on activity at the guest stables, and the royal guards at the gate told of a dark-haired maid who passed through late during the night. Harrison came to the gates, asked who had just left, and told the guards he had suspicions about the young woman and was going to follow her.

"Lieutenant Gillfin has known Aerity all his life," the king explained. "And his instincts are strong. I believe he saw her from afar on his night watch and suspected it was her. It is my hope that he will find her and talk sense into her, or return her by force."

It all seemed highly suspicious to Vixie, Harrison being a longtime friend of Aerity's and all. But their father spoke of him as the utmost professional. *If anyone can keep her safe, it's Lieutenant Gillfin, blah, blah, blah. In the meantime no one outside of the family and royal guards shall know she is missing. I've never been more ashamed . . . worst possible timing, blah, blah, blah.*

Honestly, Vixie tired of his rant and began daydreaming, envisioning Aerity gallivanting about the lands, her hair blowing behind her, free as can be. The lucky cow.

Wyneth had shot from the room the moment the meeting

ended, leaving Vixie unable to question her.

Well, fine. If Aerity could rebel, then Vixie could break a few rules as well. She would go to the stables and ride, despite her father's warnings. The second beast had been killed and guards swarmed the royal lands. Other than Aerity's "disappearance," things were uneventful at that moment. They'd appeased the madwoman's first demand, but Vixie knew more was to come. She had to take advantage of the peace and quiet now while she could. So Vixie changed into riding clothes, already cheered at the idea of seeing her horse, Ruspin.

Four guards flanked her as she stepped from the castle into the chilly air. That was two more guards than usual. Her father probably put an extra watch on her in case she tried to follow her sister.

He knew her well.

As Vixie neared the royal stables she spotted men over at the guest stalls. At the sight of a lad with his brown hair pulled back neatly at the nape of his neck, she put a hand against her stomach . . . everything inside her stopped dead and then began to dance.

"Tiern!" Vixie ran.

Her guards shouted from behind her—"*Princess!*" "*Your Highness!*"—as they chased, but she ignored them.

Tiern's cocoa-brown eyes widened when he saw her, then became alarmed at the flock of guards running behind her. But she flung herself into his arms anyhow, laughing.

His hands touched her back for one second before a guard yelled, "Hands to yourself, lad!"

Tiern's hands went straight up, and he chuckled. "All right, then. No touching."

"He's one of the hunters," Vixie reminded the guards, releasing him. "Don't you remember?" She beamed up at Tiern, but his attention kept shifting to the men, two of whom had drawn their swords.

Vixie stepped away from him and put her hands on her hips. "He's perfectly harmless. You can put away your weapons." Then she turned back to Tiern and waved a hand at the guards as if he should pay them no mind.

Again he chuckled nervously, unable to ignore the men as easily as the princess, but after a moment he seemed to focus on Vixie and relax.

"What brings you back to royal lands?" she asked.

"I received a message from Lord Alvi and Lieutenant Gillfin about another beast, but I heard on my way here that it had been killed. Still, I thought I should come in case I'm needed again. I'll most likely stay at an inn at the local village until things settle down and the Rocato woman is found."

"Nonsense." Vixie couldn't stop smiling. "I shall see about getting you a room in the guest quarters of the castle!"

His eyebrows rose. "But—"

"Come on!" She grabbed his hand and pulled him past the glaring guards, who followed closely. When one cleared his throat menacingly, Tiern dropped her hand and gave a bashful shrug.

"This place is nearly deserted," Tiern noted as they passed the market.

"Aye," Vixie said sadly. They slowed their pace and walked side by side. "The markets reopened today, but as you can see only half of the normal trade tables are occupied, and even less than half of the normal customers have shown. Everyone is afraid since a Lashed One killed a woman in front of the castle . . . and of course there was the second beast."

Tiern nodded. "Tell me of it."

Vixie told Tiern all that had happened in his absence until they stopped at the west steps of the castle. She desperately wanted to tell him about Aerity, but the guards were standing too close, and she wasn't supposed to speak of it to anyone outside the family.

The doors swung open and they looked up to see Lord Alvi. The breeze blew his hair back and he stuck out his chest to take in the fresh air. Vixie held back a giggle as his eyes lowered to her, then Tiern, and narrowed.

"Ah, if it isn't the Seabolt lad." Lord Alvi came down the steps, and the guards backed slightly away, a show of their respect for the man.

He and Tiern made a show of grasping hands and clutching each other's forearms.

"I haven't seen you or your brother since that fateful day," Lord Alvi said in a low tone.

Tiern's face became hard and serious. "Aye."

"Any word from him?" Lord Alvi asked.

"Nay." Tiern's eyes faltered to Vixie and then looked out at the sea. She swore she saw pain in those depths, and it made her ache for him. Something had happened with his brother, but nobody would tell her. Aerity loved the older lad Pax; of that she was certain. And he'd fled when he lost her hand to the Ascomannian lord. Vixie hated that it had to be that way. Tragic.

Lord Alvi's voice lowered. "How many are there like him in your family?"

Tiern went rigid, and he spoke through gritted teeth. "No others."

"Like him?" Vixie asked. "What do you mean by that?"

Lord Alvi looked surprised, as if he had forgotten she was there. "Nothing, Your Highness. I'm joking with the lad." He grinned and patted Tiern hard enough on the back to push him forward a few inches. Tiern gave a tight smile.

Had Lord Alvi been calling Paxton a coward? Saying it ran in the family? She refused to let him give Tiern a hard time. "Let's go inside and see about getting you a room," Vixie said. She moved forward, but Tiern's voice stopped her.

"I'm not certain this is necessary, Princess. I don't want to be a bother." He stole a glance toward Lord Alvi, who had crossed his arms over his chest and watched the two of them with interest.

"No bother at all," she said. "Just follow me."

"Aye," Lord Alvi said to him. "It will be good to have another hunter around."

She turned and walked toward the steps, unease wringing her gut. Something was going on here that she wasn't privy to, and she intended to find out.

Chapter 8

Paxton's eyes shot open in the darkened tent where he slept with the other Lochlan man, Konor. He listened intently, trying to discern what had woken him. Konor's light snores were all he could hear now. His skin felt sticky from the perpetual moisture in the warm air. He sat up and crouched at the tent's opening, peering out.

All he saw was darkness and trees, but his instincts were buzzing with alertness. As he turned to get his bow, something cold and metallic gripped his arm with force and yanked him. He yelled and swung out with his other arm, only to have it grabbed as well. He was held in a way that his hands could not touch anything.

He tried to fight, kicking at air and twisting his torso,

until his eyes adjusted and he saw people stepping out slowly from the trees, with bows raised at him. One of them, a slight hooded figure with swaying hips, moved forward until she was feet away from him. She lifted back the hood and shook out her dark hair. Paxton's lungs squeezed at the sight of Rozaria Rocato. Her eyes squinted and then widened as she stared at Paxton. A smile spread across her face.

"Tell me, hunter," she said, and his hopes sank, "what brings you to Kalor?"

Deep seas . . . she recognizes me from that brief encounter on that bloody island. Ideas fired through his mind until one stuck. He thought she was probably too smart to believe him, but it was worth a try.

"Look at my hands and you will have your answer."

Her eyes skimmed over to his fingertips and back to his face. "You took part in murdering my favorite beast."

"I was there, aye. I intended to collect King Lochson's prize and instate some changes from the inside. But then that fool from the coldlands got to the creature first."

She studied him. "You would have married the girl and kept your true identity hidden in shame?"

"Not shame. Necessity. Until the king was dead and my Lashed blood was incorporated into the royal bloodlines."

Rozaria chuckled. She slowly raised her hand to Paxton's face and he flinched, cursing himself at the fear of her warm hand on his jaw. Without looking away from him she gave an order to her men. "Search their tents. Take any weapons."

Curses . . . his bow and daggers!

Rozaria cocked her head, that grin of mild amusement and power still on her lips. "You fear me." Her finger ran from under his ear to down his jawline.

By now, Konor and the Torestan campers were out of their tents, standing huddled together at sword point watching the spectacle.

Rozaria's hands drifted downward to the knot at the neck of Paxton's tunic. She untied it, exposing his chest. Paxton's arms flexed and the men held him tighter. They wore some sort of metal gloves with woven links that pinched his skin.

"What is your name?" Her hands went around his throat and slid down to the tops of his shoulders, under the fabric of his tunic.

He closed his eyes, controlling every urge to fight off her men. "Paxton Seabolt."

"Mm. Tell me, Paxton Seabolt . . ." Her hands trailed down to his chest and her palms flattened against his skin. "Where do your loyalties lie? Do not attempt to deceive me."

He tried to calm his heart as he opened his eyes, knowing this beautiful, malevolent face could be the last thing he would ever see.

"My loyalties lie with myself." Her palms pressed down and heated at his response. Suddenly, he could not take in air or exhale. *Depths of the seas, she's controlling my lungs!* His chest and throat began to sting with the need to breathe, his heart beating too hard. And all the while she stared calmly up into his eyes. He could feel his face darkening as he dug his heels into the ground.

Rozaria's hands cooled and eased up. Air poured into Paxton's lungs and he gasped, slumping forward in the men's grasp. After a few cleansing breaths his energy returned and he stood taller, facing down the woman and straining against the arms that held him. He could not afford to show fear.

"Will you make an enemy of me, Rozaria? When I am here to join you?"

Her eyes widened, seemingly thrilled by his anger.

"My loyalties have *never* been with the royals of Lochlanach." He allowed his old fury against the king to rise within him, though he couldn't seem to reach the level of rage he'd once felt, even given his circumstances. He blamed Aerity for that. He'd have to fake it. His voice rose to a shout. "What have they ever done for me? Because of them my grandmother died an untimely death, never allowed to be the person she was created to be! I refuse to let that happen to me."

Her hands lowered. "Tell me why you have come here, Paxton Seabolt."

"Because only you can help me achieve my goal of freedom. I want to return home someday. But I can no longer live without magic. Not since I've tasted it for myself. I refuse to forgo my health and die young because of a fool's old laws."

She grinned, a stunning upward curve of her reddened lips. "Lovely words, indeed. But I shall be keeping a close eye on you, hunter."

"I expected nothing less. But I will prove myself to you."

She searched Paxton's face. Seeming satisfied, she nodded to her men and they released him. Paxton shook out his arms, a scowl on his face. It was imperative he earn her trust if he was to infiltrate her ranks, but he didn't know what it would take to prove himself to the madwoman. One thing was for certain though—he'd do damn near anything to keep Aerity safe.

Chapter 9

Aerity had been so determined not to be a spoiled, pampered ninny, but the cold was truly more than she'd bargained for. The first night she'd kept warm from sheer excitement, and it had only been several hours until daybreak when the sun would warm her again. The second night when the sun dropped and the chill hit, the excitement wore down, now as thin as her commoner clothing. Still, she refused to complain.

They'd ridden thirteen hours, passing through the shallowest part of Eurona River, which still soaked their legs. Each time they'd passed travelers on the path, Aerity had been terrified, but nobody had taken much notice of them. They'd stopped to change out of their wet clothing and eat, but a chill had set over Aerity.

Harrison, seas love him, took one look at her crouched over on the horse, hugging one arm across her middle, and stopped in his tracks. He leaned over and felt her cloak.

"Is this the warmest thing you've got?"

"Aye. A thicker cloak would have drawn attention."

He pulled a bound blanket from his horse's pack and handed it to her. "Wrap this around yourself. And take these." He tossed her a pair of fingerless gloves. Regular gloves were frowned upon due to fears of people hiding lash marks.

"Won't you need them?" He'd changed into commoner clothing the night before.

"Nay." He pulled a stocking cap over his head, covering his ears. "This'll do the trick for me." He gave a carefree grin that made Aerity's heart ache with a moment of reminiscence. How many times had he given her that comfortable grin over the years?

"Thank you, Harrison. Thank you for doing this. I know you have a lot to lose if you're found out—"

"Nay, dear *Callie*." He squeezed her hand and let go, facing forward again. "I fear these days I have nothing at all to lose." He trotted forward, leaving her to ponder his words of melancholy as she pulled the gloves on and tapped her horse's side to catch up.

They rode on in silence down the dark path until both of them and their horses were too tired to go farther. They traveled into the southeastern Lochlan woods off the path until Harrison found three trees with thin trunks close enough together to support a tent with rope and linen. He lay a blanket on the ground.

"Fit for a maiden."

She collapsed onto it without hesitation, her whole body exhausted and sore. Harrison sat down beside her, staring up at the moon and stars.

"Aren't you tired?" Aerity's words came out slightly slurred.

He didn't answer. Instead he looked down at her and chuckled. "You appear to be in a tangle." Indeed, she'd lain down with the blanket still around her. She wiggled and broke into a fit of giggles to find she was quite stuck. Harrison grasped the edge of the blanket and yanked, sending Aerity rolling to the side in a rush of laughter.

"Someone is punchy." He laughed when she reached out and punched his arm.

Aerity sat up beside him now, replacing the blanket over herself. "Is there another blanket?"

He shook his head. "It's all right."

"Don't be silly. We'll share this one. I'll not object to extra body heat, if it's all the same to you." She unfolded and tossed the blanket over the both of them, and they lay back. Harrison propped his forearm behind his head.

"I'm not sure your betrothed would approve of this arrangement."

A bark of laughter issued from the princess. "I don't quite care for his approval."

Harrison was quiet. Aerity wouldn't tell him of Lord Alvi's affairs. She was certain Harrison already didn't care for the man. Aerity lifted the blanket to her chin, her eyelids feeling heavy.

"Would you truly have married me if you'd killed the beast?" she whispered.

"If you had wanted me to, of course."

She smiled to herself. "Even though you only love me as a friend?"

"Aye. I would have done whatever you needed of me."

"And what of you? Don't you want to find love someday?

He paused so long Aerity though he might've fallen asleep. She looked over at his wide eyes, staring at the night sky.

"Perhaps not everyone is meant to be with the one they love," he said.

Aerity turned and propped up on her elbow to face him. "Do you love someone, Harrison?"

"All my life," he said wistfully. "As long as I can remember."

This shocked her to the core. She gave him a playful shove and demanded, "*Who?*"

"No one who loves me back."

"Tell me!" She pushed him again, and he sat up, laughing. "Is it someone I know?"

Harrison took her by the shoulders and pressed her down, pulling the blanket up over her face until she laughed and flung it down. Then he kissed her forehead and lay back beside her. "Never you mind. It was doomed from the start. Go to sleep, rebel princess."

"Will you truly not tell me?"

"Truly."

He was maddeningly private and always had been. Aerity was dying to know what secrets were held in that chambered heart of his, but she knew he would tell her nothing.

"Harrison . . . is your love a man or a woman?"

Harrison blinked up at the sky, his face filling with mirth. "I think I'll not answer that."

Worry struck her. "Have I offended you?"

"Nay. It's fun to keep you guessing."

She nuzzled her cold nose against the fabric at his shoulder. "Fine. I shall leave you alone. But your secrets would be safe with me if ever you decide to let them out. It can't be healthy to keep things trapped within."

"You're probably right, but it would change nothing to speak of it. Now, worry not, and get some rest."

She rolled toward him and took his arm in a hug, soaking in his warmth until she drifted to sleep.

By the fifth day of travel, Aerity began to experience a deep sense of pride that she'd never felt before—the pride of accomplishment. Out here, she had no maid to help her dress or bring her tea or warm her a bath. And she didn't miss those comforts as much as she thought she might, though her scalp itched and her skin longed for the tropical oils she used daily for moisture. Caring for herself made her feel stronger. Capable. She wondered what Paxton would think of this version of her. The version with her hair wound into a bun, hands red from scrubbing stockings in a stream, eating stale bread and hardened cheese, and still smiling.

Her primary concerns were a sore bottom and aching legs. She did her best to stretch the muscles each time they stopped, reminding herself that this pain was temporary.

When they reached the River Kalor, Aerity immediately became nervous. It was deeper and rougher than the shallow part of the Eurona River they'd crossed.

"Are you certain the horses can make it?" she asked.

He nodded. "I've brought us to the narrowest part. You'll need to hold on tight and trust your horse. Follow me. We'll rest on the other side."

Aerity lifted what she could of her belongings and raised them from the horse's side to its back, then hiked up her dress to her hips. By the time they got to the middle of the river, she could sense her horse pushing hard to battle the current and stay straight on course behind Harrison.

Harrison peered out at the river and yelled something she couldn't quite make out. She looked as well and saw darkness moving in the water. Within seconds something slid against her leg and Aerity screamed. She let go of the reins, and her horse gave a buck of fear. Aerity splashed into the water, going completely under. She came up sputtering to the sound of Harrison yelling, "Swim!"

She got her bearings and tread water as the school of wide-mouth fish finished swimming past. For sea's sake! She'd been frightened by fish! Thankfully her horse had calmed and was moving quickly now. She felt her hair against her neck and realized it had come out of the bun. When she looked at the water by her shoulder she could see dye spreading and disappearing.

"My hair!" She tried her best to grasp it and pile it atop her head as her feet kicked and she swam toward the shore.

Harrison was atop his horse on the bank, laughing at her as she trudged out, panting, still holding her wet locks. She let her hair fall to the side and gave it a gentle squeeze, whimpering when she saw more dye spill to the ground.

"My hair," she said again.

"Really, princess, since when are you so vain and frightened by water?"

"It's the dye," she told him. "Has it all been washed away?"

His laughter stopped. "Nay, it is still brown."

Aerity worked to dry it, trying to handle it as little as possible. It looked dark from what she could see, but hair always looked darker when wet.

"Harrison, you must swear to me you will tell me if the color lightens. I have more dye, but I have to use it sparingly. You have to make a habit of keeping an eye on my silly hair since I have no looking glass. I cannot afford to be recognized."

"I swear it, Aerity."

His solemn eyes were sincere, and she started to relax.

Her horse drank from the edge of the river while Aerity changed. She approached the animal and scratched his jawline.

"I'm sorry I startled you in the water," she told him.

He turned and nuzzled her neck, making her laugh. Then, as had become his habit, he reached around and pressed his nose to her chest, snorting.

"No! Those aren't apples, you silly thing." She pushed his head gently away and stood, patting his neck. Even her fear of horses had slightly diminished. But only slightly.

"Are you hiding your treats from him again?" Harrison asked from his place by the fire. Aerity walked past him and swatted his head with her damp stockings. He merely chuckled and continued to roast a wild rabbit that he'd caught.

"I've never seen you with hair on your face," Aerity mused.

Harrison brought a hand up and ran it down the stubble there. "Aye. Do I look dapper?"

"Nay, you look like a rogue version of yourself. But I rather like it. I think your secret love would, as well."

He gave a grunt, and Aerity bit back a smile.

Through the woods, Aerity heard a group passing in a horse-drawn cart. Harrison stood, managing to appear menacing.

"Stand near your horse, Aerity. Be ready to mount, if needed."

The traveling party seemed to slow when they caught sight of Aerity and Harrison's camp. The princess quickly tied her pack to the side of her saddle and tried not to appear as panicked as she felt. They'd seen few travelers since they'd been in the woods, and all had made her anxious.

Harrison whispered, "Looks like a Lochlan-style cart and workhorse."

As they neared, Harrison raised a hand in friendly greeting and the unsmiling man at the reins slowly raised a hand in response. Aerity's heart pounded as the two men in the seat and a man in the back of the cart stared until they passed from sight.

"How much longer until we reach Kalor?" Aerity asked.

"Two or three days, perhaps. We're making good time since we're keeping near the path and riding so long each day. But we'd be making even *better* time if you'd agree to allow your horse to go faster than a walk."

He gave her a wink, and Aerity glared. "It's better for their stamina if we don't push them too hard."

"I am at your mercy." He tore a piece of meat from the rabbit and held it out to her. Aerity hesitated before taking it, trying her best not to imagine the adorable animal hopping without a care just an hour ago. She was thankful for the energy it would bring. She was also thankful that the weather was at least ten degrees warmer than in southern Lochlanach.

After they'd eaten and packed, they mounted their horses and set forth again. Aerity let herself fall into her usual daydream of what it would be like to see Pax. In her musings he was sometimes tentative when he saw her, worried, and then he would soften. Other times she imagined he'd run to her straightaway. Always his reaction ended in happiness. Oh, how she longed for that.

She was in the middle of a particularly honeyed daydream when Harrison suddenly slowed and whispered, "Aer . . ." Her entire body immediately went on alert, tensing, as she stared ahead to where he looked. Deep in the trees to the left of the path was the horse and cart they'd seen earlier, but the three men were nowhere in sight.

It could be nothing. They could have stopped to eat and rest, but where were they? It felt strange.

Turning his head slightly toward Aerity, Harrison whispered, "Follow my lead, and hold on tight to your reins. We'll get as close as is safe, and then we're going to gallop into the trees on the right to bypass their camp."

Aerity braced. *Gallop.* What if she fell? What if her horse spooked and threw her off? Harrison must have sensed her fears.

"Squeeze with your legs and lean forward. Your horse will follow the lead of mine, but you must keep control of him. You can do this. I won't let anything happen to you."

She swallowed.

Her stomach was in a tight knot as she searched the trees for the men. She began looking around her, expecting someone to jump out at any moment, or an arrow to fly at them. They could be bandits or angry Lashed.

"*Now.*" Harrison heeled his horse hard in the sides and

leaned forward, turning them from the path. He took off in a flash, straight into the trees. Aerity followed his form, her heart in her throat as she felt the world go topsy-turvy beneath her. She bit back a scream and held on tight, squeezing her thighs around the creature and leaning forward to help it gain momentum. She watched Harrison and his horse, leading hers right and left to dart around trees, too focused to take notice of their surroundings . . . until an arrow whirred past, just ahead of Harrison, and male shouts abounded from the direction of the path.

"Faster!" Harrison yelled. He hunkered further and shot forward. Aerity gritted her teeth and kicked, spurring her horse with a shout.

They ran and ran for what felt like ages before Harrison peered over his shoulder and finally slowed his steed.

"What do they want?" Aerity asked. She was breathing hard.

"Thieves, most likely. Or outlaws. We've got to keep at a quick clip to stay ahead of them. Their single horse won't be able to keep up, especially pulling three men in a cart."

Onward they went at a quick trot, staying off the path and winding through trees and brush. Aerity suddenly broke out in a cold sweat and sucked in air raggedly. Her chest felt constricted, like her heart was failing. Harrison glanced back at the sounds and quickly spun his horse around until they were sidled close together.

He cupped her face on both sides and held her with strong

hands, forcing her eyes to focus on him. "Breath, Aer. Big breaths. That's a girl." His thumbs stroked her cheeks. "You're in a panic, and well you should be. But it's all right now. We're safe. You were amazing."

Her eyes fluttered closed as she felt her heart righting itself, her breathing regulating.

"You did it," he said. "You put Vixie's riding to shame."

Aerity laughed at the ridiculousness of that idea and took Harrison's wrists. "I think not. But thank you. I'm sorry—let's not stop any longer."

He gave a nod and pulled his horse forward again, cantering off. Aerity took one long look behind her into the vacant trees and then pushed onward. A newfound confidence filled her from head to toe. With each muscle that moved within the horse, her own body responded, moving with him in sync. She found that she could anticipate the animal's forward-and-back movement and wave of motion in its hips. It felt more natural to her now. Instinctive. She ran a hand down her horse's mane as far as she could reach and gave him a strong pat.

"Good boy. Good, handsome boy."

His head bobbed, as if responding to her compliment, and for the first time ever she realized she'd bonded with a horse. Did he actually *like* her?

"Harrison," she called out, "what's this horse's name?"

"Not sure," he said over his shoulder. "He's new to the guesthouse."

Aerity patted him again. "I shall call you Jude."

Chapter 10

After five days, Tiern still felt absolutely out of place as a guest in the castle. He'd stayed there once before in High Hall, with the other hunters during the flooding rains, but to have his own room in the guest wing felt . . . strange. His quarters were nearly as large as his family's entire house. He would have been more comfortable in a spare room in the soldiers' barracks where he didn't have to worry about manners and niceties.

Truth be told, he wasn't feeling like his old, carefree self these days. The past months had opened his eyes and made him into a man, putting burdens and knowledge on his back that weighed down his smile. Between the great hunt and his brother leaving after saving Tiern's life with his magic, a heaviness had settled about him. Add to that the things he'd witnessed in the towns of Lochlanach during his travels . . . those visions had rid him of the last vestiges of innocence in his heart.

Each day he'd been invited to dine with the royal family and Lord Alvi, and though he knew they saw his presence as a necessary precaution—a hunter on hand in case another beast invaded—he could not settle in and relax. The royals were too preoccupied to notice things that plagued him, like the way Lord Alvi sometimes watched him as if he didn't trust him. Or the fact that he couldn't hold his fork and knife in a proper way to cut his food and gently push pieces onto the edge of his fork to bring them to his mouth. He always dropped something, but the only person who noticed was Vixie. She was there with a smile and giggle every time.

Princess Vixie was the happiest, friendliest lass he'd ever met. His mood had been so dark since Lord Alvi killed the beast and Paxton left. The only time Tiern felt a fraction of himself was in Vixie's presence. Her ability to lift his spirits was addicting. But ever since he'd learned he was of Lashed blood, and seen how the people of the land were reacting to Lashed Ones, his romantic ideals for the future had taken a dive into the depths of the seas.

The things he'd seen on his journey to the royal lands and in his own town, barely being held together by a few peacekeepers forcing the hotheads not to act in violence, had disgusted and saddened him to his core. He'd been prepared to help their local Lashed man if the townspeople had attacked, but thankfully it hadn't come to that.

Towns were not faring well, and he shivered to remember. Burned homes and funeral processions. Eyes full of distress and mouths spewing malice. Normal people being worked up into mobs by hysterical leaders.

In one town he'd passed a man hanging from a tree by his neck with a sign that said Lashed Not Welcome Here. That could have been his brother, the best man that he knew. The sight nearly made him sick. Tiern had taken one look at the man's unlined nails before sprinting down the path in a cold sweat to put distance between himself and those people. The man's blank eyes haunted him. Had he been one of their registered Lashed who followed the law and never did magic? Or a sympathizer? Or merely a family member of a Lashed, like himself?

An irrational fear had risen inside him after that: Could people simply look at him and know he had Lashed blood, though he didn't display magical abilities? Had people found out about Paxton and spread the word about the Seabolts? Was his family in danger?

Nay. He knew none of that was the case, but still his mind was cautious.

At breakfast on his fifth morning, a messenger entered and handed King Charles a parchment. The entire table stopped eating and stared, even the children, waiting to see how he'd react. Some mornings he simply read the note with a stoic face and excused himself. Other mornings he would shut his eyes or bang a fist on the table. Yesterday he flipped his plate of eggs and sausages over before barreling out of the room with his lords and the queen on his heels.

"What's it say, Papa?" Prince Donubhan asked, just as he had every morning. And once again the king ignored the eager boy, lost in his own thoughts.

As they waited, Vixie sent Tiern a nervous glance from across the table. But the king simply stood without opening the parchment, and left them. The lords, ladies, and queen shared heavyhearted glances before they got up and followed, accompanied by Lord Alvi.

Lady Wyneth didn't get up, and Vixie nudged her, whispering, "Go find out what's going on!"

Wyneth appeared hesitant. "It's not good, Vix. It's never good."

"Will you tell me what's happening? They won't let me in."

Tiern followed Wyneth's eyes to where maids descended upon the royal children at the other end of the table, helping them focus on cleaning their hands and faces.

Wyneth looked toward Tiern and Vixie, then lowered her voice. "Each day a commoner in different towns throughout Lochlanach has turned up dead. In Rozaria's original notice she said people would be killed by new beasts. But these deaths have all been done at the hands of unknown Lashed. No blood or injury to be seen. All young men and women."

Tiern's gut churned, and Vixie gasped in horror.

"What is he going to do?" Vixie hissed.

Wyneth gave a sad shrug. "She won't stop unless the laws against magic are lifted."

Vixie's eyes met Tiern's, so expressive in her dread and dismay. He bit his tongue against all the things he wanted to say. Why would a Lashed One do this? Did they not value human life? Tiern shut his eyes. No, he couldn't say "they." That wasn't fair. It was not all Lashed—his brother would never act that way. But it frustrated him to no end that a select few had decided to act in this extreme way. Did they have any clue how they were hurting their own cause?

"And to make matters worse," Wyneth whispered, "they still have not discovered which of the king's advisers was the traitor. He's decided to dismiss most of them and keep only the two oldest councilmen who date back to his father's reign."

Shock zinged through Tiern, and he leaned forward against the table. "There was a traitor?"

Wyneth slapped a hand over her mouth. The princess waved off her cousin's worries. "Tiern can be trusted. You must know that on instinct or you wouldn't have blurted it out."

Wyneth's face turned red.

"I won't say anything," Tiern promised. "I swear it."

They explained to him what had happened with the list burning. All he could do was shake his head, powerless. This, all of this, was greater than any beast. This was terror within terror. The people were afraid of everything and nothing, the seen and unseen, the known and unknown, all at once. Rational people were turning on one another. Lochlans were turning on their kingdom.

"But if he declares the laws to be overturned," Tiern thought out loud, "more than one person will die each day. The entire *kingdom* could revolt. The towns . . . deep seas, the towns are not in good shape right now."

Wyneth and Vixie both were quiet. What was there to say? They could do nothing.

"It makes me nervous for Princess Aerity to be studying abroad in the coldlands this month," Tiern pondered. "I know she's to marry a man from Ascomanni, but it still seems a poor time to send her on a trip."

Wyneth and Vixie reacted strangely to this, blinking through a stretch of awkward silence. He immediately regretted saying a word.

"I meant no offense. I'm certain she's being watched carefully."

Wyneth muttered to Vixie, "I thought you'd told him."

"Told him what, exactly?" Vixie muttered back with apparent annoyance. "Seeing as how I do not know anything about this trip abroad."

Wyneth turned to her completely. "I assumed you would figure out the truth. Did she not write you, Vix? Where do you imagine she's going?"

Vixie stared at her, thinking.

"Whoa, wait a moment." Tiern held up his hands. "She's

not in Ascomanni? But a maid told me—"

"Nay," Vixie said. "That's the story Father made up to keep the staff and people from panicking. Aerity has . . . run off. Taken time to herself." She tilted her head toward Wyneth. The two stared at each other, Wyneth waiting expectantly, until Vixie's eyes went big. By now, Tiern was utterly confused and bloody curious.

Vixie began to sputter "Did she— Has she gone to . . . his brother?" She pointed to Tiern, and his heart sped up. Wyneth nodded.

"She's gone to find Pax?" he asked.

The girls turned to him now.

"Aye," Wyneth whispered.

Deep blue seas. His heart suddenly hurt, a massive longing for his brother's presence overwhelming him. He had an urge to run for his horse to join them, but it had been at least five days since she left. He couldn't believe the oldest princess would take such a dangerous risk. How many times had he himself thought of trying to find Pax? But his parents and duties to his town and kingdom had kept him planted in place.

"Is she alone?" he asked.

"Seas no," Wyneth whispered. "Harrison accompanied her."

"Did he?" Vixie asked with interest.

"Aye. But Uncle Charles believes Harrison went to find her and bring her back. So, as far as I know, he hasn't sent anyone else out, though I think that might change now that a bit of time has passed. He's getting impatient and worried. He'd have the military after her if he wasn't so preoccupied."

"Tell me everything, Wyn," Vixie demanded. "I can't even believe you'd keep me in the dark like everyone else."

"I truly believed you'd figured the truth of it by now. And, besides, can you honestly say you wouldn't have insisted on joining her?"

Vixie crossed her arms, scowling. She knew Wyneth was right. Vixie would have gone. "Just tell me how she did it?"

Tiern sat riveted at the tale of Princess Aerity's transformation, and while Wyneth talked he felt himself warming at the thought of Aerity searching for his brother. She wouldn't have done it if she didn't love him. Their future queen loved his brother and was putting herself in danger to find him. And to think his brother could have killed the beast and married Aerity . . . if only he had not chosen to heal Tiern instead.

A flood of sour guilt made him woozy. He stood abruptly, his palms flat on the table as his head spun. Vixie's large round eyes peered up at him in worry.

"Are you all right?"

"Aye . . . I just need a moment."

Tiern walked from the dining area, trying to breathe away the tightness in his chest. But sea winds seemed to be blowing in the wrong direction for him at that moment because he ran into the last person he wanted to see. Lord Alvi was exiting the king's office, a grim look on his face as he came to Tiern's side.

"Let's walk," the coldlands man said.

Tiern exhaled and stayed at the man's side as they walked down the halls and exited the castle. Several soldiers rushed out from behind them, and the hunters moved to the side to let them pass.

"They're sending more troops to quell the restlessness in the kingdom." Lord Alvi led them to the side of the cobbled road overlooking the sea to the west.

"Another killing?" Tiern asked.

Lord Alvi stared darkly out at the sea and gave a single nod. "They've scarcely any soldiers to spare. They're all out searching for the Lashed woman and her henchmen, or hench-*women*, as it may be."

A sharp gust of wind hit them, and Tiern felt a lock of his hair come dislodged from its binding. He shoved it back behind his ear, muttering, "This is madness." The king had to consider some sort of compromise.

"I need you to listen to me, Tiern." The seriousness of Lord Alvi's voice brought back Tiern's earlier feelings of unease, but his next words were a punch to his gut. "Keep your distance from the younger princess."

Tiern clenched his teeth. "I have no intentions of courting Princess Vixie."

"And yet, it seems she has every intention of being courted by you. And after giving his first daughter away, I daresay the king would be remiss if he gave his other daughter whatever she wants. Unless, of course, there is a need to offer Vixie's hand in a future proclamation."

Tiern's hackles went up in an uncanny moment of ferocity. "He can't do that!"

"Oh, he can. And if necessary, he will. But settle down, lad. It's not on the table yet."

Tiern's chest felt as if it were caving. If the king wanted to kill Vixie's bright spirit, giving her away would be the way to do it.

"You'd do well to rein in your feelings for the lass," Lord Alvi said. "You wear them openly. Think of the future of the kingdom. Think of your bloodline and what the people will do if one of their precious future royals turns out to be Lashed? Imagine the kingdom revolting, ready to tear down the monarchy and replace it. Always imagine the worst and never underestimate the people."

"Enough!" Tiern leaned forward, hands on his knees, afraid he might be sick. "You're only saying this because the princess preferred a Lashed over you."

Tiern felt Lord Alvi's hand press firmly against his shoulder. "I'm saying it because it is the truth. As royals we must think always of the people and the kingdom. What they want or don't want will always be most important. Aerity understands this, but Vixie has not yet grasped it."

Tiern stood upright again. As much as he hated Lord Alvi for saying it, he knew the man was right, and he could read between the lines. Princess Vixie would not leave him alone, so it would be up to him. The thought of hurting her feelings in any way was a massive blow to his system. He'd been a fool to pretend there was a drop of a chance between them to begin with.

He gave Lord Alvi a nod and made his way down to the docks to be alone.

Chapter 11

Rozaria Rocato and her supporters were thorough about weeding through the people at the camp to be sure they were loyalists, willing to do any sort of menial work for the cause of Lashed rights in Eurona. She'd given rousing speeches about the worthiness and necessity of her cause. She made it sound damn good, as if it were truly the only way—that peaceful tactics were a waste of time and not an option. Paxton was not swayed, but he watched Konor succumb, eyes alight with worshipful vehemence.

The sun was setting, dulled by the thick surrounding trees and vines, like walls of green surrounding them. Paxton, Konor, Chun, and his family sat on one side of an unlit pile of sticks while Rozaria faced them, front and center, her men around her in a large semicircle. Paxton noticed that one woman was never far from Rozaria's side. She was shorter and thinner, and always kept the hood of her cloak up, hiding her face. The woman turned away from the others when she ate and never spoke to anyone, but her attentiveness to Rozaria was unmistakable. He kept an eye on her, knowing the silent ones were not to be underestimated.

Paxton also noticed that the largest man of the group, who was always at Rozaria's right hand, was overly attentive as well, but in another way. He gazed at the Rocato woman like a lovelorn sap and sought her approval in all things. Paxton couldn't understand everything the man was saying in Kalorian, but he imagined it was something like "Is the meat cooked to your liking, my lady?" "Shall I strangle anyone for you today?" "Here, let me rip down this tree and hack it into a comfortable seat for you."

And anytime Rozaria turned her attention to Paxton, he could feel the brute's jealous eyes boring into him. Paxton paid him no mind, and sweetened his disposition toward the Lashed leader a wee bit, hoping he could cause smoke to curl from the man's ears.

But for Paxton, a sweeter disposition simply meant he was willing to nod his head, make eye contact, and pretend not to hate her. He even spared a couple half grins for her sarcasm. Throughout the day, her keen eyes had followed his every move as he'd set about helping in the camp, skinning a rabbit, tending the fire, and fetching buckets of water to boil. He was certain she didn't trust him, but he felt there was a warmer undercurrent in her interest—something he was willing to use in his favor if needed.

His heart nearly stopped as he watched a Kalorian man lean over the sticks, just as he himself had in Toresta, and light them with his hands. It was a wondrous thing. And to do it with no fear of repercussion. Paxton wanted that open freedom for himself and all Lashed everywhere.

But not for the price Rozaria had put on it. He couldn't let himself forget how she sent the first beast into Lochlanach, having taught it to kill men. And kill it did. Hundreds of hunters, commoners, and soldiers, all dead so that she could manipulate King Charles into succumbing to her demands. There had to be a better way.

Once the fire was crackling, people put their catches on the end of long sticks and turned them over the flames. Paxton, like most of the others, had fish from the freshwater lake, striped bass and catfish. One of the men had a snake, and another had gutted a turtle.

Rozaria's lovesick goon had two fish over the flames, no doubt cooking one for her while she sat back, her legs crossed, assessing the campers until her eyes stopped on Paxton and a mischievous smile bloomed.

"What do you think of our kingdom of Kalor, hunter?"

He rubbed the half inch of scruff that had grown on his chin. "I like your heat but don't care for the muggy air." Lochlanach had its bad days in the summer, but nothing like this.

Her oaf must not have approved of Paxton's tone, because he gave a grunt and glared hard at him. Even Konor and the other campers watched their exchange with interest. Paxton kept his eyes on Rozaria.

"You grow accustomed," she said.

Paxton nodded, though he doubted he could get used to the dampness. Rozaria watched him for another quiet moment before turning her gaze to the former chef of the Cliftonia royals in Toresta.

"Mister Chun Aval . . ."

He bowed his smooth head. "Yes, Miss Rocato."

She stared at the man, as if contemplating. Then she stood and began to pace before the fire. Everyone's dinner was cooked by then, but nobody ate. They watched the woman, waiting to hear what she would say, what grand scheme she was plotting. Finally, she decided to enlighten them.

"For one year I have been gathering people who agree that change is needed throughout all lands, at any cost. But each person in my ranks must prove themselves worthy and loyal."

She stopped and turned to face them. As if some silent cue had been given, Rozaria's brutes rose behind her and began to circle the campers until they were surrounded. Hair rose on Paxton's arms. Chun's wife wrapped their young daughter in her arms and peered around at Rozaria's men. Chun's brother was older, and his two sons were teenagers, but still young enough to show fear in their eyes. They moved minutely closer to their father. Paxton couldn't take it any longer. He stood to face the Rocato woman.

"What exactly do you have in mind?" he asked in a steady voice.

Rozaria smiled as if she found him to be eager. She gave a nod to the hulking man at her side and called him by name. "Martone . . ." She gave him an order in Kalorian and he set off, leaving their group and moving toward the dilapidated building. She appeared quite pleased with herself. A feeling of dread pooled inside Paxton. The campers looked around at one another with anxious expressions.

Moments later, Martone came out of the building holding a hunched man by the arm. The man's hands were bound behind his back, and he stumbled as he was pulled along, as if he didn't have the energy to put one foot in front of the other.

When they reached the fire, Martone gave the man a shove, and he fell by Rozaria's feet. She sneered down at him. He was filthy, his hair matted and his tunic torn down the center.

"We encountered this piece of rubbish in southern Lochlanach," Rozaria told them. "He was spying on our camp by the river's edge, and do you know what he said?"

She nudged the man with her foot and he mumbled, "Please, miss."

"Silence!" She stared from Paxton to Chun to his relatives. "He said he saw what we were, and he told us he was going to the authorities. He said we would all be killed." Her eyes shone as she stared down at the man now. "Tell them what you called us."

He shook his head and curled into a ball. "I'm sorry, miss! I'm—"

"'*Unnatural vermin!*'" she yelled down at him. "That is what you called us! 'Devils of the sea!'" Her eyes were wild with fury and indignation as she looked out at the campers now. "Come forward, Chun."

Paxton wanted to stop this. Everything in him screamed against the thought of Chun being asked to hurt a bound man.

Chun's wife covered her mouth as he walked around the fire. Rozaria looked down at the prisoner.

"Get to your feet," she ordered. The man struggled and flailed until Rozaria rolled her eyes and motioned for Martone to lift him, which he did.

Shaking and hunched, the man was the same size as Chun, who looked at the prisoner with trepidation. Then Chun turned his questioning eyes to Rozaria.

"In my army, you must always be prepared to protect our kind. Men like this"—she jutted her chin—"cannot be changed. His hatred of our kind will be passed along to the next generation. It is not enough to change laws in our governments. If the people still treat Lashed as evil entities, what life is that?" She glanced over at Chun's family. His daughter's face was hidden in his wife's embrace, and his teenage nephews kept their faces down.

Rozaria shook her head. "I want to see your eyes. All of

you. Your children's as well." She waited until the parents reluctantly nudged their children to look at her. "Whether you are Lashed or not, you carry the blood. You are one of us. You are in danger of being poorly treated, of being killed no matter how well you behave. You must not fear what must be done. In this way, you will be safe. In this way, you will prosper. I will let no harm befall you." Again, her eyes gleamed with that maniacal zealousness. "I vow that one day, you will each be respected in your community. You will be treated like the noble-blooded citizens you are. You will each be kings and queens in your own right."

Her words, her sure tone, her radiance—she had the entire camp bedazzled. The people nodded, some of the fear dissipating from their postures. But Paxton could not relax. Chun was not a killer. He was a harmless chef. This would change the man irrevocably, and his family along with him.

Rozaria faced Chun, the fire lighting her face with a fluttering wickedness.

"Put your hands on him, Chun. Stop his heart." The Torestan stared at her, then at the prisoner, then back at her as if uncertain of her seriousness. "He is not worthy of pity. He would have you killed. He would gladly have killed your *daughter*." She pointed at his girl, who watched with big eyes.

Chun's hand slowly lifted, but he hesitated. "I—I've never killed someone."

"Do not think of him as a man. He is your enemy. Focus

on stopping the movement of blood through his heart, and it will happen."

"Nay, please!" the man cried out.

Chun hesitated, his breathing heavy. Konor watched, riveted, a partial smile on his face. Paxton had the feeling the man would step in to offer to do it if Chun could not. Paxton stayed very still, but his eyes darted around him for any possible weapon. This was the worst of circumstances. He was surrounded by men who weren't just armed, they were Lashed. Attempting to escape or stop this madness was futile. His mind whirred. He couldn't let Chun do this. He couldn't watch a man be killed.

"Let me be clear." Rozaria's voice lowered to a deadly tone. "There is no going back from this camp. Those who get this far know too much. Your family either proves their loyalty to this noble cause or you choose to die. Your death would be an unnecessary shame." Chun began to visibly shake as she continued. "Imagine that this man has a knife at your daughter's throat. He would if he could. He would *kill* her."

Chun's Adam's apple bobbed as he swallowed hard and his hand rose an inch, then fell, rose two inches, then faltered. *No* . . . Rozaria's lips began to tighten.

Raging seas.

"I'll do it," Paxton said in a rush. All eyes turned to him. Every pulse point on his body banged as his eyes fastened on Rozaria's. "Let me be the first to prove myself."

It seemed as if the entire camp drew in a breath and held

it. A feminine chuckle rose from Rozaria, and she pulled her hair over her shoulder, twisting it as she pondered him. The glee on her face was enough to make him ill, but he held his ground and composure.

"Surely you'll have another opportunity for Chun," Paxton said, stepping between Chun and the prisoner. "He's a chef, you know. He'll be good to have around when you get tired of Martone's subpar roasting skills."

At this, Rozaria's face lit up, and a delighted peal of laughter rang out as she clasped her hands under her chin. Her attention was all for Paxton.

Please let this work, he begged the seas.

He gave Rozaria an imploring look, as if to ask May I?

She pulled her bottom lip between her teeth, and Paxton forced a conspiratorial grin to his face.

Rozaria held out an arm as if waving him forward. "If you feel so inclined."

Relief rippled through him, and he met the prisoner's wild eyes. He raised both hands and took the man's face in his.

"Please, sir," the Lochlan rasped.

"Sh . . .I think you've said enough in your day."

Paxton's heart thrummed wildly.

The man frantically looked deeper into Paxton's eyes, and when he found no sympathy there, the prisoner's look of panic morphed into hardened hatred. He rasped out one word as his eyes bulged: "*Monster.*"

Behind the man, Rozaria sucked in a breath. Paxton's

stomach turned over. He held the foolish man's head harder, willing him to be silent, and began to concentrate. Rather than pushing his magic down to the man's heart to stop it as Rozaria wanted, Paxton pushed it upward into the man's mind. He'd never done anything like this—never tampered with a person's consciousness. He pressed the magic harder than absolutely necessary and the man whimpered.

Sleep, Paxton thought. He felt his energy inexplicably searching, probing, surging, then a burst of heat flamed from his wrists down to his fingertips. The prisoner shuddered violently, then he became heavy until Paxton felt his magic bumping up against something, as if it were as far as it could go. The man slumped forward, and Paxton caught him. He looked up at Rozaria.

"Where do you dispose of bodies?"

Her eyes—the way she was gazing at him—he'd only seen that kind of passion in women he'd bedded. It pulsed through him, along with the buzzing of magic within his blood.

"Martone will take him," she said in a husky voice.

Paxton shook his head. Then he bent and lugged the man's limp body over his shoulder, feeling the desperate need to go before the prisoner awoke from his magical slumber. "He's my kill. I want to finish it myself."

"Spoken like a true hunter." Rozaria pointed at Lake Rainiard where the moon reflected off its dark, glassy surface. "Take him into the woods for the animals on the other side of the lake."

He began to walk away when he heard her say, "And when you return, see me in my tent."

Oh, bloody seas. He cursed himself for using his wiles to distract her from the truth. Still, he forced himself to look at her and say, "Of course, Rozaria."

As he turned to leave he caught the eye of Chun and was hit with the full force of the man's gratitude. Paxton left the camp, glad he'd "proven" himself enough to have some time away from them all.

While a strong part of him wanted to take this chance to flee and never return, he knew he needed to see this thing through to the end. He would earn Rozaria's complete trust, find out exactly where her army was located, along with its numbers and any other strategic information. He would find a way to return to his home and warn the monarch of everything he'd learned before they were blindsided by an attack. He couldn't allow that to happen to Aerity or his family. Perhaps in this way he could prove to the king and his people that Lashed could be good and worthy.

Or perhaps, more realistically, the entire thing would blow up in his face. That was a chance he had to take. It was the least he could do to show Aerity he still cared.

Paxton stayed at the outskirts of the woods that lined the lake. Kalorian wildlife was not familiar to him, and he did not trust it. He checked behind him several times to be sure he wasn't being followed. When he felt far enough away, about a quarter of the distance around the lake, he took the man several yards into the trees and laid him down on a bed of moss.

Paxton shook his shoulders, but the man slept soundly. He felt the pulse of lifeblood at his throat, which was slow and steady. Paxton patted the man's cheek a couple of times, and then smacked him. The man's eyes flew open, and Paxton pressed a hand to muffle his shouts. His eyes were like a trapped, panicked animal.

"Sh, you're safe." Still, the man flailed and yelled, muffled by Paxton's hand. "Shut up and be still, before they find us out!" he hissed.

The man stopped moving, his eyes darting around in the dark.

"Listen carefully," Paxton said. "Head north, following the seastar constellation, and you will come to the path back to Lochlanach. Stay off it, but near it, or you will be found again. You must go straight to King Charles and tell him Rozaria Rocato is gathering an army of Lashed, and she might be working with Prince Vito. You saw for yourself how she is taking Lashed refugees and forcing them to work for her. Do you understand what I'm saying?"

The man nodded fast. Slowly, Paxton let up his hand and the man sputtered, "They're crazy! She's evil! The Lashed are—"

"Be careful how you finish that sentence," Paxton told him. He held his fingers very close to the man's eyes. "Do you see this newest lashing here? It's the one that saved your life.

Remember that when you speak of all Lashed being evil."

In the moonlight, the man's eyes filled with the same hatred he'd shown at the camp. "You didn't care about saving me. You only wanted to use me to send a message!"

Paxton took the man's torn tunic in his hands and pulled him up a few inches, only to slam him back into the ground. He pulled his face close. "A message that will save you, your family, and the people of Lochlanach. *My* people. Pull your cursed head out of your arse, man!"

Paxton shoved off and stood, glaring down at him. "Seas be with you. You're going to need it."

"You're leaving me out here?"

Irritation scratched at Paxton. He squinted at the floor of the forest before he found two edible things, plucked them, and squatted at the man's side. "Look. These types of mushrooms, and these berries from that type of bush are edible. And I assume you can fish?" He pulled a rusted hook and string from his tunic pocket and handed it to the man. "If you come into sight of our camp, I *will* kill you this time. Keep to the forest until you are past us, and then align yourself with the path."

Paxton stood.

"It could take me weeks to get back!" the man cried.

Paxton spared the man one final look of warning, and then walked away.

Chapter 12

Paxton had no faith that the man would do as he'd been instructed. He wished he could get his hands on his bow for protection in case the not-so-dead prisoner was caught again. Being defenseless behind enemy lines did not suit him. What suited him even less was worrying exactly what was in store for him in Rozaria's tent. She was beautiful, no doubt, but her wicked intentions and fanatical madness erased every ounce of that beauty for Paxton. He wasn't certain how far he could stretch his charade, especially when it came to the attentions of Rozaria, even though he ached every day for the touch of a woman.

One in particular.

He thought of her soft lips and long silken hair as he

trudged back to the camp. For a moment he even imagined he could smell the coconut and berry-scented oils that graced her lightly freckled skin. He recalled the fierce look of defiance and understanding in her eyes when she'd seen his lash marks, knowing it was his reason for keeping her at bay. He recalled how her fierceness changed to soft passion as she went up on her toes to kiss him.

Seas, he would have kissed her longer if he'd known it would be his one and only chance. He would have memorized the curve of her waist and hips, the arc of her back as she leaned into him.

Smells of smoke rising from the campfire dislodged him from the memory and plunged him back into the harsh reality that faced him. All eyes were on Pax as he approached, some with wonder and awe, some with respect. Their misled opinions gave him no satisfaction, though he was glad not to be under a cloud of suspicion any longer.

Paxton made his way to Rozaria's tent, where Martone stood outside with his arms crossed. The two were the same height, but Martone's shoulders were broader, his neck thicker. His hair was shaved on the sides, and the strip of black down the middle was knotted at the back of his skull. The man's eyes narrowed into a smug scowl.

Paxton widened his stance and crossed his own arms. He welcomed a scuffle with the brute; perhaps it would postpone this cursed meeting.

Rozaria called out a question from inside—he recognized

the word "who" in Kalorian. Then the flap opened and her dark eyes peered out, glinting in the firelight. She smiled at Pax and gave Martone an order. The man reluctantly took one step aside.

Paxton passed him and hunched through the doorway. A candle burned on a small wooden table in the middle. On both sides were thick pallets with ornate coverings of bright colors and designs. On one sat Rozaria's guest, the mysterious young woman. Before she could pull her hood up all the way, Paxton caught sight of a jagged scar down her otherwise pretty face. The girl said something softly to Rozaria and then left them.

"Please . . ." Rozaria motioned to where the girl had been sitting. "Join me."

Paxton sat sideways, one leg out straight and the other bent. Rozaria sat on the other side, a satisfied look of contentment on her face as she poured two cups of red wine and placed one in front of him. She raised hers and drank. Paxton took his with a fleeting thought of poison, but drank anyway. It was sweet at first, then tart. He waited to become dizzy or ill, then felt ridiculous when nothing happened. All the while Rozaria watched him, her long fingers running over the rim of her wooden cup.

"Tell me about King Charles Lochson." Her voice carried a husky warmth that might have been alluring had she been anyone else.

Perhaps this meeting was strictly for her to obtain information. If so, he could handle that. Paxton weighed how much to say. "He's . . . disconnected from his kingdom. For too long he's had nothing to focus on except the joys and entertainment of his own family and the other royals. Worries of the towns and Lashed are dealt with by local authorities—I doubt most issues are even brought to his attention, as they're considered unimportant." He believed what he was saying, but still suffered a twinge of regrettable disloyalty to his kingdom. He took a heady gulp of wine, and Rozaria was quick to refill his cup.

She then sipped her own wine, tapping her cup thoughtfully. "As I suspected. Now tell me about you, hunter."

Paxton cleared his throat and took another drink as well. "I'm from a village on the main bay, north of the royal lands. My father worked in sea fare as a fisherman and oysterman. My mother helped with sales. My brother and I hunted. Fairly average family on the surface." He knew he was being clinical and vague. He hoped it wasn't too obvious that he was trying not to give much information about his family or their whereabouts. When Rozaria gave a sly grin, he knew he wasn't fooling her.

"I still frighten you," she said.

Paxton hesitated, then opted for honesty. "I can't say I've ever met a woman with your level of power. Few people have had the ability to intimidate me, but you, Rozaria . . . you do."

Her low laughter filled the tent, and her smile was bright in the flickering light.

"Have you left behind a sad maiden in your village?"

"Nay." His heart gave a pound. "I swore off love or marriage."

"Smart man, considering the suffering thrust upon families in your land who cannot use their magic for its intended purposes."

His heart pounded harder, and he nodded. "To save pregnancies. Aye. That was the first time I worked magic. I was seven."

Rozaria sat up straighter, her eyes filling with interest. "Tell me."

This time he did not hesitate or hold back. He told her every detail about his grandmother and the pregnant woman who'd come seeking her help, only to be healed by young Paxton instead. It came rushing out as it had when he spoke to Mrs. Rathbrook, the Lashed healer at the castle. Caught up in the story and the feelings that emerged, for one moment Paxton locked eyes with Rozaria and sensed her understanding. He felt a kinship he longed for. Then he remembered who she was, and his babbling stopped. He gave a rueful shake of his head and finished his second cup of wine in a big gulp, immediately wishing he'd opted for just another sip. He had to keep his wits about him.

Rozaria moved closer, her gaze too intense. "You have no one you can trust with these things of your past. I can hear it in your voice—you are not accustomed to speaking openly of your magic. However, I assure you, hunter, you are safe with me."

Only if he didn't dare defy her or speak out against her methods.

Her hand reached out for his face, and though his entire body tensed, he did not flinch. His heart kept a steady drumming as her warm hand cupped his jaw, her thumb grazing the stubble of growth on the hollow of his cheek. Paxton's instincts rapidly fired warnings, but he didn't move. He realized with a pang that part of why it felt so wrong had nothing to do with who she was—the madwoman who terrorized the lands—and everything to do with who she was *not*. Aerity.

He didn't want another woman, but he had to set that feeling aside, probably forever. His heart might always be with Aerity, the first woman to know his secret and want him anyway, though the seas and stars had not aligned for them. He would likely never see her again, but perhaps he could still keep her safe in this way.

Right now, right here, with Rozaria . . . this had nothing to do with his heart. This was strategy, and he hoped it would be worth it in the long run. Still, scheming or not, he could not bring himself to move. Instead he watched her eyes with great care. He watched as she grazed his messy hair and stubble, the angles of his face, down his throat to his chest and back up to his eyes.

That familiar hunger was in her gaze again—the unmistakable concentration of a woman who has laid claim. She didn't simply want him as an ally or a servant; she wanted him as a man, and to deny her would ruin any chance he had of gaining information and possibly escaping. Rozaria stepped closer. His stomach clenched in dreaded anticipation.

Rozaria was the type of woman to take what she wanted. So, he waited. Her hand moved into his hair, her nails scratching along his scalp.

He had to make himself want this. He had to make his actions believable. He forced himself to focus on the way this woman understood the torment he'd been hiding since childhood, the way she wanted to empower him and all Lashed. But it was impossible to feel softness toward Rozaria, knowing what she had caused.

She pulled his face down as she leaned in, lifting her chin. And in that moment just before their lips met he thought only one thing: *She could kill me now.*

Instead of the softness he'd tried to force, what roared to life inside of Paxton was a great anger. A rage he'd long ago caged within himself. For the first time in his life he gave himself permission to unlatch the door to that pent-up fury, and it tore through him like the beast he'd hunted—bitterness at having to run from his home and family, indignation at being an outcast, resentment that he felt a kinship with this madwoman, and worst of all a vile sense of wrongness that he was here in this woman's arms while another man would lay his hands upon Aerity Lochson.

When her lips took his, colder than he expected, he kissed her back hard. His arm went around her waist, yanking her closer, his mouth and hands rough. Rozaria groaned and both of them were pulling, scratching, mouths punishing. Paxton was surprised by the surge of temper that fueled him forward, moving on top of her with harsh force. Rozaria gave a feminine groan as her back hit the pallet, her hands in his hair again, her legs twining around him, welcoming his anger in a way that made him forget everything but the release of these grueling emotions.

Half a second later Paxton heard a shout and felt his hair grabbed by a much bigger, stronger hand. His head was yanked up, sharp pain searing his skull. A punch in his mouth threw him sideways. Then he lost all breath as a boot kicked his abdomen. He looked up blearily into the raging face of Martone. Rozaria was on her feet, screaming in Kalorian, and smacking Martone across the side of his head. He backed away, lifting an arm to block her hits. He snapped at her in Kalorian, and she yelled back, raising her arms. Great seas, the man thought Paxton had been forcing himself on her.

Martone turned to Paxton with a snarl.

Pax pushed to his feet and wiped his swollen mouth with the back of his hand. Despite the pain in his face and ribs, he was overwhelmed by gratefulness at the man's interruption.

Rozaria's face was blazing. She raised a hand to Martone and he cowered. She lowered it and pointed to the tent flap, shouting a Kalorian phrase. Martone huffed through his nostrils like a bull before leaving the tent.

Paxton touched the corner of his mouth with his tongue, tasting copper and salt. Rozaria moved to stand before him and raised her hands to his face. Anger was obvious in her tight, stern features. He closed his eyes, still breathing hard, and let her heal him, feeling heat radiate through her fingertips as she ran them over his mouth, chin, and cheek. She murmured softly as she worked, and when she finished their gazes met.

He knew from the trust in her eyes that he had achieved what he'd set out to do. Relief and guilt pummeled him. He'd never been so out of control. It all felt wrong. Wrong, but necessary. He hoped tonight would do the trick, and he could avoid future alone time with her. Then again, Rozaria was a determined woman. What had he gotten himself into?

He forced himself to show one last moment of affection, pushing a dark strand of hair from her eye. "When do we leave this camp for your royal lands?"

"In two days' time. I expect two more of my men to return by then. Tomorrow I must tend to my creations." Her creations? She moved forward until her body brushed against his thigh. The touch of her brought back his actions moments ago, when he'd been on top of her, and the feeling of wrongness invaded again.

The beating had been worth it. Paxton had clearly not been in his right mind, carried away by the onslaught of every emotion and desire he'd been suppressing. He could not let that happen again. And no more wine. The slight fog over his senses did not help things at all.

"Get some rest, Rozaria."

"Perhaps I am not tired," she said with defiance.

"Perhaps I am." He gave a slow grin, feeling weariness in his eyes.

Her lips puckered in annoyance, but he turned and lifted the tent flap, exiting into the night, wishing he could wipe his mouth and memory of the things he'd done. He'd prefer to avoid another run-in with Rozaria's lips and Martone's fists, seas willing.

Chapter 13

Paxton was up before the sun the next morning, preparing the fire for breakfast and tending the horses. Konor joined him down at the lake with a bucket, and together they carried the water up to camp to be boiled in pots over the fire. They got the first one started and sat together on a log.

"What was it like?" Konor asked him.

Paxton looked into the man's wondering eyes for a moment before he realized what he was asking about: the man he'd supposedly killed. Konor's keenness made Paxton uncomfortable.

"Taking a life is no small thing," Paxton muttered.

"It seemed simple enough when you did it."

Curses. Paxton gritted his teeth. "He was not a good man. It was . . . necessary, but it brought me no joy, if that's what you're asking."

At this, Konor seemed disappointed. "There were lots of men like him in my town. I never did anything wrong, and they still looked at me like I was scum, especially this one man, the town's messenger, Davito. He had to pass my house every day, and every day he spit on my door. When I heard about Rozaria, and found out things were changing, I knew I had to find her. But first"—he held up his lined fingernails, a frightening smile on his face—"I killed Davito's cow and goat." Konor let out a chilling laugh.

Paxton had to turn away from the man. "I'm sorry to hear you were treated that way." And even more sorry to hear he'd reacted to hatred with more hatred.

"Everything is going to be okay now," Konor said wistfully.

Rozaria emerged from her tent, and Konor jumped to his feet. Paxton was slower to rise, but her eyes found him straightaway and she made her way over to him.

"I'd like to show you something." She looked from him to Konor. "Both of you. Come."

They followed, and Paxton realized she was leading them to the building where they'd held the prisoner. She spoke over her shoulder as she walked.

"At each camp I have a place where I work on my creations. Two were sturdy enough to be transported from our last camp, though I'm not certain one will make it."

"You mean your monsters?" Konor asked with a thrill.

Rozaria nodded, fondness in her voice. "My beastlings."

Paxton's stomach turned to a heavy, plunging stone within him as he remembered the unnatural creature he'd fought in his homeland. He did not want to go into that building—to see her at work—to witness magic being used in ways that were not good for anyone. But he held his tongue and followed. One of her guards stood at the door. When he opened it for them, Paxton nearly doubled over.

The stench. He'd come across carcasses in the wild, half-eaten by vultures, so he recognized the smell of death. But this was concentrated and unfiltered. Even Konor covered his nose with his arm. Rozaria grinned.

"That is the smell of years' worth of hard-won conquests. Let yourself become one with it."

No, thank you.

Konor dropped his hand, but his face was still pinched. They followed her into a dim room where she lit a torch with her fingers, then used it to light others along the wall. Paxton could not believe his eyes. He and Konor stood there, gaping at the giant, elongated room with iron cages holding young animals and older ones that appeared pregnant, all sitting in their own excrement.

Rozaria clucked her tongue. "I am glad to have new people at camp. I shall get Chun's daughter and nephews to clean these cages."

Paxton eyed the animals: chimpanzee, ocelot, jaguar, panther, and leopard. There were also giant lizards that he had no name for, and smaller cages with predatory birds and enormous spiders. At the end in the largest cage was something large and black, with thick, curved tusks.

"What's that one?"

"That is a cape buffalo. Very strong. They have quite a temper when roused. But they are not fast runners. This one will deliver soon, and I will fuse the babe with the panther's body."

Konor's mouth made an O of wonder. Paxton was caught between morbid curiosity about how any of this was possible and an urge to set all the animals free and burn the building to the ground.

She led them around a corner into a smaller room with more cages.

"These are my newest."

A small furry ball the size of a lap dog uncurled itself in an upper cage, blinking large black eyes in a lion cub face. It flopped onto its belly and sat up, appearing to have the body of a black bear with overgrown paws and claws. Rozaria shook her head as she peered at it. She grabbed a stick and poked through the bars, shouting a command in Kalorian.

The cub immediately pounced on it, grabbing it in its paws and rolling onto its back as it playfully licked the stick. Konor laughed, but Rozaria sneered, shutting him up.

"This one shows no inclination toward attack," she said. "I

should have known better than to take the newborn cub of a traveling gypsy's tame bear. Worthless." She nudged it harder with the stick, jabbing its tough belly, and the cub yelped, pressing against the back of the cage and giving her the saddest look. Paxton had to keep himself from pushing her away from the thing. Rozaria sighed and dropped the stick.

"He'll be a waste of food. If he can't get his act together I'll get rid of him."

Paxton watched the cub as it curled up and eyed them warily. Aye, he was a hunter and he ate animals, but he had compassion for all living things. This one, in particular, tugged at his heart.

A loud hissing from below made Paxton and Konor step back, but Rozaria squatted with a smile. They peered in at a reptilian creature. It had the body of a dragon lizard, with extraordinarily long legs and a whiplike tail, but its neck and head were that of a python.

Rozaria thrust her face forward and made a vicious hissing sound. The young creature swiped at the metal bars with its long claws and hissed in return. Rozaria chuckled. The creature was relatively small, but it would no doubt eventually grow to be as long as Paxton. The sight of it gave him chills.

"How'd you do that?" Konor asked. "Make two animals become one?"

Rozaria smiled, as if she had hoped someone would ask this question. Without a word, she went back into the main room and they followed. She came to a crate in the corner and took out a small, stiff, furry carcass, laying it on the nearest table.

"This one did not make it. It had complications while I was away. In the early stages they need constant care."

Paxton and Konor inched closer to see the creature. It appeared to be a miniature version of the beast that had ravaged Lochlanach. A warthog's face, scales along its torso, and arms and legs like a bear.

"I take the strongest, most dangerous parts from animals and fuse them together. Living things are fragile, but there is a small time span when they can die and be brought back—just enough time to be cut and pieced together. I have to be sure each has the working parts that it requires on the inside. It takes great concentration to bind flesh and bone of one to another." She ran a finger along the line of the creature's back, where it seemed that a rectangle of reptilian skin had been patched. "It only works on younglings that are still growing. If the binding works, I then infuse magic to enlarge them and strengthen certain parts."

She took its stiff paw, pressing the oversized claws into the pads of her fingers. "When I send my energy into these creatures, it's almost as if they are made of countless tiny entities, and I must speak to each one. To rework each thought process about what its limits are."

A chill of fascination overtook Paxton. He remembered feeling that way when he healed Tiern, as if his magic were encompassing the smallest of rogue particles and forcing them to his will. But to hear her say it, in this context, appalled him.

Konor stared at her in open awe. "And then you train them?"

She nodded. "Once they are strong enough and I know they will survive, I begin tests of strength and loyalty, then instill a desire to protect at will and attack on command."

"How long have you been doing this?" Paxton asked.

A fond look crossed her face. "My entire life. My father was the one who started this work. His first creature was an ugly, small, mutilated thing, but it lived. He didn't know he could grow it at that time. We learned much together."

"Where is he now?" Konor asked.

"Dead. When I was ten I watched as a beast with a tiger's face took his throat in its mouth during training. I swear, he was smiling with pride when he died. He could not be saved."

She looked at Paxton and Konor matter-of-factly before dropping the dead beast into the crate and wiping her hands on her skirts. "You will both be required to do rotations guarding this building and keeping watch over the beasts, helping as needed."

Both men nodded, Konor a bit more enthusiastically. The door opened behind them, and they all turned to see the hooded girl enter.

"Ah, Nicola," Rozaria said. She looked at Paxton. "It is time for us to begin our work."

He nodded. "I would be happy to hunt today for the

camp . . . if you see fit to return my bow."

She squinted at him, causing his heart to race, then she gave a slow nod. She called out something in Kalorian to the guard outside.

"*Roza . . .*" said the girl, Nicola, in a warning tone. Paxton looked at her, but could only see her lips and nose. She seemed to be staring pointedly at Rozaria. Was she warning her against giving him back his bow? Rozaria said something soothing to the girl before returning her attention to Paxton.

"You shall have your weapons."

Triumph raged inside him as he calmly said, "Thank you." Perhaps if he could find a wild boar to feed the camp, he'd be able to gain the trust of the others. Regardless, he had seemed to earn the trust of Rozaria Rocato, and for that he thanked the seas.

Chapter 14

Vixie was concerned about Tiern. He wasn't at breakfast that morning, and he'd been awfully quiet since he'd arrived. He had to be worried about his brother, and missing him, as she was missing Aerity. But his entire being seemed to carry a darkness that had never been there before, and it had worsened after his conversation with Lord Alvi. She intended to find out what had stolen every morsel of his joy.

She had stopped trying to gain admittance to her father's study. She knew Wyneth would tell her everything. So after breakfast she'd rushed to her chamber to change into riding clothes. The first winter cold had set in, so she donned a forest-green woolen hat with fur lining, a matching scarf, fingerless gloves, and a fitted riding jacket. She set off toward the guest chambers planning to ask Tiern to join her. She was wary of bringing up his brother, because, to be honest, she couldn't understand why Paxton would up and leave for good. Even if he had fallen in love with Aerity, as Vixie suspected, it was still selfish for him to leave his family forever.

At the entrance to the guest hall, a maid was coming out of a room carrying a tray of dirty breakfast dishes.

"Is that Tiern Seabolt's chamber?" Vixie asked her.

The older maid stopped at the sight of the princess and made an awkward curtsy with her hands full. "Aye, Your Highness, it certainly is."

"Is he well?"

"Seems to be, aye." The maid tilted her head with interest at the princess's questions.

Vixie knew better than to try to enter his room on her own—it would bring a scandal upon the both of them and her parents.

"I need for you to fetch him, please. I'll hold this." Vixie tried to take the tray from the woman's hands and had to pull harder than expected.

"But, Princess!" The woman sputtered in horror at the sight of Vixie holding the dishes.

"I'm fine, miss." Vixie looked up and down the empty hallway. Only a bemused guard was watching. "Please let Mr. Seabolt know that he'll need a coat."

The woman wiped her hands down her apron before

clasping them together nervously. "Very well, then." She bustled to Tiern's door and knocked. When it opened, Vixie couldn't hear what they were saying. Tiern stuck his head out, and Vixie smiled at him, suddenly feeling foolish with the tray. His brow creased and he dropped his head. She heard him say, "One moment."

The maid hurried back to Vixie and took the tray, looking relieved to have it in her own hands. "Shall I stay, Princess?"

"No, but thank you. The guard's supervision will do."

The maid stood there another moment, unsure, before giving a small bow and scuttling away.

Vixie pulled off her hat and pressed down the curls. After what felt like too long, Tiern's door opened and he walked to her, unsmiling, holding a short winter coat over one arm and his bow and quiver in the other. He gave a small, formal bow and looked at her, waiting. A bit of enthusiasm left Vixie. He looked as put together as always—tall and lean, without a single wrinkle in his tunic or a hair out of place. It was the air around him that seemed to have changed. Dulled and still. And it made Vixie sad. She fiddled with the hat in her hands. Tiern set down his coat and weapons on the hall table. All the chatter she'd wanted to unleash simply died into one simple request.

"Ride with me?"

Avoiding her gaze, he wiped his hands down the front of his tunic. "I'm supposed to scout the royal lands with Lord Alvi."

Vixie narrowed her eyes. He scouted with Lord Alvi

every day between the morning briefing in the king's office and lunchtime. He had nearly two hours until it was time to go. Seas alive, he was making excuses not to be near her!

"Have I offended you in some way, Tiern?"

His brown eyes became vibrant, and he shook his head. "Nay, Princess. You're . . . as lovely a person as ever."

He flushed and clenched his jaw, looking aside as if he regretted saying it.

"Then why in Eurona are you suddenly treating me as if I'm plague ridden?"

He glanced anxiously over her shoulder at the guard. In a low voice he replied, "I'm doing no such thing. I'm here for the safety of the kingdom, to scout and hunt, not for recreation. Have you forgotten you're a princess and I'm a commoner?"

Vixie scoffed. *That* was his excuse? "I don't care about that!"

"Perhaps not, but many do. It's not proper for the two of us to gallivant around royal lands together while the kingdom is in turmoil."

"What else am I to do?"

"Sh . . ." Tiern held out a hand and pressed it down, glancing at the guard again.

Vixie threw her arms out, refusing to be quiet. "Oh, I don't give a swimming rat who hears! You are my *friend*, and there is no reason why we should sit about on our haunches, twiddling our thumbs and not speaking. How does that help the kingdom?"

Tiern's hands went loosely to his hips, and he closed his

eyes. Each word he said seemed to come out with reluctance. "Things have changed, Princess. Friendship is no longer on my mind. I'm sorry."

His words hurt, though she couldn't help but feel he was being evasive. Something else had to be going on here. "Open your eyes and tell me you don't want to be friends, Tiern Seabolt."

He opened his eyes, stood taller, swallowed hard, and said in choppy words, "I . . . don't want to be friends."

"Liar!" Vixie pointed at him and laughed. "That was a *terrible* lie. What is this about? Tell me!"

A truly worried look crossed his face, as if the conversation had taken a turn he hadn't expected. He blinked, at a loss for words. And, seas, he was adorable when he was flustered. Vixie shoved the hat down over her ears and patted the top of her head.

"You're taking a ride with me," she said. "As your princess, I order you. Come along."

Vixie turned and swept from the guest hall. The guard brought a hand up to scratch his lip, and she could have sworn he was covering a smile. Well, he could laugh all he wanted. This was nonsense.

Tiern followed, just as she knew he would. He shrugged the hooded coat over his shoulders, fastening it at his neck with a grumpy expression, then flung the quiver across his back. At the castle's exit he mumbled, "Just a short ride, Vix. I mean, Princess Vixie."

She was about to tell him to call her "Vix," when the doors opened and they were hit with a blast of cold air. She pulled her hat down tighter and Tiern lifted his hood. Then they set off down the stone steps with two guards following.

The trees were nearly barren, clinging with lackluster energy to their last yellowed leaves. With a gust of wind, the large oak they were passing seemed to sigh and open its fingers, releasing a handful of leaves at them.

Vixie quickly tired of the silence between them. When they reached the shelter of the stables, she began readying Aerity's horse for Tiern. The guards checked all the stalls, then went back to the entrance to stand watch.

"You'll ride Doll," she told him.

"Are you certain? I don't mind using one of the guest horses."

"It makes no difference."

She felt his eyes on her as she worked. He shifted from one foot to the other before asking, "May I help?"

"I'm almost finished." She smiled at him and patted Doll's back. "There."

He moved closer, reaching up to mount, and his arm grazed Vixie's. She reached out and took hold of his forearm, whispering, "Wait."

Tiern froze where he was, staring at the horse's side. Vixie peeked at the guards, who could see only their faces over the tops of the stalls and were too far away to hear a whispered conversation.

The nearness of Tiern and the semiprivate feel of the stall made Vixie brazen, as if this might be her only opportunity. So many things went through her mind that she could say or ask. But what she finally blurted out made her face go hot.

"Have you ever been kissed?"

His head swung back to check for the guards before turning to Vixie. She had to be as red as a beet.

"Wh— I'm not sure this is a proper discussion. Shouldn't you be readying your horse?"

Stubbornness burgeoned, overriding her initial embarrassment. "Yes or no?"

He lowered his arm from Doll and turned to face her. "Aye. I have. Twice. Now, let's ride." He tried to turn back, but she grabbed his arm again. A bout of jealousy burned her stomach, but her curiosity was stronger.

"Did you . . . enjoy it very much?"

Tiern let out a huff of low laughter. "Well, when you're a young lad and a lass is willing to kiss you, what's not to enjoy? Now, come on. Let's go, Princess."

This time he didn't let her stop him. He mounted Doll and peered down where she still stood, staring up at him.

"Aren't you curious whether or not *I've* been kissed?" she asked.

"Nay." He took the reins and would not look at her. "Not one bit."

A flare of anger heated her thoroughly, and she had to fight the urge to stamp her foot in a childish manner. Instead she marched out of his stall with her head up and entered the next stall, where Ruspin nudged her with his cool nose. She gave the horse a good scratch before saddling and mounting. She led Ruspin out of the stable, with Tiern just behind her.

One of the guards held up a hand.

"You can ride unguarded since the hunter is armed, but your father's orders are to stay in sight of the castle and guards at all times. No entering the woods."

Vixie nodded her understanding, thrilled that they wouldn't be closely followed.

"We won't be long," Tiern told the guards. Vixie gave him a sideways glare before ushering Ruspin forward with a tap of her heels. She soaked in the clunk of hooves on cobblestones—one of her favorite sounds.

When they were out of earshot of the guards, she stated, "I haven't been, you know."

"Not my business," Tiern replied.

"It could be your business if you wanted. . . ." She bit her bottom lip. Vixie didn't know what had gotten into her. It was like the more uninterested he was, the greater need she had to push for his notice. It was backward, really, but she couldn't help herself.

Tiern's mouth was set in a hard line. "You're being terribly forward, Princess. I doubt your parents would approve."

Vixie gave a mirthless laugh. "We both know what I am to my parents. A pretty jewel in their treasure chest. And not the biggest or most valuable gem, either. Not worthy of being privy to the important information. Not the future queen."

Tiern's eyes widened as he took her in, and for half a moment she thought she saw sympathy there, or perhaps understanding. Just as quickly he was closed off again, turning his head to the path as they passed the west commons.

"Are you angry at your brother for leaving?" Vixie blurted.

Tiern shifted, his face showing a gamut of emotions. "Nay. Though I suppose I'm angry at the circumstances under which he had to leave."

"Because Lord Alvi took the beast?"

Tiern slumped a bit, eyes glazing. "Aye. Along those lines."

There. Right there in those words lay the mystery. Vixie stared at him, trying to figure out what piece of the puzzle she was missing. *Along those lines.*

"Why else did he go, then?"

Tiern gave a stiff shrug. "My brother was always a bit of a loner. I don't pretend to fully understand him."

She sensed more partial truths, and frustration bubbled.

"Why is it that nobody trusts me? You, Aerity, the rest of my family. Nobody thinks I'm capable of bearing the weight of the truth. I'm bloody tired of being given the mushroom treatment—kept in the dark and fed shite! Why is it? It's because I let the Rocato woman go, isn't it?" Her chin trembled as shame surged through her. How many days and nights had she spent reimagining that moment on the island when she had the woman at arrow point, when she let someone sneak up behind her? She'd been completely unaware. If only she had sensed the other person. She could have ended it all then and there, and proven herself to her parents and everyone who looked upon her as the silly, frivolous second daughter.

Tiern's mouth popped open, and Vixie spurred her horse, moving ahead of him, hoping she wouldn't cry.

"Vixie, wait!" Tiern trotted up beside her. "Stop, Princess. Please."

She slowed, fidgeting with her gloves.

"Listen," he said softly. "Paxton's secrets are not mine to tell. But if ever I needed counsel, I know you are trustworthy. And brave. And able to help." He clasped the back of his neck and winced, as if he'd said too much. And in that moment Vixie knew for certain Tiern was still inside that closed-off body, and he still cared for her. So what had changed? She couldn't help but remember what he'd said . . . about the kisses, and that sour feeling of jealousy returned.

She peered up at him now, into his honest eyes.

"Tiern, when you returned home after the hunt, what happened to make your feelings toward me change? Did you . . . that is, was that when you kissed one of the lasses?"

"What?" He shook his head. "Nay. It has nothing to do with a lass. I've just had time to think and to see what's happening in the lands. I realize now that a Lochlan princess should be with her own kind, even if it's only for friendship."

Vixie stared. "Own kind? We are both Lochlan. I don't

care about the class differences. My mother was a commoner, as I'm certain you know. These things did not seem to hinder you from my company during the hunt. I can't understand why they should now."

He looked to the side, his jaw locked. Vixie wished she could see what burdened him so. His face . . . he seemed almost to have aged, the way his brow was in a constant furrow of worry. She wanted to climb across the expanse between them and sit in his lap, erasing those lines with kisses.

The thought shook her and she spouted a nervous laugh.

"What?" Tiern asked, tilting his head in curiosity at her sudden outburst.

"Nothing." Her heart pounded.

He stared at her curiously as a strange sound rang out overhead. Vixie and Tiern both turned toward the castle. There it was again—a guttural cawing. Voices yelled from afar.

"What in the depths?" Tiern whispered. Vixie held her breath, listening. Tiern whipped his bow over his head and had an arrow nocked before she could blink.

Again came the caw, like a grand bird in peril, closer now. And then above the stone turrets flew the most enormous bird Vixie had ever seen. She'd grown up with all manner of gulls, herons, and hawks, but nothing like this. Its wings spanned at least a dozen feet. When it swooped lower over the west commons, she saw with horror that its body was as large as her own, with talons that could shred a man.

Its feral eyes were directed at the two of them, its face like a bat's. Vixie wanted to shriek, but air was stuck in her lungs, frozen in terror.

"Vixie, go!" Tiern shot an arrow, which narrowly arced just short of the bird as it took a sharp upward swoop. "To the castle, now! Tell your father!"

Tiern shot again, puncturing a wing. The bird's pitying howl shot through Vixie, and she charged forward down the cobblestoned path, dodging guards and soldiers who were coming in her direction, swords and bows drawn. When she got to the castle entrance, she leaped from her horse and gave him a hard smack on the rump to send him back to the stables. "Go, Ruspin!"

A guard stood with the door wide, waving her frantically inside. "Your Highness!"

She panted for breath and dared to take one last look at the group of men on horseback, Tiern among them, as the great bird swooped down to attack. Men were knocked from their horses by its strong wings. The beast struggled against an onslaught of arrows, but managed to grab one of the men by his arm. Vixie gasped as the soldier was lifted high into the air, flailing. It was then that the princess released the piercing shriek she'd been holding in, and she sprinted up the castle steps.

Chapter 15

Wyneth stood in the king's office, overtaken by chills from what they'd just learned. A monstrous sand serpent that could slither, run, and leap had been on a killing rampage in Zorfina. It was able to bury itself and move in the sand, and therefore had eluded their forces. Each day it killed more people, because King Addar refused to change the laws, just as King Charles had.

And in the mountains of Toresta, King Gavriil had opened a refugee camp for Lashed—a haven against the onslaught of persecution, in hopes that this would earn Rozaria's approval, at least until she could be stopped. They had no reports of beasts yet, but Lashed were killing people each day, just as they were in Lochlanach.

“There’s a catch,” King Charles said softly as he read the parchment. “Once the Lashed go into the camp, they are not allowed to leave.”

“They are made prisoners?” Queen Leighlane asked.

Councilman Duke Gulfton clucked his tongue and chuckled without humor. “I suppose they’re saying it’s for their own good. That they are protecting them.”

“Smart,” muttered Duke Streamson. “Very smart.”

The two older dukes had been the only councilmen approved to attend official meetings with the royal family again. One younger councilman, a guard, and an officer were still being held for daily questioning. All others had been let go. Their possible treason was so despicable and saddening that nobody spoke of it.

“As for Kalor,” King Charles said, “it is no longer safe for Lochlans to travel there. We’ve had reports of people attacked and rumors of Lashed uprisings. Prince Vito has neither confirmed nor denied that his kingdom is in a state of unrest. It seems he does not trust written communication, which I can understand. In a message with his seal received before dawn, he says he has sent ambassadors to speak with us directly. They will arrive before dark.”

This piqued everyone’s interest.

“That should be interesting,” Lord Baycreek said sarcastically. Wyneth knew from past stories of interkingdom balls and functions that Kalorians and Lochlans did not always play well together.

"Aye, lock up the wee ones." Duke Gulfton's jowls shook as if he'd shivered in fear.

"Now, now, gentlemen," the king admonished. "Remember, Prince Vito allowed many of his kingdom's best hunters to come here and fight the beast. Every one of them was killed."

A respectful silence filled the space until Lord Wavecrest spoke. "Any news from Ascomanni?"

"No." King Charles and the entire room all turned to the man at Wyneth's side. Lord Alvi rocked back on his heels and nodded.

"My uncle tends to be a private man when it comes to kingdom matters. He's not likely to send news of trouble, lest it be perceived as a call for help."

"Seas forbid," Queen Leighlane said with a sigh.

Lord Alvi gave a wry shrug, unoffended, as if that's simply the way it was.

A commotion sounded outside in the hallway. Wyneth's pulse quickened and on reflex she grabbed Lord Alvi's arm. Without hesitation he brought his hand over hers. Wyneth's mother, Lady Wavecrest, glanced at Wyneth and did a double take at their joined hands. Wyneth quickly dropped her arm from Lief's just as the door flew open.

Vixie, disheveled and panting, burst into the room with a veritable army on her heels. The king rushed from behind the desk and held out his arms, which she ran straight into.

"What is it, Vix?" he asked.

"A flying beast, Father!" The entire room gasped and went still, except Lord Alvi, who ran from the room to join the fight.

Vixie pulled away enough to peer up at the king. His eyes darted around at the faces of his family and advisers, all at a loss. Wyneth pressed a shaking hand over her mouth. Vixie's eyes were rimmed in red. "It took one of the soldiers." At the memory of it, Vixie broke into tears. Wyneth stepped up and took her from the king, who rushed away with his men.

"I must check on the children." Lady Wavecrest ran from the room with Lady Baycreek.

Vixie trembled in Wyneth's arms. "Wyn . . . it was so big. Oh, my seas. Its eyes!"

"It's okay, love. You're safe now." Wyneth stroked her hair, feeling faint with fear. The queen joined them, taking Vixie's face in her hands.

"You're not injured?" She looked her daughter over as Vixie shook her head.

"I need to go. I need to make sure Tiern is okay."

Both Wyneth and the queen grasped her.

"You're not going back out there," Queen Leighlane said firmly.

Vixie still had panic in her eyes. "When will this end, Mother? Papa can make it stop. He can change the laws!"

"It's not so simple," the queen whispered. She stroked Vixie's cheeks, drying her tears.

"He must never change the laws," came a grainy voice

from behind them. "It is imperative that we not give up control."

Wyneth, Vixie, and the queen turned to Duke Streamson. He seemed to be addressing Duke Gulfton, who leaned on his ornate walking stick, eyes glazed.

"Perhaps it will never end," Duke Gulfton whispered. He hobbled from the room, green robes dragging across the floor, and Duke Streamson followed, shaking his head.

Wyneth thought with sadness that they should both retire. She looked to the queen. Her aunt Leighlane gave her a tight smile that was meant to be reassuring, but it wasn't. It felt as if everyone in the entire kingdom had lost their wits along with their control over the situation. If they'd had any control to begin with.

Something had to give.

Vixie walked to the window, looking out at the sky and grounds. "I hope they've killed it."

Wyneth's stomach turned at the thought of what her young cousin had seen. She prayed Tiern and the other soldiers were safe against it.

"Aerity is out there with monsters on the loose," Vixie whispered. "She needs to be brought home."

The queen pursed her lips. "I've been thinking the same thing. She could be anywhere by now, the foolish girl. She knows we don't have enough people to chase her down." She shook her head and walked to her daughter's side. Winter light shone against her deep red curls.

Wyneth moved to her cousin's side. Vixie looked straight at her, and in that moment the girl's terror morphed into an intensity Wyneth had never seen from the lass. It was as if a thought had taken root in her cousin's soul and was growing to massive proportions before she could attempt to stop it.

Aye, the kingdom lacked soldiers to find Aerity. But Princess Vixie, it seemed, was willing, able, and ready.

Chapter 16

Vixie waited impatiently at the entrance of the castle for Tiern to return. When the doors finally opened, she rose up on her toes, eager to see if he was all right. But it wasn't Tiern at all. It was a mass of guards surrounding a group in bright clothing: trousers and tunics of reds and greens with buttons up the sides. Vixie recognized the garb of high-class Kalorians. She stepped aside into an alcove to watch as they passed. They were a dour bunch of serious faces.

She gave a slight shiver at how the colorful dresses and long black hair of the women reminded her of Rozaria. She noted the difference in hairstyles between upper-class Kalorian men and tribesmen. Men of the tribes shaved their heads on the side while the lords did not. They wore it down and straight. But all Kalorian men wore the center strip of their hair pulled tight and knotted at the back of their heads.

Vixie stepped out to see what was going on when someone gripped her arm. She looked into Tiern's worn face.

"Tiern!"

"Are you all right?" he asked.

"Aye." She wanted to circle her arms around him in a hug, but guards were watching. Always watching.

Lord Alvi swept into the castle with a cold breeze and followed where the Kalorians had gone in the direction of the king's office. Vixie wrapped her arms around herself.

"What happened after I left? Was it killed?"

"Let's get away from the door." Tiern led her to a nearby hall. If possible, he seemed even more withdrawn and dark than an hour before. This time Vixie could very well understand why.

"It lives," he whispered. "It flew out over the sea. They tried to follow in boats but couldn't keep up. It's injured, though. Of that, I'm certain."

"Good," Vixie whispered weakly. "Tiern . . . " She glanced surreptitiously around before continuing in an even softer voice. "I'm terribly worried about Aerity."

His wide eyes met hers, as if reading her thoughts. "Don't even think about it."

"Too late."

"It wasn't smart for her to go in the first place," he said hotly.

"That's neither here nor there at this point. I've decided to go and I would appreciate your companionship. But with or without you, I must find her."

Tiern's jaw set. His nostrils flared. Truth was, Vixie's plan would only work if Tiern was willing to help her. She hoped he wouldn't call her bluff. He cursed under his breath.

"What exactly is this blasted plan of yours, Vixie?"

She held back from showing her relief. "This afternoon when the castle makes the bread run to the soldiers' barracks, I will be hidden in the cart."

Tiern threw his head back and closed his eyes. "Oh, deep seas."

Vixie pressed on. "You will be at the stables, readying a horse and cart full of hay. I will roll from the cart as we pass the stables and hide under your stack of hay. You'll take us to the nearest village and I can get out."

He gave her an incredulous look.

She crossed her arms. "What?"

"It will never work. How do you suppose you will get onto the cart without guards seeing you in the first place?"

"Mr. Shellfine in the kitchen adores me and lets me have run of the pantry, but he does not allow guards to come stomping through the kitchens to follow me. He'll whack them with a wooden spoon if they dare get near his rising dough." She grinned triumphantly.

Still, Tiern shook his head. "I'll be thrown in the dungeons when we're caught."

"Nay, I'll say I was forcing you or bribing you or threatening you or something." Vixie waved a hand. "But we won't be caught."

He continued to stare at her as if she were mad.

"Be ready at the stables. Tell the guards you're doing whatever hunters do around the perimeter."

"Scouting? Why would I need a hay cart for that?"

Vixie leaned her chin on her palm and thought. "Say you're going to do some long-term scouting for beasts, into the woods. You'd need hay to feed the horses since grasses are dying off right now. It should work!"

Tiern's eyes held sheer skepticism, but his body slumped in a way that told Vixie he was tired of arguing.

"And one more thing," Vixie whispered. "I'll need you to bring a set of commoner clothing for me to change into. I'll take care of food since I'll be in the pantry."

"This is absolute madness. I can't even believe we're discussing it. I won't put you in that sort of danger."

"I'll be safe with you."

He pinched the bridge of his nose.

"Tiern . . ." Vixie prepared to pull out her biggest card. "This could be your only chance to see Paxton again."

His entire being stiffened as his eyes became unfocused in thought. She stood very still as he pondered.

"Curses, Princess." He exhaled sharply. "When does the bread cart come?"

Vixie smiled as he relented. "One hour."

He raised his arms and smacked them down at his sides. "One hour? That's it?"

"Aye!" She wanted to clap her hands in delight. Down the hall she heard the murmur of voices. She and Tiern stuck their heads around the corner and saw Wyneth and Lord Alvi. They seemed so serious that it made her curious. Then she remembered the Kalorian guests.

"Let's see what's happening," Vixie said.

They approached the pair, who smiled politely.

"What's going on?" Vixie asked.

"Prince Vito has sent his royal council to speak with your father about their current situation," Wyneth said. "They refuse to speak in front of anyone else. Prince Vito apparently has trust issues. They made the family and council leave. They wanted to be alone with the king and queen, but the guards refused to go. I mean, really! Who do they think they are, coming into another kingdom's castle and making such demands?"

"I don't like it." Lord Alvi shook his head. "I highly doubt they'd leave their own king or prince alone in a room with a bunch of Lochlan lords. Your king should have refused their demands completely."

"Well," said Vixie diplomatically, "a king must sometimes compromise to make others comfortable in order to make revelation possible."

They all looked at her as if surprised. Vixie shrugged and rubbed her belly.

"I'll be needing to visit the kitchen soon." She turned and gave Tiern a sly wink before nodding her good-byes to Wyneth and Lord Alvi. Inside, she was glad to be the one with her own secret this time.

Vixie's escape from the castle wasn't glamorous, seeing as how she was dirty and bruised from her tumble from the bread cart. Now, breathing in the dusty air under a pile of hay, she knew she was out and that was all that mattered. She had to hold back peals of giddy laughter as she listened to Tiern's muffled conversation with the guards at the gate. She grinned to herself the entire way to the village of Dovedell.

When they got there and parked in the town stables, Tiern stood beside the cart and whispered. "Nobody is in sight. You can come out." She pushed her way up, and he helped her by the hand, brushing straw from her shoulders. She had pulled her hair into a low bun, so the straw was fairly easy to pick out, although the small pieces would just have to stay until she could bathe. She wondered when that might be. . . .

"Here are your clothes." Tiern handed her brown rags. "I'll turn my back and tell you if anyone is coming." Vixie held up the breeches and tunic.

"You've brought me *lads'* clothing?"

"I couldn't very well go traipsing through the maiden's laundry, could I?" There was laughter in his voice. Vixie held back an aggravated growl.

She tried to pull at the lacing strings at the back of her

dress, straining to undo the knot. "I think I need help."

He slightly crooked his head and peeked, then turned fully and got to work on the knots, gently loosening them and probably going a little lower than was necessary. Vixie had to hold up the loosened dress in the front. She turned to face him. He didn't move. Just looked at her.

"Thank you," she whispered.

"You do know you're quite mad for a princess, right?"

"Aye." She smiled.

He turned back around, crossing his arms. Vixie dropped the dress and made quick work of the breeches, pulling the string tight around her waist so that the fabric bunched. She rolled up the legs since they were too long. Then she pulled the tunic over her head and rolled the fabric at her wrists. It was baggy, but warm enough. Lastly, she pulled out a scarf and wrapped it about her head to cover her hair. The red curls would be a beacon to any royal guards who might happen to be in town.

Vixie peered down at herself, feeling dowdy. "I look ridiculous!"

Tiern turned and gave a snort. "Only you could manage to be adorable dressed like that." He flushed and dropped his smile. "Come on. We need to find a hearty meal and then we'll be straight on our way. We'll have to ride hard. I took the biggest, strongest horse from the guest stables to pull the cart, since he'll have to carry us both."

Vixie admired his selection and followed him to the inn.

When they entered the warm room filled with chatting people, Vixie first felt apprehension as people turned to look them over, and then euphoria as they all turned back to their own conversations, clueless as to her identity. Her heart danced as they took stools at the end of the bar. Vixie stared around at the lived-in space with its worn counters and knobby chairs, the fire roaring in a blackened hearth. It was cozy and she felt free. Inconspicuous.

"What can I getcha?" the barkeep asked.

Vixie dreamily said, "Your largest ale, my good chap."

The older, thin man let out a whelp and slapped his knee. "Lil' thing like you?"

Tiern laughed nervously and pinched the top of Vixie's thigh. "She's only joking. Water and meat pies will do us."

Oh, fine. "And two coffees with sugar, please," Vixie added. They would need it to keep them awake on the ride.

The barkeep raised his eyebrows at her, then looked to Tiern, who nodded. "It's her birthday." The man looked Vixie over again before walking away.

"Why must it be my birthday to have a coffee?" Vixie whispered.

"Coffee and sugar are luxuries," he whispered back. "Very expensive. Most commoners opt for a weaker herbal tea blend with milk."

"Oh . . ." Vixie stared down the bar at the hands holding wooden cups. Some wore grungy fingerless gloves. Ungloved hands were leathery and clearly hard-worked. Not one of them held a coffee mug. Her abdomen twisted with an unfamiliar guilt, and the coin pouch at her waist felt particularly heavy. She'd never thought of them as worth much until that moment.

When their coffees came, Vixie finished hers as quickly as possible and pushed the mug away. She felt guilty enjoying it in front of the others. Tiern did the same. The meat pies were filling, though the crusts were far denser and the meat less seasoned than the castle's. Vixie slipped coins to Tiern and he stood to go pay, just as two boys her age came up behind them.

"You two leaving? Can we have these stools, then?"

"Aye, in a moment," Vixie told them.

The boys cocked their heads, stared at her, then looked at each other with mirth. They had cute faces, albeit too thin.

"You a lad or a lass?" one asked.

Vixie propped a hand on her hip. "Do I sound like a lad?"

"Maybe a lad who hasn't gone through the change," the other said. They bumped each other, laughing. "Why you wearing a lad's clothes, then?"

Perhaps Vixie should have been offended by their gruff teasing, but she found it quite humorous. Nobody ever treated her this way. "My dress is in the laundry, you gits."

"Nah, nah," one said, pushing a mass of curly light brown hair from his eyes. "If you're a lass, prove it."

Oh, now, that was going a bit too far. She wanted to prove it with a punch to his groin, but suddenly Tiern was at her side, wrapping a hand around her waist. His face came down and he pressed his lips to hers, warm and soft. It was over before she'd had a chance to process it. "Ready, love?" he asked. Then he turned a glare at the two boys. They backed away and let Vixie and Tiern pass.

Vixie blinked, in a daze, as Tiern took her hand and led her out. He didn't release her hand until they got to the horse.

"We'll have to leave the cart behind," he said. "Is there anything else hiding under the hay?"

What? Was he going to act as if he hadn't just kissed her? He set to work unhitching the horse. When he finished he turned to her. "Vix? Are you going to check the cart?"

He'd called her Vix. . . . She shook her head to clear it and then began roughly tossing hay from the cart, riffling through the straw for her pack.

Tiern grasped the back of his neck. "Look, Vixie, that was nothing, okay? The lads had taken an interest and I had to claim you or they might have tried to follow." He moved away from her to fiddle with the saddle and bridle.

I had to claim you. Vixie shivered with strange pleasure, but then the idea that he'd done it out of an obligation took the wind from her sails. She couldn't understand the ways of lads.

"It's ready." Tiern pointed to the horse. Vixie obliged, still unable to find her voice.

She'd just had her first kiss! While it may or may not have been a "real" kiss, it was one of the sweetest sensations she'd ever experienced. *Seas, his mouth had been so warm.* She climbed atop the horse, followed by Tiern's lithe form behind her. Together their body heat kindled between them.

"Are you comfortable?" he asked.

She nodded and let him take the reins. Just as they were setting off, two soldiers came charging up from down the lane. *Seas! There was nowhere to hide. They would have already been seen.* Vixie couldn't believe her sorry luck, to be caught so quickly! Tiern whispered a curse as the men approached, out of breath.

"Have you seen any foreign riders?" one of the soldiers asked.

What in Eurona? Vixie shook her head, and Tiern responded, "Nay, sir."

"Any carts or wagons of any kind?" the other soldier's voice was persistent, desperate. "Anything suspicious at all?"

"Nothing," Tiern said. "Can you tell me what's happened? I was part of the recent hunt."

The soldier caught his breath and said gravely, "The king and queen have been kidnapped by Kalorians."

"*What?*" Vixie yelled. She fought for breath. Her body felt disjointed, as if she'd just done a horribly faulty trick on horseback. Tiern's hand went around her waist, holding her tightly.

"Aye. Our navy ship followed their vessel out to sea and took control, but it was a decoy. We believe the Kalorians escaped on foot. They were Lashed. They left a trail of dead. Spread the word. All must be on the lookout."

They took off toward the inn, and everything inside Vixie constricted.

"Oh seas, oh seas, oh seas." She was going to be sick. "Tiern . . ." She struggled to say his name. "We have to go!" She fumbled to pull the reins from his hands.

"Sh, sh. You're panicking, Vixie. I've got it."

Dry sobs rose up as she fought for air. Her mum. Her papa. What had their captors done to them? "We have to find Aer," she said fiercely.

"Seas . . . if your parents are gone and Aerity is gone, there is no one on the throne."

"Aye. Go!" Vixie said, never more certain in her life. "Find her!"

"*Yah!*" Tiern called out, urging the horse with his heels, and the two of them leaned forward as they shot down the path.

Chapter 17

Traveling south for days, Aerity was taken by surprise at the climate shift. She began the journey cold, and now she couldn't stand the thought of putting that cloak around her. She was glad for the thinness of her shift and dress, even though they clung to her. She rode, swatting all manner of biting flies from her face. It wasn't hot, exactly, just warm, but the air held moisture and gave the atmosphere a stifling consistency.

She rode behind Harrison through the thick forest. It wasn't the dry-barked, straight-up-and-down sort of trees she was accustomed to. No pine needles littered the ground. No full canopies of soft greenery. These trees had large, thick leaves and seemed to bend in all directions as they rose high above, weighed down by vines. And not the leafy vines of Lochlanach, but wide, veiny creepers like snakes that wound around trunks and branches.

When they came to a fork in the path, Harrison stopped and opened his map. He pointed to the southeast path.

"This will take us south and we'll turn east just before a lake. We'll cut through this patch of woods eastward until we hit the path to Zorfina. It's not much farther, Aer. Two days, perhaps. The Zandalee tribe is said to be just inside the border in the south, over the hills."

She nodded, happy. Not much longer. Aerity pulled the damp hair from her neck. She still felt a moment of surprise and confusion whenever she caught sight of her dark locks. Harrison gave her a small smile.

"You look so unlike yourself. Each day I have to stare a moment to find you inside that disguise. Mostly because you're so filthy."

Aerity returned his rueful smile. "Very funny. At least I don't have a furry critter growing on my face."

He rubbed his cheek. "Speaking of growing, though." He pointed to her hairline. "There's a tiny bit of light hair showing. Just a sliver. Not sure anyone would notice but—"

Oh, no! Aerity's hand shot upward. She absolutely could not allow any of her natural color to show. "I have a small jar of the dye. I can patch it up."

"Now?"

"I really must," she said. "And I'll need your help."

"You've got to be kidding." His face froze, making her laugh.

"I don't have a looking glass! I'm likely to stain my entire forehead."

He gave her a you-owe-me glare. They pulled their horses off the path and Aerity made quick work of stirring the liquid with a stick. Harrison sighed loudly and took the stick, heeding her directions. He was very careful to dab the stick in the dye and comb upward along her hairline, only touching the new growth and not her skin. His tongue protruded from the corner of his mouth as he concentrated. He worked from one of her ears, up and around her hairline to the other ear.

"There. Do you need to wash it?"

"I suppose I can't," she said. "It'll have to do for now. Thank you."

Seas alive, she'd give anything for a long, proper bath. She swatted a bug from her arm and shuddered. Flying beetles had taken to falling on her from trees, and she was only glad they weren't the hairy spiders she'd heard of. As they remounted and turned to head down the south path, Aerity glimpsed something white sticking out from under the brush. "What's that?"

Harrison stopped, climbed down, and plucked it out. He smoothed it against his leg and shook his head. "It's in Kalorian."

Aerity held out her hand and took the parchment, which appeared to have once been posted on a tree. She read, and her heart began to race.

“‘Lashed Ones. A haven can be found at Lake Rainiard in return for your services.’” Her eyes went wide. “Harrison! Do you suppose Paxton saw this? Is that the lake up ahead on the map?”

Worry filled Harrison’s eyes. “It’s the only lake in the south, so I assume it is, but I don’t have a good feeling about this. What services are they asking of the Lashed?”

“Aye,” she agreed. “And who posted this? Obviously Kalorians, but is it perhaps a group of ill or injured people who need magical help?”

“Or part of Rozaria Rocato’s ranks?” Harrison added.

Aerity chewed her lip. It did seem a little worrisome. But she couldn’t shake the feeling that Paxton would have seen this notice and been curious too.

“Come on,” Harrison said, mounting again. “We’ll check it out when we get closer.”

Onward they rode for hours. Aerity munched a handful of dried berries and nuts to appease her ceaseless hunger pangs. She was ashamed at how vastly she’d underestimated the heaviness of her castle meals.

Just as her thoughts were headed dangerously along the lines of coconut cake, Harrison held up a hand and signaled her into the woods. Dusk was falling, casting dimness over the already shadowed forest.

“I think I smell smoke, and I saw fresh hoofprints on the trail,” Harrison whispered. “We’re not far from the lake now. This is right where we’d need to veer off to cut through to the Zorfina border.”

She could tell from his imploring tone that he wasn't comfortable going forward, and he wanted to cut through now. But what if Paxton was here and they wasted all their precious time traveling to the Zandalee tribe?

"Just a wee bit closer?" Aerity pleaded with her eyes until his lips tightened and he blew out a breath.

"*Fine.* We'll have a quick look, but we'll have to tie the horses in the forest and go on foot to stay quiet. If we don't see Paxton straightaway, we'll continue to Zorfina—"

"Entrudios." Intruders . . .

Aerity gasped, and Harrison spun his horse toward the voice. He reached back for an arrow, but one whizzed between the two of them, a warning shot.

Great seas! At least five men stepped out from deep within the forest, all pointing arrows at them. Harrison held up the palms of his hands and leaned slightly to the side as if to block Aerity.

The princess took in the sight of their dark bodies, shirtless, and hair that was shaved on the sides. Kalorian tribesmen. Aerity put her hands up as well, giving them a wary smile. She'd met tribesmen during the hunt and they'd been perfectly reasonable.

"Hello," she said in Kalorian. "We are traveling through. We mean no harm to anyone."

All eyes went to her with interest. The largest man moved forward. He sniffed the air and eyed the two of them. Aerity saw his hands, clutching his bow, and her stomach tightened at the sight of purple lines on his nails.

"You are not Lashed?" he asked with a grunt, speaking in Kalorian.

Aerity swallowed and responded in his native tongue, "No, sir, we are not. But we are Lashed supporters."

His eyes narrowed with skepticism. "How do you know Kalorian? You appear Lochlan." He spit on the ground.

Aerity's heart sank. She hadn't thought about how she would explain her language knowledge. Generally, only wealthy families learned foreign languages. Curses! She should have pretended not to understand. She fumbled for a quick idea.

"My family does trade mostly with Kalorians. Coffee beans and spices for wheat and soybeans. I befriended a Kalorian merchant's daughter and we taught each other."

Harrison watched their exchange carefully, most likely not understanding more than a few words here and there.

"Tell your man to throw down his weapons," the tribesman ordered. "*All* of them."

"He says to throw down your weapons."

Seeming unsurprised, Harrison slowly slid his bow and quiver off and lowered them to the ground. Then he pulled the daggers from the sheaths at his waist and boot and tossed them out too. One of the men rushed over and snatched them up, turning them over with a grin.

Aerity kept a sizable dagger in her horse's saddlebag, but she didn't dare tell. The large man told them to dismount, so they complied. Two of the men took their places on the horses, though the horses were unsure about it all, whipping their heads side to side. Aerity wanted to stroke Jude and tell him it was okay. Then again, maybe with any luck he'd throw the man to the ground.

The large Kalorian and one other took ropes from their waists and grabbed Aerity and Harrison by the wrists.

"Please," the princess said, starting to tremble. "We are harmless."

Quick, blinding pain stung the side of her face. He hit her!

"No!" Harrison shouted. "Keep your hands off her!"

Aerity had never before been hit by another person, and she was shocked by her urge to cower at the simple act of brutality. Then she heard a scuffle and thump, followed by a prolonged grunt from Harrison. She lifted her head to see him bent over, clutching his abdomen.

"Stop it!" she shouted in Kalorian. Her eyes watered as the large man tightened the ropes around her wrists and yanked her forward. "Don't hurt him, please," she whimpered.

"Tell your lover to shut his mouth and come with us. No more struggling."

Her first foolish instinct was to correct him, to say he was not her lover, but she dared not. The side of her face throbbed.

"They said be quiet and come with them. Don't struggle."

Harrison's eyes were wild, like he wanted to fight. Aerity shook her head. They were tugged forward, through the trees and back onto the path. Each step closer to their fate turned Aerity's stomach. Ten minutes later, wrists burning from the ropes, the trees opened into a clearing. In the dusky, dim lighting, Aerity saw a tall, dilapidated building and a camp with several tents and a fire raging in the center.

Her eyes darted about as people shuffled over to see them. Bald men with a woman in a Torestan-style shift and a young girl stared. A thin man in a Lochlan farmer's tunic watched. Aerity's hopes plummeted at the unfamiliar faces, though they seemed harmless enough.

They stopped in front of the largest tent, where candlelight flickered within.

"Madam Rozaria," the man holding her called out. Ice slithered down Aerity's back and she froze, her breaths ragged with terror. *Great seas. No.* Then the man said proudly in Kalorian, "We have captured intruders."

Aerity clenched her teeth, shaking. If it was the Rocato woman, would she recognize the princess? If so, she would surely kill them immediately. Or worse—kill Harrison and use Aerity as leverage to manipulate her father. Sick bile rose in her throat.

The tent flap opened, and a beautiful face peered out. *Her.* Aerity had a bow and arrow the last time she'd faced Rozaria; this time she was unarmed, her hands bound. Despair trickled into her like drops of toxin, making her dizzy. Deep oceans, help her. Rozaria pushed out through the tent flap, seeming somewhat annoyed. She stood, looking Aerity up and down, then at Harrison, with no signs of recognition. The princess held her breath, prepared to struggle and fight with all her might, come what may.

And then the flap opened again, and a man came out. His brown hair . . . those unruly waves . . . a sob nearly choked Aerity. When he stood fully, he glanced at her, then at Harrison, then back to Aerity. Their gazes locked, then abruptly his eyes seemed to erupt as he stared at her. *Aye*, Aerity wanted to cry out, *it's me*.

He was in terrible need of a shave. He inspected her intensely but remained silent. Aerity watched as his eyes went to Harrison again, and Paxton gave a quick, minuscule shake of his head. Harrison dropped his eyes.

"You're Unlashed," Rozaria said in Euronan. "And Lochlan." Aerity wondered how she would know they were Unlashed, other than having no marks. They could be Lashed who'd never worked magic, couldn't they?

"We're only traveling through," Harrison rasped as if he were in pain. "We meant no harm to your camp."

"Then how unlucky that you happened upon us," Rozaria said in a cool, low voice, "because we cannot allow you to leave." She turned and placed a hand intimately on Paxton's arm. He acted as if it were natural and fine, but a sickening zing ratcheted up Aerity's back as Rozaria gazed up at him. The look on her face was one of ownership and comfort. Seduction, even.

What in all of Eurona is going on here?

"You, Martone, and Robertone will escort them to the tower for questioning. Trust no one, Paxton. Ever. Even an innocent-seeming woman. Assume the worst and find out what they know. Take Chun with you so he can see how it is done. Remember: pain and fear prompt truth."

"Aye, Rozaria. I understand." The way he looked at the Rocato woman so openly, without fear—something was between them. *Oh, seas . . . are they . . . ?* No. Her mind whirred and she couldn't form coherent thoughts. Everything was wrong.

Aerity bent at the waist and dry heaved. Her empty stomach felt as if it were twisting in on itself. The world was spinning and turning and she started to topple until her captor yanked her upright and gave her a shake. She let out a weak wail.

"*Callie*," Harrison called. "Be strong."

He was rewarded by a backhand to the face from the brute holding him. Harrison shook his head like he was trying to clear away the pain. Aerity wanted to be sick again. She looked at Paxton, whose stare dropped to the ground between them, his eyes glazed in calculated thought.

Rozaria gave instructions to Martone in Kalorian, saying not to kill them—that they could be used as a test for loyalty. Aerity had no idea what that meant, but she knew they were in unspeakable danger.

Aerity and Harrison were dragged to the old building, and one of the bald Torestan men joined them, looking unsure. The moment the door to the building opened, Aerity was smacked with the rancid smell of decay. She gagged and coughed. It was the exact concentrated smell of death she'd experienced on the Isle of Loch, a gruesome stench from her nightmares that told her Rozaria was creating more monsters here.

This couldn't be happening. Why was Paxton allowing it? Aerity questioned everything she thought she knew in that moment. Paxton had carried so much anger when they'd met, but he'd still seemed to value human life. He couldn't have turned, could he? Had he been romanced by Rozaria's ideals of Lashed power?

No, Aerity refused to believe it.

In the entranceway, she saw an open room to the right. A young woman stood at a table with some sort of hairy creature wriggling under her hands. A scar marred one side of the girl's pretty cheek. When she saw them, she quickly raised the hood of her cloak, hiding her face. The small creature took this opportunity to stand and leap down from the table in a flash. Aerity screamed as it ran toward them on four little legs, claws clacking against the ground. The brute Martone tried to grab it with one hand while holding Aerity's arm with the other. It streaked past and up a dark stairwell.

The girl shouted, "*Imbecile cub!*" in Kalorian.

"I will retrieve it," Paxton told her. "I'm on duty here tonight anyway. We're dealing with these prisoners, and then I'll take care of the creature."

The girl didn't respond, causing Aerity to wonder if she could understand Lochlan. She simply glowered at Paxton and then tugged her hood down farther, rushing past them and out of the building.

Martone pulled Aerity toward the dark staircase and she stumbled on the first few steps before finding her footing. They seemed to wind up and up forever until they came to a round room where Martone shut them in. Aerity expected the tiny monster to jump out at her at any moment, but she saw it nowhere. Harrison's captor shoved him down onto the filthy floor covered in loose hay. A single window let in the last of the early evening light, swirling dust around old bed pads on the far side of the room.

The other Kalorian pointed at the floor by the empty wall. Aerity gladly moved away from them and sat, pulling in her knees. Harrison leaned against the wall ten paces away. Her eyes darted to Paxton, who was watching her intently. His lips were set in a way that made him seem furious. The Torestan stood behind him, watching with nervous, darting eyes. Martone kept his hands fisted as he paced back and forth. Aerity shrank away from the volatile man.

Paxton knelt before Harrison. "Tell us your name and why you are in Kalor."

Harrison cleared his throat. "I am Broden Spanner of southern Lochlanach. It has been said I hail from Kalor roots, that my grandmother was a Kalorian vagabond."

Martone marched over to Aerity and gave her hip a hard

nudge with his foot. He pointed to Harrison and said in Kalorian, "What does he say? Translate!"

Paxton's eyes went round with horror when Aerity began to speak in Kalorian for Martone. Paxton pinched the skin between his eyes and told Harrison, "Go on."

"My parents have both died and I'm without family, so I wanted to venture to Kalor to try to find my kin." He paused for Aerity to translate. "I offered to pay my friend to join me because she's the only person I know who speaks Kalorian."

"How convenient," Paxton muttered.

While Martone and the other tribesman concentrated on Aerity's translation, she could have sworn she saw an interaction between Harrison and Paxton: a movement of lips. Yet both of their faces remained fiercely determined.

Paxton reached out and gripped the side of Harrison's neck, pulling him back. "I need you to tell me the truth now, Broden Spanner. . . . Who sent you to Kalor?"

Harrison's chest arched up, and he let out a growl that escalated into a howl that made Aerity's skin prickle. Paxton held on tight to Harrison's neck as his legs kicked out beneath him.

Aerity could not believe her eyes. She screamed, "Stop it!" and pushed up on her knees, ready to knock sense into Paxton herself, but he stopped just as Martone grabbed Aerity by the shoulder and wrenched her back. Her head hit the wall with a thud and she scrambled away. She and Harrison were both breathing hard. Paxton was glaring at her. *How could he?*

Her entire world shifted in that moment into something ugly. Her heart had never ached so.

"I work for no one," Harrison panted. "I swear. I am a wheat farmer who wants to find my family."

Martone turned his head to Aerity in expectation and she weakly translated.

Paxton now put both his hands on Harrison's neck, as if he might strangle him, and looked him in the eye. "This is your one and only chance to come clean. If you tell us the truth, everything you know about those hunting Rozaria, and express your loyalty, we will consider not killing you. We can perhaps find a use for you."

Aerity murmured a translation, her stomach clenching. Then she said to Paxton, "Please . . . please don't."

His jaw clenched, but he did not look at her. His forearms flexed and a gurgle came from Harrison. Harrison's entire body shook, and he fell over to the side. Paxton pulled his hands away and shouted, "Tell me what you know or each time will get worse!"

Harrison gasped. "I . . . know . . . nothing."

The man, Chun, who practically hid from the display, spoke Kalorian in a shaky voice, "I think he's telling the truth."

"This man is weak," Martone said in Kalorian to his partner, hitching a thumb at Chun. The other tribesman nodded, sending a sneer to Chun, who stepped away.

Aerity's vision was spotty in the shadowed dimness. She

felt numb. Dead. Until Martone's hard smack hit the same spot on her face he'd hit before. A throb of pain filled her entire head and neck. "Tell us what you know, *gluta*," he snarled. *Gluta* . . . a foul word for Lochlans that meant colorless pig.

She brought her arms up to shield herself from further abuse as Paxton yelled, "Oy! I'll handle her." He crouched before her now and ordered her to tell what she knew.

Aerity slowly lowered her arms. Paxton was so close. Her chest rose and fell rapidly. Her eyes burned. She knew now that his allegiance had turned, but her heart was so foolish. Even now, after seeing him hurt her friend, she wanted so badly to take his hands and tell him he didn't have to be this way. That she missed him terribly. That it wasn't too late to turn from Rozaria's clutches and come home.

She swallowed a dry lump and repeated the story she'd told the men in the woods, first in Lochlanian, then Kalorian. Martone grunted and looked down at Harrison's still body. He pushed him with his foot.

"Is he dead?" The man laughed. "Rozaria said not to kill him, you fool."

Aerity's heart gave a great bang. "*No!*" She tried to push away from Paxton to get to Harrison, but Paxton held her by the arms. "Is he dead?" She thrashed and screamed until Paxton pressed his palm hard over her mouth, speaking roughly.

"He is alive. He's only passed out. Tell Martone."

Oh, thank the seas. If anything happened to Harrison she'd never be able to live with herself! Aerity drew a deep breath of relief.

He took his hand away and she obeyed, staring at Harrison and feeling better when she saw the light movement of his chest. Then she turned her face to Paxton and felt more anger than she'd ever felt in her life.

"How *could* you? How could you do that to him?" She struggled, trying to kick or hit or hurt him in any way she could. A scream tore from her throat as the helplessness of utter betrayal took over.

"I think they are innocent!" the Torestan man said, his voice filled with panic.

"You are too soft." Martone sneered at him before turning to his partner. "We are getting nowhere with these prisoners and I grow bored."

Oh no. "Watch out," Aerity breathed, though to whom, she could not say.

Martone shoved Paxton aside and grabbed Aerity's throat with his meaty hand, lifting her to her feet and then off the floor. Spots swam in her vision.

"Tell us what you know, girl!" His voice was monstrous.

She grabbed his wrists with her bound hands to hold herself up, kicking her feet. Her throat and jaw pulsated with pain. Oh, seas, she couldn't breathe!

"She can't tell us a damned thing if you've got her by the throat!" Paxton shouted. "Put her down!"

Aerity wanted to tell Paxton that Martone couldn't

understand him. She vaguely heard shouts. From the corner of her eye she saw a blur of fur come across the room. The tiny beast? She was pitched slightly to the side as Martone kicked the thing and it soared into the wall with a yelp. Then she felt herself losing consciousness—loud voices and stomping seemed so far away, then quiet and blackness as she was dropped to the ground. The last thing she felt was a firm hand on her cheek, and then nothingness.

Chapter 18

Heaviness upon her body.
Tender lips grazing her own.
Warm breath against her cheek.

A whispered voice. "What in the bloody depths of the seas are you doing here, Aerity Lochson?" Close, but so far. "Have you any idea how it broke me, the way you looked at me tonight?" In a more urgent whisper, "Wake up, Aer. It's time to wake up." It was a strange sort of dream. It made her long for something lost.

Like wading upward, slowly, from deep and afar, Aerity felt her senses opening with drowsy awareness. She tried to remember the dream, but it was miles away now. She forced her heavy eyes open to see a dark figure looming above her. In fact, the dark figure was lying on her body with a hand over her mouth, covering her, holding her down with a strange, dominating gentleness. Aerity suddenly lit into full awareness and she struggled, trying to roll or fight, but his body overpowered her, holding both her wrists with one hand and muffling her voice with the other.

"Sh . . ." he whispered. "It's *me*, Aer."

A large, dark splotch came at her from the side and there was a sudden loud snuzzling of air at her ear that made her squirm. Then a lick directly inside her ear.

"Get out of here, you mad little fiend," the familiar voice said, gently pushing the creature away and looking down at her.

Her eyes adjusted and she stilled. His hair hung loose between them, tickling her cheeks. His pupils were wide and dark. This was unmistakably her Paxton. And then she tensed.

Her Paxton . . . who had tortured Harrison.

Slowly, when he must have assumed she was going to behave, he released her hands and mouth. Aerity swung and smacked the side of his head. He hissed and grabbed his ear.

All her earlier betrayal and hurt surfaced with a vengeance and she railed on him with all her might. When he tried to grasp her hands she cried, "Traitor! Get your hands off me!" Feet, hands, knees, and elbows. She made her way out from under him and sat up, still swinging as he attempted to restrain her.

The tiny monster made a gurgling growling sound and

pounced onto her lap, pawing at their flailing arms and scratching her skin. It was attacking! Paxton pitched it off with a single swipe, then grasped Aerity's wrists and pushed her down with the weight of his body, looming over her again. They were both panting.

"Be. Quiet." His voice was low but stern. "We have less than three hours until dawn, but it's imperative that you're quiet."

"What has happened to you?" Aerity whispered harshly.

"*I didn't hurt Harrison,*" Paxton said. There was hurt in his voice. "He was faking the pain, and then I put him to sleep, just as I did to you."

It took several long moments for Aerity to process this information—for all the pieces of painful emotions to backpedal and right themselves, still somewhat askew. It was too much.

"You're playing both sides?" Aerity asked.

"I'm gaining information for Lochlanach." He moved off her and they both sat up. Paxton bent his knees and rested his arms on them, but he seemed tense. The creature walked around him, sniffing him, then came to Aerity and did the same. She shrank away.

"It's one of her creations, isn't it?"

"Aye. Just a babe. She wants to kill it for not being fierce enough."

Every ounce of her fear for the creature was wiped away with those words. It was just a baby. She hesitantly held out her hand and it came forward. It sniffed her, then licked her palm. When it lifted its paw to playfully swat, she yanked her hand back. Those claws were no joking matter. After pawing at her a bit more, the creature abruptly seemed to tire, and it curled up beside them.

Aerity's fascination turned from the creature to Paxton. Their legs were touching where they sat. She looked up at him, and he peered down at her. He was really here. She couldn't believe she'd ever doubted him. He laid his hand gently over the top of hers and Aerity felt her entire body warm and soften to his touch.

They moved at the same time, his hand going to her hair as her palm cupped his face. He grabbed her wrist with his other hand. His face was inches from hers but filled with tension.

"We need to get you and Harrison out of here, right now."

"What about you?" she asked.

"I have to stay." His voice was firm.

"Why?" Panic rose. "Do you stay for *her*?"

He tilted his head at her. "Do you think the worst of me, Aerity? You believed I was one of them. I saw it in your eyes."

Her heart ached and her eyes burned. "Not until I thought you were hurting Harrison. You can't be mad at me for that—you were both damned convincing!"

"Tell me why you're here," he said softly.

How could he even ask? In a gentle but confident voice, she told him. "For you, of course."

There was a pause in which neither moved. And then Paxton's hand tightened in her hair, the other sliding down to her waist, and he pulled her to him until their mouths met in a sweetness of yearning. Her arms circled his neck, holding him tight. Oh, how she'd craved this from him. She came up on her knees before him, needing to be closer. Their mouths moved together as if they could make up for every moment they'd spent apart.

Paxton pulled Aerity down to his lap, eliciting a moan from her, and that was when they heard the clearing of a throat against the wall. Their lips went still.

"Before you get too carried away, we should probably hear Paxton's plan of escape," Harrison said.

Aerity practically leaped from Paxton's lap. "How long have you been awake?" she sputtered.

"Long enough to cry happy tears for the both of you," Harrison teased. Embarrassment swept over her as Harrison chuckled. "We came all this way. I wasn't about to ruin the moment too soon." He got to his feet and so did Paxton. The two of them met with a clasp of hands and a hard pat to the shoulders.

Paxton moved to the window and looked out. He whispered, "I've got your horses ready below this window. We'll have to shred these old beds and perhaps some of your clothing to make a rope."

"Can't we take the stairs?" Aerity asked.

"Nay. One of the Kalorian tents is near the front doors,

and there is always someone on watch in the lower levels with the creatures. Right now it happens to be me, and I can't raise any suspicions against myself. Chun added a sleeping herb to the evening tea, so hopefully the camp is sleeping soundly. Let's get going."

He took out his knife and set to slicing pieces of the bed-covers, while Harrison pulled off his tunic. Aerity pulled straw out of the beds to give Paxton better access to the fabric. As they finished cutting strips, Aerity began knotting them together with shaking hands. She prayed to the seas that this would work. They were quite high up, and though she wasn't afraid, if these rags gave out, they could face broken bones, being knocked out upon impact, or even death.

She gave each knot an extra hard tug.

"That's it," Paxton said. "And by the way"—he looked back and forth between them—"Rozaria's plan was for Chun and his brother to kill the two of you in the morning to prove their loyalty to the cause. So Chun, his wife and daughter, his brother and his two nephews, will all be riding with you. They're waiting below."

Aerity's eyes bulged, and she rushed to the window. Sure enough, five horses were hidden in the nearby trees with people atop. She had to squint in the dark to see them—a young girl was riding with a woman, but the rest were males.

"If you believe they can be trusted," Harrison said, "that is good enough for me."

"Thank you." Paxton sounded relieved. "It was Chun's

idea. When I came to him after leaving you tonight and told him Rozaria's plan, he confided in me. Said he wanted to make it look like he'd helped you escape."

"Do our companions know who I am?" Aerity asked.

"Nay. The fewer who know, the better." Paxton quietly wrenched the old window open. Aerity's nerves were on edge, waiting for any noise that might ruin their chance of escape. She went to the ledge and slowly let the rope down. It was hard to see, but she was certain it didn't reach the ground.

"Curses," she whispered. "It's too short."

Paxton moved past her and leaned out, then pulled back in. "You'll have about a seven-foot drop. I think you're both graceful enough to make it."

Oh seas, oh seas, oh seas . . .

"You go first, Harrison," Aerity told him. She wanted another moment with Paxton. But Harrison shook his head.

"You're more important, Aer. If I break the rope, you'll be stuck. You go."

She wanted to argue, but the two of them were likely to haul her out the window if she tried. So she reached up to give Harrison a quick hug and then moved over to Paxton for a longer one. As they held each other, sudden sadness invaded, cold and disappointing.

"I had so much I wanted to say," she whispered. Her face was buried in his hot neck and soft hair.

"Me too," he whispered back.

"Please come with us," she begged, not willing to let go. Paxton held her harder.

"I want to so badly you can't imagine. But this is where I will do the greatest good."

Aerity looked up at him. She knew she had no right to cling to this man. She was soon to be married to another. Paxton's business was not hers. But part of her would always think of him as her own and wish for his well-being. The thought of Rozaria with her claws in him made her want to rage.

"Do you share a tent with her?" she asked.

His eyebrows pulled together. "Nay."

Aerity exhaled raggedly. "Be careful, Pax. She wants you, and she's not one to handle losing very well."

"Noted." He kissed her lips one last time, then led her to the window. "Don't worry about me, Aer."

Aerity climbed deftly to the edge, her legs dangling over. She turned back to look at Paxton one last time.

"I will always worry about you. All my days."

His eyes softened with gratitude and something even deeper. "When it is safe, I will find a way to send news. Just know for now that Prince Vito is not to be trusted. I'm not certain of their plan, but when I find out I will alert Lochlanach straightaway." Aerity nodded. That would have to be good enough.

The sleepy cub creature shuffled over and came up on its hind legs, its front paws on the window, watching Aerity. In the moonlight she could see its adorable face, in complete contrast to the oversized fangs protruding from its mouth. She remembered what Paxton said about Rozaria wanting to destroy it.

"Can I take him?"

Paxton rubbed the back of his neck and looked to Harrison, who shrugged noncommittally. "I don't know about that, Aer."

But the idea was in her mind now. She couldn't let Rozaria kill him.

"He appears part bear," she said. "Put him on my back and see if he holds on." Again the men shared a look, as if it weren't a good idea. "Just do it. Please."

Paxton sighed and hoisted the creature to her back. It must have sensed the height because right away its arms went around her neck and its legs hitched under her arms, clinging tightly. A sort of nurturing pride filled Aerity and she gave Pax one last smile. He shook his head, but managed a tight smile in return.

She wound the fabric of the improvised rope around her feet and grabbed hold tightly with her hands, then lowered herself down, shifting her foothold as she went. It wasn't nearly as stable as the silks she was accustomed to climbing, but it would do.

She moved cautiously but swiftly downward until she heard a stretching sound in the fabric and she stilled. When she didn't hear it again, she moved down more slowly. At the bottom she released the rope with her feet and used her upper body strength to climb down to the last knot. She eyed the dark ground but saw nothing in her way, so she dropped. Aerity landed on her toes, then heels, and bent her knees. Her palms hit the ground and she breathed a sigh of relief.

The cub clung so tightly that she had to pry him from her back and move him to her chest. She ran to Jude and pulled up onto his back one-handed, then watched the window where Harrison sat on the edge. *C'mon, Harrison . . .*

His descent was much less graceful. He didn't know how to use his feet as effectively as Aerity, so he was putting the heels of his feet together, sliding them down to the next knot, and then the next. Aerity glanced up at the window. Paxton's hands grasped the edge as he stared at her. She raised her hand in a weak good-bye. He nodded and turned, then was gone.

Harrison was three quarters of the way down—so close—when a ripping sound wrenched the air. It was the same spot where she had heard the fabric stretch. Harrison moved faster, and the fabric broke. He tried to land gracefully on his feet as she had, but his ankle seemed to give away and he toppled to the side. To his credit, he made not one sound. She was about to dismount, when Chun and his brother dismounted and ran out from the woods. The two of them got to Harrison and helped him to his feet.

"I have problems with this cursed ankle," he muttered.

"Let's get him on the horse," Chun said. "I can heal him when we are safely away."

Harrison used his arms and good leg, along with their

help, to get on his horse. Aerity peered around at the darkness, eager to be gone from there. They made their way slowly into the woods so as not to make a ruckus. Then as soon as they were out of sight from the camp, the seven horses blazed forward, the beast cub curled in her lap.

Aerity should have felt the rush of freedom in escaping her captors, but what she felt was just the opposite. A confining sense of loss all over again. Her love was now a captive of Rozaria, feigning his loyalty and interest in her. She couldn't imagine a worse situation. Aerity vowed to send help to him as soon as she could. She only hoped it wouldn't be too late.

Chapter 19

As they rode fast to the border of Zorfina in the final hours of night, the vegetation changed, the altitude rose, and the climate slowly shifted. Buttressing roots of jungle trees gave way to thinner trees as they moved upward over the low-lying hills in the morning light. When they finally crested the peak, trees turned to sparser shrubbery on the other side. Rich, fertile soil of clay and silt morphed to something grittier as they descended and the land flattened out. The blazing sun beat down on them. Aerity's skin felt tighter with lack of moisture.

A dire sensation pervaded her with each mile that brought her farther from Paxton. Aerity couldn't shake the awful feeling. She knew they couldn't go back, but she also couldn't see the point of going anywhere other than home now. Her father needed to know what was happening in Kalor. Something had to be done.

"I think we've crossed the border!" Harrison called once they'd finally left the hilled forest in the far distance. Chun and his brother gave a holler of triumph. Their voices made the monster cub stir from its slumber on her back. Chun had given her a rucksack to keep it in. She didn't want it to try to climb out. Aerity carefully pulled the strap over her head and shifted the pack to her front. The little beast poked its head from the opening. It sniffed the air and twitched its whiskers. Then it opened its mouth for a wide yawn, revealing the full length of its large, white, sharp teeth.

When it closed its mouth and ran its pink tongue over its fangs, it appeared so young and innocent. Aerity reached in her pack and pulled out a piece of dry jerky. It nearly jumped from her arms when it smelled the dried meat, but she held it tight.

"Easy, boy." She slowly brought the food to its mouth. When he tried to snatch, she made a sharp clicking sound and gave him a yank back. "Gentle." She brought the meat forward again and this time let him have it. Harrison glanced back over his shoulder.

"We'll let it hunt for its own food when we stop. He'll probably do better than even I could."

They surged forward into the cracked dirt, the beast blinking its little eyes in the movement of air. Aerity had to shield her eyes against the glaring sun.

When it was time to stop and rest the horses, Aerity pulled the beast from its pack and held it like a baby. It was shockingly compliant, lying back lazily and turning its head to look about them. She checked and saw that it was, indeed, a male. It probably weighed twenty-five or thirty pounds. It had to be very young still. She set him down on the ground and he stretched, digging his massive claws into the ground. Harrison had been right; within minutes the beast sniffed out a snake in a shrub and pounced, effectively killing it and playing with it before eating it.

She doubted her parents would approve of bringing one of Rozaria's beasts home. The creature would no doubt be dangerous full-grown, but right now he was such a little thing. Perhaps if he wasn't raised to kill people he would lose that instinct? She cringed a little as she watched it thrash the snake around between its teeth. When he finished eating, he bounced back to Aerity and swatted at her loose skirts.

She turned to Harrison. "May I see the map?"

He took it out and they knelt in the dry dirt to spread it out. The afternoon sun was unhindered by clouds or tree cover. There were occasional patches of shorter trees and bushes, yellowed grasses, and out beyond was more of the same. If they continued east it would turn to desert sand.

Chun's wife set to feeding her daughter and two nephews while the men joined Aerity to peer at the map.

"Where is the Zandalee tribe?" Aerity asked Harrison.

He pointed to a spot further east. "A day's ride from here."

Aerity shook her head. "We can't go. I must return home." She looked at Harrison, and then turned to Chun. "It is imperative that you take your family, though. You will be safe with the Zandalee."

"Zandalee?" asked Chun's brother in surprise. "But they hate men!"

"They are matriarchal," Aerity explained, "but they do not hate men. They are Lashed supporters. Be honest with them that you escaped Rozaria's camp and be willing to share everything you know."

The men looked skeptical. Chun asked, "What if they think we're trying to trick them?"

Harrison sighed. "Ask for Zandora and tell her Lieutenant Harrison Gillfin of the hunting party sent you."

Chun's mouth bobbed open. "You lied about your identity? You are a soldier?" He looked upon Harrison with complete distrust.

"Of course I lied," Harrison said with a tone of frustration. "The Kalorians would have killed me on the spot if they'd known I was a Lochlan soldier. But I wasn't there to hunt Lashed or spy or infiltrate. We were truly traveling through and I wouldn't have taken Callie anywhere near that bloody lake if I had known who was there."

His impassioned words must have done the trick because Chun and his brother seemed to relax again. Then Chun asked, "What did you say the Zandalee woman's name was again?"

"Zandora," Harrison said.

Chun looked at his brother. "We met her! Do you remember the first day Paxton came? The women were only there a short while before they left." Both men grinned at the fact that they had, indeed, met the notorious Zandalee women.

"That makes sense that they'd been traveling together," Aerity said. It made her glad that he hadn't been alone.

"They'll likely remember you then," Harrison told them. He pored over the map with them, giving specific instructions. Then he and Aerity mapped out their own route home along the borders. This time they would have to go through Toresta to get back to Lochlanach. She hoped the Torestan border patrol would allow them in without papers. Kalorian lands had to be completely avoided. The Torestan route would take a day longer, but Aerity was willing to stop less and ride faster this time. She *had* to get home. The sooner her father's army could foil Rozaria, the sooner Paxton could be free of the madwoman and everyone could be safe.

Paxton was not looking forward to breaking the news to Rozaria, but he could wait no longer without looking too suspicious. She would already be furious that they escaped under his watch.

He took a deep breath, set his shoulders, and sprinted from the building, glad to at least be away from the stench.

"Rozaria!" he called. The camp was quiet, wisps of smoke still rising from last night's fires. "Rozaria!"

Seconds later she and her men burst from tents, some

half-dressed, bleary-eyed. Her face set in agitated worry when she saw Paxton running to her.

"What has happened?"

He bent and put his hands on his knees, looking up at her. "They're gone. They went through the window." He panted. Her worry turned to hardened anger. "They shredded the bedding into ropes. I never heard a thing."

She shoved past him and began barking orders in Kalorian. Her men scattered, yelling to one another.

"I can hunt them," Paxton said. "I'm a tracker. They can't have gotten too far on foot. If we take the horses—"

Martone ran from the stables, shouting words Paxton couldn't understand.

"Seven horses are gone," Rozaria whispered in horror.

"You've got to be kidding," Paxton said.

Konor came out of his tent rubbing his eyes and staring in confusion at the chaos.

"Wake the others!" Rozaria ordered Paxton. "See if they heard or saw anything."

Paxton nodded and ran to Chun's tent. "Chun, get up." He flung the tent flap wide and stared in, then stepped inside only to run back out and sprint to Chun's brother's tent and do the same.

"They're gone!" he shouted to Rozaria. "Every one of the Torestans!"

She raised her chin and pierced the air with a scream that seemed to uncoil from deep within her.

"Check the lake!" she commanded.

Paxton and Konor ran down to the lake and scoured the beach area.

"They really left?" Konor asked.

"Aye," Paxton said. "With the prisoners, it seems."

Konor's eyes bulged from his thin face. "The cowardly traitors!"

Paxton nodded and they ran back to camp just in time to see Rozaria scream and throw a kettle into a stack of wood. Her chest heaved and she stared dangerously around at all her men and the mysterious woman. Ultimately, her eyes landed on Paxton. He awaited her wrath, but instead a frightening sense of calm suddenly pervaded her being.

"If they escaped during the night, they could be in Zorfina by now. Word will spread, and it is just as well. The time has come to take back what is ours. We leave now for Castle Kalor." A zealous gleam filled her eyes, and Paxton forced himself to smile.

Chapter 20

Wyneth had never before seen the underground tunnels. In fact, until yesterday she'd thought they were a fable. Indeed, that if there'd ever been actual tunnels, they'd long since collapsed. Now it was a single shaft. After spending nearly twenty-four hours stuck in the underground room with her family, a handful of guards, and Lord Alvi, she hoped she'd never see the fabled room again.

"How much longer must we wait?" Lady Wavecrest demanded of the guards.

"Until we receive communication from aboveground that all is safe," the guard told her again. But even he sounded doubtful at this point.

None of them had slept well on the military bedrolls.

Wyneth felt everyone's nerves stretched taut and wondered who would be first to break. Most likely one of the lords: her hotheaded father or uncle, or Lief. As for Wyneth, she'd lain awake wondering about Vixie, who couldn't be found during the chaotic roundup.

Lord Alvi's knee bounced up and down from his spot on the bench. His arms were crossed and his face was as etched with unhappiness as it had been the moment they had gotten down there. He had only meant to help Wyneth and her family into safety, and then he'd expected to be let back up to join the fight.

Wyneth had never seen a person as angry as Lord Alvi when he'd been told he would have to remain below or risk giving away their hiding place.

Over and over, Wyneth ran through yesterday's events. She had gone straight to the library after speaking with Lord Alvi, Tiern, and Vixie. The nearest guard had swept Wyneth down the hall. It was as if some well-rehearsed plan of action had been put into place. The entire royal family converged, brought by guards and flanked by Lord Alvi, on a small cupboard room beyond the cellar. Once inside, a panel was lifted from the bottom of a large chest, and down the musty tunnel they went.

"Where is Princess Vixie?" one guard had asked as soon as they were to safety.

"In the kitchens!" Wyneth had been unnerved at the thought of Vixie caught in the fighting. The panic rose again now because Vixie was never brought to the shelter, nor was

Tiern. All they knew was that fighting had broken out in the king's office, where he and Queen Leighlane met with the Kalorians.

Thankfully the shelter room had been well stocked with food, water, and toys for the children. Wyneth imagined the toys had been Leighlane's touch.

Lord Alvi stood and paced again. He said grumpily, "Perhaps the reason no one has come for us is because they're all dead."

"We are following protocol—"

"Ach!" Lord Alvi waved the guard's words away and crossed his arms tightly.

Wyneth's youngest cousin, Merity, let out a whining howl from her place on the floor.

"What is the matter now?" her mother called. Lady Baycreek had long since lost patience, accustomed to having maids to help with the children.

"She's trying to take my doll!" her older sister, Caileen, cried.

Lady Baycreek put her face in her hands.

"Here." Wyneth came over to the girls and squatted. "Shall I draw something for you? How about I draw each of you as an animal?"

"Me first!" Caileen yelled. Merity fell over and set to crying. Wyneth pursed her lips.

"You cuddle your doll, Caileen, and I shall draw Merity first. Then you."

She thanked the seas for her mother's forethought to grab

their outing bag with drawing utensils and a bound notebook, along with playing cards and other games to entertain the children.

Merity sat up with puffy eyes and even poofier red hair, and gave Wyneth a watery smile. "Can you make me be a dolphin, Wynnie?"

"Of course. And what a darling dolphin you shall be." Wyneth lost herself in doodling, not noticing as the children crowded around, even the older lads. When she was finished they all laughed and remarked on the silliness of a dolphin with red hair, swimming in a sea of flower-strewn water.

"Now me!" Caileen said excitedly. She shoved the doll into Merity's arms. "Make me a bird!"

"Only if you ask nicely . . ." Wyneth smiled.

"*Please*, make me a bird?"

"Actually . . ." Wyneth raised her eyes to Lord Alvi, who had moved to stand just over her shoulder. "I know someone who can draw a birdie even better than I." She looked around at the children and they stared back in wonder.

"Who?" Cousin Leo asked. "Not me or my family."

Wyneth glanced up at Lord Alvi again and held back a laugh at the look of *No, no, no!* on his tight face.

"Lord Alvi, is it?" Leo exclaimed. "Can you draw, sir?"

"Oh, come now," he said with a dark chuckle. "I'm . . . busy."

"Busy brooding," remarked Wyneth's twelve-year-old brother Brixton. At that Wyneth barked a laugh and the other children did as well.

Lord Alvi dropped his arms and actually gave a grin. "I never brood."

Wyneth grasped him by the wrist and tugged him down. He sighed dramatically and took the notebook that she pressed to his chest. He spared her one last threatening glare before looking around at the waiting faces.

"All right, then. Who is to be the bird? Is it you, Donubhan? A hummingbird?"

"No, sir! I am to be a killer whale!"

"It's me!" Caileen raised her hand, beaming.

"Ah, yes, it is Lady Caileen. I remember now." He examined the freckled little beauty for a moment before setting to drawing. Raucous laughter ensued as Lord Alvi depicted the girl, covered in red curly feathers, eyes crazed with mischief—even Lady Wavecrest and Lady Baycreek had taken peeks and giggled behind their hands—until the rusty-hinged door to the room creaked and flew open. Lord Alvi dropped the drawing book and stood.

A pale guard peered around the room with a frown. "It is secure for you to come up, but . . ." He swallowed and his forehead gleamed with sweat. "The king, queen, and Princess Vixie are all missing. We're scouring towns now."

Seas, no! Wyneth pressed a palm to the floor and her other hand over her forehead as the room spun. Adults shouted questions and children burst into tears.

"Mum!" Donubhan's voice nearly shattered Wyneth. She pushed through the other kids and wrapped her arms around him.

"Sh, Donnie, it will be all right." She pressed her cheek to his head as his body heaved in sobs. "They'll be found."

Please, let them be found.

"Hush!" Lord Wavecrest shouted. "I cannot hear the man!" Wyneth grabbed the crying Merity and pulled her into her embrace to shush her. Then all eyes went back to the guard.

"It was a Lashed attack. We believe all the Kalorians who came were Lashed. They were checked at the gate, but nobody saw any lines. We think they used a paint of some sort. Ten guards were killed plus four of the Kalorians. They must have somehow subdued the king and queen to change their clothing—we're not certain—but when they came out of the office and attacked, they broke into two groups and went in opposite directions." The guard grimaced. "They knew the castle better than any guest should."

"The traitor gave them more information," Lord Baycreek whispered.

"Aye. And they had more people lying in wait outside. A whole caravan they pretended were their maids and servants. They were all trained. The caravan fled up the path to the royal gate, but our soldiers said they saw a group of them taking the king and queen to the docks, so we set off after them, prepared to capture their vessel." He shook his head. The room was silent as they clung to every word.

"Their boat was a decoy," he said. "A distraction. And when we seized their boat, the five aboard laid hands on one another in a circle, and they all just fell . . . dead."

Now Caileen let out a frightened wail, and Wyneth pulled her in with Donnie and Merity.

Lord Alvi must have heard enough. He pushed past the guard and climbed up the ladder. Nobody stopped him. The guard moved aside and motioned for the others to follow, but Lord and Lady Baycreek and Lord and Lady Wavecrest all turned to one another instead.

"The castle has been compromised," Lord Wavecrest said. "I think we should retreat to somewhere safer and more remote while the army searches."

Lord Baycreek nodded. "The Isle of Evie?" Lord Wavecrest returned the nod.

Wyneth watched the exchange with mixed feelings. They wanted to flee to the royal vacation island. It made sense as far as the safety of the children went, but Wyneth would go mad that far away right now. The island was chosen for its natural barriers: cliffs and a magnificently rugged landscape. A nearly impenetrable villa had been built atop the cliffs, and it would be easier to thwart an attack there than in the royal lands. But she knew she could not go.

Wyneth said nothing, not wanting to upset the children again, but when the time came for them to leave, she would state her case. She was of age to make her own decisions now. Aerity was set to return within days, if all went well. She was certain that the remaining army would not be allowing visitors of any kind into royal lands, and the naval guard was likely to secure the port with heavier measures now that a threat was apparent. She felt safe enough.

She kissed the heads of her cousins and stood. "Come along now, little lassies. Let's all pack our favorite things and set off on a grand adventure."

This seemed to raise their spirits. The little ones trooped after their mothers, anxious to leave the musty room. The four oldest boys—her brothers Bowen and Brixton, and her cousins Donubhan and Leo—stayed behind. Wyneth looked about at them, each with hair of varying shades and lengths of red, from radiant auburn to deep reddish-brown.

"Are we to run as cowards do?" Bowen asked.

"Bow, it's not like that at all," Wyneth insisted. "We're royals, and it's important that we keep ourselves safe so someone can run the kingdom."

"I want to join the army and fight," he said.

"Yeah!" said the other three.

"You're fourteen!" she reminded Bowen. "They won't consider any lads under seventeen—you know this. Pack your bows and arrows and practice while you're at the Isle of Evie. If the island comes under attack, seas forbid, you can shoot arrows from the high turrets and you'll need to be good shots."

"Come along," said a guard from the doorway. "We're closing up."

They did as he said, all inhaling deeply of the fresh air as they entered the tall castle hallways again. While the other three boys bounded off to prepare to leave, Donubhan lagged behind at Wyneth's side. She turned to face him, clasping his shoulders. He was only inches from her own height, still far too young to deal with this. Her heart hurt knowing the lad was all alone, his entire family gone or missing. Where in Eurona were they?

"What if they're not found?" he whispered. "What will happen to Lochlanach? And when is Aerity coming home? She needs to be here!"

Wyneth had never seen the carefree boy so serious. It was as if he were maturing before her very eyes. She pulled him forward and he let her, wrapping his arms around her waist tightly.

"They'll be found," she promised. "I just know it. And Aerity will be home soon. Go and enjoy your time on the Isle."

It was a dangerous time to make promises she couldn't keep, but Wyneth had to be hopeful, and so did Donnie. It would be the only thing to get them through.

Chapter 21

"I don't blame you."

Paxton peered at Rozaria, who'd slowed her horse to ride beside him. He kept his eyes straight forward, keenly aware that the woman in arm's reach had the most powerful magic hands he'd ever encountered. "Well, I blame myself."

She chuckled. "They were sly and quiet. I am a light sleeper and I heard nothing."

He could feel Rozaria watching him, and he wondered at her genuine kindness toward him. If Martone or any of the others had been keeping watch, she would have had their heads. For a clever, powerful, distrustful woman to be so malleable in his hands after such little time, he could only thank the seas for his luck.

From in front of them, the hooded girl slowly turned her head and gave a hard glance at the two of them over her shoulder. Paxton could only see her nose, mouth, and chin before she turned back around. He nearly shivered.

Rozaria gave a small grin and lowered her voice. "Nicola is not as convinced of your innocence, but she is not prone to trusting men in general. And she is particularly protective of me."

Paxton nodded, mentally making note. "Her devotion to you was clear to me from the start. It is good that you have her."

"Mm. Her father was not Lashed. He did not know his wife was of Lashed blood until Nicola first worked magic as a child. She was trying to revive her mother after something ruptured inside her while delivering a dead child. Her father attempted to kill Nicola when he saw what she was—took a knife to her—but he didn't expect her to fight back, timid as she always was. He was only able to cut her face before she grabbed hold of him and burst his heart from the inside. She lost both parents that day, but she gained me. Her energy was so strong I felt her from outside the house. I had been called to help, but I was too late."

Deep seas. For the girl to have done that, survived that, as a child . . . it's no wonder she was so loyal to Rozaria and so distrusting of men.

"That town," Paxton said. "They knew what you are?"

She shook her head. "I was young myself at that time, only fifteen, and already a seasoned midwife. I knew Prince

Vito, so I knew things were going to change in Kalor, but the towns still held many bigots. Lashed were only working openly in select groups. That was ten years ago. Things are different now."

A low animalistic rumbling sounded from behind them, and several of the men spoke loudly. One man howled, apparently bitten or scratched.

Rozaria gave a roll of her eyes and yelled over her shoulder, "Subdue it, you fools. Don't bait them with your shouts."

After a few moments it quieted down. Only three of Rozaria's beasts were ready for the journey. It had taken quite a lot of hands to calm them and force them into a deep enough slumber to transfer them to the cart-pulled steel cages. He'd double-checked the locks himself.

In that moment, Rozaria's horse reared with a great whinny, and she tightly grabbed hold of its mane. Paxton looked ahead and saw a giant snake with a diagonal design that had slithered into their path. It was as thick as Paxton's upper arm. The creature rose up with a vicious hiss at the horse. Beside it, Nicola gave a scream and her horse ran, nearly throwing her off.

Without thought, Paxton let loose an arrow and pierced the snake through the spot beneath its head. Rozaria soothed her horse and stared down at the serpent as it jerked its way back to the side of the road before going still.

"You are good to have around, hunter."

She gave him a beaming smile of laughter, and in that

moment she was just a woman. A beautiful woman who, in one vulnerable moment, had needed saving. And it was almost possible to forget she was a ruthless murderer. In that fleeting moment, Paxton had half a mind to try to reason with the woman about her methods. But then he remembered who she really was.

He nearly laughed at himself. He could not afford a single speck of weakness toward Rozaria Rocato.

As they trotted past his kill, a man from their caravan behind them jumped down and nudged the snake, then picked it up and threw it over his shoulders with a smile.

"Dinner," Rozaria remarked, still with lighthearted laughter in her voice.

This time, when Nicola made her way back to the path and turned to stare at Paxton, she lifted her chin so he could see her dark eyes within the hood.

Two days of traveling through the thick terrain of foliage made Paxton long for home worse than ever. As soon as he learned a bit more about Rozaria and Prince Vito's plan, he would abandon the Lashed ranks and race to his homeland with the information as fast as possible.

He thought of Aerity during every quiet moment. Nobody in all Eurona could have made him experience the gamut of emotions he'd had when she showed up at camp in that ridiculous disguise. It's a marvel Rozaria hadn't recognized her—those hazel eyes were a dead giveaway for him.

The rest had only confused him for a moment before the farce became clear.

But to have done all that for him. *For him.* Deep seas, she could have been killed. And she must have known the risks. But still she came charging into Kalor to seek him. But why? To bring him home? To merely say hello? Was she married now? Or would she be soon? These were all things he'd had no time to ask.

In the course of that night she'd broken his heart when she'd believed him capable of evil, and then she'd revived him again and filled him with fuel to continue on.

He was in the midst of these musings when a high-pitched yipping sounded from above. Within seconds it grew and seemed to move. He peered up into the canopy of stretching, leaning trees. Rozaria was also staring up, smiling with mischief.

"The first line of defense," she said. "We're nearly to the fortress. It is entirely surrounded with tree ranks." Ranks of soldiers in the trees? Did she mean those yipping sounds were people?

As they moved closer, he could make out a series of rope ladders and planks. His eyes roamed; they were everywhere! A complete series of treetop transportation. Men ran lithely through the canopy with their bows, arrows pointed. The soldier-like tribesmen were painted in greens and blacks, making them hard to see until they moved.

Rozaria cupped her hands over her mouth and sent up

a high-pitched call to the trees, making the same yipping-chirping sound. The men up high gave a cheer.

Unease rolled through Paxton. It was one thing to fool a single woman. To fool an entire tribe and royal family was bound to be a bit more difficult. Especially if he was expected to perform further acts of atrocity.

Paxton took a silent, deep breath, and followed Rozaria through the maze of jungle to the fortress entrance. Around the grounds were wooden stakes with pointed tips, a barrier wall of them. The wooden gates swung wide and music poured out. Inside was a veritable festival.

The first thing he noticed was two people in multicolored outfits with oversize hats walking on wooden stilts above the crowd. Everywhere were bright colors, festive flags and banners strewn across the streets between rooftops, masks of wild animals worn by adults and children alike, scents of grilling food from street vendors. His stomach gave a deep growl.

Rozaria turned to him with a look of pride. "Welcome to the royal fortress of Kalor, hunter."

"I'm surprised they allowed me in without question," he said.

Rozaria grinned. "It is because you are with me. Nobody enters or leaves the fortress without permission."

He nodded, tucking that information into his mind, feeling a noose of entrapment tighten around his neck. Escape from here would be nearly impossible. His facade of loyalty would have to be stronger than ever. He inclined his head to a tiger walking on his hind legs for its master. "Is it always like this?"

She watched the spectacle fondly. "Only when we are celebrating."

She said nothing more, and in truth he was afraid to ask what was being celebrated. They moved at a slow pace through the crowded streets. Paxton sighted their destination ahead: a tiered building faced with smooth terra-cotta. Each level was smaller, topped with a dome on the fourth level.

When they neared the entrance, they slid from their horses and gave them over to eager stable boys. Paxton and their entire party followed Rozaria up the grand palace steps, where ornately dressed guards pulled open heavy doors for them. Straight ahead, down the wide hall, Paxton could see into their great room, where a man sat upon a golden throne at the top of a set of regal steps.

From afar, Paxton could make out no details except the long black hair, red robes, and scantily clad women flanking him. Before they could move any closer to that room, a woman dressed in bright green walked into their path, stopping.

She eyed their group and said something in Kalorian, pointing to an adjoining room to the left. And then she motioned Rozaria forward to the great room. Rozaria looked at Paxton.

"Go and eat with the others, hunter. I will find you tonight." She disappeared into the great room, with Nicola a step behind, and its gold-trimmed doors shut tight behind them.

Paxton followed the other men toward the smells of spiced rice and marinated, roasted meats with vegetables. They set upon the table of food like animals. The maids could not refill their platters and glasses fast enough. Even Paxton found himself immune to basic manners in that moment.

Afterward they were ushered into guest quarters, which consisted of stalls of washbasins and a warm room lined with soft-looking pallets. As Paxton cleaned his hands and face he heard laughter and mumbles in Kalorian. The word *Lochson* stood out to him. He tensed a moment before continuing. They were speaking of the king. He wished he could understand.

He listened intently as he made his way to a pallet, but it was no use. Only a few words here or there were recognizable. Paxton lay his head on the downy pillow and forgot to listen anymore as sleep swiftly took him.

Chapter 22

Aerity and Harrison rode fast along the tree line that separated Kalor and Zorfina. Several times they'd passed traveling Zorfinans, who watched them with interest or suspicion, but nobody tried to stop them. Twice they'd run into a Zorfinan border patrol and had to explain their situation. Aerity was thankful for those moments to pass along the dire information to local authorities.

Water was scarce on the Zorfinan side. On the rare occasion when they came across a dawdling stream, they drank until they might pop, then filled every container they had.

They'd opted to ride through the night, much to Harrison's dismay. The chill of the night air, along with sheer determination, had kept Aerity awake. And now in the late morning sun, lack of sleep was finally catching up to her. Several times she'd slumped forward as they rode, only to be awoken by the wiggling creature in the pack in her lap. And the princess couldn't help but notice that the pack was much tighter and a bit heavier; the little beast had grown overnight. Now he poked his sleepy head out and licked across his enormous teeth with a long, pink tongue. His big, black eyes stared up at her.

"I think he's hungry," Aerity called. She patted Jude's wide neck. "And the horses are tired."

Harrison slowed his horse and they pulled to the side of the path among short, stout trees and brush. He eyed the creature warily as Aerity climbed down and tugged it from the pack. It immediately bounded into the bushes, sending birds scattering upward.

"He needs a name," Aerity commented. She scooped a handful of oats into a cloth bag and fed Jude.

Harrison's voice was gentle. "I'm not sure it's a good idea to name it, Aer. It seems harmless now, but it's not a pet. We have no idea what to expect of it."

Aerity watched as it prowled low to the ground and then pounced on a bush. Some birds escaped, but the little beast grabbed one in its mouth midair and set to chomping it with ferocity, feathers flying. Aerity pulled a face.

"I can't help but think that if we raise it not to be a killer of humans . . ."

"Some things are in an animal's nature."

He put a hand to her shoulder and she nodded. For now, the furry monster was hers to care for. She understood Harrison's need for caution, but she couldn't worry about that right now. She let the horses rest as long as possible and then stood.

Aerity made a clicking sound with her tongue. "Come along. You've had your breakfast." She took a swig of water from her pouch as the creature came cantering up. "Can you pass him up to me once I've mounted? He's getting a bit . . ."

"Large?" Harrison lugged him up into his arms as Aerity took to Jude's back. Then the creature licked Harrison's cheek, and the man craned his head away. "Ugh. Don't get used to the taste of me, *furball*." Harrison looked down into its face. The beast lay comfortably on its back in Harrison's arms, happy to be cradled. His tongue lolled to the side. "By the seas, you are rather cute in an ugly sort of way, aren't you?" Harrison sighed and passed him up to a giggling Aerity.

They rode on for hours. In the afternoon, Harrison held out a hand and stopped, signaling Aerity to do the same. He seemed to be listening. In the distance, she could scarcely discern the sounds of a running horse.

"Into the forest!" Harrison pointed to the Kalor side where they'd be better hidden. They rode until they were far enough in to still peer out.

Minutes later a fine horse with two riders pulled up and halted abruptly where they'd left the path. Aerity squinted. The man seemed to be pointing at the ground, trailing his hand toward the forest where they'd fled, as if he were tracking them. Aerity's heart gave a pound.

"Wait a moment," Harrison whispered. "Is that . . . ?" He stared hard a moment longer and then his face beamed. "Tiern Seabolt!"

"What?" Aerity sat up straighter, and as she looked she surely recognized the straight brown hair, pulled back, and the Lochlan tunic. And he seemed to have a lad with him . . . with a hair covering?

Harrison burst back through the forest with Aerity on his heels. They were greeted by Tiern's arrow pointed straight at them. But the lad in front grabbed his arm and shouted, "That's Lieutenant Gillfin! And Aer!"

Aerity recognized the voice immediately, and it wasn't a lad at all.

"Vixie!"

The sisters slid from their horses, Aerity less graceful with the creature in her arms, and they sprinted for each other. But when they got close, Vixie shrieked and jumped back, pointing.

"What the seas is *that*?"

"Oh! Don't worry, it's . . . Furball. He's only a babe. We saved him. Or stole him. Both, really."

"But what *is* it?" Vixie's face was scrunched in confusion and disgust. Rather than explain, Aerity set down the creature and hugged her sister senseless.

"I have so much to tell you," Aerity whispered into

Vixie's head covering. They clung for what seemed like forever. Then they pulled away, surveyed each other, and said simultaneously, "You're filthy."

Aerity laughed, but Vixie's face darkened quickly. Warning bells rang in the older sister's ears.

"What is it, Vix? Why are you here?"

Vixie's eyes watered. "It's Mum and Papa. They've been kidnapped by Kalorians."

Aerity felt the ground tilt beneath her and a heady rush of blood. She grasped Vixie's shoulder. Both Tiern and Harrison leaped down to join them.

"Kidnapped?" Harrison went straight into military mode, his eyes alert. "Do we know for certain they're still alive?"

"Nay," Tiern said. "We only know they were taken nearly a week ago."

Aerity was going to be sick. She pressed a hand over her stomach. "What of the rest of the family?"

"Is Lady Wyneth well?" Harrison broke in.

"We don't know," Vixie said weakly. "We left to find you before it happened. The Kalorians had just shown up. We weren't there for any of it. We just heard of the kidnapping from two soldiers in Dovedell."

"Oh, seas." Aerity's eyes roamed the dirt at her feet, searching for understanding, seeking answers and wisdom. If only she had been there. She felt riddled with painful guilt for abandoning her family at such a time.

"Why were you away from the castle?" Harrison asked.

Vixie chewed her lip sheepishly. "I was coming to search for you all. But that doesn't matter now, does it? Aer . . . you've got to act as ruler until they are found."

Her gut clenched further. *Ruler.* All eyes were on her as they processed that information. Her mind reeled. Lochlanach had been attacked by an outside force. The throne was empty. The kingdom vulnerable. And only one person could rightly rise up and fill it.

Her.

Determination rang out inside her, clearing away all doubts and fears before they had a chance to surface. She had no time for any of that. Aerity clicked her tongue and patted her thigh. "Come, Furball." The creature obeyed and she scooped him up. "We have to go."

"But what about all the things you have to tell me?" Vixie asked. Aerity looked from her sister to Tiern, whose lips were pressed tightly as if holding back a slew of questions for her.

"It will have to wait." Aerity lifted Furball onto Jude's back, then grasped the saddle and heaved herself up. "Home needs us. Now."

Chapter 23

Paxton awoke to soft fingers trailing across his stubbled cheeks. The room was dark, and all around him rose a symphony of snores. His eyes slowly adjusted to Rozaria leaning over him, her dark hair pulled to one side.

"Come with me." Paxton smelled wine on her whispered words.

He let her take him by the hand and lead him out of the guest dormitory and down another torch-sconced hall with vivid rugs depicting tribal customs, nakedness, and war. It had to be the dead of night, but he could still hear revelries at a distance. As they walked, Rozaria stumbled into him a few times or leaned to the side and had to be righted by his hand.

She giggled uncharacteristically, and he wondered how much wine she'd had.

He guessed with a bout of nausea that she was leading him to her personal chambers. After being with Aerity again, it made this farce with Rozaria all the more difficult. Before, when he kissed Rozaria, he believed Aerity was no longer in his life. Now he realized she would always be. The thought of being touched by Rozaria—of touching her back—it felt wrong in a way he hadn't allowed to stop him before. And yet he continued to let her lead him into her chamber.

Rozaria's room was spectacular. A four-poster bed of dark wood was draped in beaded silks of deep red. The rugs were plush and the pillows plump. Plants of various large species were along the walls in ornate terra-cotta pots. The windows were round and looked down at gardens three stories below.

Rozaria turned to Paxton and pressed her body against his, draping her arms over his shoulders. His heart picked up speed. He eyed a bottle of wine with two glasses on a table by the bed. The perfect distraction.

"More wine, I think." He slipped from her grasp and poured them both a glass, filling hers higher than his own. He handed it to her and lifted it in a toast. She gave him a heavy-lidded, seductive grin and then drank. He touched her glass to encourage her to drink again.

"You have news?" he asked.

She set down her glass on the bedside table and sashayed to the window, leaning against it. Paxton tipped part of his wine into hers before she turned back around. She walked to where Paxton stood at the side of the bed. This time when she got to him she placed her hands on his chest and firmly pushed him back.

Curses. His spine went rigid and he forced himself to relax before she noticed.

Now he was on the bed and she was climbing atop him. Her mouth came down on his, soft and sour. She moaned and placed all her weight on him, seeming unable to keep herself up. Paxton flipped them so she was on her back and he was on his side looking down at her. He gave her pliant lips another kiss. *Betrayal.*

"What did you learn, Rozaria?" He touched his nose to her cheek. *Deception*. It was the only way. He shoved his feelings of infidelity aside.

"It went off without a hitch. King Charles and his wife were kidnapped."

His eyes flew wide, and Rozaria burst out into a husky laugh.

"Right from their very own castle." She giggled.

Paxton's instinct was to jump from the bed and run. Do something. To find Aerity and warn her, if she didn't already know. Where would she be now? Surely not home yet. But he forced himself to be still. To place his lips against Rozaria's jaw, and take her waist in his hand.

"Brilliant." The word pushed past the sickening lump in his throat. "Are they to be killed?" He kept his voice light.

"Not"—her eyes fluttered—"yet."

He kissed her again. "When?"

"The princesses. They could not be found." Paxton's heart pounded furiously. He traced his lips down her jawline and neck as she went on. "The prince wishes to flush them out. Then . . ." Her eyes closed. Paxton gripped her waist.

"Aye? Then?"

"Then he will advance and take over the kingdom of Lochlanach. You'll be able to return to your homeland with more power and respect than you dreamed possible, hunter."

Paxton ground his teeth. Rozaria, in a sudden burst of renewed energy, climbed atop him again. Paxton quickly sat up, gently moving her from his lap to sit beside him, and grabbed both glasses. He pressed hers into her hand.

"To the prince. And to change. Drink up, gorgeous."

"To change." She brought the glass to her lips and drained it, then let it fall to the bed beside her. "I want to celebrate with you." Her words smashed together and she pulled at him.

Paxton moved her so that she lay on the bed and he hovered above her, stroking her hair. She raised a knee, pushing back her skirt, and rubbed her bare leg between his thighs. *Ugh.*

"How long will he wait to advance?" Paxton whispered, placing more of his weight on her. She arched and her head fell heavily onto the pillow.

"When . . ." she slurred and Paxton had to ask her to repeat. "When our insider sends word about . . . princess. . . ."

"Ah." That was not good news. He cleared his throat quietly. "Who is this mole?"

Her eyes closed and she mumbled incoherently. Paxton's jaw clenched. This time when her eyes didn't open again, Paxton let her sleep. He'd never been so thankful for wine. He waited until her breathing was heavy and then he slipped from the room, back to the dormitory.

Aerity could return to Lochlanach in a matter of days, and she had no idea what was in store for her. And where was Princess Vixie? He could only hope she'd been taken to safety. Paxton considered leaving the Kalorian fortress that very instant and returning to Lochlanach, but he knew it wouldn't be so simple. He remembered what Rozaria had said: nobody in or out without permission.

He rubbed his face in frustration as he fell back onto his pallet. There would be no more sleeping that night. Not unless he knew Aerity and the kingdom were safe again.

Chapter 24

As they rode, taking breaks only for the sake of the horses, Aerity formulated a plan. It was clear that the foe was much larger than her father anticipated. He thought he was dealing with a rogue enemy in Rozaria Rocato, a few monsters perhaps, and a group of her zealous Lashed followers. He believed that if their band of evildoers could simply be caught and destroyed, they could go back to life as usual.

Now they knew better.

This was so much larger than anything they could have anticipated. Prince Vito—and possibly the entire kingdom of Kalor—was against them. It was up to Aerity now to implement changes that would hopefully benefit all Lochlans, appease Prince Vito and Rozaria, and get her parents back.

Seas, don't let them be dead, Aerity silently begged. Pain shot through her chest at the thought. She leaned forward and rode harder. She heard a shout of surprised laughter from Vixie behind her.

"Look at you go!" her sister said with apparent pride.

Aye. Fear of horses was no longer a luxury Aerity could afford. Neither was sleep, for that matter. Her eyes were heavy.

But onward they rode.

They stopped only when Tiern said his horse was tiring. Aerity considered telling him about Paxton, but something held her back. She'd left Paxton in a dangerous situation. Tiern would no doubt be worried, and possibly want to seek him out. Aerity couldn't allow it. So instead they took their break in silence, all exhausted. She would tell him when they reached the castle.

As they set to tending to the animals' needs, Tiern began casting furtive glances toward Aerity, but she pretended not to notice. Perhaps if they could ride a bit farther before he found out, it would lessen his desire to turn back.

"Tiern," Aerity said, "how about you take Furball to lighten your horse's load and Vixie can ride with me."

"Erm . . ." Tiern stared down at where the creature was digging at an anthill, gouging its claws deep into the soil as if cutting through butter. Even Vixie eyed Furball with misgiving.

"He's only a cub," Aerity promised. "And he rides well. Naps like a babe."

"I'll take him," Harrison said. "Let Tiern and his horse rest a bit." Tiern looked relieved.

Aerity paced while the animals were fed and watered. Then she followed Vixie's lead and set to rubbing down the horses' legs and hind muscles. Jude let out a whinny of joy at his massage.

"By the depths, Aer," said Vixie. "He actually likes you!"

Aerity laughed. "I know. Madness, right? I've named him Jude."

Vixie smiled, then looked over Aerity skeptically. "Your hair has turned a shade of grayish brown now."

Aerity groaned and smoothed back the top of her head. She could only imagine how awful she appeared. "When we return, I'll have Caitrin try to fix it somehow. Red dye, perhaps." Though her hair and appearance were the least of her concerns at that point.

"What will you do when we get home?" Vixie asked with seriousness.

Harrison and Tiern both stopped what they were doing to watch her.

"I'll do what I've wanted father to do all along. I'm going to set up a post, probably on royal lands: a safe area where Lashed can work. It will be guarded. If it works, I'm going to open a second in Dovedell outside the gates. And then another."

"Like infirmaries?" Tiern asked.

Aerity nodded. "Exactly. They will be the only place where Lashed are allowed to work their magic. For now. And only under guardian eyes. Any persons needing Lashed attention can come, unarmed."

"You'll want to address the people first," Harrison suggested.

Aerity had already thought of that. "I'll need you to round up soldiers to help at the entrance to royal lands as people are allowed in, and then to keep an eye on the crowd as I address them. Tiern," she said. He raised his chin. "I will need you to visit the local towns with a message. I'm certain the people are in fear after news of their king and queen gone missing. We should probably get going straightaway."

Tiern gave a nod. After a quiet moment, when Vixie had left to water their horse, he said, "I thought . . ." Then he hesitated.

Oh, seas. Aerity peered down at her dusty boots and waited for it.

"I thought perhaps you would have Paxton with you."

At the sound of Paxton's name in his brother's saddened voice, Aerity wished she had forced him to come. Thinking of him with the madwoman jolted her with stark terror. It took a moment for her insides to right themselves. She took a deep breath and looked at him. So be it.

"I will tell you as much as I can while the horses rest, and then we must be on our way again. But you must remain with us, Tiern. You cannot go back for him. Vixie needs you. Lochlanach needs you."

He clenched his jaw and nodded.

Though Tiern was visibly upset at the news of Paxton's situation, he did not wish to seek him out. Aerity realized with a lightness of heart that his need to protect Vixie seemed to override his need to find his brother. Paxton would have approved.

Aerity and the others were bone weary by the time they crossed into Toresta. Unlike the border between Kalor and Zorfina, the Torestan border was lined with soldiers. Five of the nearest ones held their bowstrings taut with arrows pointed at them. Aerity and the three others raised their hands.

"You might want to lower your weapons from the faces of your neighboring royalty," Harrison said to the brown-clad soldiers.

"I've got this," Vixie said. She turned to them and removed the scarf from her head. "I have returned," she said in Torestan. "With my sister, as promised." She motioned to Aerity.

The men were immediately at attention, shouting orders. Aerity squinted at her sister, and Vixie smiled.

"We came through days ago and explained everything. It took some detailed information to convince them who I was without papers, but once they believed me they swore to escort us back to Lochlanach when we returned."

Aerity breathed a sigh of relief. "So they know of the

Kalorian raid on our castle?"

"And the kidnapping, aye."

"This is good news," Harrison said.

Two Torestan soldiers approached on horseback and inclined their heads at Aerity. The superior said, "We will escort you to your border. It should take two days and one night."

"I thank you," Aerity said. "Any news?"

"None, Your Highness."

She nodded gravely. "We must get to our castle at once."

They rode swiftly, stopping to camp and catch a handful of restless hours in the night. Then they were on their way again. The temperature dropped. They were half-frozen when they finally spied the Lochlanach border.

Only three Lochlan soldiers stood guard at the path. Their eyes seemed to bypass the women and go straight to Harrison.

"Lieutenant Gillfin?" one asked.

"Aye, cadet. And your two princesses."

Their eyes narrowed with confusion and then went huge as they turned to the Lochson girls and recognized them, giving deep bows.

"We would escort you, sir, but we're on foot," one of the soldiers said.

"We'll be fine. Any news of my parents?" Aerity asked. The men shook their heads gravely. *Curses.*

"All the royal hounds are out with the guards, searching for their scent in the towns."

"Your Highness," called a Torestan soldier in his native tongue. "We shall return to our king at once with an update."

"I thank you for your assistance, sirs. Please give King Gavriil my regard. And . . ." She swallowed her pride. "Any assistance he can spare would be greatly appreciated."

The men nodded and set off.

Aerity had a dreaded feeling her parents were nowhere in Lochlanach. She hitched her heels into Jude and took off. They still had two days of hard riding before they'd reach royal lands. And though things weren't stable in their kingdom, and she had no clue what to expect upon her return, it felt so, so good to be home.

Chapter 25

Upon their arrival at royal lands, one thing became distinctly clear to Aerity: their military forces had been stretched too thin, to the point that the royal lands may as well have been unguarded. Soldiers had been sent all across Lochlanach—to try to keep peace in the towns and to secure the borders. But it wasn't enough to have a few men everywhere. If any of those places were attacked, it would be overpowered in no time. Young men were being trained as quickly as possible, but it wasn't enough.

They were not safe.

The royal lands were too quiet. The market had been closed and people were not allowed in. Everything appeared eerie: the trees barren of their leaves; the stalls empty; the wind-whipped sea, lined with ready vessels. A winter-gray sky loomed, blowing frigid air along the paths.

Harrison waved down a fellow officer and called him over. It took the man a moment to recognize Aerity as she dismounted her horse, sore and cold. He bowed.

"Princess! Thank the seas for your safe return."

"Get her inside where it's warm," Harrison told him. He was still atop his horse with Furball bundled in a blanket on his lap. "I'll be in shortly. We'll need a debriefing on every detail."

Harrison clomped away, most likely to find a safe place for Furball. Aerity, Vixie, and Tiern climbed down and relinquished their horses. The three of them took the stone steps to the castle, dried leaves crackling underfoot. The moment they reached the top of the stairs and the doors were opened, Aerity heard a familiar voice.

"Princess!" Caitrin rushed forward and hugged her hard, earning headshakes from the guards. Aerity didn't care; she hugged her back just as tightly.

"Oh, seas, look at you, Your Highness. Your hair." The girl had tears in her eyes. "Come, let's bathe you and get you into warmer, proper clothes."

"Not yet, Caitrin," she said gently but firmly. "After I meet with the council. But I could use some help with the color at that time. And I need a guest chamber readied for Tiern Seabolt."

Caitrin twiddled with her apron, seeming reluctant to let

Aerity go a moment longer looking the way she did. "I'll alert the guest maids and start warming the water for your bath." She rushed off.

Wyneth heard voices and she ran to the library window. The sight of Harrison's back as he rode down to the stables sent a jolt of pure joy through her. He was here! And safe! Did that mean Aerity had returned as well? She grabbed her warm cloak and threw it over her shoulders as she sprinted through the castle to the entrance. The guards held open the door, and she nearly fell down the steps moving so quickly.

She finally caught up with Harrison near the stables. But instead of going inside he dismounted and sent his horse away, heading toward the hounds' kennels. He had a bundle in his arms.

"Harrison!" she called, jogging.

His head shot to her and his face lit up with a joyful smile that made Wyneth catch her breath—he must have been happy to be home, and she was certainly glad to see him again. The bundle shifted and jumped from his arms—he swiped out to catch it but missed. Wyneth stopped in her tracks, skidding in the sandy dirt as something strange and furry charged at her. Harrison yelled. Wyneth saw thick fangs and claws as long as her fingers. She gasped and choked on a scream as she turned, only to fall over her twisted skirts like a clumsy oaf.

She scrambled to her feet, but it was too late. The beast jumped onto her back. She turned, screaming, and felt a wet lick up the entire side of her face. She walloped the creature and it fell to the side with a pained yap.

"Wyn! It's okay!"

Harrison got to the creature and grasped it by the scruff of its neck. Wyneth pushed herself into a sitting position and crab walked backward a few feet. She stared at the creature, panting.

"It's okay," Harrison said, softer this time. "It—he . . . he won't hurt you. He got excited, is all."

"He— What is it?"

She stared at its lion head with a short, furry mane, and its bear-like body with thick, coarse fur of brownish black. The creature tried again to get to Wyneth, but Harrison lifted it into his arms and held it tight.

"I think he likes you," he said, squatting on one knee. "He wants to meet you. We saved him from Rozaria. He's just a cub, but he's nearly doubled in size already since we took him."

Rozaria? Wyneth's mind spun. *This was one of her beasts? But . . . how? What in Eurona had happened while they were away?* The more Wyneth looked at the wiggling monster, the more she could sense its innocent excitement. She pushed to her knees and moved forward, holding her palm out. When she got to the creature, it sniffed her hand fervently and then set to licking. Wyneth laughed. She met Harrison's eyes, and they both stared at one another in wonder.

"All right, Furball, enough of that," Harrison said. "You

can get to know Wyn later. Right now you have a big meal and a warm kennel calling your name." He looked at Wyneth and stood, helping her to her feet but not releasing her hand right away. "And we've got a lot of catching up to do."

Aye. Her forgetful moment of fun came to an end as she thought of her aunt and uncle, somewhere out there with Kalorians, and all that had happened in Aerity and Harrison's absence.

Aerity wondered where the rest of the family was. She thought perhaps they would be in the king's office, but when they'd reached it, there was only one person within. Old Duke Gulfton sat in his adviser's chair, his hands on his staff, his eyes glazed. It took him a moment to turn his face to them and focus. A momentary look of frozen fear crossed his features.

"Are you all right?" Aerity asked him. "It's Princesses Aerity and Vixie."

"I know who you are." His voice rasped.

"Good seas, sir," Aerity said. "How long have you been sitting here? Have you eaten?" The man seemed to have aged decades in her short absence, from all he'd witnessed in the kingdom, no doubt.

"Everyone left after the king and queen were taken. Duke Streamson, even. All of the council. I didn't think anyone would ever return."

"Duke, why don't you let one of the guards see you to a guest room for a rest? I will have a meal sent." He peered up at her with the saddest glossy eyes.

"Nay. I will leave today to return home to my lands."

Aerity nodded. "Be safe, good sir." Then she turned to the nearest guard at the door. "Where are the lords and ladies?"

"At the Isle of Evie, Your Highness."

"Except one," came a sweet voice from the doorway.

Aerity looked up into the gorgeous face of Wyneth, and she rushed forward, nearly barreling her cousin over. They laughed and clung to each other, their happiness turning to a deeper joined emotion over all the things they'd felt in Aerity's absence. Wyneth pulled back, holding Aerity's shoulders.

"You are a sight." Wyneth wiped her eyes and stood taller. Lord Alvi rushed into the room behind Harrison and looked about at their faces. He honed in on Aerity.

"You're back. By the stars, Princess, something must be done around here! Your military must be brought together." He made passionate gestures with his hands. "They need to decide a focus point and a plan of action—"

"I couldn't agree more," Aerity said.

Lief stopped and stared as if surprised, then dropped his hands. "Good. You're a smart woman."

"I need to be caught up on what's happened and then we will form a plan."

Harrison arrived, bringing five of the highest-ranking military officers. They informed Aerity of all that had happened, allowing her to stop and ask questions. When all was said, they took a few moments before Aerity addressed them.

Her voice was strong, but inside she felt herself shaking from the weight of responsibility.

"The first thing we need to do is call in the troops from throughout the kingdom," Aerity said. "The towns will have to police themselves for now. Send half the soldiers back here and the other half to the Kalorian border to strengthen our line of defense there.

"I am issuing a proclamation throughout Lochlanach: let them know that I am their acting monarch until my parents are returned. Beginning tomorrow, the royal lands will once again be open. We will have full military and royal guard in force. All hands will be checked—any suspicious persons will be detained. Let the people know I am seeking Lashed who wish to help others with their skills, and Unlashed who are in need of medical attention. The west commons will become a camp, a safe place for magic to be worked under supervision, but laws against magic throughout the kingdom are still intact."

Lief crossed his arms. "What are the rules for the Lashed while they are here? Torestan camps are not allowing their Lashed to leave the premises."

"I will not force them to stay," Aerity said. "Some of them will have families to tend to. But no one may roam freely on royal lands, just in case Rozaria's people try to infiltrate. Lashed must be escorted to and from the west commons and the royal gate by armed guards, and suspicious persons will be detained without question. We can take no chances, but I don't want the Lashed feeling like criminals. The guards will be just as much for their protection." Shocked faces stared back at her. "We can no longer afford inaction. Am I clear?"

Slowly, everyone in the room gave resolute nods.

"Prepare the tents and tables for use inside the west commons," she said. "Gather our warmest blankets, spare clothing, and wood for fires. Hire lads from local towns to help, if needed. Send out the proclamation." Harrison and the officers quickly left to begin.

Aerity leaned upon her father's desk and exhaled, allowing herself to outwardly tremble now. Lord Alvi, Vixie, and Wyneth stood there quietly.

The old adviser had said nothing the entire time, which was uncharacteristic.

"Duke Gulfton," Aerity said carefully. "Are you certain you're all right?"

He lifted his drooping eyes to her and said in a scratchy voice, "Nay, child. But not a one of us is all right these days, I suppose." And with those ominous words he pushed achingly to his feet and shuffled from the office.

Aerity looked at the other three and shook her head. "I'm not sure it's smart to leave the towns without coverage. Especially once they hear the proclamation."

"No course of action will be perfect," Wyneth told her. "But I think you're making the right decision in this. You're showing Rozaria that you're trying."

She hoped her cousin was right.

"Aer," Vixie said, "I think it's time for that bath."

Chapter 26

Chun had never had a keen sense of direction, and he was quite certain that he'd lost his way. In Toresta, the common direction was up the mountain or down the mountain—it wasn't as difficult to discern as these flat stretches of Zorfina with its dry ground and patchy foliage. In a sickening moment, he wondered if the Lochlan men, Paxton and Harrison, had fooled him.

"I am hungry, Baba," his daughter said in a weak voice, calling out from his wife's lap on the next horse.

"I know, sweet one. We all are. I'm certain we'll find a camp soon." But that was a lie.

"I think I see something," Chun's brother said. They stopped and stared at the horizon. He was right. Three black-clad figures on horseback were headed straight for them at a quick pace, sending up plumes of dust in their wake.

Chun's heart raced. They hadn't encountered a single soul on their journey. What if these were outlaws? More evil Lashed? Or simply haters of foreigners? Chun held an arm out to his wife and waved her back.

"Get behind me."

His wife quickly obeyed, turning her horse, but when she faced the opposite direction she and his daughter let out screams. Chun turned to see three more figures draped in black on sleek horses, all with bows and arrows aimed at them and definitely within shooting range.

Chun shuddered and told his family, "Raise your hands in peace." His wife, daughter, brother, and two nephews did as told. The figures slowly advanced as the other three rode up from the side.

"Torestan, *jes*?" one of the riders called to them. A woman.

Chun nodded and sputtered in universal Euronan, "Yes. We are peaceful."

The people circled them, and Chun couldn't help but take in their feminine figures, in such contrast to the male warriors in Toresta. Their hair and faces were covered in black cloth, showing only their striking, light eyes. These were them, the Zandalee. He remembered three of them from the day they'd ridden in with Paxton. He let out a ragged breath.

"I recognize you from the camp in Kalor," the woman said. Chun nodded.

"We have been seeking you," he said bravely.

Several of the women made hissing sounds that prickled the hairs on his neck.

"Why?" asked the same woman who'd spoken before.

"T-two men . . ." Chun swallowed. "Two Lochlan men, Lieutenant Harrison Gillfin and your traveling fellow, Paxton Seabolt, they sent me. The camp you saw—it is run by the one who creates the beasts and plans to attach Lochlanach. We came to warn you and seek refuge."

The woman's eyes enlarged. She turned to the other riders and spoke to them in Zorfinan, translating. Several murmured the names *Harrison* and *Paxton*. The woman looked at Chun. "How do I know you are not lying? That you are not on her side?"

He outwardly shook now. Their bows gleamed wickedly. "Paxton . . . he said he hunted with you, and that . . ." His cheeks warmed at this next part of the message; would they be angry? "And that if you give us refuge, Paxton will reward you by serving Tiern Seabolt to your sisters on a platter."

The woman stared a moment and then threw her head back in laughter. She turned her head to translate and the women all laughed, slapping their legs and commenting to one another in Zorfinan. Chun exhaled once again.

"You are Lashed?" she asked.

"I am. And one of my nephews. The rest of my family is not." Once again he swallowed, trying desperately to wet his dry mouth. "Please. Please do not hurt the children."

The woman's eyes narrowed. "Did Paxton fail to tell you that we are not monsters?"

"No. No, I'm very sorry. I meant no offense. I speak foolishly when I'm afraid."

The woman moved closer. "Why did you leave the Rocato woman's camp?"

"Sh-she wanted us to kill people. To prove we're loyal. I could not. And Paxton wanted you to know that he believes Prince Vito is working with her. He fears they may soon attack Lochlanach."

Zandora hissed. "We must go." She pointed to one of the horses. "That one has gone lame during our patrol. Caught his hoof on a root. He is skittish and we need him fixed before we can proceed."

"I can heal him," Chun said. He wasn't afraid of horses, and he was glad for this moment to prove himself. He climbed down and made his way carefully to the mare. Its rider dismounted and held the reins tightly while Chun calmed the animal and ran his hands deftly down its muscled legs. Within minutes, it was healed. The horse stomped its foot and whinnied. The Zandalee woman gave him a nod.

"You will come to our tribe's land and tell me everything you know."

"Thank you." Chun shared smiles with his family before mounting his horse and following, filled with a zing of energy and gratitude.

Duke Gulfton's family had owned the southernmost piece of Lochlanach waterlands for countless generations, bordering Kalor. He'd always been fair to the villagers who resided on his lands, collecting not a copper more in taxes than was necessary. He'd been loyal to King Charles and his father before him, just as Duke Gulfton's father had been to the kings of old. He'd lived a prosperous life of respect. He never thought he'd see the day when his soul would slip into the slimy depths of the sea.

His joints creaked from traveling as he walked the sprawling overgrown lawn from his grand home to their sturdy docks. His land and everything about it was too quiet. Too empty. His home, like everywhere else in Lochlanach, had become a hopeless place with no security. A place that hardly felt like a home any longer.

Normally the duke would ask his grandson to ready the boat for him, but he hadn't seen the boy in nearly two months. His eyes watered at the thought. Duke Gulfton's aching legs took much longer to walk the long dock of his property than they used to. When he got to the end, he struggled to lower his boat, using all his might to crank the tight wheel until his vessel was in the water.

He climbed aboard, grasping the rail to keep from falling, and cursing all the while. Once aboard he set the sail, taking breaks to breathe. *One last time*, he told himself. Finally, the sails were set and he was headed south to the part of the shore where Lochlanach met Kalor. He steered the vessel until he came to the place with the statue on the shore that signaled the border. And then he turned another crank to lower the anchor.

Duke Gulfton stared toward the milky statue that he knew to be a giant sea gull carved from stone, but his old eyes could no longer make out the details. In the time of King Charles's father, it had been given to King Kalieno of Kalor as a sign of peace.

So much for that offering. Duke Gulfton laughed drily until it became a cough that racked his entire thin frame and made him ache all over.

Moments later a much grander vessel of dark wood showed itself around the corner of land, heading directly toward him. The duke stared, his heart full of hatred. The boat slowed as it neared, and sidled up next to his, allowing dark-skinned shirtless men to tie the vessels together. Then a man stepped aboard and strode toward the duke. His hair was smooth and straight to his elbows. He wore a bright green tunic buttoned up the side, and came to stand before Duke Gulfton with his hands comfortably clasped behind his back.

"My men saw your signal of smoke from your chimney. What news have you, old sir?"

Duke Gulfton wanted nothing more than to bash this man's head with his cane. Instead he gritted his teeth and practically snarled.

"The princess has returned. She is at the castle now. She is opening the royal lands tomorrow and allowing Lashed to work their magic on anyone in need. They're pulling all the troops from towns and focusing them on royal lands and the Kalorian border. That is all I know."

The royal Kalorian lifted an eyebrow. "Indeed?"

"Aye, indeed," the duke said gruffly. "You said once she returned that would be my last message. I've done my part. Now release my grandson back to me." He held his staff tightly and gave it a single bang on the wooden deck at his feet. He'd watched as these fiends killed his son and daughter-in-law two months ago in his own home. And then they'd taken his grandson.

"You have done well, good sir. The boy shall certainly be released. Just as soon as you perform one final task."

Duke Gulfton was stifled by the words. He wanted to crumple. "You said this was my last task!"

"Ah, but things have changed," the Kalorian said calmly.

The duke lifted his cane, pointed it at the man's chest, and said through gritted teeth, "I will do nothing more until I see my grandson again!"

The Kalorian shed his calmness as his eyes brimmed with annoyance. He called something in Kalorian over his shoulder. On the dark vessel, a Kalorian tribesman brought out a twelve-year-old lad, hands bound and mouth gagged. The boy's eyes bulged when he saw Duke Gulfton and he bent, crying and reaching for him.

Duke Gulfton lifted a hand across the expanse. His grandson! For the past month he'd begun to wonder if it was all a ruse. If they'd really killed the lad and he'd been a traitor for nothing. Seeing him now filled Duke Gulfton with a sweet waterfall of relief. The boy was all he had.

"All right," he said weakly. "Let me have him, please. I'll do whatever you want."

The Kalorian man chuckled and flicked his wrist toward the tribesman. He said something and the man disappeared belowdecks with the boy again. Duke Gulfton cried out.

"You shall have him soon enough. Now listen closely."

Chapter 27

With each day that passed without the king and queen being found, Wyneth felt her cousin's anxiety rising. The tension and stress within the castle was stifling.

"Where are you going?" Lord Alvi called from behind Wyneth as she donned her warm cloak again. She nearly told him she was only going for a walk, but considering the current circumstances there was no room for deception between any of them.

She spoke quietly. "Aerity and Harrison took one of Rozaria's baby beasts when they escaped—"

"They did *what*?" His eyes rounded.

"Sh." She smiled reassuringly at the nearest guard, who

watched them. "It's like an overgrown pup, Lief. They saved it. Nothing to worry about."

"Yet," he murmured, but he seemed to have softened at hearing her use his name. "And you're going to see it?"

"Aye." Aerity and the others were busy and the creature was all by itself. She felt bad for it. Someone needed to tend it.

"Not by yourself. I'm going with you."

She lifted her eyes skyward and said, "Fine. Come see for yourself."

They walked through the biting winds down to the kennels. As they got closer, Wyneth gasped. The beast had climbed up the high wooden door and was sitting atop it, watching them.

"Skies!" Lord Alvi reached back for his bow, but Wyneth smacked his arm down. He lowered his arm and stared at the creature. The cub let out a pathetic *rawr* that made Wyneth giggle in delight. And then it leaped deftly down from its perch, rattling the door.

"My lady . . ." Lord Alvi was not at all comfortable when she squatted and patted her knee.

"Come, Furball," she said.

"Furball? That's its *name*?"

The beast climbed her, putting his paws on her thighs, and then her shoulders, and licking at her ears. She felt its claws dig against her upper back. Wyneth laughed in earnest, trying to angle away from its huge tongue.

"I cannot believe my eyes," Lord Alvi mumbled. He

walked to the kennel and opened the door. Then he let out a curse.

Wyneth looked and her stomach plummeted. The inside of the pen was shredded with claw marks.

"Oh, dear," she whispered. Wyneth pulled Furball down and peered at his paws. One of them was bleeding where the claw met his skin, from scratching at the wood so hard. She ran a finger down the smooth claw to its sharp tip. Furball brought the paw up and licked the wound. They could not keep the little beast in the hounds' kennels anymore.

Crackling leaves and footsteps sounded from over the hill. Lord Alvi and Wyneth raised their eyes to see Harrison joining them. He stopped, looking back and forth between them, then came forward. Lord Alvi stomped his way to Harrison, close enough to bump chests.

"What were you thinking bringing this beast here?"

Harrison, as calm as ever, met the coldlander's eyes. "I was thinking it was one less creature she could use against us."

"Then you should have put it down! Not kept it!"

"I realize this," Harrison said. "I've spoken to Aerity of my concerns."

"No!" Wyneth stood. The cub wrapped its arms around her shoulder and its legs around her waist. She held it like an overgrown toddler. "It is not a danger."

"Look at *that* and tell me the thing is not a danger!" Lord Alvi pointed to the destroyed kennel.

Harrison hissed and ran a hand over his hair. "I wondered

if that might happen. I was just coming to check."

"And the cursed thing can climb," Lord Alvi added. "It will be far larger than any of us men when it's full-grown, and then it will be a greater challenge to kill."

Wyneth thought of the creature she'd seen killed in the forest, the empathy she'd felt for it. She couldn't help but believe the beasts were capable of something better if they were not raised to kill. The thought of anyone hurting this innocent cub sent a protective instinct shooting through her.

"You're not putting it down," Wyneth said, holding Furball tighter. "He stays with me. If the Rocato woman can train an army of creatures to be loyal to her, I can train *one* to be loyal to me."

Lord Alvi clenched his jaw and Harrison dropped his gaze, his hands hanging loosely at his hips. Wyneth walked away from the men, earning herself another warm, wet lick in the ear.

Chapter 28

Aerity wanted to lie in the hot water forever and forget her worries. She'd moaned like an ailing woman when she climbed in the tub. The water was a cloudy shade of brown from the dye washing out, but she didn't care about soaking in dirty water. It felt glorious.

She'd wanted to be left alone to wash and to think. Was she doing the right thing? Would towns further revolt upon hearing her proclamation? And what if nobody came? Most of all, what would it take for the Kalorians to return her parents? A nagging voice at the back of her mind kept whispering one loathsome thought: *they're already dead*. Aerity squeezed her eyes shut and submerged herself under the water, where all was muted.

When she slid back up and wiped her eyes, two faces were leaning over her, one quite furry. Aerity let out an automatic squeak and covered her chest. Wyneth laughed as Aerity caught her breath and smiled.

"I should have known you'd take to Furball," Aerity said. The cub seemed quite comfortable and happy with her cousin.

"I can care for him if you'd like," Wyneth said.

Aerity felt relieved. "That would be a huge help. He was a spontaneous decision. A sort of parting gift from Paxton, but I'm not sure he'll be well received."

"Don't worry about that."

The creature suddenly wiggled to get down from her cousin's arms. "Oh, no," Aerity whispered. And sure enough, the moment he broke free, Furball bounded to the tub and pulled himself up the side. Aerity jumped to her feet inside the tub just as Furball dived over the side with a splash. The princess snatched her towel from Wyneth's outstretched hand and climbed out, not at all interested in bathing with the beast. Wyneth was in a fit of laughter.

They both watched Furball dunk himself over and over, pawing the water and making a grand mess on the floor. And naturally that would be the very moment when Caitrin appeared, a look of confusion on her face as she peered from Lady Wyneth to Princess Aerity to something splashing about and snarling in the tub.

Caitrin let forth a scream and jumped back. "What the raging seas is that?"

"He's our . . . pet?" Wyneth said.

"But . . . but . . ." Caitrin stared at its claws and face as it peered over the edge at them, blinking away drops of water.

"We saved him from Rozaria," Aerity explained.

Wyneth grabbed a bar of soap and converged upon the creature in the tub, careful not to slip on the puddles of water as she set to cleaning him.

Aerity looked at the sealed bottle in Caitrin's hand. "You found red dye?"

"Yes, Your Highness." Caitrin spared one last quizzical look at the beast before turning her full attention to Aerity. "It won't be your natural color, but it will be beautiful, and eventually the darker red will fade into your natural color better than this brown has." Caitrin touched a strand of her faded, mousy colored locks.

Aerity nodded, shivering.

"Come, Princess," Caitrin said. "Sit before the fire while I dry your hair. I'll have you ready to face the people in no time."

Aerity sat on a stool, thankful for the crackling fire, and let Caitrin work, drying her strands with a comb heated by the fire, and then applying the new dye. She was glad for the respite of the bath and laughter she'd been able to share with Wyn, but those good feelings were quickly replaced by dark wonderings. If Prince Vito and Rozaria were working together, that meant the prince was seeking Lashed rights throughout Eurona as well. Would the infirmaries be enough to show them she was attempting to change things in Lochlanach? Would it be enough to make them stop the daily killings, give them back her parents, and perhaps focus on another kingdom instead? She felt horrible at the thought, but they needed time to regroup and prepare, just in case it wasn't enough to appease them.

That evening after supper, Aerity gathered the entire castle staff into High Hall to inform them of all that was happening. She walked into the room with her chin lifted, her hair as vividly red as her mother's had been, wearing her best sea-green gown. The staff gasped. Some of the women sighed and murmured, "Beautiful." "Fit to be a queen!"

She felt humbled by their appreciation, and it made her long for her mother. What would the actual queen think of her older daughter at that moment? She so wanted to make her parents proud.

"Thank you for coming," Aerity told the staff. "I want to thank you for all you've done. I know the past week has been especially difficult and frightening for you. To have enemies in your midst and then left without a ruler . . . I imagine some of you felt quite powerless." A few nodded their heads and brought handkerchiefs to their eyes.

"I apologize for not being here, but I learned much while I was away. I learned that the enemy is vaster than we first imagined. And I learned that it's time to make a few compromises to allow for peace as long as possible." Aerity told them all of the proclamation herself. And though the atmosphere became tense and fearful, nobody spoke out against the news.

"And lastly," Aerity said. "I don't like the idea of you being unable to protect yourselves. I'm issuing a bow and arrows and a dagger to each of you who want them, along with personal lessons from our royal guard instructors on how to use them. Training begins tonight. Not one of you is too old or young to learn how to defend yourself."

Whispers of interest went up. People smiled at one another. Lord Alvi appeared at her side and squeezed her shoulder. "I'll be happy to help train," he said to the room in his booming voice.

More murmurs, and quiet giggles from maidens in the back. Aerity gave a tight smile and turned, taking Lief by the hand in a united front, and giving him a side glance.

He chuckled. "I'll behave myself."

They left High Hall together and Aerity whispered, "Any news from your family?"

"Nothing. But I sent a message by trade ship to my uncle today telling him what you learned of Kalor."

"Do they know of my parents?"

"Yes," he said. "I've been communicating with them all along."

"One-way messages is hardly communication," Aerity said. The king of Ascomanni expected Lief to keep him updated on every detail of Lochlan news while sharing nothing in return.

"The Ascomanni way is that no news is good news."

"Humph." Torestans and Zorfinans had been open about their situations, so Aerity had been sure to send a message of her predicament and their next step, along with what she'd learned on her travels.

Aerity was about to return to her chambers when Lief gently took her wrist.

"About the beast you brought—"

"It stays," Aerity said. He pursed his handsome lips and dropped her arm. "That is my final word on the matter, Lief."

Before he could protest, she turned from him.

Lief called out, "Highness." She stopped and awaited his argument. To her surprise, he said, "You look stunning."

She held back a grin and disappeared into her chambers for the night.

Chapter 29

Paxton woke edgier than he'd ever been in his life. He felt a veritable pull toward home, though he had learned nothing new over the past twenty-four hours. Yesterday he'd waited for Rozaria to come to him. He'd wanted to learn more, *needed* to know more, but the thought of what he might have to do to find out made his gut twist. It ended up not mattering, as he'd merely caught glimpses of her as she was dragged from meals to meetings with the prince. Paxton had no choice but to sup with the other lackeys and try not to draw attention to himself. At least the food was good.

He sat on his pallet after breakfast, sharpening his arrow-heads with a stone. Excited voices from the hall caused him to lift his head. A few men hooted in gladness and then rushed into the room, grabbing their belongings. Were they leaving? Paxton's heart banged, and he began gathering his own things. He strapped his daggers across his chest and threw a tunic over his head, followed by his bow and quiver. Then he grabbed his pack and followed the other men out.

When they got to the palace entrance it was pandemonium. It seemed the entire staff was running about, carrying things, shouting excited orders, shouldering their way past Rozaria's men and the Lashed army. It seemed chaos to Paxton, yet nobody was angry. A hand grabbed his from behind and he turned to see Rozaria's beaming face.

"It's time," she said over the din. Paxton's muscles clenched.

"To take over Lochlanach?" he asked. The words felt foreign and wrong.

Rozaria smiled. "Yes. The army is preparing to march. Prince Vito's carriage is ready. It is time."

Her voice, her eyes, were maniacal with the thrill of impending war. All at once Paxton remembered exactly who he was dealing with, and the duplicity of his thoughts toward her made him ill. This woman, whose affections he'd taken with a grain of salt, yet still managed to build a sense of companionship within him, was willing to kill Lochlans, to kill Aerity and her family, if it would ensure that her vision of rightness came true. She squeezed his hand and he nodded, afraid to speak.

Paxton felt powerless as he stared around at the thousands of people preparing to descend on his homeland. Lochlanach had no idea what it was about to face, and he had no way to warn it.

In the chill of the morning, Aerity stood on the castle's balcony amid a line of guards, leaning against the stone railing, watching as timid Lashed made their way into the west commons. With each person who entered, Aerity's heart swelled. She'd wanted to be down there, greeting those who came, but Harrison and her guards had adamantly warned against it.

The guards had been told to usher all Lashed to the long table, and ailing Unlashed to the rows of cots. So far there were eleven Lashed, all haggard in appearance, both men and women. No Unlashed had entered the west commons, though the royal lands and courtyards were beginning to fill with bystanders. She was glad she'd allowed the market and street vendors to open so the people would have food and be able to do some much needed trading, selling, and buying.

People were bundled in cloaks, fingerless gloves, and scuffed boots. All were milling about having hushed conversations, watching as the Lashed were escorted into the west commons. Aerity's stomach was wound tightly. *Come on, people, let them help you*, she silently pleaded.

In no time at all, the area outside the commons was bursting with people, watching and waiting expectantly. Nervous energy filled the air. Guards and soldiers were everywhere, but they were outnumbered. Harrison and Lief were down there somewhere, trying to help keep the peace. If a revolt were to break out now . . . The princess shuddered at the thought.

"Shall I fetch you a warmer robe, Your Highness?" asked her nearest guard.

"No, thank you," she whispered.

An hour passed.

Two hours. The grassy knoll and street outside of the west commons were filled to bursting. Twenty-two Lashed sat waiting by a fire in the west commons. Not a single citizen had approached to be healed. The volume seemed to rise. A scuffle broke out along the cobblestoned pathway where a cart was trying to get through the crowd, but it was quickly subdued by ready guards. Aerity's heart was in her throat. Too much time had passed. Something had to be done. This was a disaster and had the potential to get so much worse.

"I'm going to address them," she told the guards.

"Are you certain?" one asked. She knew it was foolish to speak unplanned, but this camp had been her idea, and she would do whatever she could to make it work. She prayed to the seas for the right words and then nodded and stepped to the edge, gripping the barrier.

"Good people of Lochlanach!" Her voice quavered. It took a minute of shushing and pointing within the crowd before everyone settled and stared up at her. Aerity had never been more nervous. She inhaled a cleansing breath and let it out slowly. Then she allowed her voice to reverberate through the heavy winter air.

"We have all been told a great untruth!" All was quiet as she paused, pushing herself to keep going. "You, and I, have been led to believe that Lashed and Unlashed can live apart." A symphony of tense murmurs rose and Aerity shouted over them. "*It is my belief* . . . from what I have seen and learned . . . that Lashed were created to heal others, and Unlashed are meant to allow this healing and to protect the Lashed. We were created for a symbiotic relationship." She brought her hands together in the air and twined her fingers.

"We *need* one another to survive. If I did not believe that with all my heart, I would not have organized this gathering today. I bring us together, not to appease the enemy, but to help my people thrive." Her small fists banged down on the balcony railing in emphasis.

"Are there evil Lashed?" she yelled. "Aye, my good people. We know this to be true. We battle Lashed Ones this very day who choose to do harm to others. But I tell you, there are evil Unlashed as well. And all evildoers must be stopped and punished. It is time that we begin looking at one another as individuals rather than grouping one another into separate entities." She fought for breath. "My parents have been taken. You all know that. It is time for this kingdom to come together, to join as one, if we are to have any chance at a future against our adversaries!

"I have brought you here today so that we may begin to

embrace the truth, together as a kingdom. Apart, we are helpless to fight any powers of evil that threaten our peace." She pointed down at the waiting Lashed. "Brave men and women have come today, and they have come to help you. These Lashed are not our enemies—they are your own neighbors! They are your fellow Lochlans! I know there are those among you with ailments that human healers have not been able to cure. I know there are women out there"—at this Aerity's eyes burned—"who have lost countless babes.

"Why do you think the population in Eurona has dwindled over the past hundred years since magic was outlawed? Because it was never meant to be forbidden! Pregnancies *need* help. That is nature. And nature has provided a way. *Let these good people help you!*"

The side of her fist absolutely stung from banging it against the stone. Her chest heaved with emotion. Sweat trickled down her back despite the cold. Aerity's eyes scanned the unmoving, silent people. Many had dropped their eyes. They waited. And waited. It wasn't working. She pressed her lips together, trying desperately not to cry.

And then the crowd began to move. *Oh, seas . . . were they leaving?* But no. A young woman was being ushered to the front by a young man. Her husband, perhaps? From afar she seemed lethargic. She held her rounded stomach. They approached the west commons gates, and two guards swung them wide. The crowd shuffled to be able to see, and it was as if the entire royal lands held its breath.

One of the Lashed women stood as they entered and hooked the pregnant woman's other arm over her shoulder. She led her to a cot and immediately set to work. Aerity wished she could hear what they said to each other. She leaned heavily against the railing, not wanting to blink. The pregnant woman did not look far enough along to give birth, but she must have been having complications to come forward.

The Lashed woman slid her hands onto the bare belly and the pregnant woman arched her back, giving a loud moan. Her husband held her hand against his cheek. The Lashed healer worked for several minutes. And then they watched as the woman began to sit up, the healer helping to gently lift her. A beautiful sound broke the air at that moment—laughter from the couple.

The pregnant woman placed a hand on her swollen stomach and laughed with joy. Whatever difficulty she'd been having with the pregnancy was obviously gone. Her husband said something and he laughed as well, taking her into his arms. And then the couple was crying. And Aerity quickly swiped hot tears from her own cheeks. The couple stood, smiling, and were led by a guard out of the west commons, back to the crowd, who converged with questions and wonderings. The Lashed healer clasped her hands under her chin.

Another woman broke through the crowd, raising a hand high and crying out, "Heal mine! Please!"

A man pushed his way forward carrying an older man. "My papa's leg is broken!"

One by one, people came forward. A line formed. Aerity sniffed hard. She refused to let any tears fall.

"You've done it," whispered the guard beside her.

Aerity shook her head. "This is only a start." There were plenty of skeptical faces still in that crowd. Plenty of onlookers just waiting for the wrong move from a Lashed One—waiting for a reason to strike, to prove Aerity's beliefs wrong.

But it was a definite start.

Aerity felt a light hand on her shoulder and she turned to the royal healer, Mrs. Rathbrook, her eyes watery. The woman cupped Aerity's frozen cheek with her papery hand, nails lined from those she'd recently helped. "Blessings of the seas, Your Highness."

Aerity gathered the woman into a hug and held her tight. "Thank you, Mrs. Rathbrook. I want to make it right."

"You will, precious girl. You will."

"Come," said Aerity, taking her hand. "Let's get in from the cold."

Chapter 30

By the end of the day, when no rioting or rebellion had broken out, Aerity, Lief, Harrison, and four senior officers met in the king's office to choose three villages throughout Lochlanach to implement supervised healing infirmaries: Dovedell, Craw Coorie, and Duke Gulfton's southern town of Fetchko. She hoped word would quickly spread about the good that had been done that day.

Thirty-seven people had come forward for healing. People cried and rejoiced. Lashed and Unlashed shared grateful hugs. Aerity felt as if she were floating all day with the rightness of it. If only her parents were there to see . . .

They were just concluding business when a knock came

and two guards entered with lined faces. Aerity's lightness suddenly dropped.

"What's happened?" she asked.

"Nay, Your Highness, nothing has happened, per se. . . ." They glanced at each other.

Harrison stepped forward. "Then what is it?"

"Well, it's just that, you see, we heard rumor that a beast had been captured on your travels, and we just now saw Lady Wyneth struggling to take the thing out of doors . . . she had it by a rope but I'm not sure what good that will do. It very nearly outweighs her." They shared another worried glance.

"By the stars . . ." Lief shook his head.

Aerity and Harrison looked at each other with pursed lips.

"You needn't worry, sirs," Aerity said. "This beast is quite different, I assure you."

The men all furrowed their brows in skepticism except Harrison, who stared down at his hands and sighed. Lief looked ready to say something.

At that very moment a giggle sounded down the hall and Wyneth could be heard saying, "Slow down, Furball!"

Now was their chance to show these men just what a threat the creature was. Aerity called out for her cousin to come into the office. She hadn't seen Furball since the day before. When Wyneth came through the door holding the end of a rope, and the beast bounded in beside her, Aerity sucked in a breath.

Deep seas! How was it growing so quickly? It walked on four legs, but if it lifted onto its hind legs it had to be as tall as Wyn.

Harrison and the other men gawked.

"What are you feeding it?" Harrison asked.

Wyneth laughed. "He's not picky, I'll give you that! Any type of meat or fish, vegetables, grains. Whew!" She stared around at the faces and her smile faded.

"My lady," Lief said carefully, "where did it stay during the night? It's hardly detainable." He eyed Furball's claws as the cub swatted at tassels hanging from chair cushions. He swatted again and the tassel was swiped clean off.

Wyneth stood straighter and jutted out her chin. "Furball is a he, not an it. He's quite smart. I've house-trained him. And he sleeps in my chambers."

Mouths fell open. More silent glances of horror were shared.

"I'm not sure that's wise," said a guard.

"It's *not*." Lief's face had gone fierce.

"To be honest," said Wyneth, "I feel more protected with him by my side than any human guard. No offense." The guard who had spoken looked at the playful cub and shook his head.

"Watch this," Wyneth said to him. "Grab my arm."

"Wyn . . ." Harrison's voice held warning.

"Don't worry," she told him. Then she looked to the guard again. "Grab my arm."

He hesitated before he reached out and grasped her. Wyneth let out a dramatic "Ow!" and the little beast suddenly changed. His ears perked. A ridge of fur pricked up along his neck and back, and he stood on his back legs, letting out a growl and baring sharp fangs. The guard released Wyneth and jumped back with a yell.

Lief moved forward in warrior stance, the muscles in his arms bulging.

Wyn made a double clicking sound with her tongue against the roof of her mouth and said firmly, "Down." Furball immediately went to a sitting position, never taking his eyes from the guard who'd grabbed her. Wyneth put a hand on the guard's shoulder and said soothingly to Furball, "Friend." Then she clicked her tongue again and snapped her fingers, pointing to her side. "Come."

Furball walked forward, swaying his wide bottom, and sat at Wyneth's feet. He licked his jowls.

Aerity gave a nervous laugh of shock. Wyneth grinned at her.

"You've certainly been busy," Harrison remarked. Lief crossed his arms and scowled.

"Aye." Wyneth eyed the guards and soldiers. "Please let your men know that Furball is a danger only to anyone who tries to hurt me. He will stay at my side, and this castle is his home."

The guards and officers nodded, albeit with seeming reluctance as they stared at the strange creature.

"*Furball*, my lady?" said an officer, trying to hold back a grin.

"Aye, sir. Apparently you can blame Lieutenant Gillfin

for that mighty name." Wyneth gave a gorgeous full smile at Harrison, and Aerity could have sworn his cheeks became pinker as he stared at Wyn and let out a dry laugh of his own. Lief gave a grunt and stalked from the office.

Wyneth was on her way to the gardens, where Furball could run through the maze of bushes. She had been training him nonstop, marveling at his ability to obey, but she wanted to see if she could call him to her when he was a distance away. The gardens seemed safe enough, since only royals could use them, and the royals, well . . . they weren't there, were they?

Another bout of sadness descended on her as she walked Furball down the stairs, accompanied by a guard. He peered around at the empty garden with its high wall of shrubbery and gave a nod that it was safe.

Wyneth stood there a few minutes, staring into the manicured space as her warm breath made clouds in the air. Everything was still. The sky was gray. Wyneth had never liked winter. She found it depressing, except for the first snow, which was pure beauty. But the lack of warmth and the abundance of darkness had always felt soul sucking to her. It was so much worse now without the joyful sounds of her siblings and cousins running about. So much worse without the comfort of her parents and presence of their seasoned ruler.

Aerity had done well today, but she was too young to be forced into ruling. Wyneth couldn't help but think it was only a matter of time before things went awry. Those who had taken her aunt and uncle would surely be back. How would they protect themselves? And was her family safe on the Isle of Evie? She hoped to receive word from them on the morrow.

Furball pressed his nose hard against Wyneth's hip and snorted where he knew dried sardines hid within her deep skirt pockets. She clicked and pointed to the spot before her. Furball jumped to that spot and turned. She raised a hand and he went up on his hind legs. Wyneth tossed him a sardine, which he crunched happily and licked his lips.

She then tested his skill to stay. She started small, ten feet apart, then twenty, then around a corner of bushes. Each time he seemed a little edgy as she left him, as if he wanted nothing more than to follow. But he remained where she left him, telling him to *stay*, until she clicked her tongue and called for him. After an hour and a half, as the skies darkened, he had managed to stay at the far corner of the maze of bushes until she called. But much to her surprise he didn't wind through the maze to get to her.

In his lack of patience, he made a straight line to her *through* the bushes.

Wyneth stared at the trampled plants with a hand over her mouth. Oh, Queen Leighlane would be furious. She was still staring, wondering if the bushes were salvageable, when Furball gave a small growl and stared behind her toward the castle. Wyneth spun and saw Harrison sitting on the steps. The guard was gone. Harrison clapped his hands.

"Remarkable, Wyn."

Her heart rose and danced as it always did when he complimented her. "Thank you."

"But he growled at me," Harrison said, standing. "He's never done that before."

The creature seemed unfazed now, happily tuckered out as he lay at her side. Perhaps he'd just been startled, or maybe it was the darkness. But she couldn't have Furball growling at her friends when they came near. He needed to recognize the difference between friendly interactions and danger.

"Come to me, Harrison," Wyneth said.

He looked upon her, and in that moment there was a heavy sort of strangeness between them that made her blush, as if she'd asked him to do something inappropriate.

"To see how he'll react," she amended.

"All right," he said softly. And he did as she asked, walking forward.

Furball watched him carefully. As Harrison got closer, the creature went from lying to sitting, definitely more attentive. When they were a few feet away, and Harrison paused, Wyneth whispered, "Closer."

He took a step forward, and then another, until there was only a foot between them. Wyneth peeked down at Furball, who craned his neck up at the pair but did not seem upset.

"He seems okay with you now." Wyneth spoke softly.

"Aye," Harrison whispered. "Good." But he didn't move.

Wyneth swallowed. She didn't want him to move away

yet. "Perhaps you should touch me . . . just to be sure?"

She stared into his eyes and shivered all over when she felt the warmth of his hands surrounding hers, twining their fingers together. Furball snorted. Harrison released her fingers and ran his hands up her cloaked arms to her shoulders. His eyes had her mesmerized, the way he gazed at her unflinchingly as if searching. Wyneth didn't understand what was coming over them.

This is Harrison, for seas' sake. Breckon's cousin. He was as familiar and comfortable as a hearth flame or a hot bath. And right now all she wanted was to be submerged in the warm feeling he gave off. Her breaths hitched as his hands moved up and pulled back her hood.

His palms ran up her neck, the heat of his skin a stark contrast to the cold air engulfing them. When he took her cheeks she quaked at her core.

"Harrison?" she breathed. She hadn't meant his name to come out as a question, but her entire world was off its axis at that moment.

"Aye, Wyn," he whispered.

And then his lips touched hers. They didn't move. His breath warmed her face, and his lips began to explore hers with absolute gentleness, as if he were savoring each curve and crevice. Wyneth grasped his wrists, afraid her legs would stop working the way her mind had. She clung to him.

He pulled back and pressed his cheek to hers, his warm breath at her ear. "Forgive me, but I've wanted to do that for far longer than is proper."

"I . . . what?" Her mind broke.

He looked at her with something akin to sadness. "I shouldn't be saying this." He stopped and swallowed. "Let's get you inside. It's cold."

He dropped his hands from her face and began to turn.

"No!" Wyneth grabbed his hand and pulled him back to face her. "What shouldn't you be saying?" Her heart was racing. She'd never seen his eyes like this before. So solemn and intense, as if he were afraid. And the things he was saying—each word was a thrilling zap that reached to her core. "Tell me."

"I don't want to lose your friendship," he said. "It means more to me than anything. And some words, once spoken, cannot be taken back. Some words have the power to ruin friendships and . . . change things."

Deep seas. She could hardly find her voice. She whispered, "Tell me."

His face inched closer to hers, his eyes still so serious. "I've loved you as long as I can remember, Wyn. Since we were a lad and lass. Even when you were with Breckon, I wanted you."

She stared, dumbstruck. And in that moment it was as if the empty, raw places within her heart began to fill with a warm salve, and an earnest sense of home covered her. She thought of the times she'd caught him watching her throughout the years. She'd always thought he was admiring Breckon, looking up to his cousin, and that his devotion to Wyn was an extension of that. Could it truly have been *her* that he was admiring all along? The very idea bent and twisted Wyneth's mind, reshaping years of their history together.

The castle door opened, casting a dim light over the three of them.

"Lieutenant Gillfin and Lady Wyneth, the curfew is in effect," called the guard.

Harrison slowly stepped back and broke the gaze between them. He waved her forward like the gentleman he was. Wyneth moved up the path and stairs with Furball at her side. She stared around at the castle walls, everything seeming new and different. And suddenly the edges of dullness shed away from winter.

Harrison walked her to the entrance of her chambers and although her heart and soul were brimming with new awareness, all she could bring herself to murmur was "Thank you."

Harrison gave her a polite bow and put his palm out to Furball, who sniffed him and seemed satisfied. So Harrison set to scratching the beast on the head. Without looking away from Furball, Harrison asked, "Are you upset with me, Wyn? Shall we pretend I never behaved wrongly?"

"Wrongly?" The word chafed her. "What part of that felt wrong to you?"

He looked at her now, a sense of grateful disbelief in his eyes. And Wyneth was done with gentleness.

She grabbed the sides of his uniform collar and pulled

him down until their mouths crashed, and then her arms were around his neck and his hands held her waist. In a swift move, he pinned her heavily against the doorframe and kissed her with what she now knew to be years of pent-up passion, his hips pressing against hers.

I didn't know, she wanted to say, but they never broke away long enough to speak. She'd always wanted him to marry Aerity, but only friendship was there. Wyneth thought for years that Harrison must have fallen for a woman while he was out on duty. He'd always been so private.

But now she knew. There'd been no mystery woman. Only her. And she knew if Breckon had lived, Harrison would have taken his love for her to the grave and never told a soul. That kind of dedication and willpower . . . her respect for him grew to new proportions. And all the feelings of friendship she'd had for him all her life, they grew and morphed into something bigger and more spectacular. *And, oh, seas, his mouth was a glorious thing.* Their hunger was well matched.

A dark, unamused chuckle sounded nearby, and Harrison broke away from her, brandishing his dagger in a flash and pressing her behind him. Lord Alvi stood there, his arms crossed, a deadly look on his face that Wyneth had never seen before.

Furball tensed and growled.

"Down," Wyneth warned him. She was suddenly shaking.

"You've taught him to fear me?" Lord Alvi asked. His eyes

bore into her, filled with pain and torment, and unfounded guilt kicked within her abdomen.

"Of course not. He can sense your mood," Wyneth warned. "What are you doing in this hall?"

"I came to check on you." His eyes flashed to Harrison and back to Wyneth.

"Well, I don't need you to do that. Please, just calm down and go. Now."

"Indeed," Lord Alvi said. He glared at Harrison. "You're a lucky *flekk*."

He turned and walked away. Wyneth ran a shaking hand down her face. *Flekk* was Ascomannian for *thief*. But Lief was wrong. Harrison had stolen nothing from anyone. Did the coldland lord think he could collect women like toys and keep them all for himself?

"Don't worry about him," Harrison said softly. "He'll cool his head tonight and soon move along. But you need to tell me if he becomes a problem."

Wyneth nodded. She still felt rather ill. Harrison didn't attempt to touch her again. He could read her so well.

"Get some rest, Wyn."

"Aye," she whispered. She went into her chambers with Furball, and Harrison gave her one last look before closing the door and leaving her with her thoughts.

Chapter 31

As they marched through the Kalorian jungles at sunrise, thousands in their party, one thing became clear to Paxton: the Kalorian majority was afraid of them. Villagers ran for cover when they saw them coming. Doors were shut tight and windows shuttered. The villages appeared empty. These were not people who wanted to cheer for their ruler as he came through. They wanted to hide from him.

It felt extremely strange to Paxton, and even stranger that the army seemed to be okay with it, as if the people's fear was a sign of respect and proof of the army and prince's power. And then Paxton began to see just why people were hiding. Throughout towns, bodies were strung from trees, left in shackles to rot, beheaded at stumps, or simply lined along the ground in neat rows, without an injury in sight. Those had obviously been victims of Lashed hands. And all the dead were left out as morbid reminders to the living.

Paxton fought the urge to cover his mouth and nose as they passed places with the dead on display. The smells were as sickening as Rozaria's beastly experimentation rooms. He tried not to look at the despicable exhibits. He faced forward and kept his expression blank.

He racked his brain as they rode, trying to figure out a way he could warn the people of Lochlanach that they were coming. Along with their ground forces of military ranging in the thousands, there were at least a hundred Lashed who'd been amassed by Rozaria through her camps, three detestable monsters, and a fleet of naval vessels set to attack. Half the army remained to protect Kalor in case fighting filtered back over, and to keep their own lands protected while the prince was away.

"Hunter."

Paxton turned his head toward the sound of Rozaria's voice coming from the prince's coach. She was leaning out of the open doorway as it moved. It was a gaudy thing, draped in bright silks and trimmed with gold. Paxton lifted his chin in response. She waved him back. He turned his horse and rode next to her.

"The prince wishes to speak with you," she said. In her eyes was something like pride, but Paxton felt only apprehension.

He dropped from his horse and passed the reins to a nearby soldier, then grasped the gold handles of the carriage and pulled himself into the dim interior. He was immediately hit by the strongest burst of magical aura he'd ever felt. His skin tingled as if he stood too close to a fire. It smelled strongly of burned incense, powdery and flowery. Paxton took a seat on a cushion and pushed his unruly hair behind his ears before looking up at the smooth face of Prince Vito.

He hadn't been allowed this close to the man before now. He couldn't be much older than Paxton. He was of slight build, but heavy robes with padding made him appear larger. His hair was perfectly straight as if it'd just been brushed, and his entire face appeared sharp with the way his brows, nose, cheekbones, and chin jutted out. The prince stared unsmiling and Paxton dropped his eyes, waiting silently.

And then he saw the prince's hands. *By the depths . . . his nails are entirely purpled*. Not a slice of white could be seen. Perhaps it should not have surprised Paxton that the prince was Lashed, and yet it did. A Lashed monarch was unheard of. This was a well-kept secret that would not go over well with the rest of Eurona.

"Prince Vito," Rozaria said huskily, "I give you the hunter Paxton Seabolt."

All was silent. Paxton could feel himself being studied and wondered if he should say something, but he decided against it.

When Prince Vito finally spoke, his Euronan was heavily

accented. "You may look upon me." Paxton raised his eyes. "Roza tells me you have met Princess Aerity Lochson."

Trepidation ripped jaggedly through Paxton like a vile, burning poison, and he was glad to be sitting. He hoped his panic didn't show on his face or in his voice.

"Aye. Yes, Your Majesty. I have met her."

"Tell me about her. I only knew her as a child. Roza says she is beautiful."

Rozaria waved a hand and rolled her eyes. "I said no such thing. I merely gave you an account of her appearance."

"Is she beautiful?" the prince asked him.

Paxton had never wanted to put an arrow through someone's head at close range until that moment. Why in the deep, dark seas was he asking this? Paxton wanted to say that Aerity was hideous, anything to keep him away from her.

"I suppose beauty is subjective," Paxton said. "Some might call her beautiful."

Prince Vito laughed, a high, creeping sound like a strangling vine. "Ah, a politician."

"Nay, Your Majesty. A simple man who prefers a lower-maintenance, more natural beauty from his women."

Rozaria sent him a seductive grin, as if pleased by his suggested slight against a royal Lochson.

"I can handle a demanding woman if she is beautiful," Prince Vito said.

Paxton could choke him with his bare hands. The satisfaction of it would last a lifetime. But it would mean he'd have to get within reach of the prince's hands, which were quite possibly the most deadly weapon there was. He didn't move.

"How well do you know her?" the prince asked. Paxton hated the laziness of the man's voice.

"We spoke a few times, always surrounded by guards, so nothing in depth. I have seen her interact with Lashed, always surprisingly openly and without fear. I was there with her the night she and Rozaria . . . met. And the beast was killed."

"So you would say that the princess trusts you, yes?"

Paxton's pulse was wild in his throat. "Yes. I would believe so."

"That is good." The prince stared at him with uncomfortable intensity. "We will use you to get into the castle."

Paxton nodded, his pulse out of control.

Rozaria shifted and spoke. "We do not foresee a problem taking over royal lands, but the castle will be heavily secured. If we send you in first, and have you on the inside to let us in . . ." She spread her hands as if enough had been said. Again, Paxton nodded. This was perfect. It would get him inside to warn the others and possibly get them to safety.

"Of course. I will help in any way I can."

She grinned at the prince, who continued to stare at Paxton.

"Why does your heart beat so hard?" the man asked. Paxton blinked in surprise, and the prince said, "I can feel it in your energy."

He could feel Paxton's pulse? The kind of power that must

be in this man's blood was unreal.

"I suppose I'm . . . excited, Your Majesty." Paxton rubbed his sweating palms on the knees of his breeches. "This is the moment I've been waiting for."

Prince Vito linked his long fingers together on his lap and Paxton couldn't help but stare at those purpled nails as the prince responded.

"Freedom from the oppression of Unlashed rulers is upon us. Things will finally be as they should. First Lochlanach, then Toresta, Zorfina, and lastly Ascomanni. Though we may simply have to kill that entire kingdom of tyrants."

Paxton gave a humorous snort at his irony. If ever there'd been a tyrant, it was the prince himself. But he said, "Aye. There is not much hope for the coldlands. I nearly broke my hand on one of their noses during the hunt."

The prince let out his chilling laugh again. "Shame you couldn't have just killed them all while nobody was looking. All their supposed *warriors*. Those people are nothing but muscle and hate."

"Soon enough," Rozaria crooned.

"Yes, Cousin." *Cousin?* Prince Vito patted her hand. "Soon enough. And the princess is just the tool I need to gain the trust of the Lochlan people. When I make her my queen, we will join lands, and nobody can question the validity of my rule."

Paxton tried to swallow the bile that had risen in him, but it stuck. He had to kill them. Right now. He stared at their hands, wondering how quick their reflexes were. He had never killed a person before. It would take him a long moment to find their hearts and stop them. But these two . . . they could kill him in less time than it would take him to blink.

Paxton sat back and met the prince's sinister eyes. He gave the man a nod. He could not kill them now. He would get to the castle first and get Aerity to safety. He would never let this man near her.

Never.

Chapter 32

Wyneth had been up since before the sun, patiently awaiting the moment when Aerity would be awake so she might speak with her. She hurried down the hall with Furball lumbering along behind her on his giant paws—she no longer bothered with the pretense of the rope leash—and hordes of guards in front of Aerity's wing made a path for them. Wyneth got to Aerity's chambers just as her maid was coming out with the laundry.

"My lady," Caitrin said with a curtsy.

Wyneth inclined her head. "Good morning, Caitrin."

"Wyn!" Aerity's eyes brightened as she came out of her chambers. And then her eyes bulged at the sight of Furball. "Great raging seas!"

Wyneth rushed in and closed the door behind her. "I know. Try having him sleep in your bed."

"He doesn't!"

"He does," Wyneth admitted. "Let's just say there's no need for a fire with this one curled up against your back."

Aerity did not look like she enjoyed the idea of the beast cub in her bed, but Wyneth didn't mind. She knew it sounded mad, but he gave her such comfort. She watched him fondly as he nosed his way through her cousin's room, sniffing everything, his claws clicking and scraping against the wood floor.

"Listen, Aer, I know you've got your morning meetings, but I need to speak to you for a moment." Wyneth paused, wondering if she should bother her cousin with such trivial matters when there were legitimate important issues to be dealt with. "You know what . . . never mind. It can wait."

"What?" Aerity grabbed her arm. "Don't you dare pique my curiosity and then say never mind!"

Wyneth loved the glow of interest in Aerity's eyes, and she wondered if maybe a tiny distraction from the kingdom's woes might not be such a bad thing. She glanced down the hall. The guard was out of hearing range.

"All right, then, but I'll make it quick. Yesterday . . ." Wyneth's mind went into a blur of warmth and confusion and guilt, the swirl of emotions that had kept her tossing and turning all night.

"Well, go on." Aerity grasped both of Wyn's hands now.

"Harrison kissed me!" she said in a rush.

Aerity's face froze, and she rocked back on her heels. Then she gasped, let go of Wyneth's hands, and slapped her palms over her mouth. Wyneth pressed her lips together, waiting for it.

"Oh, my seas!" Aerity screamed. "It was you all along!"

"What do you mean?" Wyneth laughed as her cousin danced around her, clapping her hands before stopping in front of her.

"The mystery love of Harrison's life is solved!" Aerity sang. "He told me while we were away together, but I never suspected. What with Breckon . . ."

Both girls lost their smiles. Wyneth couldn't look at her now. Was it wrong to feel this way for her lost love's cousin? His best friend?

"Wyn, you don't need to feel bad. I daresay you'd have Breckon's blessing."

Wyneth swallowed the onslaught of stupid tears that threatened. "Perhaps," she whispered. "And as if things weren't complicated enough, Lief saw us kissing and acted like a jealous ogre."

"He has no right!"

Again, Wyneth's heart felt as if it were stretching and collapsing, like a tug-of-war being played in her chest. The look on Lief's face . . . She hadn't wanted to hurt him, but the two of them were never meant to be.

"Do not feel guilty about Lief, Wyn," Aerity said softly. When Wyneth didn't respond, the princess went on. "I wasn't going to tell you this, but now I think I must."

Oh, no. Wyneth looked into her cousin's serious eyes, wondering what had happened.

"Lief slept with my maid, Caitrin."

A bout of nausea kicked Wyneth in the stomach. It made her jealous and sad and disgusted all at once. She shook her head, unsure what to do next. Furball grunted and came over, nudging her hand until she absentmindedly scratched his head.

"I'm sorry," Aerity said. "Maybe I shouldn't have said anything."

"No." Wyneth stood taller. "I'm glad you did. I've known all along what Lief is like. He's not the type to change his ways for any woman. He is who he is, and I was foolish to have allowed affections to grow between us in the first place." Her heart absolutely ached.

Until she thought of Harrison. That familiar comfort wrapped itself around her like silk. She closed her eyes. He *loved* her.

"That must have been some kiss."

When Wyneth opened her eyes, Aerity was watching her, grinning.

"I didn't think I could ever feel that way again. I mean, I know it hasn't been long . . . since Breckon was killed, but so much has happened since the summer. Sometimes it feels as if he's been gone for years."

They were quiet a moment, and then Wyneth asked,

"Will you still marry Lief? Even if your parents . . ." Wyneth shook her head. "No, I know they will return. I'm sorry."

"I still have to keep my end of the agreement," Aerity responded quietly. "Ascomanni will make sure of it." Aerity sighed, making Wyneth wish she could take some of that burden from her cousin's shoulders.

"Wyn?" Aerity's eyes looked so much older in that moment. "What if my parents don't return? I have this terrible feeling."

She took Aerity's hands again. "We must continue to hope until we know for certain."

Aerity turned to stare out at the gray morning. "I don't know if I'm ready for this. I thought I'd have years to prepare for my role as queen. I feel unqualified."

Wyneth could not even begin to imagine. "It's too heavy a burden for you to have to shoulder, Aer, but you're doing *wonderfully*. What happened here yesterday was nothing short of a miracle from the seas. I felt a sense of peace and excitement in the air that I haven't felt since the summer festival, before all this madness began. You *must* continue to have faith and be strong."

The weight of the burden didn't leave Aerity's frame, but she lifted her chin in a show of strength. "Will you accompany me to the meeting?"

"Aye. I won't leave your side."

"Thank you." They took hands and headed to the door until Aerity pulled her to a stop. "And I'm happy for you. And for Harrison. You deserve each other."

Wyneth smiled, flushing with warmth. She clicked her tongue. "Come, Furball."

Together, the three of them left to face the day, whatever it might bring.

Chapter 33

Aerity couldn't help but notice the tension throughout her father's office as Harrison, Lief, and two officers filtered in—a tension that had nothing to do with the danger at hand. She held in an inappropriate smile as Harrison and Lief shifted, looking everywhere but at each other or Wyneth. Tiern and Vixie were the last to arrive. Vixie had a bow and quiver of arrows across her back.

"I see you're staying armed these days," Aerity admired, "even within the castle."

"I've been practicing with Tiern. I just . . . I feel more comfortable having it."

"All right, then." Aerity moved to the map of Eurona on her father's desk. "The eight of us will have to come up with a plan to protect the kingdom from imminent attack. We don't know when or how, but we know it's coming. I want another proclamation issued throughout the lands today. Homes and businesses should prepare as needed. Everyone should be on the lookout."

"Should we hold off on the Lashed infirmaries, Your Highness?" asked Harrison.

"No. Life should proceed as normal. It could be months before the Kalorians decide to attack. Perhaps the existence of the infirmaries will deter the Rocato woman when she sees we are making changes, though I'm not counting on it."

Harrison nodded. Aerity listened to their counsel and together they decided how many soldiers to place in which areas, mostly to protect royal lands.

"There's simply not enough manpower to protect all the villages," one of the officers said. Aerity swallowed her bitter disappointment. Hundreds of new, young faces had joined the army and navy after her parents were kidnapped, but their forces were still stretched too thin.

"Your Highness," said the senior officer, "perhaps you, Princess Vixie, and Lady Wyneth should join your family on the Isle of Evie while we wait this out—"

"No," Aerity said.

"It's not a bad idea," Lief interjected.

"My answer is no. Wyneth and Vixie have my blessing to go, but I must stay."

"Absolutely not!" Vixie huffed.

"I'm not leaving you," Wyneth said firmly. They both

looked defiantly at the faces around the room, and the men did not argue. Harrison looked down and rubbed his jaw.

Aerity said to the officers, "Go. Send out the next proclamation. And have our fastest messengers deliver word to Toresta and Zorfina of our circumstances."

When the senior officer opened the door, they saw a guard standing there, about to knock. He gave the princess a quick bow, his eyes alight.

"Your Highness, we have visitors."

Aerity's heart beat a heavy hammer. "Who?"

"The king and queen of Ascomanni and their council, Princess."

Lief gave her a surprised look before bolting from the room.

Suspicion flapped through Aerity like an angry crow. She peered at Harrison. The last time foreign royalty had come to the castle, her parents had disappeared. But Harrison gave her a nod.

"They are allies," he reminded her. "And Lief's people. You will be surrounded by armed guards at all times. I'll make sure of it."

"All right." Aerity looked at the guard. "Let them in. Have the kitchen prepare breakfast in the formal dining room. That is where we shall meet."

The feeling of unease did not leave Aerity as she stood before the doors to the dining room, dressed in finery, an emerald heavy against her forehead. As the doors opened, she saw that Harrison had been true to his word about guards. They lined the room, but they were not alone. The Ascomanni had brought many guards of their own.

King Dagur and Queen Agnetha Vikani stood when Aerity entered, along with Lief and a couple Aerity didn't recognize. All were wearing the finest fur-lined leather vests, with kilts and boots. Harrison and Wyneth stepped to the far end of the table. Aerity went to her father's spot, feeling extraordinarily strange at the head of the table. Vixie took the queen's chair at her side. Still standing, Aerity addressed the visiting king and queen.

"We meet again, King Dagur and Queen Agnetha."

The king inclined his head. "We have much to discuss, Princess."

"Surely you are weary from your travels. Please, accept our hospitality before we discuss any matters."

The king looked down at his plateful of food before nodding his agreement. As they all sat, Lief remained standing.

"My lady Aerity, I give you my parents, Lord Daan and Lady Hanna Alvi." Lord Daan was a beefier, thinner-haired version of Lief, and he gave her a lazy grin that had probably swept many women off their feet for years.

"We finally meet," said the senior Lord Alvi.

"It is a pleasure, my lord and lady," Aerity said. "Our kingdom owes much to your brave son."

Lady Hanna, a formidable woman, smiled proudly up at Lief, who finally sat and sent Aerity a grateful look. The coldlanders dug into their breakfasts without further ado. Aerity tried to eat. Between small bites of eggs and sausage she sent furtive glances down the table to Wyneth and Harrison, who seemed as alert as her, not eating much. Same with Vixie at her side. Her sister was being uncharacteristically quiet, which was good.

Aerity was glad that one of the officers had been willing, and even slightly eager, to take Furball out to the gardens for a bit of exercise. She wasn't ready to spring that surprise on their guests.

Once they'd finished their meals and the plates had been cleared away, King Dagur smoothed down his beard and crossed his hands over his belly. He eyed her closely.

"Shall we speak in front of everyone, then?"

"Aye, King Dagur. I would prefer it, if you don't mind."

"Fine. Any word on your parents?"

She forced strength into her voice. "Nay, sir. Not a word."

King Dagur looked around at the tapestries that told of Lochlan history.

"Our fathers were good friends," he murmured. "Your grandfather and my father, that is. Your papa and I used to play in this castle when we'd come to visit. He never wanted to break the rules, your father." King Dagur grinned mischievously. "But I made him. While the kings worked, we explored every inch of this castle and beneath it. . . ."

His eyes glazed, remembering. Aerity wondered what he meant by beneath it. Surely he wasn't speaking of the tunnels. She'd only just learned of them herself.

He sighed heavily, disrupting her thoughts. "My sources

say that Kalor means to take over Lochlanach in less than a week's time. Days, perhaps."

Days? She tried to hide her surprise. Her own military spies had not been able to give an estimated time, but she didn't want to admit that. *Days* was not good. *Breathe, Aerity, breathe . . . bluff your way through this.*

The king rested his elbows on the table, tenting his fingers. "I daresay your army is not prepared."

"They are preparing as we speak."

A slow smile came to his lips. "You put on a brave face for a young woman, but surely you must be terrified at the prospect of war."

Responses vied in Aerity's mind, but she chose not to say any of them.

"Would it ease your mind, Princess, if I told you my troops are ready to move on your behalf? To fight alongside your army?"

Oh, great seas, yes! Aerity wanted to press her hand to her heart and laugh at the sweet relief coursing through her, but she remained steady. She glanced at Lief, who watched her with an oddly remorseful expression of seriousness.

"Any forces you would be willing to offer against this foe would be much appreciated."

"Good. That is good." King Dagur sat up and leaned forward on his elbows, his fingers linked. "I can make that happen just as soon as our kingdoms are properly united."

Aerity went very still as she stared into his calculating eyes. She dared not look away or show weakness as she fought to keep her breathing even.

"You speak of my marriage to Lord Alvi?"

"Exactly. With your father currently . . . out of the picture, I would hate for our agreement to be put aside much longer."

Hot, rigid fury filled Aerity. She felt her spine straighten as she sat up taller.

"I intend to honor my father's proclamation whether he is on the throne or not. Our wedding will go on this spring, as planned."

Again he smiled slowly. "I had heard it was moved up to this winter."

Curse it!

"There was talk of moving it up to distract the masses, but that was before war became imminent. I hardly think this is the proper time for a wedding. I want to give the people something to celebrate once all the madness is over."

"And if you die in said madness?"

Vixie gasped. Aerity did not take her eyes from King Dagur as she held her index finger up to Vixie to silence her. She knew what was going on here: Ascomanni believed Lochlanach would fall, and they wanted it for themselves in the aftermath.

"If anything happens to me, my sister will reign, and my brother after her."

"But they are so young. Is it wise?" His show of worry made Aerity ill.

"My aunts and uncles are safely hidden away, and they will

return to advise our ruler, however young she or he may be."

"Do you truly believe anyone in your family is safe right now? Do you think they will not be targeted out on that island? Kalor wants Lochlanach for its own. I am offering to prevent that." His voice had risen, and a war broke out inside her. Of course he knew about the royal island. Was there anything he didn't know?

If her parents were here, they would absolutely have her marry Lief that very moment to secure the country. They would fold to King Dagur's demands.

"If you are to marry my nephew in a matter of months, what does it matter?" he asked. "Be reasonable. This is not the time to dally, Your Highness."

Seas, his words were so much like what her own father would tell her, but his voice held an arrogance that set her on edge, as if he couldn't believe he had to deal with her. Aerity gritted her teeth. In her heart of hearts, she believed her army and navy could defend the lands against Kalor once they set all their plans into motion. Would it be pretty? No. But it would be their hard-earned victory. And after all was said and done, she would have to face all Eurona, possibly as queen. These first impressions of her reign were important.

Aerity hated making decisions. Up until now she'd had everything decided for her, like it or not. In that moment the pressure piled upon her, and she knew that what she decided now would determine how she would be treated throughout her entire reign.

She had watched her father's will bend to others too many

times to count in the past six months. She had thought his decisions were made for the benefit of the kingdom, and she'd admired his humility in the face of it all, but now she couldn't help but think her father had been driven by fear, just as King Dagur was being driven by greed.

Aerity could not afford to begin her rule by allowing the coldlands to bribe her. She had to set a higher precedent.

"King Dagur," she said steadily, "if you fight alongside me, I will marry your nephew the moment Kalor is defeated."

His eyes narrowed and his jaw locked. This was not a man who was accustomed to hearing no. He pressed his index finger against the table. "Marry him. *Today.*"

"I will not."

Queen Agnetha clucked her tongue, and Lady Hanna sucked in shocked breath. King Dagur pushed his chair back from the table and stood.

"Do not be a fool, girl! This is a sensible arrangement. We both know your father would agree."

"I am not my father, as you can clearly see." Aerity pushed back her own chair and stood tall. "Lochlanach is an ally of Ascomanni and will adhere to all promises. But I will *not* allow my hand to be forced in a time of despair." And shame on him for trying.

The coldlander king placed both of his fists on the table and scowled at her. "You will regret this."

"I am not your enemy," Aerity told him. "Please do not leave here angry."

King Dagur gave a growl, turning with a flourish. "Our

business here is done," he said to Lief's parents.

Queen Agnetha gave Aerity a disbelieving stare before following her husband. Aerity stood her ground, careful not to return any of their furious looks.

Next was Lady Hanna, who raised her chin. "You dishonor my son."

"I will honor him, my lady, in due time," Aerity promised. But Lief's mother humphed, leaving the room. Lord Daan Alvi took his time standing, his entire being like a keg of gunpowder, prepared to blow at any moment. His glare was deadly, making Aerity's heart hammer, but he never said a word. Just moved like he owned the place, shrugging his heavy furs over his expanded shoulders.

"See them out and leave us," Aerity said to her guards.

After the four Ascomannian royals left the dining room, followed by the clomp of guard boots, Aerity stared down at the table, feeling as if icy water had been poured over her head. She began to shake.

What had she done? Her actions had probably made an enemy of a viable ally. *What have I done?* She planted her palms against the tabletop and breathed. She felt Vixie rubbing her back but could hear nothing over the rush of thoughts pummeling her mind.

Fool.

Your pride just lost you this war.

You've killed the kingdom, and for what? Pure stubbornness? Concern for yourself?

Oh, seas! Aerity wanted to chase them, to fall at their feet and beg forgiveness, to tell her staff to ready High Hall for a wedding and do what she must to save her kingdom. Why had she made such a rash decision? She should have told King Dagur she needed time to discuss the matter with her council! She could have put them in comfy guest quarters, given them Lochlanach's finest wines, and loosened them up a little.

"I've ruined everything," she whispered to herself.

"Aerity." She blinked up into Vixie's pale face. Wyneth and Harrison were right beside her, looking aghast. She turned her head and saw Lief on her other side.

She whispered to him, "What have I done, Lief? That was awful!"

And to her utter surprise, Lief palmed her cheek and gently said. "No, Princess. *That* was incredible." And then he began to laugh.

Chapter 34

Had Lord Alvi lost his mind? Leif bent at the waist, holding his stomach, and laughed with all his might, one hand gripping the edge of her chair.

"It's hardly funny!" Aerity shouted.

Vixie let out a laugh of her own, but covered her mouth when Aerity leveled her with a frown.

"Never in all my years"—Lief stood, wiping tears from the corners of his eyes—"have I ever seen my uncle so irate."

"Yes, highly amusing," Aerity said without humor.

"Princess." Lief laid a heavy hand on her shoulder and looked her in the eyes. "He liked your father but never respected him. Not fully. And you may have just injured his pride, but, I assure you, you've also earned his respect."

Aerity felt the fury from earlier rise inside her at the

memory of King Dagur's attitude. "Well, a fat lot of good his respect will do as he watches from the coldlands while we're slaughtered by Kalor!"

"I hardly believe they'll allow it to go that far," Lief reasoned. "You may have angered him, but anger is temporary. His hatred for Kalor is long-standing."

Aerity looked at Wyneth's and Harrison's sober faces. They appeared as worried as she. After watching King Dagur storm off, there hardly seemed room for hope of his help.

"We in the coldlands are hotheaded," Lief said simply. "Don't expect an apology in words, Princess. His way of apologizing will be something more substantial."

"I cannot imagine receiving an apology of any sort after that," Aerity said. "I think you're assuming quite a lot. Are you not offended as they were? About my refusal to marry you today?"

He patted her shoulder. "Perhaps I'm just as uneager for marriage as you are, Princess." And with those loaded words and a wry look, he walked from the room.

Harrison ran a hand through his hair, then followed Lief. "I'm going to see that they're sent off with due respect."

Aerity nodded as he left. She was horrified that the king and queen of Ascomanni had come all that way only to turn around and leave after a single meal. No, she did not share a speck of Lief's positive outlook about making any sort of amends after that.

"I don't think I'm going to enjoy this whole being-queen thing," she said to Vixie and Wyneth.

"I could not have handled that the way you did," Vixie said. "I had to keep myself from shouting and cheering. I've never been prouder. You're doing a grand job!"

Aerity pressed the heels of her hands into her eyes. "Nay, Vix. This is the worst job ever. I feel as if every response is a wrong response. I cannot win."

Wyneth snorted. "I'm not going to lie. I fully expected you to give in. I'm still somewhat in shock."

Aerity collapsed into her father's chair. "I should have sought counsel before I responded."

"Perhaps," Wyneth said. She and Vixie sat on either side of her. "But there will be times, like today, when you need to make a decision from your gut. You heard what Lief said. He seems to think it was a good move to stand your ground."

Aerity let out a laugh and rubbed her eyes again. "I'm going to need cake today."

"I can make that happen," Vixie said. She stood, grabbed her skirts, and ran for the door.

"Bless her," Aerity whispered, as her thoughts returned to the looming threat they faced.

Days, King Dagur had said.

She shivered and wrapped her arms around herself. "I have to be stronger than this."

"Look at me," Wyneth commanded. Aerity opened her eyes and peered at Wyneth's stern face. "You are the strongest woman I know. I'm amazed by you. Today, yesterday, when you agreed to your father's proclamation. Vixie and I, neither one of us, could have done the things you've done."

"You could if you had to."

"No." Wyneth adamantly shook her head. "Not with the grace you have. You are a queen, Aerity. You were made for this, and I believe the seas have breathed their blessing over you. You may not feel strong inside, but I promise—to the people, to me—you are the very picture of might." Aerity swallowed. "But it's okay to show weakness with us. That's what we're here for. With me and Vix, you don't have to be perfect. You can curl up in a ball and cry and stuff your mouth with cake, and then, when it's time, we'll clean you up and you can face all Eurona with your head held high."

A small smile graced Aerity's lips. Despite everything, she felt lighter. "Thank you, Wyn." Aerity took a deep breath and stood. "I don't know what I'd ever do without you."

"Let's never find out."

Arm in arm they left the dining hall, ready to face the ensuing war together. When they got to the door, Harrison was jogging up the hall toward them, face grim. The princess and lady dropped their arms.

"What is it?" Aerity asked.

Harrison was nearly out of breath. "Our naval watch just returned from sea. There is activity in the Kalorian naval yards. They're preparing their fleet."

Aerity nodded, her heart pounding. "And our fleet?"

"Prepared. Stocked. Larger than theirs."

"Good," Aerity said, exhaling in a rush. "Now to prepare the castle." And eat cake.

Chapter 35

Paxton didn't know what he'd been expecting when they got to the border of Lochlanach. An army, perhaps? But there was nothing. The Kalorian troops had kept them a mile away from the coast on a very specific path, and they entered what seemed to be private Lochlan property. They converged on a large home and Paxton wondered whose it was. He wasn't familiar with the south or its dukes and landowners. Whoever owned this property seemed to be gone.

They began setting up camp on the property, erecting makeshift tents and building fires. The prince's carriage pulled up right in front of the stone house. Paxton watched as Prince Vito and Rozaria went straight inside with their handful of elite Kalorians as if they owned the place. He waited to see if any Lochlans were inside, but there wasn't a sound from within. It was all very strange.

Paxton set to taking care of his horse before washing up at the well with the other men. While some napped or lounged, playing cards, Paxton decided to explore the garden he'd spied earlier. The plot was overgrown and weedy, as if it hadn't been tended in a while. He stared down at the crops with his hands on his hips. The garden's fall vegetables were full-grown and had not been harvested.

He squatted and grasped the leaves of a carrot, tugging it back and forth until it came loose. Though the weather was colder than Kalor, the southern Lochlanach grounds weren't frozen, so the carrots were still in decent condition. He wiped it on his breeches and took a bite. Definitely edible. The sweet crunch sent a burst of homesickness through him. He grabbed a small shovel at the garden's entrance and began to dig.

Paxton relished the feel of Lochlan soil on his hands. He'd amassed a nice pile of differing root vegetables when he heard footsteps behind him and turned to see Rozaria with damp hair and a clean scarlet dress. She gave him a half smile.

"An all-around provider, aren't you?"

Paxton stood and brushed his hands together.

"We'll put your wares to good use for the troops tonight." Rozaria glanced at the pile of food. "But I'm afraid it's time for you to prepare to leave." Her eyes gleamed as she took him in, and Paxton held his breath while she continued. "It's two days' ride to royal lands from here. That should put you there by sundown tomorrow. We will arrive in the early morning hours before sunrise the following day. Do you think you can have the castle ready for our entry by then?" He felt his pulse thump in his throat as he swallowed. They had two nights before Kalor would attack.

"Aye, Rozaria. I can make it happen."

She smiled seductively. "I know you can. From what I can recall during my time there, the castle has entrances in the front facing the sea, on the side facing the markets where the maids and staff do their business, and on the back of the castle at the garden." The thought of her on royal lands gave him chills. Paxton nodded along as she continued. "We think it will be easiest if you get rid of the guards at the back entrance. The gardens will keep us hidden."

"How many are you sending in?"

Rozaria chuckled. "All of them. The royal lands will be well protected. As we attack, the primary mission is to keep the Lochlan soldiers and navy busy so that we may get Prince Vito into the castle with his personal guards."

Paxton nodded. Forced a partial smile. "And what of the king and queen? Will you barter for them?"

The moment he said it, and her wicked smile spread, things seemed to slow down and fall into place. A sickening sense of understanding settled like sludge. Rozaria's head tilted. She peered up at him as if he were something adorable.

And then she gave that husky chuckle that tingled his scalp.

"Oh, no, no, no, hunter. We have no use for prisoners. Once Prince Vito is in . . . it is ours. No bartering necessary. And there is no question we will take the castle."

Do not react. "So they are dead?"

"As of this morning." His stomach roiled and bile rose, burning the back of his tongue. Rozaria reached up, and he forced himself not to flinch as she stroked his cheek. "The people in your lands who once oppressed you will now grovel at your feet. The Lashed will rise. You are free of your bigoted rulers now, Paxton Seabolt. Free in every way."

Nay. He was more burdened than ever before.

"I'll prepare my things straightaway."

Paxton was probably pushing his horse too hard, but he was desperate to get to the castle. The only thing that stopped him in the dead of night was the village of Fetchko in his path. He slowed when he saw several men gathered on the path, holding bows.

"I am Lochlan," Paxton called from a distance as he came closer.

They squinted at him in the lantern light. One bravely brandished a club while another hesitated and then raised his bow, pointing an arrow. Paxton realized he was wearing a Kalorian tunic and was fully armed. He held his hands up.

"I am Lochlan," he repeated. "Whose land is this?"

"Duke Gulfton's," one of the men answered. "If you're

Lochlan, why are you wearing *that*?"

"It's a long story," he said. "But you need to be warned. Kalorian troops are currently at the main estate in the south. They will advance on royal lands sometime tomorrow. Prepare your village." Their eyes widened in fear. Paxton pointed to the one who'd brandished his bow. "And when they arrive, raise your bow without hesitation."

Paxton didn't stop to answer the questions they shouted as he left. He took to the path again and hoped to the seas they would get their children out of the line of the Kalorians, and quickly.

In the light of the morning he crossed the Bay Bridge and took the path northeast to stop at the town of Dovedell before he reached royal lands. It took him out of the way, but it would give his horse a rest, and he couldn't live with himself if he didn't warn the people. He accepted offers of food and set back toward royal lands. He was nearly there. For hours his mind had been turning, working. He tried to devise plans to fight the forces that were headed their way, but the thought of Aerity anywhere near Prince Vito made him sick. Nay, the only thing he knew for certain was that he wanted to get her out of there before the Kalorians arrived. They would take what they wanted and kill anything in their way.

Paxton still couldn't believe King Charles and the queen were dead. He thought of Aerity, Vixie, and the lad Donubhan. Aerity was now queen and she had no idea. They would all be holding out hope that their parents would return. He hated that he would have to be the one to tell her. But better him than Prince Vito.

Paxton leaned forward and urged his horse due northwest. The sun was lowering. For the first time that day he realized how cold it had become. His ears and face were freezing in the wind, but he felt no pain. All he felt was determination.

Chapter 36

Vixie hated waiting while ominous dangers loomed on the horizon. She'd taken to practicing archery with a vengeance, and patrolling the royal wall alongside Tiern, her trusted bow across her back. Without her parents to order her inside, the guards let her out whenever she wanted. She could see the disapproval on their faces, though. They probably thought she should stay inside the castle like a proper girl. And while she loathed the idea of being that girl and the annoyances that came along with it, she did truly miss the protectiveness of her parents.

They rode beside the stone wall in the dry, yellowed grasses. The walls had been fortified since late summer, built thicker and higher. Now there were platforms along the length for soldiers to climb and defend. Each scaffold also had a strong pulley system to raise small cannons or vats of hot tar and oil. The sight of war preparations made Vixie uneasy. Danger was on its way.

"Tiern," Vixie said, "do you suppose my parents are still alive?" It's all she could think about lately.

Tiern's spine went rigid as he rode. "I don't rightly know, Vixie. I wouldn't put it past the Kalorians . . . but, then again, if they kept them alive, they could use them for bargaining."

"What could they possibly want to bargain for?"

He shook his head gravely. Vixie exhaled, her stomach churning.

She'd spent the past year fighting against everything they wanted her to be, searching for who she really was, being angry at her father for the great hunt. And now the thought of them gone forever left a gaping pit of desolation in her heart. She'd never imagined a life without them. She'd taken them for granted and never shown her appreciation.

Vixie glanced at Tiern, his face so serious as he scanned the area. They'd never spoken about the kiss. In fact, Vixie had put it from her mind. It hadn't been a proper kiss. She believed now that he'd only done it for the reason he said: to keep the lads at bay. With all that was happening, romance seemed ridiculous. Still, she enjoyed his company, and trusted him above all others.

"You should have seen Aerity and the coldlands king this morning," Vixie chattered. She told him everything. Tiern seemed to enjoy her stories as they trotted in the cold sunshine, reacting with all the appropriate shock, awe, humor, and upset that she hoped to convey. In fact, now that she'd stopped pressuring him about his feelings, he was almost his same old good-natured self with her again.

Yet, as they neared the southern gate to royal lands, Vixie heard raised voices. Her head spun to Tiern.

"Something's happening," he said. He pushed his horse ahead and Vixie followed. There was a crowd of soldiers and guards at the gates and several horses. They were surrounding someone.

"He's Lashed!" she heard a guard say, which was followed by more raised voices, shouted questions, gruff responses. She couldn't make it all out.

Through the moving bodies she spotted a long-haired man with a short beard and dirty face. His tunic was bright blue, Kalorian style.

"Pax?" Tiern whispered. Vixie's eyes shot to his and she saw Tiern staring, wide-eyed. And then he yelled, "That's my brother!" He leaped down from his horse and ran, pushing through the people. Vixie's heart went into her throat and she pressed a hand to it. This couldn't be Pax . . . they'd called this man Lashed.

When Tiern reached the man, he threw his arms around him and the two of them embraced, holding tightly. The brothers pulled apart and she could see Paxton's face.

"It's really him," Vixie breathed.

He's Lashed.

She rode slowly forward, forcing the guards and soldiers to part further. Her eyes were set on Paxton. Surely they had been mistaken. Or perhaps they spoke of someone else. Her eyes roamed the crowd but there were no others. Tiern and Paxton both turned to her.

"Princess Vixie," Paxton said, "I need to see your sister *at once.*"

Her eyes went to his fingernails and she felt as if she'd been blasted by the coldest of winds. She fought to breathe. She looked to Tiern and his eyes were pleading. Absolute confusion and fear became a hurricane between her ears. Lashed . . . Kalorian clothing . . . her parents' kidnappers.

With a shout, Vixie forced her horse to rear, causing all the men to back away, and then she turned and charged toward the castle.

She could hear herself whimpering. What was going on? Paxton was Lashed? Could he be trusted? He'd been in Kalor all this time and now here he was. Vixie rode to the front of the castle and dismounted, smacking Ruspin on the rump and then sprinting to the stone steps.

"Princess!" the guards called when they saw her. She ran past them, shouting when she got into the hall.

"Aerity! Where is she?"

"What's wrong?" the guards asked. She ignored them and ran to the king's office. More guards were outside it, a sure sign Aerity was within.

Vixie burst in, making Aerity jump to her feet, the blood draining from her face.

"Paxton is here!"

Harrison, Lief, Wyneth, and all the officers present jumped to their feet.

Aerity's mouth hung open. "Are they here? The Kalorians?"

"Nay." Vixie's voice shook. "It's just him. But he's—" She stopped and stared around at the faces watching her. "He's . . ." Should she tell them all? What if they hurt him?

Aerity's face smoothed. "I know what he is. Where is he, Vix?"

"You *know*?" Vixie stared at her sister, who seemed inexplicably calm. "But, Aer, he looks like one of them!"

Aerity faced the officers, speaking quickly. "The hunter Paxton Seabolt is Lashed. He is one of us but was able to infiltrate Rozaria's army. He must have been able to escape. He'll have information. Have him brought to me at once."

The men rushed from the room, including Harrison and Lief.

Vixie stared at her sister. Aerity's face paled.

"I'm sorry." She tried to step forward and touch Vixie's arms, but the younger princess yanked them away. "Seas, I don't even know what day it is half the time anymore, Vix. I can't remember who knows what—"

"You don't tell me *anything*!" Vixie shouted. Anger rose in her like a demon of the deep sea, and she let it loose. All the times she'd been kept in the dark and left out, all the unfair treatment and secrets. Vixie screamed in frustration, squeezing her hands into fists. She was throwing a veritable tantrum and she could not stop herself.

"Vix!" Wyneth said in shock, but Vixie ignored her, staring down Aerity.

"Stop treating me like a child! Stop trying to protect me, and keeping me ignorant about every last thing! I'm sick of it!"

"All right," Aerity said. And truly, she did appear remorseful. "I'm so sorry. I should have told you everything—you're right."

Vixie's chin trembled as the fire went out of her, and her shoulders hunched. Aerity came around the desk and wrapped her arms around her.

"Please forgive me," she murmured into her hair. "No more secrets, I promise."

Vixie sniffed hard against her sister's shoulder. "Aerity?"

"Aye?" she pulled back to look at her.

"Paxton looked . . . bad. What I mean is, he seemed . . . like one of them or something. He frightened me. And his eyes were a bit crazed."

Aerity took her face in her hands. "I'm certain he did, but you needn't be afraid of Paxton. I can promise you, his loyalties are to us."

"Is Tiern . . . ?"

"Nay. He is not Lashed." Vixie breathed a sigh of relief . . .

and then questioned herself. Would she really have cared if he had been Lashed? Nay, she did not believe so. But if he *had* been and he'd kept it from her, that would have upset her grievously.

Aerity went to the desk and grabbed her cloak that had been thrown over the chair. She slung it over her shoulders and rushed from the room. Wyneth gave Vixie's shoulder a squeeze before following Aerity. Vixie stood there alone, recalling the look in Tiern's eyes and how she had left them in fear. No wonder Tiern could not tell her. She'd reacted shamefully. Guilt clutched her. She wouldn't blame him if he wanted nothing to do with her now.

Chapter 37

Aerity didn't dare leave the safety of the castle. She waited inside the entrance hall with Wyneth by her side, her heart dancing with anticipation, which parried with worry. If Paxton was here, she knew they must be one step closer to something happening. From one of the tower entrances she saw Mrs. Rathbrook peek out, her guard behind her. Aerity waved her over.

"Please, join us." The Lashed woman and her guard came to her side.

"What is happening?" Mrs. Rathbrook asked.

"I'm not certain, but you can remain with me. I want you kept safe."

A rush of sound filtered down the hall as the doors opened

and bodies poured in. The doors were tightly closed again and barred. Through the group of men she saw Paxton's unruly brown waves and she couldn't contain herself. She ran to him and grasped his hands tightly, locking her eyes onto his brown ones.

"You're okay," she whispered. He looked frightfully weary. "How much time do we have?"

"They'll be here in the early morning hours," he said. "Possibly before sunup."

She looked at Harrison and motioned with her head back down the hall toward where the office was. They lived in that room these days. She caught Lief's eyes over her shoulder. The man had seemed to go into warrior mode with the impending battle.

Vixie ran up alongside them with a worried expression and asked, "Where is Tiern?"

Paxton answered. "He went out with a few soldiers to warn as many villages as possible."

Vixie's entire being seemed to droop. "Paxton, I'm sorry for my reaction—"

"Nay, Princess, you needn't be," he said in a low voice. "You were taken by surprise."

She nodded before slowing and becoming lost in the crowd. Aerity peered back and saw her in the back of the group walking with Mrs. Rathbrook.

"I should have told her," Aerity said to Paxton. "She was so hurt."

"What's done is done," he told her. "She's a fighter. Tiern's worried that she's angry with him, so I urged him to go with the others to clear his mind."

Oh, dear. They didn't need this on top of everything else.

They hurried into the office. Vixie was the last one in, holding Mrs. Rathbrook's hand. She closed the door and maneuvered to Aerity's side, and then all eyes went to Paxton. Nobody bothered to sit. He didn't wait for an invitation to speak.

"I'm going to start with the worst news first so that you can understand what we're dealing with." He took a deep breath and peered at Aerity. The sadness in his eyes nearly made her collapse because she knew. She *knew* what he was going to say. Every muscle in her body braced.

"The king and queen are dead," he said softly to her and Vixie. "I'm very sorry."

Even with every muscle tensed, Aerity still felt as if she'd been kicked in the chest.

She was queen of Lochlanach.

She swallowed and tried to wet her lips. At her side she heard Vixie's deep inhale of breath. She grasped her sister's hand, and Vixie pressed her face into Aerity's shoulder. Aerity knew her sister was doing her best to be strong. She stroked Vixie's hair. There were no words. She could not believe this was their reality. Her parents murdered. How had it come to this? They were dealing with the worst kind of people.

Next to Vixie, Wyneth had covered her mouth, her eyes

wet. Harrison placed a hand on her back, his face grave.

Paxton hurried on. He gave approximate numbers of horses, carriages, and men, both Lashed and Unlashed, on land and sea.

"And by far the most dangerous are Prince Vito and Rozaria Rocato. Both are Lashed and ruthless. And cousins."

"The prince is Lashed?" Lord Alvi exclaimed at the same time Aerity said, "Cousins?"

Fear whipped through Aerity when Paxton nodded. She shouldn't be surprised by anything at this point.

"What are his weaknesses?" Lief asked.

"Beauty. Vanity." Paxton's jaw clenched. "His plan is to unite Lochlanach and Kalor by marrying you, Princess."

Aerity felt a spasm of disgust.

Lord Alvi laughed without an ounce of humor. "Seems you're a hot commodity to neighboring kingdoms, Aerity. He'll need to queue up."

"Lucky me," she gritted.

"How did you escape them?" Harrison asked Paxton.

"I didn't. They sent me ahead to make a way into the castle for them. I'm to kill the guards at the east entrance so the prince and his elite can enter the castle through the gardens in the morning hours."

Aerity looked to Harrison. "Can we spare soldiers to stop the Kalorians at Bay Bridge?"

He grimaced. "Not enough to make it an even match while still protecting the castle. They'd be better used here on royal lands."

"This will be a war of defense, not offense," Lief muttered. From his voice it was clear he preferred to be on the offensive.

They stared around the room in disquiet, all minds calculating possible courses of action.

"Of course we'll keep them locked out, right?" Vixie asked.

"There are the underground tunnels," Wyneth pointed out. "If they manage to get in, we can have soldiers waiting below until Prince Vito and his men believe they have overtaken the castle. Then when they get good and comfy, we come out to attack."

Lief rubbed his jaw. "I like that."

"I do as well," Harrison said.

"The royal lasses should be taken to safety away from the castle," Paxton said, looking from Aerity to Vixie to Wyneth.

Oh, no. Aerity pressed her lips together. A definite sense of conviction kept her rooted to the castle.

"I don't want to leave," Vixie said.

"You're next in line for the throne after Aerity," Paxton explained. "It's important to keep you safe." Vixie dropped her eyes.

"I will stay," Aerity said. All eyes went to her, and she wondered if she was being foolish and impulsive again. She couldn't explain the sense of wrongness that filled her at the thought of leaving, as if the seas were against it.

Paxton shut his eyes. "What do you think you can do here? The kingdom needs you to be safe. You are the *queen* now, Aerity."

Her heart jumped and Vixie squeezed her hand. Aerity looked around the room at the fierce but neutral faces. She knew they would support her to their deaths, but none of them would decide this for her.

"Your Majesty," Harrison said, "if your father were here, we would advise him to leave as well. Royals are usually taken to safety and not meant to be at the front line."

"I need a moment to myself," she said.

One by one, people filtered from the room. Vixie's soft hand disappeared from her grasp. Aerity leaned back against the desk, her hands covering her face. What would she do? The idea of leaving the castle and that madman getting in . . . it was the worst feeling of violation. Even if she left temporarily, she felt as if being gone meant giving up, handing it over to the enemy. She *had* to be there.

Aerity sensed warmth in front of her. Breath on her hands. She lowered them from her face. Paxton's hands were on his hips.

"Don't keep me out, Aer. Tell me what you're thinking."

She paused, knowing he would not like her line of thought. "You said he wants to marry me. . . ."

She could sense Paxton's pulse rapid firing by the intensity of his set jaw. "Which is exactly why you should be kept away from him. The man is lethal and narcissistic."

"Perhaps you're not the only one who can play both sides."

"Aerity." He stepped closer. "This is not like when you faced the beast and I stood by and allowed it. I had hope in that moment. When it comes to Prince Vito, there is no hope. He is the worst kind of monster. *He. Cannot. Be. Charmed.*"

Aerity sucked in a shaking breath as Paxton released her and began to pace. She gripped the edge of the desk behind her. What was she to do? Flee and hope for the best?

"I need to think," she said softly.

He came to her and lifted her chin. Their eyes met and heat filled her.

"Promise you'll consider what I've said."

"I will."

He kissed her forehead and left her with her jumbled thoughts. Aerity went around the desk and sat down in her father's grand chair. She placed her elbows on the desk and her face in her hands.

Her father. He would never sit on this cushion again. He would never decide the fate of the lands. He would never again look to his loyal wife for her support. And her mother would never be there, filling the room with her calming strength.

Aerity wanted to cry, but the tears did not come. She knew if she broke down now she might not recover. There was no room in her life for weakness. She breathed deeply, trying to clear her mind and think straight.

Everything within her fought to stay in her rightful home, but the people she trusted were telling her to go. To protect herself. To let them clear the enemy from their midst so she might return and rule. And she knew that if she stayed,

Vixie and Wyneth would stay as well. Their lives were her responsibility.

A quiet knock came just before the door opened. Aerity lowered her hands and saw Duke Gulfton, his watery eyes peering through the barely opened door.

"Come in, good sir," she said.

He did, and as the door opened she noticed an empty hall.

"Where have my guards gone?"

He closed the door behind him. "There was smoke in the kitchen and a disturbance at the servant's entrance."

Aerity stood in a rush, but Duke Gulfton held a hand out as he walked to the desk.

"Everyone is on edge. Most likely burned bread and a fight between messenger boys. It is fine." He leaned both hands against his staff. The man appeared heavily burdened, his eyes sagging and dark circled, his back more hunched than ever.

"I thought you had returned to your land," Aerity said.

The duke nodded. "I did, briefly, but I am back. It does not feel safe there. As you know, my property neighbors the Kalorian border."

"Of course." Aerity shook her head. How had she not thought of that? Her father would have insisted the duke and his family stay in the castle or in a northern property.

"I hope your family has fled to safety," Aerity said.

His face drooped, and it took him a moment to respond. "What will you do now, Your Majesty?"

Aerity swallowed. "Though it goes against my every instinct, I think I must leave until the war is over. Not to the Isle of Evie, though. Some place different. Do you have a suggestion?"

She expected him to be relieved by her choice, but he continued to look frightfully downtrodden. His voice was dry and raspy, and he appeared to fight for strength to speak.

"Your Majesty. There are certain things your father meant to tell you when it was time for you to reign someday. Secrets of the castle. I'm sure he thought he had more time. . . ."

"Like the underground tunnels?" she asked.

He nodded. "Aye. And a vault of safety here in this very office."

"Indeed?" Aerity perked with interest as the man began to shuffle toward the bookshelves along the wall behind the desk.

His hands shook with tremors as he grasped the top of three books and pulled them down with a creak—the books appeared to be stuck together, and moved like a lever—then he pushed with a weak grunt. Aerity moved forward to help him. She expected to see a dusty cavern but what she found was a simple elongated space that was extraordinarily clean.

"Why did he never tell me?"

"Children tend to think of secret passageways as playthings, but they are old and dangerous."

Aye. He likely hadn't wanted word to trickle down to Donubhan.

The room appeared to have supplies in the far corner. She

walked to the corner and bent to examine the jugs of water and bag of food. All this time the room was here, ready in wait to keep her family safe. If only they could have used it. A shuffle and click sounded from behind her, and Aerity was suddenly immersed in pitch-darkness. She sucked in a breath and yelled.

"Duke Gulfton?" Aerity's heart pumped hard as she felt along the wall. There had to be a handle of some sort. "Duke! The door has closed!" She pounded with her fist and pressed her ear to the wood. "Hello? Open the door!"

The man was old and weak, and had moments where his mind seemed absent, but he had to know the door had closed with her inside. Surely if he didn't have the strength to open it again himself he would get help, right? Aerity pressed her palms against the door. She felt disoriented in the dark as if she might suffocate. Her heart, her breathing, were both ragged with panic. Again she pounded and smacked at the door, kicking it until her toes throbbed.

Seas . . . the vault walls were too thick for her to be heard.

Aerity pressed a hand against her chest, trying to calm herself. Why was this happening? Had Duke Gulfton gone mad? Did he think he was protecting her? But she'd told him she was going to leave. Why would he do this?

Her stomach suddenly turned and Aerity slid to her knees, overcome with nausea. The duke . . . was he the traitor? She shook her head, whispering, "No. No. It can't be." He was the wisest in the council. The most trustworthy. Why would he do such a thing?

Paxton would come. Vixie. Wyneth. Harrison. But they didn't know about the vault. Surely someone in the castle would know. The military? The guards? Someone had to know! Aerity crawled forward to the door. She started feeling from the bottom, slowly running her hands over the door, taking her time to feel every single inch. Her fingernails dug along the crevices where the door sealed itself.

There was nothing. Why would they make a vault where the inhabitants could not get out? Aerity felt short of breath. Perhaps it wasn't for safety at at all. Perhaps it was a holding place for captives.

She quickly crawled to the corner and fumbled for the supplies, hoping they would have something, anything, that she could use. She found a wooden pail and pushed it aside. Then she grabbed the bag and fiddled with the strings to open it. Cloths. A blanket. A bag of something heavy. She tugged the strings and pushed her hand inside. Oats? Useless! She pushed the bag away.

Aerity crawled until she felt the door, and sat, leaning her head back against it. She listened hard but could hear nothing except her own ragged breaths echoing in the room. And suddenly this was the proper time for that breakdown she'd been holding back.

Chapter 38

The feeling of nervous anticipation never left Paxton as he bathed and shaved. His skin felt rough from his time in Kalor. He grabbed a clean tunic and brought it to his face. The scent was fresh and reminded him of home. Paxton strapped his daggers to his chest, then put the tunic over his head and shook out his damp hair, all the while wondering how his parents were faring.

Seeing Tiern had been like cool rain on his face after trudging through a desert. He'd missed his brother more than he'd let himself admit. He also wouldn't admit how much he wanted to pack up Aerity and the others and force them to leave. Paxton grasped the sides of the washbasin and leaned forward, closing his eyes.

Deep seas . . . let Aerity make the right decision. He wouldn't force her, but surely she would see reason. In a matter of hours, five or six at the most, they would be under attack. The time for her to leave was now. Paxton readied his bow and quiver and set out to find his princess.

The halls were busy with staff and guards rushing around, preparing the castle. Tensions were high. Everyone was fully armed. Even maids had bows and quivers across their backs and belts with blades. He was glad to see it.

When he came to the king's office a single guard was outside.

"I need to speak with her," Paxton said to him.

The guard shook his head. "She's not inside."

"Do you know where she is?"

"No, sir."

Paxton went to Aerity's chambers first. The guard at her hall said she wasn't there either, but Paxton passed him and knocked at her bedroom door anyway. No answer. It was evening now, but he didn't expect her to be sleeping. He doubted anyone in the castle would sleep that night.

He went next to High Hall, then the dining rooms, which were all empty. Where was she? A flicker of worry began to spark. Paxton saw her maid rush past with a stack of towels.

"Have you seen Prin— er, Queen Aerity?" he asked her. The girl's eyebrows furrowed.

"Nay, Mister Seabolt. Have you checked the office?"

"Aye." He left her and jogged down to the far halls. He

looked in the library, then in the archery room. Wyneth, Harrison, and Lief were all there with a handful of staff members, feverishly practicing. Furball sat on a mat in the corner. They all turned to Paxton.

"Have any of you seen Aerity?"

They looked around at one another and shook their heads.

"I've looked nearly everywhere," he said.

"I know that Vixie was going to the kitchens," Wyneth said. "Perhaps there? I'll look too."

They joined him, with the beast on their heels. They jogged through the castle, calling her name, asking every guard and soldier they passed, telling everyone they saw to search. He went to the tower where Mrs. Rathbrook had returned, but Aerity wasn't there.

Paxton was unnerved by the time they reached the kitchens. Only one man was in there, a robust baker with a red face, pulling trays of bread from the oven as if winning the war depended on feeding the masses.

"There's Vix!" Wyneth pointed to the far corner, where Vixie sat at a table, absently dabbing at half a coconut cake with the tines of a fork.

"Have you seen Aer?" Wyneth called.

Vixie shook her head and slid off the stool, coming to them. "You can't find her?"

"We've searched the castle," Paxton said.

Vixie pushed past them all and ran into the hall. They sprinted to the doors at the back of the castle where the gardens were. Paxton's stomach turned. These were the doors he was to keep unguarded and unlocked for Prince Vito. As Wyneth, Harrison, and Vixie ran, Paxton saw an old man sitting alone on the corner bench in the hall.

"Duke Gulfton," Vixie called. The man slowly lifted his head. Paxton and Lord Alvi went to him as the girls jogged to the doors.

"Have you seen Queen Aerity?" Lief asked.

The duke's eyes wandered aimlessly to the doors where Vixie and Wyneth screamed for Aerity outside. "They are coming. . . ."

"Yes, we know," Lief said impatiently. "We need to know if you have seen the eldest Lochson girl, the Queen." Vixie and the others came back inside, shaking their heads. They all looked at the duke.

"I daresay we have all seen the last of Aerity. Seas forgive—"

Paxton grasped the man by his velvet robes and heaved him up until they were face-to-face, and shook him. "What do you mean by that?"

The man moaned helplessly, his eyes fluttering shut.

"Pax!" Wyneth grabbed his shoulder. "He's mad. He doesn't know what he says."

Paxton dropped the man back to the bench, flexing his trembling hands into fists.

"Great oceans deep and wide," the old man murmured. And then he dropped his head and began to heave great sobs.

Vixie looked at the nearest guard. "He should probably be brought into the tunnels to be kept safe. He needs to lie down." The guard nodded and bent to put a hand under the man's arm, but Duke Gulfton suddenly seemed to come to his senses and pushed the man away.

"Leave me be! I'm staying right here until it's time."

Vixie gave the guard an exasperated look. "Leave him, then."

Paxton began to pace an angry line back and forth across the hall. "Something has happened. She wouldn't run off without telling any of us. How is it that not a single person in the castle has seen or heard anything?" He raised his hands and shouted, "*Where is she?*"

Harrison and Lief both nodded. "I'm going to alert the military in case she left the castle so they can keep an eye out on the grounds."

Paxton eyed Wyneth and Vixie, who clutched each other's hands. "I think it's time for both of you to go into the tunnels until we find Aerity. If there is a threat in these walls, you'll be safer there."

"But—" Vixie began as Paxton cut her off.

"Please, Princess. *Please* do not argue."

She pursed her lips tightly, but something in the sincerity of his voice seemed to deflate her. "All right. Fine."

"I'll take you," Harrison said.

Wyneth, Vixie, and a lumbering Furball followed Harrison, and Paxton looked at Lief.

"We need to decide a strategy while we search for Aerity,"

the coldlands man said. Paxton nodded and began walking. "I say we clear the castle of staff, send them north so they're out of the way, and then we fill the castle with as many soldiers as can be spared. Rooftop, balcony, windows, and parapet lined with archers."

"Aye," Paxton said, but he couldn't stop thinking about Aerity, still in disbelief that he couldn't find her. He led them back to the office where that same guard stood. "This is the last place I saw her," Paxton said. "I'd like to have a look."

The guard moved aside with a wave of his arm. Paxton and Lief went into the silent office. An eerie sort of presence filled the room, perhaps an ancient power of some sort. It was strange to be in the room where kings of Lochlanach had held countless meetings and made centuries of the kingdom's decisions. Paxton looked under the desk and opened the largest cabinet doors. He shook his head. *Where are you, Aer?*

A light series of *bangs* sounded and Paxton stilled to listen. "Did you hear that?" he whispered. It sounded close, but faint. Perhaps knocking from somewhere else within the castle? Lief stopped and inclined his head toward the wall to listen.

BANG.

Outside the window the night lit up in a display of bright orange.

"Great skies!" Lief ran to the window with Paxton just behind him. The naval yard was under attack. Another boom sounded, this time farther away, in the opposite direction, perhaps at the royal gate?

"They're early," Paxton said in disbelief. He'd been duped.

They must have left mere hours after him. He gritted his teeth in anger. And where the curses was Aerity?

The two men ran from the room as a closer boom shook the floor, rattling the windows. Screams rang out inside the castle now.

"Get below!" Paxton shouted to terrified staff members who ran into the halls. "Take your weapons!" He stopped and faced Lief. "Listen. They think I'm one of them. I can stay. But there's no time to get the military inside the castle. The people in the tunnels are going to need a strong leader, someone who is ready to strike when the time is right."

Lief narrowed his eyes and leaned into Paxton's face. "If this is a trick, you will be the first one I kill."

It bothered Paxton to the very center of his being that this man didn't trust him after all they'd been through. Paxton held up his palms within striking distance. Lief leaned away, eyeing his hands.

"If I were a traitor, you would have been the first one I would have killed by now." Paxton dropped his hands. "All I want is to keep Aerity safe and to defeat the Kalorian army. I was sickened by what I saw while I was with them. You have *no* idea."

Lief's jaw rocked from side to side. "Can you truly say you will be fine with letting Aerity go when we defeat them? That you will not stand in the way of our union?"

Paxton huffed hot air from his nose, livid at the thought. "Nay. I will *not* be fine with letting her go, but neither will I stand in the way of her responsibilities to the kingdom."

The floor shook beneath them again. Harrison came sprinting up the hall.

"Any word on Aerity?" Paxton shouted.

Harrison shook his head, panting. "Nay. I've no bloody clue where she's gone! Their fleet is upon us, every sea vessel fights. I think our navy can overcome theirs, but the land battle is a different matter. The royal wall has been damaged and the gates compromised. We thought we had more time. We weren't in place yet. Soldiers are running amok with no direction!"

Curses! Paxton grabbed Harrison's shoulder. "Tell your men to be on the lookout at the garden entrance. And then gather as many soldiers as you can spare and go below into the tunnels with the staff. Be sure to get Mrs. Rathbrook. If the prince's men overtake the castle, I can get exact counts of how many we'll be up against within the castle walls. I will alert you when the time is right to come aboveground and strike."

"When they least expect it," Harrison said, nodding. "Perhaps when they're celebrating."

"Exactly," Paxton agreed. "Be patient."

"I will," Harrison said.

They both looked at Lord Alvi's frowning face. The man let out a low growl.

"So be it. We go below." Lief stalked away, and Paxton shook his head at Harrison.

"I cannot deal with his hostility. And where in the bloody seas is Aerity?"

Harrison's face was tight. "Don't worry about Alvi. But as for Aerity . . ." He shook his head. "She had to have been taken. There's been a traitor in the castle for some time now. It has to be one of the guards or soldiers. My men and I are all eyes and ears. I pray to the seas she's safe."

"It makes no sense. Prince Vito wanted Aerity to be here. Why would he have her stolen away?"

The ground rattled and the men met eyes.

"They're getting closer," Harrison said. "I've got to go."

They grasped hands.

"Seas be with you, Paxton."

"And you, as well."

Paxton moved quickly toward the back entrance overlooking the gardens. To his astonishment and dread, the end of the hall was filled with smoke. When he got closer he could make out six Lochlan guards strewn across the stone floor, and the heavy scent of gunpowder. He covered his mouth and squinted to find the doors wide open and Duke Gulfton sitting in the same exact spot as he'd left him. He had to have seen the whole thing.

"What happened?" Paxton shouted.

"Smoke bomb," the man said. "He'll be safe now. I'll have him back."

Paxton stared at the gnarled metal device on the ground by the old man's feet, still smoking, and the unmoving bodies of the guards.

"Who is safe?" Paxton asked.

The man smiled wistfully. "My grandson."

What the seas? He was *mad.* "Who set this bomb?" Paxton squatted and looked for wounds on the men, but there were none. Had the smoke made them faint? But it hadn't hurt the duke. He felt for a pulse on a guard, but there was none. Seas . . . he had to get the doors closed. His scalp tingled as he slowly looked toward the doors and saw the back of a castle maid standing in the opening, her hair long and dark brown. She slowly turned and met Paxton's eye. The scar on her pale face gleamed in the moonlight.

Paxton's stomach sank. His heart went erratic. Soldiers in bright colors rushed up the steps, led by Martone, who motioned that Paxton was an ally. He moved to the doors, still wondering if he could close and lock them, but it was no use. Kalorians were rushing to the steps. Nicola stared past the gardens, where the prince's carriage barreled down the path surrounded by Kalorians shooting arrows and holding up shields.

They had made it. As the horses and carriage went straight through a set of low bushes, the army surrounding them fanned out to protect the prince. Someone opened the carriage door and soldiers ushered him and Rozaria out, forming a wall of protection around them as they rushed up the garden path to the steps and up to the door.

Paxton stood at the top, schooling his face to hide his shock. Rozaria handed Nicola a cloak and chuckled. "The clothing of Lochlan maids does not suit you, dear."

The girl took the cloak and put it on, pulling the hood up over her head. The three of them hurried inside with about twenty more guards, and they shut the doors behind them. Prince Vito was all smiles as he surveyed the bodies and stepped over them. The Kalorian guards stared down the empty hall, holding spears. Paxton noticed, appalled, that Vito wore the king of Lochlanach's crown.

"They're all gone," Paxton told them. "Everyone fled or joined the fight outside the castle."

"Everyone?" Rozaria asked.

Paxton nodded. "I'm fairly certain. I'm sorry I don't have more information. Things turned to chaos."

"Don't worry," Rozaria told him. "Everything is under control."

Paxton's hopes sank as his anxiety rose. He wanted to ask questions, to find out if they had Aerity, but he knew those kinds of questions would raise suspicion.

Prince Vito waved a hand and half the guards ran down the wide hallway, most likely to survey and open the other castle entrances for more of their people to come in. The prince held out his arms at the expansive hallway.

"Home! And where is my welcoming committee? The place could use some redecorating. All in due time, I suppose." The prince began walking, studying the paintings on the walls, and the remaining guards circled him.

Paxton felt a hand on his arm and jumped. Rozaria laughed up at him.

"No need to fear. You have done well."

"You were earlier than I expected. I nearly didn't make it to the doors." He was having a hard time reining in his anger, but she didn't seem to mind.

Rozaria shrugged. "The prince was eager. And we had another man on the inside, just in case."

"Just in case?" Paxton asked. They hadn't trusted him.

"The prince trusts no one but me. You were the backup. In case the other man couldn't do what was necessary."

"My grandson," mumbled Duke Gulfton from the bench. He was looking straight at Rozaria. Paxton was about to tell the man to quiet down, for his own protection, but to his shock Rozaria replied to him.

"All in good time." She stared at him.

"Wait." Paxton looked back and forth. "That bag of bones is the other inside man?"

Rozaria smiled. "He has been most helpful these months."

Paxton tried to process it. There was no way this old man could have overpowered Aerity. It had to be someone else.

"Listen," he said to Rozaria. "Aerity Lochson isn't here. I took my eyes off her for twenty minutes and she disappeared. I lost sight of the younger princess and lady in all the madness as well, but I assume they were ushered away."

Again, she gave him a knowing, wicked smile. "Duke," she crooned to the old man, "be so kind as to lead us to the king's office."

The man pushed to his feet and shuffled down the hall.

Paxton's heart had not slowed one bit. He peered at Nicola, who trailed behind them. He did not like having her at his back.

"I can show you the way." He moved impatiently past Duke Gulfton and the prince and his men. Why were they going to the office? He just wanted to find out where Aerity was. If they hurt her, or worse, he would kill every last one of them with his bare hands.

Paxton gritted his teeth as he reached the office door. It felt wrong, so wrong, leading them into the Lochlanach royal room. He pushed open the door with reluctance. They all looked around, touching things, making unimpressed remarks. Paxton moved against the wall near the door and stood with his feet apart, hands clasped in front of himself, and watched. Waiting. His quick-moving blood made his skin feel like it might ignite at any moment.

The prince looked to a tall Kalorian dressed in impeccable silks and gave him an order in Kalorian. Paxton held his breath as the man looked at Duke Gulfton and asked, "Where is she?"

"My grandson, first," said the duke.

"Of course. He awaits you, as promised. Give us the young queen."

To Paxton's utter horror, the old man walked behind the desk and pulled down several books, pushing the bookshelf inward with much effort. Paxton nearly flew across the room when he saw Aerity on the floor within. She brought a hand up to shield her eyes, squinting.

She was alive! He crushed his teeth together to keep from yelling her name. So help him, if anyone tried to hurt her . . .

"My grandson! I've done everything you asked." The old man's voice shook. "I've given you my whole kingdom. Now give me my grandson!"

"Of course, papa," said the Kalorian royal. "He awaits you this very day. It is time for you to join him."

"Aye," the duke said in a joyful whisper. He stared up at the man, who patted his sunken cheek once, twice, and then settled his hand on the duke's face until his blissful look fell away, and he collapsed on the floor in a pile of robes.

Chapter 39

Aerity screamed as Duke Gulfton crumpled, and then clapped a hand over her mouth when all eyes turned to her. Her vision was still adjusting. She scrambled to push to her feet and stand, staring back at all of them, so many Kalorians. Her eyes landed on the man with the most ornate robes and bands of gold around his neck, and then her eyes went up to the crown on his head—her *father's* crown—and she fought for composure.

In a quick, calculated moment, she recalled what Paxton had told her about the Kalorian ruler, and she made a decision. The only way to beat them would be to join them. Or to pretend. She begged the seas to make her act believable.

She cocked her head at the prince and wet her lips.

"Is that you, Prince Vito?"

At the sound of his name a smile played on his face. "You remember me?"

"Of course. You were the most handsome lad at that dreadful ball." She'd been nine at the time, and he thirteen. She had never met such a sour, spoiled, unpleasant lad in her life.

His eyes narrowed as if suspecting deception, and then he chuckled. "I always did hate forced entertainment." He steadied his crown, making a show of it.

Aerity stepped slowly forward until she was in the bookshelf doorway.

"Don't come any closer," warned Rozaria. Then she narrowed her eyes and studied her. "You look . . . different."

Oh, no. Would Rozaria recognize her as the woman who'd escaped from the camp? That would put Paxton in jeopardy. Aerity raised her palms and looked into the woman's eyes. "Perhaps it's because I'm unarmed this time."

Rozaria sneered. "Exactly why you should hold your tongue."

Again the prince laughed. "You injured my cousin and killed her finest creation. Her wrath was quite a spectacle."

Rozaria crossed her arms and glared at Prince Vito.

"Cousin?" Aerity said with interest. "She left that part out when she spoke so fondly of you that day."

Rozaria uncrossed her arms and moved forward. The prince grabbed her arm in a graceful reach, but that didn't stop the woman from unleashing a tirade at Aerity.

"Do not stand here and pretend to be a friend of Kalor! I recall everything you said that day."

"I was angry," Aerity said with just as much passion. "You were the cause of upheaval in my life. Because of your creation my father was giving me away like some disposable item."

"You poor darling," Rozaria spat. "You were to be forced to marry a coldlands brute, and meanwhile Lashed were being slaughtered by your ignorant townsmen."

"I did not want that to happen! I tried to get my father to see reason, but he refused. Did your precious insider tell you that?" She pointed at Duke Gulfton's body and swallowed hard. Then she looked straight at Prince Vito, preparing to tell a lie that sent pain throbbing through her. "You did me a favor by removing my parents from the throne. I have done more good for Lashed in mere days than has been done in a century. I have lifted the magical restriction laws—"

"Not everywhere!" Rozaria rebutted. "We saw your proclamation."

Aerity shook her head emphatically. "It was a start, and it was just as much for the protection of the Lashed as anything else. Look, Rozaria, I don't agree with your methods. I made that clear when we met. But I do have the same vision as you: for Lashed and Unlashed to live in peaceful equality. Surely there is a compromise."

The prince placed a hand on Rozaria's shoulder and pulled her back, stepping forward. Aerity's heart rate picked up as he came nearer. He stared, taking in her hair and clothing, the shape of her. And before his eyes even made it back up to hers he said, "I'm not certain you have the same vision as we, dearest."

Aerity tried to control her breathing and not move. He finally met her eyes again, and she wanted to rock back on her heels from the feeling of revulsion.

"You see, Your Majesty, I want to rule Eurona. All of it."

Oceans deep . . . She braced herself, remembering what Paxton had told her of the prince's plans. "I assumed as much."

Again that creepy smile came to his smooth face. He raised a hand to move his hair behind his shoulder and Aerity saw his fingernails, as dark as if they'd been painted with blackberries.

"I will require someone by my side," he said. "Someone the people trust who can ease my transition into power."

There it was. Her heart had slowed to an eerily calm beat as she let herself slide into the role that it would take to overcome this foe.

"Am I to be that someone?" she asked.

Prince Vito studied her as he would a butterfly under a pin.

"Leave us," he said quietly to the room as he stared at Aerity.

Nervously she began to second-guess her acting skills. What would he want from her? Would he call her bluff and kill her? Or expect her to prove her affections right then in a more substantial way? She wanted to vomit at the thought.

"She's not to be trusted, Vito," Rozaria said. "She told me her father was a good man."

The prince and Aerity kept their eyes locked.

"It matters not," he murmured. "I said *leave us*."

As people began streaming out, Aerity glanced over the prince's shoulder and saw something that made her muscles seize. Paxton stood beside the door, staring with a wrathful intensity that frightened Aerity. He'd seen and heard it all.

Seas! He would ruin everything! As Rozaria got to Paxton she took his hand and glanced over her shoulder, sending a glare back at her. Aerity wanted to rip their hands apart, but mostly she needed Paxton to get hold of himself and trust her.

"You heard him," Aerity said in a voice weaker than she'd hoped for. "Leave us."

She was speaking more to Paxton than Rozaria. Thankfully Rozaria was so busy glaring at Aerity that she didn't notice the sheer look of fury on Paxton's face. Rozaria spun in a huff and pulled Paxton by the hand. He stood like a rooted tree until Rozaria looked up at him and tugged again. Then, to Aerity's relief, he stiffly allowed her to lead him out the door.

Within half a second, as her eyes met Prince Vito's, her relief morphed into unease. He stepped closer, far too close. Pretending to be interested in him was the very worst idea she had ever had. As he leered down at her, Aerity was willing to bet it was the worst idea anyone had ever had in the history of

Eurona. He stepped closer, and she accidentally stepped back. She fought for composure.

"You were pretty as a girl, but now . . ." He touched her hair, let it run through his fingers. Aerity made an involuntary sound that brought a grin to the prince's face. "I make you nervous."

Aerity felt her face heating, but not with the good kind of blush. She was scared senseless. Any wrong move from her and this man could reach out and kill her before she blinked. "I'm not accustomed to being alone with men," she said carefully. "Especially not powerful . . . handsome ones." *Do not gag.*

He moved forward until she was backed against the wall.

"You find me handsome?"

"More than handsome," she whispered. "Like no one in Lochlanach." She dropped her eyes to her hands. There was no possible way he'd buy this. But when she hesitantly raised her gaze to his, that heavy leer was still there, taking her in like a delicacy.

"You would be my queen? Willingly?" he asked in a voice like hot oil.

"If you would have me." Her voice quavered and she swallowed.

"You are an innocent. Only an innocent would be so nervous with a man she found handsome."

Oh, the abhorrence she felt. Aerity's eyes fluttered closed and she nodded. "It is the ultimate union, and I will hold to it until the day vows are made and blessed by the sea."

Prince Vito chuckled. "Superstitions."

Aerity forced a small smile. "Perhaps. But I hope you will allow me to hold to my beliefs."

"What of your betrothed from the coldlands? Will you miss him?"

Aerity's face tightened in an honest scowl. "I *never* wanted to marry that scoundrel."

Where was Lief? Had they all gotten to safety? *Please, let them be safe.* She didn't know if any of this would be worth it if so many of the people she loved were killed.

Based on the prince's pleased expression, it had been the right thing to say, but then he inclined his head toward her, almost as if smelling her. She was so afraid he would kiss her. So afraid she would freeze up or convulse at his touch.

She saw his hands come out from under his robes, watched them reach for her hands, and she was powerless to do anything except let him take them. Her entire body trembled out of control. As he took her hands, she let out a quiet laugh.

"I'm sorry that I'm nervous. I was going to reach out to you myself, to invite you here, to tell you of my plans for my rule as queen and the changes I'll be instating . . . but here you are."

"Here I am." He brought her hands to his chest and looked at her fingers. He ran his purple-nailed thumbs over the top of her pinkish ones. And finally he looked at her. And when he did, a line of pain ratcheted from her fingers, up her arms, shoulders, neck, and into her mind like the most severe headache she'd ever experienced. A scream caught in her throat like a thistle.

"I hope you understand that I've got to keep a close eye on you," he said, her head splitting. "And that your lies are not necessary. In truth, I prefer your fright. Such emotion is . . . real. . . . It fascinates me. So, tell me, does my new crown suit me?"

Aerity shook uncontrollably as she looked into the monster's eyes and spat, "No."

He laughed heartily and lowered her hands. The pain in her head immediately waned, and she sucked in air, no longer attempting to hide her feelings.

"Oh, my beauty. In honesty or lies, I will never trust you." He spoke in a soft tone that gave her chills. "You will remain in your chambers until we have secured the kingdom. I will send messages to you, when necessary. And if at any time you choose not to be loyal . . ."

Aerity stared hard.

He gave a slow smile. "You should also know that when I decide to make you my queen, it will happen immediately. I am not a man to be kept waiting." He trailed the back of a finger up her throat to her chin, then laughed low when Aerity shivered. "When I was ready for the Kalorian throne, I took it."

Curiosity fueled her. "B-because your father was too ill to rule?"

"Because the man called King Kalieno was never fit to rule. Nor was he my father."

Aerity's mouth popped open, and the prince seemed amused by her dismay.

"My mother, Kalieno's queen, was the sister of Rozaria's father—Rocato's blood heirs who no one in Eurona knew of. . . ." His voice was smug. "She was planted into a royal family with the purpose of marrying Kalieno. My father was another powerful Lashed One from a family who had been banished, but he was smuggled back into the kingdom. It was an elaborate plan, and it worked until a year after I was born, when my mother was caught with my father. Kalieno had them both executed."

Prince Vito was an imposter. Not of royal blood at all.

"He never knew you weren't his son?" Aerity whispered.

"Not until I visited him on his deathbed and explained what had been ailing him all along. Small touches from the man he thought was his son. Touches that closed the vessels to his heart over time. Touches with fingers whose nails were carefully painted each and every day."

"So, he's dead now too?"

"Very much so, though the people do not yet know. And this is what our countries need. Young rulers. Fresh ideas. Change. When I return I will be King and conqueror. Those who clung to their loyalty to Kalieno will have no choice but to bow to my power."

Aerity could not bring herself to respond to his self-satisfied admissions. He obviously thought this was all okay. And that she should be impressed by his cleverness.

"Now if you would be so kind," he murmured, "I wish for a tour of my new home and the king's chambers. I require rest."

She was glad to give him a tour, anything to get out of that office with him, but this castle was not, and never would be, his home. It was the place he would die.

Aerity would make sure of it.

Chapter 40

Paxton felt sickened as he stood in High Hall and watched Rozaria's army of Lashed tear the royal Lochlan tapestries from the wall and push them from open windows to be burned outside in the dark of night. His head throbbed and his stomach was on the verge of heaving. How long had it been since he had eaten or slept?

And what in the bloody deep seas was happening with Prince Vito and Aerity? His stomach rolled again, his hands clenching. Paxton had never killed a human being, but he would take pleasure in ending the prince's life. How could Aerity consider baiting a serpent like him?

In truth, he begrudgingly admitted that she'd handled him brilliantly, playing on his weaknesses of vanity and seduction, but they needed to overpower the Kalorians and Lashed rebels quickly before Prince Vito had a chance to officially make Aerity his queen. Paxton would not allow that to happen, even if it was him against a thousand.

Rozaria came to Paxton's side and watched the spectacle with a sparkle in her eyes. Then her mood seemed to darken.

"Your princess is up to something. I don't trust her. Vito has always been a fool for a pretty face."

Paxton crossed his arms. He wanted to remind her that Aerity was queen now, but held his tongue. "I can tell you it's true that she harbored anger toward her father, and that her views on Lashed were far more open than his. I don't think you need to worry about her. She would appease the Lochlan masses and keep them from revolt, and the prince could easily overrule her when needed."

Rozaria observed him skeptically. "Are you a fool for her pretty face as well?"

"I don't find her pretty," Paxton said matter-of-factly.

Rozaria's eyes softened, and she seemed appeased for the moment.

I find her absolutely gorgeous, he thought.

A crash sounded, followed by laughter, and Rozaria raised an arm in frustration. "You're not to break general valuables, only Lochlan artifacts!" She marched into the crowd and began shouting in Kalorian.

Paxton's eyes glazed as he thought. When they'd left the king's office, a swarm of Kalorian soldiers and Rozaria's

Lashed Ones had been let into the castle. From what Rozaria translated for him, the land takeover had been tragically fast. It seemed that the Lochlan navy had bested the Kalorian fleet, sinking every single one of their vessels, but the remaining Lochlan ships sailed north rather than returning to the royal port that was now overrun by the enemy.

Rozaria was still shouting orders to people as she made her way back to Paxton's side. "This hall is being cleared for our injured who need healing. They're bringing them in now."

"I'll help," Paxton told her.

He was glad of the distraction and the excuse to leave the castle. It was pitch-dark out, but fires had been lit around the castle, burning piles of Lochlan artifacts and trees that had caught fire during blasts. From afar Paxton could make out the naval quarters and army barracks, all burning brightly. Out in the port was a line of Kalorian cannons facing the sea, ready to strike any Lochlan ships that dared return. Battle-weary hotlands soldiers who'd escaped injury flooded into the gates of the west commons, where tents had already been erected. Shivering Kalorians passed him, carrying wounded men.

It didn't feel real to Paxton. In the darkness and cold with foreign words spoken all around him, it felt like a nightmare of confusion and wrongness. Paxton saw a soldier struggling to pull an injured man, and he ran over to take the feet and help carry him into the warmth of the castle. Once they got him in High Hall, Paxton set to healing the man himself.

Many of the men were missing limbs and died before they could be healed. To Paxton's disgust, those bodies were thrown from the windows into a heap. Aye, High Hall was becoming overcrowded, but he was appalled that anyone would treat their dead with such lack of respect.

Paxton's injured man had been burned on his shoulder and arm. He cried out and tried to move away when Paxton went to remove his tunic.

"Sh, I'm going to heal you. You'll feel better soon."

The man struggled, in pain, not understanding a word Paxton said. He worked quickly, holding the man down with a knee and pressing his free hand to the man's good shoulder while he worked with the other hand.

A blissful sensation of energy filled Paxton as fresh, new muscle and skin began to form over the man's arm. His head thrashed back and forth, but Paxton continued until all of the blackened spots were pushed outward and wiped away, showing only golden skin. The man lay panting, his face sweating. He slowly opened his eyes and dared a look at his arm. Then a disbelieving smile came to his face. He babbled in Kalorian and Paxton nodded.

"All better."

The hunger and exhaustion from earlier had disappeared under the influence of magic flowing through Paxton's body now. If he could keep healing people, perhaps he could continue to go without sleep for a while longer. He had no idea how he could get the forces underground to safety, and he needed time to think. He couldn't imagine that they'd been able to cram more than forty soldiers into the tunnel with all the staff. There was no possible way they could come above and fight the hundreds of Kalorians who still lived.

He needed to find a time when he could sneak to the basement past the cellars and pantry, where stores of wool, cotton, and feathers were kept to replenish bedding. It was said that the entrance was hidden beneath a rusted chest that had been bolted into the floor. He had to warn them and see about restocking their food and water. But they couldn't stay below forever. He'd have to find a way to get them out.

Paxton ran outside to find another person to heal. On his way back inside with a man draped over his shoulder, he was passed by soldiers carrying armfuls of wine cases up from the cellars. They spoke animatedly, laughing.

They were planning to celebrate.

Paxton brought the man into High Hall and lowered him to the floor, concentrating on his shattered knee until every shard of bone had fused. When finished, Paxton wiped his brow. Fine skirts of deep blue swished next to him. Paxton raised his chin to look at Rozaria's face. She'd changed and brushed her hair. When she held out a hand, he took it and stood. In her other hand was a bottle of wine.

"I enjoy watching you work," she said. "But now it is time to relax." At the sound of those words, his insides did the exact opposite of relaxing. If she was referring to more time alone, he couldn't stomach it. No more. Touching Rozaria was wrong on too many levels. She held out the bottle of wine, but he held up a hand.

"I cannot relax when there is still work to be done," he said. "You enjoy it."

"You do not know the meaning of relaxing, do you, hunter?"

Paxton huffed a laugh from his nose. "I suppose not."

She ran a hand up his chest. "Well, I think we are all tired. I imagine they'll drink every drop in the castle and then sleep half the day away tomorrow."

"Sounds like a solid plan," Paxton said. What he really wanted just then was to find out what happened between the prince and Aerity and to see if she was okay. He had to carefully fish for information. "I take it the prince has found suitable accommodations within the castle?"

"Mm, he found the king's chambers and he's probably sleeping like a plump babe as we speak. He needs as much sleep as a youngling. As for the girl, she's not to leave her chambers."

His chest jumped at this mention of Aerity. "Under the watch of guards, I presume," he said.

"Yes, though I think he will not waste any time before marrying her. Possibly even tomorrow." Paxton stopped breathing for several long moments before forcing himself to respond.

"I suppose that makes sense for him."

"Yes. She is key to getting the people to accept his rule.

But she will always be under lock and key. That is his nature. To control. The girl may believe she'll be queen in all ways, but she will be a puppet of Vito. A plaything. And he will eventually tire of her." This seemed to delight her to no end.

Paxton cursed the prince to the darkest depths of the seas. "He is a smart man."

He is a dead man.

Rozaria raised the bottle and took a drink.

"I'm going to patrol," he told her. "I'll try to find you when I'm done."

"I'll be in the south Lord and Lady chambers."

Paxton nodded and walked from High Hall, breathing deeply once he was away from her. When he was at the end of the hall he glanced back and saw Nicola walk out of High Hall alone. He went down the next hall, down the steps, and toward the library. He wanted to get a better idea of how many were in the castle, and which rooms they occupied. The library was completely empty, but he noticed the shelves had been ransacked and the books torn. He gritted his teeth at the shameful display.

Back in the hallway he headed toward the indoor archery range, but he could have sworn the wall tapestry swayed. He slowed and watched. It didn't move again. Paxton stepped into the doorway of the range and found it surprisingly empty, as well. Nobody was using this wing.

From the corner of his eye he saw the tapestry move again. So slight, like a flimsy branch in a breeze, but definite movement. Paxton slid into the archery room and hid behind the door. He pulled a dagger from under his shirt. Seconds later, Nicola slowly and silently moved into the room. Paxton reached one arm around her, pinning her arms to her sides, and stuck the tip of the dagger to her throat.

"Why are you following me?" he asked.

Somehow she was able to maneuver her hand upward so that one fingertip touched his forearm. A singe of pain burned Paxton's skin and he flung her away. She spun to face him, her hood falling back to reveal her angry face.

He took a stance in front of the door to block her, brandishing his blade. "Why, Nicola?"

"You do not care for her, Lochlan," she spat. "She is deceived but I am not."

Curses. He had no time for this. Paxton stood and shoved the dagger back into its sheath at his chest, then tugged his tunic back down. She seemed taken aback and stood taller as well.

"You're not the first to accuse me of not *caring*," he said. "I've never been good at showing feelings and all of that nonsense when it comes to women. But what Rozaria and I have is mutual. She understands me. I appreciate your concern for her, but it's wrongly placed."

"I don't trust you."

"Get in line," Paxton told her in a raised voice. She scowled. "I need to get back to patrolling. I know this castle better than your men, so I want to check everything out myself. You're welcome to join me and watch my every move if you feel you must."

He turned and walked out of the room, keenly aware of just how far she was from him while his back was to her, and what distance he needed to keep in case she decided to leap and grab at him with her deadly little hands.

When he passed High Hall he was relieved to see her go inside and stay there. Aye, Paxton would not be able to sleep anytime soon. She didn't trust him, and he sure as the depths didn't trust her either.

Chapter 41

They were getting drunk, Aerity realized. She stared from her bedroom window, watching the revelry below as the sun rose, turning the horizon from dark blue to gray. Kalorian soldiers were everywhere. These weren't the respectful tribesmen who had come to fight in the hunt. Those men valued life. These men were something altogether different. They were wild, without rules or boundaries. They threw one another to the ground, threw empty bottles, shot arrows straight up into the air.

And worst of all were the caged beasts in the middle of the west commons. They taunted them with spears and torches. Aerity couldn't make out the creatures in detail, but she could hear their maddened howls and see their paws swiping at the perpetrators. She rushed away from the window and curled up at the headboard of her bed with the heels of her hands pressed firmly into her eyes. She rocked back and forth.

This could not be happening.

She thought of all the ways she could escape. The windows were definitely out. She'd lower herself right into the west commons with the madmen. She thought about opening the door and smashing her vase over the guard's head. But what if there were more than one? And surely the halls were filled with them.

Aerity's eyes scanned her room, looking for anything that might be used as a weapon. But what her gaze landed on was her bookshelf. She stared at it. At nine years of age she'd begged her parents to remove the dusty old books and allow her to fill the shelves with more interesting stories. They'd given her the bottom three shelves for her own tales but told her the top shelf of books was to remain—that she would appreciate them someday and not to bother with them yet.

Hope sprang to life as she ran to the bookshelf. She pulled at the books on the top shelf, flinging them to the floor one by one to reveal plain boards behind them . . . until she got three-quarters of the way through, and those books stuck. Her heart absolutely pounded now. Three of the books were fused together, just as the ones had been on the bookshelf in her father's office. She grasped the top of them and pulled down with all her might until she heard a click. And then she pushed the bookshelf.

Oh, seas! It was moving! She glanced at her chamber door. All this time there'd been a hidden place in her room and she hadn't known it! How many more were there throughout the castle? She held back an exhilarated laugh.

Unlike the hidden room in the office, this one smelled musty, and a small cloud of dust plumed out as the bookshelf swung outward. She glanced toward her door again and listened to be sure no one was coming. When she heard nothing, she stepped in, careful to keep the bookshelf from shutting.

What she found in the dim light was not a room at all. It was a passageway. Aerity examined the back of the bookcase and found a lever just where the set of books was. Unlike the vault in the office, this door could be opened from within. She looked down the narrow passage and saw an old torch on the wall. All she needed was to find something to light the torch and then she could leave. The passageway was pitch-dark otherwise.

Aerity went back into her room and tugged the bookshelf doorway closed before rushing to the hearth. She knew Caitrin kept a box with kindling, tinder, and flint around there somewhere. They weren't on the mantel, only boring old urns and candelabras. She rushed to the side table and was about to open the drawer when voices sounded from the hall. Aerity sucked in a breath and spun around. She looked to the bookcase to be sure nothing was amiss and saw the books she'd flung to the floor.

Seas alive! She fell to her knees and snatched them into

her arms before leaping to her feet again and shoving them haphazardly back onto the shelf and rushing away from the bookcase, brushing dust from her skirts.

Go away, go away, go away, she silently begged to whoever was out there. But they didn't. Footsteps got closer. Low, male voices. The door handle was moving. When it opened she felt her mouth open in a gasp.

Paxton. His expression was hard and guarded. She had to keep from running to him because he wasn't alone. He had a large Kalorian man with him who Aerity recognized at once as the brute Martone. Her eyes went large, remembering their time together in that tower room, and she looked down. He was the first to speak, using his native tongue.

"I am told you speak Kalorian." His voice was gruff.

Aerity nodded, afraid to respond, worried he might recognize her voice.

"Prince Vito will rest today, and marry you tonight."

Aerity brought a hand to her throat, tasting bitterness.

"Very good," she whispered.

"He says for you to write a declaration to send to the people telling them of your union. He will approve it before it is sent out."

Aerity nodded, swallowing hard. Martone walked to her tall chest of drawers and opened the top drawer, lifting her undergarments in a meaty fist and peering beneath them.

"What are you doing?" she asked in Kalorian.

"Removing any weapons." The brute pointed to her desk. "Write."

Aerity walked to the desk and sat, her hand shaking as she opened the top drawer and slid out a piece of parchment, quill, and ink. Once she wrote this, things would forever change in Lochlanach. The people would never trust her again if they thought she was willingly uniting with the enemy, handing them over to his rule.

"A seamstress is on her way," Martone said as he tore another drawer open and rummaged through it.

Aerity's eyes flitted to Paxton, who made a show of opening her wardrobe and pushing gowns aside while sneaking a look at her. She could see the calculating thoughts in his eyes as he tried to come up with a way out of this. She needed to be alone with him to tell him of the passageway.

Aerity turned her head enough to speak quietly over her shoulder.

"Sir, if you would be so kind, will you please relay a message to the prince on my behalf? It is important, so I need it to be conveyed by someone worthy of the prince's trust."

Martone stood taller. "What is the message?"

Her mind desperately cranked out a weak idea. "Please tell him I am also writing letters to the other three kingdoms. I need to know if there is anything he wishes me to include. They'll need to be issued straightaway to keep the other kingdoms from interfering in our plans."

Martone paused, then nodded. He looked at Paxton and pointed to Aerity, as if he was to keep an eye on her. Paxton nodded his head. Her hopes soared. *Blessed seas!*

Martone stomped his way out of the room and pulled the

chamber door shut harder than was necessary. Before Aerity could even stand all the way, Paxton was in front of her, grasping her shoulders and hissing.

"You are *not* marrying him!"

"Sh!" She grabbed his hand and pulled him to the bookshelf, whispering. "There's a passage!"

"Wha—"

She reached for the books and pulled, releasing the old lever.

"Great seas," Paxton whispered. Before she could get it open all the way he was pressing her inward and pulling the door closed. They were immersed in darkness and Aerity's heart was thumping so loud he could probably hear it.

"I forgot flint!" she whispered. "We won't be able to see!"

"You've got me, aye?" he whispered back.

There was the dry sound of his hand against the wall, and then the scraping of the torch being pulled from its spot. A tiny spark of light, the scent of smoke, and then the flame was crackling, filling the hall with flickering light as he pulled his hand away.

Aerity beamed up at him.

"Let's get as far from your chamber as this passage will take us." He held the torch high in one hand and grabbed her hand with his other, then led them forward. Aerity's skin was alight from the hot thrum of blood through her body. She'd never been more nervous.

"I never knew this was here until I tried it today," she

said. "I've no clue where it leads."

"We'll find out soon enough."

"They'll know you're against them now," she whispered. They turned a tight corner. "Martone will return any moment and they'll know. It's only a matter of time before they find us, and then—"

"Sh, Aer, we can't do that." He stopped and turned, holding the torch above their heads. His other hand went around her waist and pulled her until their chests were together, their pounding hearts pressed tight. She leaned her face against his shoulder and breathed him in, feeling his cheek rest on her forehead. The comfort of him was just enough to slow her heart.

"Let's keep going," she whispered.

He obliged. At the end of that long stretch he pointed to another lever on the wall. "It definitely connects with other rooms. This is good. But I think we should go farther."

"Aye."

They walked and turned for what seemed like forever. Aerity's sense of direction had never been keen, so she had no idea where they might be at that point. But with every lever they saw and every corner they turned, she felt greater optimism. Finally, the hallway ended in a small room with a chair and chest. There was a lever in that room with an outline like her bookshelf.

They stood staring at it. "What room do you suppose it is?" she asked.

Paxton shook his head. "I believe we went east toward the front of the castle."

"Guest quarters?" Aerity guessed.

Again, he nodded. Each pressed their ears against the wall, but the other side was silent. If someone were in that other room—if the passageway was discovered—they were both dead. But they couldn't remain within the walls forever. Paxton rubbed his temples.

"Sit down a moment," Aerity told him. He sat heavily in the chair while Aerity fit the torch into the sconce on the wall. She watched as he put his elbows on his knees and let his forehead rest against his palms. "How long has it been since you slept, Pax?"

He chuckled quietly. "I don't know. Days."

He'd been carrying the weight of the kingdom on his shoulders.

"Let's take a few moments to rest before we decide what to do," she said.

Aerity crouched next to the chest and quietly pulled up on the unlocked clasp. Its hinges creaked when she began to open it, so she stopped and went slower until the lid was fully up. Inside was empty. "Well, that's not helpful," she muttered. She left it open to avoid more creaking.

Aerity pushed to her feet and stood before Paxton, gathering his head in her hands. He brought his arms around her, above and below her hips, and rested his face against her stomach, pulling her to stand between his open legs. She ran her fingers through his hair, then over his smooth cheeks. In that one single moment, her world felt right.

"I love you, Aerity Lochson," Paxton whispered into her skirts, and her heart brimmed with fullness.

"I love you as well. Even if you were a rogue skirt raiser when we met."

His chin lifted to send her a questioning look. Aerity smiled. "It's what Wyn used to call you."

A small, tired grin played on his lips.

"What will happen to us, Pax?" she whispered.

A deep sense of desperation to grasp their time together rose within her. This could be it. This could be their last moment alone together.

He held her tighter and pressed his forehead into her abdomen. "I just want to keep you safe."

"And you have. We're safe right now, aren't we?" Her heart began a rhythmic pounding as she realized what she wanted. Perhaps it was foolish and dangerous, but she'd never felt such dire desperation. "You have my heart in this lifetime and the next, but we are not promised more than this moment together."

He lifted his chin to peer at her again, whispering fervently, "I won't let Vito touch you, Aerity. I swear it."

"We don't know what is to happen when we leave this room. And even if by some miracle of the sea we're able to escape and somehow beat Kalor . . ." Her voice caught. "I am still promised to Lief."

She licked her dry lips. Paxton's brow creased at this thought, and he dropped his gaze. She took his chin and lifted it to look at her. His eyes were full of remorse at the mention of her marrying, as if he'd lost her already.

"I am yours, Paxton. And we have now."

He stared at her a moment longer. His voice deepened. "What are you saying, Aer?"

"I think you know," she breathed.

He stared. She could see the war between yearning and fear in his eyes. She wondered if the pattern of his heartbeat matched the gallop of her own.

Aerity's voice shook with nerves and need. "Give me a memory of our love that I can keep with me always, Pax. Something no one can take from us."

His tight jawline began to relax, and she watched as the fear shed away and pure yearning took over. Slowly, with his eyes fastened on hers, his hands roamed down from her hips, down her legs, and grasped the bare skin of her ankles before sliding back up, under the hem of her gown. Aerity's breath hitched as his hands cupped behind her knees, stroking upward to the backs of her thighs. His small grin turned wicked.

"You want me to make good on my nickname?"

Aerity seemed to have forgotten how to breathe. All she knew was that she did not want Paxton to stop. In that hidden room she was not a queen. She was simply a lass in love with a lad, and wanting nothing else in the world than to give him everything and take all he was willing to give in return.

"Aye, Pax. That is what I want."

His gaze heated. His hands slid upward, under her petticoats and over her hips until his fingertips circled her bare waist and held tightly. He gave her a tiny shove back without releasing her, enough to pull his knees together and yank her forward again to straddle his lap. Then he raised her skirts and lowered her, a hand behind her back and one on her neck. Aerity whimpered at the feel of him through his breeches.

She loved that he didn't question her forwardness, didn't ask if she was sure or attempt to save her virtue, because despite her obvious nervousness he trusted her judgment. She knew he'd give her anything she wanted if it was in his power.

Their mouths met with passion and impatience, knowing their precious time together could be stolen from them at any moment. Paxton curled his fingers around the fabric at her shoulders and pulled it down her arms, below her chest as far as the chemise would allow. He kissed down her neck to the softer, fuller skin of her breasts now displayed.

"Seas!" she whispered as his hot mouth enveloped her sensitive skin. She grasped his head and arched her back. Aerity needed more.

She reached for the bottom of his tunic and lifted it. He raised his arms and let her pull it up, tossing it into the open chest. Her hands roamed over his shoulders, down the front of him where the daggers were strapped. He stripped the blades and set them on the floor. She relished the way his breathing quickened as he watched her touching him, her hands moving down his taut stomach.

Her eyes landed on his hands on her thighs. The tops of his nails still had a bit of flesh tone, but the bottom sections of his nails were all purple. A quaver worked its way through her at the power that lived inside this man.

She slowly inched back on his lap and felt for the ties of his breeches at his waist. Her hands trembled as she undid them and pulled them down. Her heart gave a bang. Their gazes struck like flashes of lightning, causing a wave of pounding heat to rise between them.

Paxton shifted beneath her and raised Aerity up by her waist, taking her mouth with his as he lowered her slowly back down onto himself. She clung to his shoulders. He caught her quiet cry in his own throat and held her tightly as they became one.

She was Paxton's, come what may. Not Lord Alvi's. And never Prince Vito's. Only Paxton Seabolt's, and nobody could take that from them.

Chapter 42

The news that reached the local town of Dovedell at daybreak had not been good. Tiern had been on edge, pacing the local tavern all night since they'd heard sounds of explosions from a distance. He'd wanted to return to royal lands that very instant, but the soldiers he was with said it'd be suicide.

They had only planned to amass willing fighters from Dovedell and be back in time for battle, three hours at the most. And now . . . *Seas alive, what the curses had happened?* One moment he'd eagerly offered to help on a quick mission, hoping to erase from his mind the look of fear and betrayal that Vixie had given him. And the next thing he knew, royal lands were infested with Kalorians.

He'd run when he should have stayed. He should have been there. What had happened to Vixie and Paxton? It was driving him mad not to know.

When news spread through the night, hundreds of commoners from local towns had shown up to see what could be done.

"Are the princesses safe?" They had no way of knowing.

"How many are there?" A bloody lot.

Nearly a hundred soldiers who'd been patrolling and doing border duty now massed in the town square. Tiern joined them, hearing shouts of "Reorganize and regroup!" "Rearm!" "Reestablish leadership!" "Plan and execute!" Big words, but laughable compared to what they were up against. The Kalorians had smashed their ground troops like a tiny anthill and taken over royal lands.

"Our navy moved north," said the highest-ranking soldier there. "If we can get word to them in the bay—"

"That will take days!" another shouted.

"Not if we send a single fast rider."

Tiern rubbed his face. The kingdom was doomed. It was only a matter of time before Prince Vito settled in the royal lands and began to send his people out to crush the towns. They didn't have the men or resources.

Horses, carts, and caravans filled with women and crying children set off, shouting their good-byes and sending kisses to the men they'd leave as they fled north. Tiern walked away from them and toward a large tent some way from the town center. When he got to it, he realized it was one of the Lashed infirmaries. He peeked inside and saw three women and two men sitting, discussing in earnest. Their heads spun toward him.

"Very sorry," he said. "Didn't mean to interrupt."

"Wait," called one of the men, standing. "Is there a plan?"

Tiern shook his head. "Not yet. We're still trying to decide and hoping for more men from other towns to arrive once people start to get word."

"We want to help," said one of the women in a strong voice. "They have Lashed among them . . . bad ones. Lochlanach will need Lashed fighting on our side as well."

"Aye," Tiern said. "But are you willing to kill with your hands?"

They looked around at one another forlornly, and nodded.

"I'll let the soldiers know."

When he left the tent he saw a trail of dust rising from afar on the path. He squinted to see many bodies, all wearing the pale colors of Lochlan clothing. Tiern broke into a run until he got to the town center.

"More men are coming."

Tiern and the others rushed to meet them. There looked to be close to fifty extra men. This was good. Now they only needed about a thousand more.

Tiern nearly laughed at the likelihood of that.

From clear in the other direction of town came a distant rumbling from the hills. The senior soldier's eyes widened.

"What the seas . . . ?"

Tiern, the Lochlan soldiers, and Dovedell townspeople ran to see, spreading out and staring at the horizon. A chill that had nothing to do with winter ratcheted up Tiern's back as moving dots rose over the hills straight toward them.

"Attack!" a townsman yelled. Others joined him, raising their sharpened sticks and bows, but Tiern and a few others hushed them.

"They're not coming from the direction of Kalor!" Tiern shouted over the din.

They stared out, powerless to do anything except watch as the forces gained ground.

"We should take cover!" another townsman said.

"Wait," said the commanding soldier. "They wear the bronze of Toresta."

Murmurs rose up around them. "Toresta is an ally, aye?" "Should we trust them?"

Tiern pushed his way through to see better, and his eyes traveled to the end of the approaching party. A large group of them rode shining black horses, and wore all black clothing from head to toe.

"The Zandalee!" He jumped and punched the sky. "These are definitely allies!"

"Aye," said the soldier. "And more Zorfinans behind them!"

The townsmen and soldiers sent up a great cheer of welcome, raising their fists in gratitude. As they got closer, Tiern couldn't wait any longer. He sprinted up the hill toward the Zandalee. There were so many of them; Zandora must have brought the entire tribe! She and the two sisters Tiern knew all leaped down deftly from their horses. He ran to them and gathered the three of them in a great big hug.

Horses barreled past them. Fierce women circled them, eyes alight beneath their head coverings, making clucking sounds and high-pitched calls.

Zandora pulled away and laughed. "You will make us look soft."

He dropped his arms, smiling hugely. The two sisters faced him on each side and both took to running hands over his light beard, shaking their heads and muttering in Zorfinan.

"They say a sweetling like you must keep his face young."

Tiern rubbed his cheeks, unable to stop smiling. "I promise to shave just as soon as we take back our castle." He looked at Zandora now, whose face had gone stony. His smile fell away as the dire situation came rushing back at him.

"Your royal lands have fallen?" she asked.

"Aye." The ache inside him began anew. "And they killed our king and queen."

Zandora gave a grim nod. "We will take back Lochlanach, I promise you. Prince Vito goes too far."

Chapter 43

Vixie sat up, panting and disoriented, visions of cannons and blood still swirling in her mind. She peered around blearily and felt the gentle scratch of Wyneth's hand at her back.

"Sh, love, go back to sleep."

"Nay." Vixie rubbed her eyes and pulled her legs criss-cross on the mat she shared with her cousin. She hadn't meant to fall asleep. She'd closed her eyes to try to rid herself of a headache. "How long have we been down here? It feels like days."

"Half a day, at most," said Harrison from the bench next to Wyneth. He leaned his elbows on his knees, a foot tapping nervously. Beside him, Lief paced from one end of the tunnel to the other, a mere five steps for him.

From across the way, Mrs. Rathbrook came to Vixie and knelt before her. "Is your head bothering you, dear?"

"Yes," Vixie whispered.

"May I?" The woman's hand hovered beside her cheek, and Vixie nodded. The princess closed her eyes as the Lashed healer touched the side of her head and weaved warmth through her mind that seemed to unravel the tight thread within. Vixie breathed and relaxed.

"Thank you."

Mrs. Rathbrook smiled and went back to her pallet beside her watchful guard.

Down the long, low-ceilinged room were forty-seven people. Soldiers, guards, cooks, maids, and them. Every cot, mat, chair, and wall space was spoken for. The baker had made loads of bread. Apparently he baked more than necessary under stress. Coincidentally, Vixie ate more than necessary under stress, so lucky her.

Vixie leaned her head back against the wall. "What do you suppose is happening up there? Can anything be heard?"

"Nay," Wyneth said quietly. "Nothing." To Vixie's surprise, Wyneth reached up and placed a hand on Harrison's knee. He covered her hand with his own. The gesture was so intimate, so loving and natural, that Vixie could only stare. She wasn't alone, either.

Lief stopped pacing, eyeballed their two hands together,

and all but snarled as he began his furious pacing again. Nobody dared tell the coldlander to sit down and be still. Wyneth gave Vixie a small, reassuring smile, but it did nothing to calm her. All she could think about was that her parents had been murdered, and how those same people were now directly above her with her sister.

Was Aerity even still alive? A sob rose and Vixie choked it down, tried to make it seem like a cough. She lifted her knees and put her arms across them to hide her face. Wyneth rubbed her back again. What would Vixie do without Aerity? And would that make *her* the queen? She'd never, ever aspired to be ruler. It simply wasn't in her. That had always been Aerity's job. Vixie quickly wiped her dripping eyes against her shoulders.

One of the chefs, a plump middle-aged man who sat atop a large chest at the rear of the room, jumped to his feet and said, "Sh! Listen! Do you hear that?"

All murmuring and shuffling stopped. The room became silent.

They waited. Another beat passed. And a third.

Then . . . a scraping. A light thump. Another scrape.

The chef spun to face the wall behind him, staring at the blank space and the chest. "I—I think it's in the wall!"

Lief, Harrison, and several soldiers ran for the back of the room, forcing the baker, chefs, and maids to move away and let them inspect. Wyneth and Vixie both stood to see, but they were too short. Vixie climbed up on the bench, her head grazing the low ceiling. She placed her hands on Wyneth's shoulders in front of her, and Wyn grabbed her fingers, watching the men.

Lief ran his hands over the wall, and Harrison opened the chest.

"Someone is definitely on the other side of this," Lief murmured.

But they were underground!

"Here!" Harrison said, peering down into the chest. He seemed to be pulling up a panel of some sort and then there was a poof sound and chaos broke out. The men all brandished their daggers and bows, pointing their weapons into the chest. *What in Eurona was happening?*

"Oh, seas!" Wyneth said, grasping Vixie's hands.

And then Lief spoke out. "Volgan? Is that you?"

"Yes, lord," came a deep, bad-tempered voice, "and I'm tired of eating dirt, so if you could remove the arrows from my face and give me a hand, that'd be appreciated."

Lief slung his bow over his back, letting out a hearty laugh as he reached down into the giant chest and helped an even more giant man out. Vixie gaped in disbelief. She recognized the man from the hunt!

"Ascomannians?" she asked.

Lief shot her a smile over the heads of the others. "At your service, it seems."

Vixie jumped down and pushed her way through the crowd. One by one, filthy coldlands men rose from the depths of the chest, brushing off their furs and beards before embracing Lief.

"How many are there?" Vixie asked in wonder.

"Why, all of us, of course," said the hairiest, Volgan. He winked at her. "Here to save your arses again."

Vixie couldn't even bring herself to be offended. She simply bounded into the great big brute's arms and hugged him with all her might.

Chapter 44

When their stolen moment had ended, and harsh reality bombarded Aerity's senses once again, she sat in the chair watching Paxton as he stood and stretched his arms. He gazed down at her, making her feel too warm all over again.

His face was serious, and she knew he was worried about what they'd do next. She watched as he leaned down into the chest to retrieve his tunic. But to Aerity's confusion, he stayed leaning down for longer than was necessary.

"I think there's something here," she heard him whisper. *What was he talking about? The chest was empty.* And then she heard a scraping as Paxton pulled.

Seas almighty! He was lifting the bottom of the trunk! Aerity ran to peer in.

"A tunnel?" she asked. Aerity leaned back as Paxton grabbed the torch and held it over the chest. Old wooden rungs embedded into the dirt wall went down a man-sized hole. They looked at each other, eyes rounded. "I think we're above the cellars," she whispered.

"I want you to stay here while I check it out." He stood and gave her his bow and quiver. "No part of the castle is safe now. But if there's nobody in the cellar I will call you and we can try to find the tunnel where the others are."

"And then what?" Aerity asked, putting the bow over her shoulder. "Be stuck there forever? It's not actually a tunnel, Pax. I don't even know why they call it that. They say it's simply one long room. A dead end."

Paxton sighed.

"We'll figure out something. At least if I can find the others, we can tell them what we know." He handed her the torch. "I need it to be dark, so if there's anyone below they don't see me."

When he turned toward the chest, fear gripped Aerity's heart and she grabbed his arm, pulling him back for one more kiss. Their mouths sealed, his perfectly tender against hers, until Paxton pulled away enough to whisper, "Don't be afraid. Listen for me. If anything happens, run."

Aerity nodded, reluctantly releasing his arm. She watched as he climbed down into the hole and lowered himself one rung at a time. Her heart sprinted furiously. It felt like forever before he climbed back up and gave her a silent nod to follow.

He pointed to the torch holder on the wall. Aerity snuffed the torch in the holder and felt her way in the dark back to the chest. She climbed down, pulling the chest lid closed and letting the bottom fall back into place over her head.

She was breathing too hard until she felt Paxton's hand around her ankle and heard his firm voice say, "It's all right. Take your time." When they got to the bottom they were sandwiched together. Paxton fiddled with something in the dark, and Aerity felt movement of air. He'd opened a compartment of some kind. Her hands felt him kneel.

"Crawl out behind me," he whispered.

She did as he said and found herself exiting an old cupboard in the pantry behind the wine cellar. Faint light filtered in from the staircase beyond the cellar. Around them were sacks of potatoes and grains. Paxton jumped to his feet and searched until he found another old trunk in the corner like the one they'd seen in the room above. They rushed to it and lifted the lid.

Low laughter rang out from somewhere above, making Aerity jump. Paxton wrenched up the base of the chest and motioned for Aerity to go first. She glanced behind them to be sure they were still alone before lowering herself. It was musty and dank as she made her way down into the dark. When she hit the bottom, she heard Paxton above her and all went pitch-dark again as he closed the lid.

She crouched and felt a wooden panel with her hands. Paxton deftly landed on his feet next to her.

"Harrison told me of a secret knock," he whispered. "So they don't attack us."

One-two, one-two, one-two-three-four, one.

Paxton then pushed on the panel as someone from the other side pulled. Aerity squinted into the bright room and heard Vixie whisper, "It's Aer!"

She was yanked through the doorway by her wrist and wrapped in a tight hug. Then another set of arms was around her: Wyneth's. They moved aside so Paxton could come in and shut the panel.

"Blessed seas!" Wyneth sized her up.

"I can't believe you're here!" Vixie exclaimed.

"Neither can I." Aerity kissed her sister's cheek and embraced her again.

"What's happening up there?" Harrison asked. "How did you get away?"

"Were you possibly followed?" asked one of the soldiers.

"Nay . . ." Paxton explained their escape.

Furball gave a low *rawr* of welcome to Aerity and came up on his hind legs beside them. Aerity jumped back and then laughed, reaching out to scratch his wiry stomach. She then looked around the room in confusion. There were only seven people down there besides her and Paxton. Four soldiers, Harrison, Wyneth, and Vixie. But bedrolls and things were strewn everywhere.

"Where have the others gone?" Aerity asked.

Paxton stopped and looked around, his eyes quizzical as well.

"Funny story, that," Harrison said.

Aerity spotted the chest at the end of the room and pointed. "Wait. Is that . . . ?"

"It is," Harrison told her. "This tunnel leads north outside the royal walls. The Ascomannians are here. They've taken our staff to safety. Their navy has met with ours and awaits further battle in the bay. And what's more, they told us there is rumor of help coming from both Toresta and Zorfina."

"Seas above!" Aerity clasped her hands under her chin and beamed, closing her eyes in thanks. If what he'd said was true, and they overthrew Prince Vito, Aerity would spend her entire rule trying to repay the other three kingdoms.

"Does this mean we can leave?" Paxton asked, placing a hand on Aerity's back.

Harrison grinned. "We've just been waiting on word from you."

A low rumble began in the walls around them. They all looked up, staring at the shaking from feet stomping overhead, and then gaping at the sounds of Kalorian war cries from above.

"They've found out you're gone," Paxton said. "Go, go, go!"

But Aerity didn't need to be told. She was already running.

Prince Vito and Rozaria stood in Princess Aerity's empty chamber, with Nicola silent behind them. In the hall Martone shouted orders to half-drunk Kalorian soldiers, who ran about, confused. A tight knot had formed in Rozaria's stomach as she considered what might have happened.

"She could have tricked him—"

"Silence," Vito said in a sinister whisper. "He has made a fool of us. Perhaps now you will finally learn not to trust." He turned to her with a sneer, and Rozaria locked her jaw in defiance. She was the only Kalorian alive who didn't fear him, but at that very moment he seemed unstable and capable of lashing out. She kept her distance.

Vito walked the perimeter of the room, skirting the edge of the bed as he ran his fingertips along the downy covers. Menace glistened in his eyes. Rozaria did not want to believe that Paxton had helped the Lochlan queen to escape. He was different, wasn't he? He'd made her feel things she never allowed herself to feel for men. But how could an unarmed girl overtake a strong Lashed? It only made sense that he had helped her. They were missing, *together*.

Rozaria sensed Nicola behind her, and felt a surge of dread: Had she been wrong about the hunter all along? Her two closest comrades, Nicola and Vito, had not trusted him, and she ignored their doubts.

A flare of disappointment singed her from the inside. Nicola must have sensed her mood because she silently moved next to her, their arms touching, as if to let her know she was still there. Still at her side. Rozaria raised her chin and felt the shame of her jaw trembling. She hadn't cried since . . . she couldn't recall. Never, perhaps. Tears were a sign of softness, weakness, which was not in her. This burning in her eyes, it was brought on by sheer rage at Paxton's duplicity.

She would look him straight into his eyes as she killed him. Better yet, she would make him watch as she killed his precious queen. The thought eased the stinging behind her eyes.

Prince Vito's hand trailed the walls until he came to a bookcase. Rozaria moved forward to see what he was staring at. Her mind went back to the king's study and the bookcase there that opened to the hidden room. Vito's head spun to her; he must have realized it at the same time.

"Martone!" Rozaria called. The man ran into the room, at her command. "Ready your weapon."

He unsheathed his wicked knife and went to Vito's side. Beside her, Nicola pulled out her dagger. The prince felt along the books until he came to three joined ones, and then he pulled downward. Martone moved to the opening to protect them, ready to attack. Rozaria held her breath, staring hard as the dark room took shape, but her anticipation fizzled to disappointment at the sight of empty space. Martone stuck his head in and whipped it back to Prince Vito, wide-eyed.

"It's a passage!"

"What are you waiting for, idiot?" Vito asked. "Go! Find them!"

Martone rushed in, with Prince Vito, Rozaria, and Nicola following. With each lever they came to, the brute yanked it down and gave an unnecessary war cry into the empty chambers they revealed. "Shut up, you fool," Prince Vito said after the second time. "You'll alert them."

Their journey ended in a small room with a chair and a trunk. Martone silently pushed the lever and charged into yet another empty room. Vito cursed and fisted his hands. If they had gone into any of those rooms, it would have put them back into the castle. Every Kalorian was on alert. They would be found.

They were quiet, thinking of what to do next, when Rozaria realized she could hear a murmur of voices below . . . coming from the chest. She pointed. Nicola fell to her knees and wrenched it open. The girl leaned into it, feeling around, and then yanked up a panel to reveal an opening with ladder rungs.

"Well done, Nic." A thrill of victory shot through Rozaria. "We've got them now."

Chapter 45

The tunnel was long. Too long. Aerity would so much rather climb to fearful heights out in the open than be confined in a low, dank space with bugs of all manner crunching underfoot. Judging by the labored breathing and frequent stifled sounds from Wyneth and Vixie, they weren't loving this either. Especially since Furball practically had to be pulled along to stop him from digging at protruding roots or swiping up crawling things as snacks.

Aerity had no idea how long they'd been moving, but it was long enough to have to stop and rest several times, and continually drink water. Though it was winter outside, they were sweating from the quick pace in the confined space. The passage seemed to go on forever. Finally, *finally*, Harrison called, "The exit is ahead!"

One by one they crouched through a smaller hole and entered a shaft that went straight up. Aerity grasped the wooden rungs and kept her mouth closed against the falling dirt from Harrison's boots above her. At the top, Harrison grasped her hands and helped her up. They came out of yet another giant trunk inside a small room with old barrels, sacks, and dusty shelving. An Ascomannian and a Lochlan soldier were there.

"Where are we?" Aerity asked, brushing herself off.

Paxton came up behind her, followed by the other girls and the officers.

"From the outside it appears to be an old lean-to shack for storage," Harrison explained. "It's a small military compound that was closed off years ago."

"And where are we within Lochlanach?" Paxton asked.

"Just north of royal lands. We'll head northeast along Parryhorn Bay, where the Ascomannians and our fleet of ships wait."

"Come along, Your Majesty," said the Lochlan soldier. "We've readied a horse for you. We must move quickly."

The sight of Lochlan and Ascomannian ships together in Parryhorn Bay filled Aerity with immense joy. She let herself be ushered onto the grandest Ascomannian vessel with Harrison and two other high-ranking Lochlan officers. Lief stood at the end of the gangway, awaiting her. He took her hand to help her aboard.

"Thank you, Lord Alvi," she said. He held her hand for a moment longer, appearing relieved to see her.

"My pleasure. Follow me."

They took steep steps belowdecks. King Dagur stood with his arms crossed in the low-ceilinged cabin, watching intently as one of his men ran his finger along a map. His eyes came up to her as she entered, and he grunted.

"You are safe, then."

"Aye, thanks to you." She went to him, and though he was unsmiling, he reached out and took her hands. Aerity swallowed hard, unable to speak. She tried to convey her gratitude with her eyes, and he nodded.

"Very well. Enough of that." He released her hands and motioned to the map. "Here is our plan. We must get them to leave royal lands and come north to this strip." He pointed to a stretch of land between Loch River and Crescent Stream. "If we can get them here, it won't matter if they outnumber us, because we'll have them in a pinch. Only limited numbers of their men can get through at a time to battle us."

"How do you propose we get them to leave the safety of royal lands?" Harrison asked.

"Well, what are their weaknesses?" Aerity asked. "Lashed Ones, aye? What if they caught wind of Lashed Ones being rounded up and killed in Craw Coorie? And that the townspeople there are revolting? Knowing his pride, the prince will wish to show his power by putting a stop to it immediately and using them as an example."

The king nodded. "We'd thought about the town-revolt idea, but I like the addition of the Lashed abuse."

Loud footsteps outside made them turn their heads toward the stairs. An Ascomannian warrior hurried down and bowed to his king.

"What news?" King Dagur asked.

"Your Majesty, a Lochlan soldier riding from the town of Dovedell says they have amassed people to fight. And more, Torestan and Zorfinan troops have joined them."

Blessed seas!

The king chuckled heartily and winked at Aerity, rubbing his thick hands together. "Good news, that. Anything else?"

"Yes, my king, the details of their plans. Half their Lochlans and the entire Torestan army are marching north as we speak to join our forces. The other half of the Lochlans and the Zorfinans will remain in Dovedell to attack the southern entrance of royal lands. They will arrive by tomorrow midday. Their plan is to attack tomorrow at sundown. They said if this plan does not work, for you to send notice at once."

The king grunted. "Waiting nearly two days is not ideal, but I suppose we have no other choice. Send a messenger on a fresh horse to respond with our plans—"

He was cut off by yet another sound of stomping boots and another Ascomannian rushing down into the cabin and coming to stand before the king with a bow. He panted.

"Speak," the king commanded.

"Your Majesty, our land spies have spotted mass movement through Kalor and over the border of Lochlanach. More of their troops are coming."

The king cursed. He looked at the first messenger. "Send a rider at once. Let those in Dovedell know of the additional Kalorian troops coming from the south so they're not taken by surprise or trapped. Go."

The warrior bowed and rushed out. King Dagur looked at Aerity.

"Seems we've got ourselves a verifiable war on our hands, Queen Aerity. May as well start your reign off with a bit of a boom."

Aerity stared at him, horrified. Lief chuckled behind her.

"Ah, Uncle, if there is one thing I can tell you from my time in Lochlanach, it's that their people prefer to avoid the booms at all cost."

Aerity sputtered a laugh in spite of herself. "Aye. I would prefer if this was the one and only boom of my reign, to be quite honest."

King Dagur patted her shoulder hard. "Then let's make it one to remember."

Chapter 46

Vixie, Aerity, Wyneth, and the no-longer-such-a-cub beast all opted to sleep in a cabin together on a Lochlan vessel that had anchored safely in the middle of the bay. Furball had actually seemed offended that he wasn't allowed on the bed. He tried to climb on and opened his mouth in a mournful roar when Wyneth told him no and pointed to a pallet on the floor beside them. Once they finally settled, the four of them slept like the dead.

Vixie was groggy when she felt slimy wetness drag along her cheek and nose. She opened her eyes and found a giant mouth with pointed fangs yawning in her face and she screamed. Aerity and Wyneth bolted upright, covers flying. Vixie caught her breath and fell back.

"Furball!"

"Oh, for sea's sake," Aerity grumbled. "You frightened me to death."

Wyneth stood. "He needs to go out. What time is it? Gracious, the sun is already halfway up the sky!"

The door to their cabin burst open and three faces vied in the doorway. Paxton, Lief, and Harrison all stared in at them, worried.

"It was only Vix being licked to death by Furball," Aerity said.

The men relaxed and put their weapons away.

Harrison snapped his fingers at the creature. "Come, Furball. I'll feed you and take you to the top deck."

"Thank you," Wyneth said. The two of them shared a gaze that made Vixie and Aerity smile at each other. Then Wyneth said, "I think I'll come with you to stretch my legs."

Harrison and Wyneth left with Furball at their heels. Lief glowered at their backs and eventually left as well.

"What time is it?" Aerity asked Paxton.

He leaned against the doorframe and watched her with heavy, dark eyes. "I'd say after ten."

"So late already?" Aerity exclaimed.

"There was no need to wake you."

Vixie watched the two of them staring at each other, and it suddenly made her cheeks go hot. She cleared her throat and untangled her legs from the blanket.

"I'm going above for some air."

They didn't even acknowledge her, just kept their eyes locked. Vixie walked past Paxton and he went straight into the cabin, closing the door behind him. She gaped. Her sister was alone with a lad! In a room with a bed! What would Father say? Her stomach dropped and she blinked back a feeling of shock, remembering her father would never again enforce rules of propriety on them.

The princess stared at the closed door for a moment longer before shaking her head and making a direct line for the steps, giving her sister as much space as possible. She met Lief at the top, looking as if he was planning to go back down the steps.

"Where are you going?" she asked.

He seemed taken aback at her questioning. "To see your sister and let her know where she will need to be during the attack."

"You can't go down there right now. She's . . . indisposed. But I'd like to hear the plans, if you don't mind."

He glanced toward the stairs before turning back to Vixie and relenting. "The plan is for you, Aerity, and Lady Wyneth to remain in Craw Coorie when the fighting begins. You will have your own troop with you at all times. They will lead you back toward royal lands, if and when the path is cleared and safe."

Vixie hummed. "So we are not to fight."

"Of course not."

She scowled at him. "I know how to shoot a bow."

He put his face close to hers. "Shooting a target is not the same as shooting another person, Princess. Be prepared for your first kill to feel as if you yourself were shot in the heart as well."

Vixie's heart quickened. "Is that how it felt for you?"

Lief watched her. "Their blood will stain you. It becomes part of you. No matter how justified the kill."

Vixie swallowed. "All right." It came out as a croaked whisper.

Lief nodded. "I'll speak to Aerity once she's dressed and above deck." He began to turn, but then paused and looked back at the stairwell, eyes scrunched. "I never saw Paxton come up."

"Nay," Vixie said. "He is still below."

She crossed her arms and waited as his face slowly went slack. The boat began to move, causing both of them to shift.

"Are we docking?" Vixie asked.

He nodded, still lost in his own mind. She saw the muscle at his temple working, and his arm muscles flexed. She had no idea what he was thinking, but Vixie was fairly certain there would be more blood staining Lief Alvi's soul that evening when the battle began. Much more.

Once they disembarked, the late morning flew past, with people whittling spears, stringing bows, and sharpening blades. It was so cold out that the royal lasses were each brought cloaks. Soon, it was time to say their good-byes to the Ascomannians and ride northeast along Loch River to the town of Craw

Coorie. Vixie had been there twice before on travels, and had always loved the historical feel of the place, with its smashed-together old, leaning shops tucked away within hills and valleys. It was one of the largest towns in the kingdom, lined with small thatched houses, sheep farms, and flower fields.

The place was deserted when they arrived at midafternoon. Soldiers and armed townsmen milled about, discussing and preparing. The girls took their horses to the stables. Vixie noticed the tremor in Aerity's hands as she petted Jude's nose, her eyes distant.

"Aer?" Vixie whispered. Her sister looked at her and reached for her hand. Vixie took it. She couldn't imagine the weight on Aerity's shoulders.

"I don't want my people to die," she said. "It's my fault. If I hadn't left . . . and then if I had accepted King Dagur's offer in the first place . . ."

"That is in the past," Vixie said. "All you can do is learn from it and look to the future."

Wyneth, having heard the conversation, joined them.

"Even if you had stayed, or accepted his offer, Kalor would have attacked and your people would be fighting. Nothing you could have done differently would have stopped him. I believe even if your father had lifted laws against magic, Prince Vito *still* would have invaded."

"You're probably right," Aerity said. Her face soured. "To think . . . if I hadn't escaped, we'd be married right now."

Vixie felt a spasm of disgust go up her spine. "Thank the seas."

A low thrumming sound came from the distance and the ground shook slightly under their feet. Their eyes went large. Paxton and Harrison came running over.

"It's probably the Torestans," Harrison said, easing their worry.

Together, surrounded by their protecting troops, they climbed the hill that hid Craw Coorie from the south. Vixie inhaled a huge breath at the glorious sight of hundreds of men on horseback, spread across the grassy field. She couldn't help but smile. The troops surrounding them let out a raucous cheer in greeting, the steam of their voices rising up into the frigid air.

When the foreign army arrived, led by Lochlan men, Vixie's eyes went directly to Tiern. Paxton saw him at the same time and jogged over. They grasped wrists and Tiern dismounted, embracing his brother with a hearty smack on the shoulder. They both laughed. Vixie's insides swirled at the sight of him smiling, safe. Tiern's head turned to her and his smile fell. Paxton looked back and forth between them before giving his younger brother one last pat and walking away.

Tiern did not come to her, though. He gave his attention to his horse. Vixie stood there, contemplating what to do as she tugged her cloak tighter around herself. Here they were, on the cusp of battle, both lucky to still be alive, and yet they were not speaking. She lifted her skirts and went to him.

"I'm glad to see you are well, Tiern."

He undid clasps and buckles, staying busy. "Same for you, Princess."

"Please, stop a moment."

He paused, his hands leaning against his horse, then he turned fully to her.

"I don't take surprises well," Vixie said. "Or being left out. I understand if you are upset with me—"

"It's you who's upset with me, isn't it?" He cocked his head.

"Nay." Her insides began to right themselves. "Perhaps at first, but no longer."

"So . . . we are all right, then?"

She gave him a bashful smile. "I do have one selfish request." He waited while she worked up the nerve. "Paxton has agreed to stay back as part of the troops who will guard Aerity and me during the battle. I was hoping you could as well."

His eyebrows drew together. "I'm sorry, Vix, but I've promised the Zandalee I will return to Dovedell and fight with them. I only came to see you—erm, all of you—before the battle."

Fear jolted her. "Surely we can send another in your place."

His eyes softened. "I must go. Our chances are good. Please don't worry."

She let out a shaky breath. How could she not worry?

"Is that you, Princess Vixie?"

Both of their heads turned toward the voice. A lean, sturdy Torestan lad with a fine face and royal uniform buttoned to his neck came forward, flanked by five Torestan soldiers. Vixie studied him. He looked familiar. Then her mind lit up.

"Prince Hanriil of Toresta?"

The lad smiled. "It has been a long time."

She tried to remember the last time she'd seen King Gavriil Cliftonia's son. "Three years," she said. "The updated Eurona pact signing."

"Dreadful," he said, and they both laughed.

From the corner of her eye she saw Tiern rock back on his heels with his hands behind his back, watching their interaction.

"Prince Hanriil, this is the hunter Tiern Seabolt. He joined the great hunt and had a hand in slaying the beast."

"Well, I wouldn't say . . ." Tiern mumbled but stopped and simply gave a respectful bow. "It's an honor to meet you, Your Highness."

"And you, hunter," the prince replied before shifting his full attention back to Vixie. "I was very sorry to learn of your parents' fate, Princess."

Vixie dropped her eyes and nodded as a sharp ache landed in her chest.

"They were the kindest rulers in all the lands," he continued. "I always enjoyed our visits to Lochlanach, and I wish I were here under better circumstances."

She finally looked at him, trying to stand tall.

"You resemble her very much, your mother," he said, the reverence in his voice making her swallow a burn of moisture.

"Remember how angry she was when they found us under the dock, collecting crabs and covered in mud?"

Vixie let out a laugh, wiping the corners of her eyes. "I only remember how much convincing it took you to go under that dock in the first place." He'd been so lanky and overcautious. He'd certainly grown out of that awkwardness, though.

The prince grinned. "I was fifteen. Too old to be playing in mud."

"But you had fun," Vixie teased.

"I did."

Tiern cleared his throat, and nodded his head toward officers who were beginning to gather and call everyone in for planning. Prince Hanriil peered over his shoulder before giving Vixie a tight look. "I've got to go."

"Are you to fight?" Vixie asked.

"I am. My first battle. I have trained two years, despite my father's wishes, and I am honored to be at your service." He gave her a bow from the waist, which she returned.

"Seas be with you." She prayed he would return to his father unharmed.

"And the winds with you."

He left, and when Vixie looked back at Tiern his mouth was in a straight line and her tummy flipped. *By the seas . . . is he jealous?*

"He's an old friend," she explained.

Tiern gave a slow nod. "A delightful prince of an old friend."

Vixie propped a hand on her hip. "If you wished to ward him off, you could have simply kissed me. I've heard that strategy works well."

Tiern's eyes rounded, and Vixie pressed her fingers to her lips to hold back a laugh at her boldness.

"Perhaps next time I will, little sea star," he said threateningly.

Vixie dropped her hand from her mouth and smiled outright. "I'll hold you to that." A quiet comfort formed between them, and Vixie lost her mirth. "Be safe, Tiern. Seas be with you."

"And also with you."

Chapter 47

Aerity stood in a small room of a house in the valley of Craw Coorie, peering down at a map of Lochlanach with Harrison and two senior officers. They had gone over every detail of the plan with her. Enticing Kalor's troops into the narrow land between the rivers was ideal because it would even their chances by thinning the Kalorian troops and not allowing them to outnumber the allies. And if the Zorfinans could sneak attack from the northern end of the waterways, it would trap the enemy. They would never make it near Craw Coorie, but a plan was in place to move the queen, princess, and lady farther north if the fighting moved farther than expected.

"What if they do not leave royal lands to attack?" Aerity asked.

Harrison sighed. "Then we will have to come up with a new plan to attack directly."

"Your Majesty," said the senior officer, "once we are able to storm the castle, we recommend taking Prince Vito captive so that after the battle is over there can be a public execution."

The room was quiet as the men watched for her reaction. Aerity thought about it. A public execution would show her strength as a ruler and send a message that she did not take enemies of her kingdom lightly. But this was Prince Vito they were talking about. She shook her head.

"I cannot take the chance of his escaping. He is not to be underestimated. My orders are to kill him on sight, any way possible. Same goes for Rozaria Rocato."

The officer gave a nod. "Do we have your permission to exhibit their bodies for the public to see?"

Her stomach turned. "Just this once, and not for an extended period. I will not make a habit of morbid displays of power."

Voices outside made Harrison go to the window. "Townspeople are arriving from Dovedell and bordering villages. We're told there will be Lochlan Lashed among them—people from your camps who are willing to lay hands on the enemy, and heal our men who are injured along the way."

"I wish to address them," Aerity said. "Gather everyone in the town center."

The officers shared a glance before agreeing. She knew they wanted to keep her hidden and as far as possible from all people and the battle, but Aerity hated letting everyone fight while she sat back, comfortable and safe. All she had to offer them were her words, and so she would give them.

Each and every life entering the battle weighed on Aerity. She couldn't believe King Gavriil had sent his son—granted, it was his second son, and his soldiers had insisted he not be allowed on the front lines. In fact, his battalion remained in Craw Coorie as the last line of defense. The insolent look on Prince Hanriil's face when he'd been overruled had so reminded her of Vixie. She'd had to hold back her amusement.

Once the people were all ushered into the town square, Aerity was led to the center, where she climbed a raised platform used for town meetings. As soon as she appeared, the crowd broke into a cheer that made her cheeks warm and her chest tighten. She looked out upon regular townsmen and townswomen who stood alongside Lochlan soldiers and Torestan soldiers. It was a beautiful yet saddening sight. She let her voice rise into the wintry air.

"Good people of Lochlanach and Toresta! My heart aches to see you, and longs for better circumstances for our gathering. Among you there are farmers and fishermen, blacksmiths and bakers, Lashed and Unlashed, fathers, mothers, sons, and daughters. I extend my fondest gratitude to each one of you for being here, willing to fight for our way of life—a life I hope to enrich during my rule—a life that will surely see further strife and wickedness if we do not take back what is ours.

"The time to rely on one another is now. Look around at those who stand beside you. Today I lift the laws against magic, for all of your benefit. Today, the Lashed who stand at your side will be there to heal you if you fall. You need not fear one another. I promise that when this battle is over, and victory is ours, I will spend my life working to repair a century's worth of injustice done against each one of you, who has suffered knowingly or not, by what you have been denied.

"The enemy claims to be a friend of the Lashed, but he is a friend of *no one*. I have seen firsthand that the ruler of Kalor seeks power through fear and hate. He wishes to use magic for his own benefit, not for the good of the people, and I will not stand for it! This is an enemy who does not value life and will kill any who stand in the way of his domination over all Eurona. I pray to the seas that justice is swift and we can begin our lives anew very soon. To each of you, I bestow my heartfelt gratitude for your courage and valor. The seas be with you."

A murmur of "Also with you" rose up from the crowd, and all were respectfully quiet as Aerity was escorted away.

Two Lochlan women and a Lochlan man, wearing rags that were splattered with blood, ran as quickly as they could toward the royal gate. Each had fear in their hearts for what they were about to do, but that fear was overridden by their desire to help Queen Aerity in any way they could.

The sky was darkening as the sun set. Their panting breaths left trails of steam in their wake. The man suddenly skidded to a halt and held out his arms to stop the women.

Their eyes followed his up to the top of the stone wall.

Their hands went up, trembling in the air, at the sight of Kalorian soldiers lining the wall, arrows pointed directly at them. The Lochlan man stepped forward and fell to his knees, his arms still up.

"P-please. We are under attack. They are killing all the Lashed!"

"My son!" wept one of the women, clutching her chest.

The Kalorians peered around at the empty fields and hills behind them, and then murmured to one another. One of them held a palm up to them, as if telling them to wait. Both women were crying in earnest, their fear apparent.

Moments later the gates opened just enough to show a Kalorian lord with a severe, long face. He stared at them, a lip curled in repulsion at their appearance, and then his eyes narrowed at the sight of the man's hands.

"Come closer . . . now stop. Hold up your hands."

Three pairs of dirty, shaking hands came slowly up for the man to see the lines on their nails.

"Ah." He relaxed a small fraction. "Lochlan Lashed. Why have you come?"

"Please, sir," said the man. "We heard you have many Lashed among you, that you're a friend of the magical folk, that you're going to change the laws around here." The man swallowed hard, still trying to catch his breath. The Kalorian said nothing, so the Lochlan kept going. "They want you gone—"

"Who?"

"The townspeople in the north. They want to stop all our Lashed from joining you. They've got our Lashed ones locked up in the town hall at Craw Coorie and they're planning to burn it tonight! They want to wage a battle to root you out."

"My son is in there!" one of the women cried. She clasped her hands together, begging. "Please save them—I'll do anything! I will be at your service for life."

The Kalorian's lips pursed into a tight bud of ire. "How many Lashed?"

"More than fifty," said the quietest woman.

"And townsmen?"

The three of them looked at one another and the man spoke. "Hundreds. And more are coming from nearby villages, dragging their Lashed as well. They're trying to make their own army. This has been boiling since the new queen opened the Lashed camps."

At this, the man laughed drily. "It was only a matter of time. We will squash this uprising like a fat berry and leave its rotting flesh for all to see."

"And the Lashed?" the woman asked desperately. "Can you save them?"

"Come through the gate and stand against the wall. If you move, you will be shot. I will fetch our general and you will tell him exactly where this town is located."

"Bless you, sir!" said the women, sending their praises as the three of them rushed to the wall, still lined with Kalorian soldiers watching the spectacle with interest.

"Long live Prince Vito!" shouted the Lochlan man. The three of them clung together by the wall, rejoicing.

The sun had fully set, sending an ominous quiet over the town of Craw Coorie. Three messengers had been sent to start the war. She prayed Vito would take the bait. It was unnerving to know there were hundreds of soldiers and townspeople in her midst, ready to fight, all hidden within the town, and yet not a single sound could be heard. Aerity sat in a complete stranger's cozy main room with Vixie, Wyneth, Paxton, Mrs. Rathbrook, and a hulking Furball.

Aerity chewed her thumbnail as her mind turned over scenario after scenario. What if Vito didn't believe the three Lashed? What if he simply didn't care that Lochlan Lashed were supposedly being killed? What if he was too busy searching for Aerity inside the castle and refused to have his men leave royal lands until they found her? What if they'd found the hidden passageways?

"Aer, you're breathing funny again," Vixie said gently.

Aerity sat up and took a deep breath. She wanted this war to be over with. She listened so hard that the quiet actually thrummed deep in her ears. "It's killing me not to know how much longer we've got, or if they're even planning to attack." She stood and went to the window where Paxton was watching through a crack in the shutters with his arms crossed. Together, they did the only thing they could do. Wait.

Chapter 48

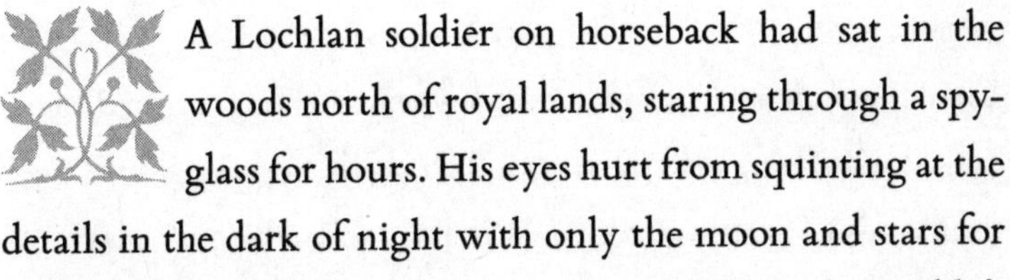

A Lochlan soldier on horseback had sat in the woods north of royal lands, staring through a spyglass for hours. His eyes hurt from squinting at the details in the dark of night with only the moon and stars for light. Something was going on in royal lands . . . he couldn't see it but he could hear it. Commotion. Movement. Voices. They were preparing. He wanted to charge away that instant to tell the Lochlan and Ascomannian soldiers waiting along the bay, but his orders were not to move until he saw the royal gates open.

It was deep in the night before that finally happened. Kalorians on horseback spilled out. With a pounding heart, the soldier turned his steed and shot northeastward. He rode faster than he'd ever gone, trees rushing past in a whir of dark movement. It took almost an hour before he came to the first soldier, also on horseback.

"They are coming!" he shouted. The other nodded and turned, riding toward the bay to warn the first line of troops.

Up the strip the soldier went, alerting other messenger soldiers until the news spread like moving fingers through the woods, up to the bay, and along Loch River and Crescent Stream to the waiting troops. He rode, finally reaching Craw Coorie where he fell from his horse and grasped a cup of water from Lieutenant Gillfin's outstretched hand.

"You did well," the lieutenant told him. "Rest. It could be hours before they reach the rivers, and that's if the Ascomannians let them make it that far."

Tiern Seabolt rode swiftly southward to the town of Dovedell. It gave him a thrill to round the hill and look down over thousands of waiting troops. When they saw him, an alertness rang through the air. Soldiers and townsmen began to rush about.

He rode to the inn, which had been made into headquarters for the army commanders. He jumped from his horse and was led straight in to find Zorfinan high officers and Zandora. They all stood expectantly. He gulped two large breaths before giving his news.

"We estimate that one third of the Kalorian troops have exited the northern gates of royal lands and headed north."

"They have taken the bait," said the Zorfinan leader. The others nodded with satisfaction. "But two-thirds remaining inside the walls is more than I had hoped."

Tiern continued. "Aye. We will be evenly matched with their numbers on land."

"When the battle begins, Lochlan and Ascomannian ships will come down from the bay into the royal port," a Zorfinan officer said. "That will provide a distraction to get Kalor away from the wall, and into cannon fire."

"We will outnumber them," Zandora said with confidence. "When will we leave?"

"I propose that we give the ships an hour or so to move into place in order to attack simultaneously," said Tiern. "Perhaps we will catch many of them comfortably asleep at that time. How many Lashed will join us?"

An officer answered, "With those who came from southern lands we now have forty-four prepared to enter battle with us."

Zandora's eyes gleamed. "I will ready my women."

"And I my men," said the Zorfinan leader.

Tiern remembered Vixie's face when he'd left her. He wanted to be worthy of that look. This was his chance.

Chapter 49

News of battle made it to Craw Coorie from another mounted messenger. Lochlan and Ascomannian forces had patiently waited while Kalorian troops squeezed onto the strip of land, and then attacked from the river side, stream side, and north. Meanwhile ships sailed down from the bay to royal lands for the battle that would take place there.

So far everything had gone according to plan, much to the joy and relief of all the leaders in Craw Coorie.

"At this rate you could be back in the castle as soon as tomorrow, my queen," said Harrison.

"Seas willing," she whispered, too afraid to hope.

Once she'd been informed, the officers left the thatched house where Aerity was to remain during the battle, surrounded by guards. She looked around at the others. They appeared as tired as she felt, especially Paxton, who had finally sat and was rubbing his face.

He brought his palms down to rest on his thighs and looked at Aerity. They stared at each other, neither appearing happy, and both steady in mutual agreement: it was too good to be real. Knowing what a cunning man Prince Vito was, it seemed unlikely he'd fall so easily for their trick. They were dealing with an evil mastermind. Others might forget it, but Aerity and Paxton could not.

After well over an hour, the confined room began to feel stifling. Aerity could not bring herself to sit still or eat the food they'd been brought. For once she had more energy than Vixie, who looked on the verge of passing out from exhaustion at any moment. Aerity so desperately wanted to fly above the lands like a hawk and see what was happening.

"Aerity, you're going to wear a path in this poor family's rug," Wyneth said gently. "And if you don't eat something your body will eventually crash." Her cousin held out a plate with a buttered roll, roasted pumpkin, and a poached egg.

She took it and sat heavily at the table, wanting to appease Wyneth. She took a nibble of the roll and pushed the pumpkin around until Wyn cleared her throat and nodded at the plate. Aerity shoved a bite of roasted pumpkin in her mouth and had to grab a cup of water to wash it down when it got stuck. She forced down several more bites before pushing it away, stomach aching.

"Give it here." Vixie sounded grumpy as she sat across

from Aerity and took the plate, absently putting bites into her mouth. Furball walked over to her, put a hand on the bench next to her, and began to lift himself up to the table.

Wyneth made a sharp click with her mouth that caused Furball to jump back, away from the table.

"Good boy," she said. She grabbed a sausage from her plate and tossed it to him, shrugging when Harrison crossed his arms and gave her a rueful look. "What? It's not as if you lot were going to eat it."

He opened his mouth to speak but didn't have a chance. A hurried knock at the door pulled him away. Paxton stood and went to Harrison's side as he opened it. One of the officers stood there with fervent worry in his eyes that made Aerity's stomach plummet.

"Bad news, Lieutenant. When the Kalorians realized they were under attack, half their forces stayed to fight while the other half fled across the stream. But instead of continuing south, they turned and headed northward. We hadn't expected that since the stream is chest deep and nearly frozen. We're not certain if they're trying to circle and hit our forces from behind, or if they're taking the long route here to Craw Coorie, but it's time for the town to brace and the queen to be moved."

"Aye," said Harrison. "Though the Kalorians will be in poor shape after going through the stream. And what of the small village on the other side of the stream? Have their people evacuated?"

"Those that remained have been told to flee."

"Very good. I want the queen, princess, and lady taken to safety straightaway," Harrison said.

The officer nodded and pivoted to leave. Harrison turned to Aerity and the other lasses. "A boat awaits to take you across the Loch of Lanach where the town of Easthaven will harbor you."

"Fine, thank you," said Aerity, knowing better than to argue. Paxton's shoulders lost their tension when she agreed.

"I'm going to get an idea of their arrival time and round up your horses," Harrison said. "This is only a minor setback. Nothing we can't handle." He gave Wyneth a warm look and she rewarded him with a small, reassuring smile before he turned to go.

"Will you come with us?" Aerity asked Paxton.

His eyes moved to the door and then back to her. He grasped the back of his neck. Aerity felt a pinch of worry in her chest when she realized he wanted to stay and probably to fight. Or heal. Or both.

"Pax, please," Aerity said, her chest expanding and collapsing with each bang of her heart. He came to her and took her hands.

"Soldiers will accompany you," he told her gently. "I'll be the first across that lake once things settle."

Aerity closed her eyes, trying to calm her anxiety. She knew she could beg and even use guilt tactics to make him leave with them, but she also knew his mind and heart would remain here, in Craw Coorie, feeling as if he'd abandoned the other men when every hand was needed . . . feeling as if he'd taken the coward's route.

"Please be safe," she implored.

He leaned his face down to kiss her when a *bang* rocked the ground beneath their feet. Vixie screamed and voices outside rose to a shattering volume of screams and shouts. Paxton's eyes went huge.

"What was that?" Wyneth asked.

"Gunpowder explosion," Paxton said.

"It sounded close." A wave of panic crashed through Aerity. "Maybe even town hall."

"We've got to get you out of here." Paxton pulled her by the hand and looked at Wyneth and Vixie when he got to the door. "Stay close!" They huddled with Furball at their side.

Aerity wasn't prepared for the shock of what she saw when they came out of the cottage. Her guards had fanned out, staring at the commotion, with their bows and arrows drawn.

Beyond the hill that hid them was the town square and town hall. Flames shot high into the air, stretching its smoke into the darkness of night. From the corner of her eye, Aerity saw a flash of light as something came soaring through the air.

"Watch out!" she screamed, pointing. Paxton pushed them back just as the flaming arrow hit the thatched roof of the tiny house next to them. It crackled and quickly spread until its roof was in flames. Heat wafted toward them.

"Where is Harrison with the blasted horses?" Paxton

yelled. The four of them peered around at the commoners with armfuls of belongings, and soldiers who were pointing, directing, and running with weapons brandished. But so far not a single enemy could be seen in their valley.

Wyneth murmured a plea to the sea under her breath.

Paxton looked at Aerity. "He must have met interference. I'm going for the horses myself. Stay behind your guards. If anything happens, run north and don't look back." She squeezed his hands and he sprinted up and over the hill.

The three girls clung to each other in silence, watching the chaos. Their guards moved in closer to surround them. A covered cart rounded the hill and sped down toward them, halting as the guard's arrows were aimed at its single driver, a Lochlan commoner.

"An army of Kalorians are just through those trees—" The moment the man said it, another flaming arrow came soaring from the woods, hitting the ground and skidding to a halt in front of them. A guard stomped it out. The man continued in a rush. "I carry two riders, villagers from across the stream, but there's room for three more: two in the carriage and one up front with me. Any takers?"

The guards looked at one another, then their eyes went to Aerity. She shook her head. "I will wait for Paxton."

One of the guards hurried forward and bent his head so only the royal lasses could hear. "Your Majesty, I implore you to go now. And to take two guards."

"I'm not leaving my sister and cousin."

"Aerity, don't be absurd!" Wyneth said.

"Go!" Vixie pleaded. "We'll be right behind you."

The guard's eyes beseeched her and Aerity exhaled, knowing she had a duty to keep herself safe. "All right." She kissed Wyneth and Vixie quickly on their cheeks. She did not want to leave them. Every footstep toward the carriage went against her instincts.

Please let Harrison and Paxton be safe. Please let Vixie and Wyneth follow me to safety straightaway.

One of the guards climbed up next to the driver in front. Her guard opened the door to the carriage and looked in at the occupants before nodding and ushering Aerity up, then climbing in himself. Seconds later they were moving. Aerity glanced at the two commoner women, both who wore dirty aprons, and she gave them nods, which they returned. If they recognized her, they didn't make a fuss. She wished there were windows in the cart, but the cloth covering was tight over the carriage.

A shout came from the front of the cart, followed by a loud grunt and a thud. The cart shifted momentarily as if the weight in the front had changed. Aerity grasped the seat to keep from falling. Her guard grabbed the door and was about to swing it open to peer out when the driver shouted back through the cloth wall overhead.

"Sorry about that! All clear now!"

Her guard sat back slowly, appearing as edgy as Aerity felt. The commoner women took the bump in stride, silently.

Aerity's eyes dropped to their hands in their laps and her stomach filled with agitated, nervous buzzing. They were Lashed.

She scolded herself for the rush of prejudice and fear that seeing their lash marks brought. She had no reason to feel distress in the presence of her own Lashed commoners, unfriendly though they may be.

"I thank you for sharing your cart," Aerity said.

The woman stared, straight-faced, and did not reply. Aerity's neck prickled.

Her guard sat forward. "This is your queen, Aerity Lochson, who has addressed you—"

"It's okay, sir." Aerity lay a hand on his forearm just as shouting rose up behind the cart.

"*Stop them!*" she heard. Was that Paxton's voice? She sat up straighter.

One of the women sprang and grabbed the guard's hand. He tried to pull away, but in a split second his face slackened and he fell forward. Aerity stared in horror at his body at their feet before a shattering scream tore from her throat. She lunged for the door, but the women grabbed her and pushed her back. She screamed, kicked, and flailed her arms against their holds. The cart moved faster.

"Stay still or we will kill you," one of the women said in Kalorian.

Aerity loathed the whimper that escaped as she went limp in obedience.

Chapter 50

Paxton had only seen the side of the cart driver's face from afar, lit partially from the light of nearby fire as he pulled away. Recognition frayed the edges of his mind. He'd reined in his horse, and Harrison stopped his steed at Paxton's side, sensing that something was awry. Paxton's eyes went to the horseshoe formation of guards surrounding the lasses. Two lasses.

"Aerity is gone," he said. His pulse shot up so quickly that he had to swallow. His eyes went toward the covered cart and all at once the recognition clicked into place. "Deep seas," he whispered. That man driving the cart . . . he could have sworn it was Konor. "Harrison, I have to stop that cart! It's one of Rozaria's men!"

Paxton shoved the reins of the other two horses toward Harrison as he charged down the hill. On the path he had to weave through townspeople and soldiers.

"Stop them!" he'd shouted.

Up ahead a crowd had formed. They slowly moved aside as Paxton pressed inward, shouting for them to clear the way. And then he came upon what they'd been staring at. A royal guard dead in the path.

"He was thrown from that cart!" a man said.

"Get to safety!" Paxton told the townspeople before charging forward again.

Was Aerity alone inside that carriage? If not, who was with her? Rozaria? He shook his worried thoughts away and urged his horse into a gallop, gaining ground. "Stop them!"

They were nearing the edge of the town when Paxton's horse was at the cart's door. He swiped for the handle, but couldn't reach.

"Aerity!" he shouted. Nobody responded, but up ahead Konor leaned to the side and peered back with wild eyes. Paxton urged his horse forward until he was riding alongside Konor. The man kicked out, landing a blow to Paxton's horse's neck. His horse faltered one moment before righting himself with a huff. Paxton leaned and grasped Konor by the back of his tunic. The man spun to try and grab Paxton, but Pax yanked with all his might, sending the man flying from the cart with a holler as he rolled on the pebbled path behind them.

Paxton tried to grasp the reins of the cart but couldn't reach. The cart horse spooked and turned abruptly up the hill. "Whoa, whoa!" Paxton cursed as the carriage tilted and then toppled over. Screams sounded from within the carriage, and the horse reared with a great whinny.

Paxton yanked his horse to a stop and leaped down.

"I wouldn't do that if I were you," said a low, seductive voice that he knew all too well.

Paxton slowly turned to face Rozaria, who had walked out from behind the very last house. The severe look of betrayal in her eyes, paired with the utter calm of her body, sent a tremor of apprehension to his core. Paxton said nothing and did not move, though his eyes darted to see who else might step out at any moment.

The door to the toppled cart opened at the top and a brown-haired woman's head rose. Rozaria called out to the woman in Kalorian, and whatever the woman said made a triumphant laugh spill out of Rozaria. Her eyes gleamed at Paxton.

"We have your precious queen, hunter. It seems all your hard work was for nothing."

His head jerked toward the toppled cart, and he watched as two women tried to pull Aerity from the doorway. She struggled and then gave a strangled scream as one of the women apparently used magic to subdue her. His love, his queen, was in the hands of Lashed, being dragged roughly away.

Never had he experienced such blinding dread. There was

no telling what torturous actions they were capable of in their offended rage. From the triumphant look on Rozaria's face as she stalked slowly forward, she knew he was afraid. She stopped just short of an arm's length away from him.

"I pride myself on reading people. Nicola tried to warn me, but . . ." She tilted her head. "I know at least part of you felt what I felt, isn't that right?" Her smug smile made him clench his fists. "I understand you at a level that no Unlashed woman ever could, don't I, hunter? Indeed, I believe part of you truly did hate your king and want him gone. So what weakened you, hmm? Was it the attention of a pretty princess? What did she promise you? Lands? A grand boat to fish your life away? A place in her bed?"

"She is *more* than a pretty face," Paxton said, unable to listen to another word. "She is compassion and integrity at its finest."

Rozaria sneered and shouted, "You have allowed the weaker parts of yourself to win out! For that, you will not be spared. And neither will your queen. But first she will belong to Vito."

He felt his face harden, and Rozaria chuckled darkly.

Paxton surveyed his situation. The two women were pulling Aerity away from him, toward the houses. Down the path he could hear hooves and voices. Help would arrive soon, but that almost made him more nervous. It wouldn't take much to make Rozaria snap. She continued to stare hard at Paxton as she spoke loudly to her women in Kalorian.

They stood eye to eye as the women tugged Aerity toward the door of a far house. Paxton had his bow and arrows and his daggers. In the time it would take him to reach and ready one of those weapons, Rozaria could have her hands on him. However, he did have one thing that could reach her in a hurry. The women were nearly out of sight.

"Oh, hunter," Rozaria began, but he did not allow her to finish.

Paxton pivoted and whipped his leg out with all his might, sending a kick straight into Rozaria's mid-chest. He connected, hard, and she flew with an *umph*, landing on her back. She was gasping for breath when he pulled his bow out and nocked an arrow, pointing it straight down at her. Before he could let loose, a whizzing sound and sharp sting burned the side of his arm.

It was a deep gash, and his right arm suddenly lost strength; he couldn't grasp his bow as tightly. He looked up to see Nicola with a bow, another arrow pointed directly at him. She rushed forward, caught between wanting to keep the arrow aimed at him and wanting to bend down to care for Rozaria. If she took one hand off that bowstring, Paxton would throw a dagger with his good hand.

Rozaria panted something in Kalorian, clutching her ribs as she pushed to sit up, and then stand. She wore a mask of maliciousness, as if every ugly thing inside her had surfaced and was now showing.

From behind Paxton, sounds of Harrison and the guards

neared. Rozaria pointed at Paxton and snarled a word in Kalorian that he recognized: "*Shoot!*" Nicola pulled back her bowstring, but Paxton ducked and rolled, feeling his bow and quiver dig into his back, then he leaped to his feet and took off toward the side of the house where Aerity had been taken. He darted side to side so as not to give Nicola an easy target. An arrow missed him, and another. He heard her scream of frustration as he rounded the corner out of view.

Chapter 51

Each time Aerity struggled, she felt a burning sensation in her skin where the women held her wrists, and something inside her would burst into pain, or she would simply not be able to breathe for a moment. They'd also done something to her jaw, locked it so that she could not open it to scream. Their power over her was terrifying.

Inside the house was dark. The women shoved her to the floor and turned to go. She felt her jaw release once their hands were off her. They left her in complete darkness. Aerity scrambled to her feet just as a flame was lit. And then another. And another. Prince Vito and two guards—one of whom was Martone. They were in a single-room house with only one door. Aerity lunged for the exit, but Martone grabbed her around the waist and flung her into a chair.

Martone stepped away, leaving her in the chair while he blocked the door and the other Kalorian stood in front of the single, curtained window on the side wall. Her eyes went to Vito, who stood too close, watching her with lazy amusement.

"I was always good at hide-and-seek, you know. And I appreciate a good game as much as the next." He walked forward and leaned down into Aerity's face, grasping the chair arms on each side of her. His breath was sour. "But I am quite done chasing you now."

His eyes lifted from hers at the sounds of tromping feet, shouting, and arrows whizzing. It sounded as if they were fighting just outside the cottage. Aerity opened her mouth to scream, but Prince Vito struck her with the back of his hand, slinging her face to the side in a starburst of pain. She brought a hand up to her mouth, tasting blood where her teeth cut her lip. Aerity pressed away from him in the chair, shaking uncontrollably as she said, "You can kill me, but you will not win this."

A slow grin came to his face. "Death is too kind for you now. You *will* be my wife. You will serve me in every way."

"Never."

"To keep your brother alive? I think yes."

Donubhan . . . Aerity turned to a statue under his scrutinizing gaze. *Seas no.* Vito began to chuckle as she envisioned the Isle of Evie under attack, and Donnie being captured by these monsters. If they had him, they had the entire royal family.

"The first thing we did," murmured Prince Vito, "was to shave those vile red curls from his head with our sharpest blade."

Aerity shut her eyes and her body convulsed. She couldn't take it. Outside voices were getting closer. The prince looked at the spare guard and ordered in Kalorian, "Bring the cart around now. The fighting wasn't supposed to get this close."

The prince turned his head to steal a look outside as the guard left. Aerity took the opportunity. She lunged forward and brought her knee straight into the prince's crotch as hard as she could, but instead of him doubling over, it was she who cried out at the blast of pain in her knee. He wore some sort of protective metal covering. He swung again, this time hitting her ear, making her entire head ring. Aerity screamed, and Vito laughed once again.

"We can keep going," he said as she cowered. "I'm enjoying this very much."

When the ringing had almost stopped she stood, bracing herself, and faced him. Outside the door, a vicious, animalistic roar split the air, causing Prince Vito's eyes to widen.

"I thought the beasts had remained on royal lands," he said to Martone. Aerity's hopes rose. *If it wasn't one of their creatures . . .*

Something crashed into the door like a battering ram and

sent it flying clean off its hinges, sliding to the middle of the room. Furball stood on his hind legs, his mane touching the ceiling, and roared so loudly it shook the walls. Prince Vito's face transformed from his usual look of smugness to an ashen pallor.

Aerity pointed at the prince and yelled, "Attack!"

Furball's paws stretched wide, his bright, sharp claws shining in the candlelight, but he was distracted when Martone brandished a sword. Furball swiped out in a fast movement that sent Martone's hand, with the sword in it, flying across the room in a gory splatter. The prince backed away against the wall as Furball leaped onto Martone, and Aerity ran out the door.

The house next to them was on fire, blinding, hot, and loud. A cart tore up next to her and the prince's other guard jumped down. An arrow swooshed by and the guard gurgled wetly as the arrow pierced his neck. He fell to the side, swiping at it.

"Aerity!" Paxton ran forward, bow in hand. Her eyes went straight to the stained, torn sleeve.

"You're hurt!"

He shook his head. "Mrs. Rathbrook healed me." He looked to the open doorway.

"Prince Vito's in there," Aerity said. "Furball attacked Martone. And, oh, seas . . . they have Donubhan!"

Paxton put a reassuring hand on her shoulder. "We'll find him." He nocked another arrow and sidled next to the doorway, peering in. His eyes went from side to side before stopping, a deep frown etching his face.

"Furball come!" he shouted. His eyes went to Aerity. "The prince must have fled through the window."

Curses! She looked in, and sure enough, the room was empty with nowhere to hide. The window was wide open, with scratch marks from where Furball had apparently tried to give chase but couldn't fit. Martone's carcass lay in the middle of the floor. Aerity covered her mouth and backed away.

"Aer!" Wyneth's voice rounded the corner of the burning building. She, Vixie, and Mrs. Rathbrook appeared, flanked by Harrison.

Paxton grasped her arm. "All four of you need to get in this cart and go north to cross the lake. I've got to find the prince."

Aerity swallowed hard, sick at the thought of Pax facing Vito, but somebody had to stop the madman.

"Wait." Harrison sprinted up, pulling something metallic from his waist and handing it to Paxton. "Smoke bomb." Pax took it and ran to search behind the house.

Seas be with him.

Aerity hurriedly waved a hand to the other girls and they ran faster. Furball came through the door, his jowls dark with blood, just as Wyneth halted, breathing hard. She made a horrified face at the gore covering him.

"Good boy, Furball," Harrison said, earning a satisfied grunt from the beast. "Now, let's go. Ladies, in. Furball will have to run beside us." Aerity took his hand and climbed up. It was identical to the one she'd been in before, and it gave her a shiver to remember. The other three climbed swiftly in, and the cart lightly dipped as Harrison took his spot at the reins. "Hang on!" he shouted.

But there was nothing to hang on to. They grasped the seats and one another as the carriage shot forward, bumping over rocks and tilting upward from the slant of the hill. Aerity's mind went to Paxton trying to find Prince Vito, and she clutched her stomach. She hoped he could get a good shot so he wouldn't have to be within arm's reach of the man. *Seas, keep him safe.*

Hand-to-hand combat did not suit Tiern. He'd been fine shooting arrows from behind an overturned market table. In fact, a sense of calm had come over him, causing his aim to be steady and more accurate than ever. One after another, he took down Kalorians. But when he'd shot his last arrow and saw a soldier preparing to shoot the youngest Zandalee, Zaleek, from behind, he snatched a dagger from his waist and sprinted, plunging the knife into the man's neck.

Nay, the crunch and blood, coupled with the dying man's last struggle to fight, was not Tiern's idea of fun. Perhaps that made him less of a man, but so be it. Zaleek seemed impressed enough. When she spun to see Tiern taking the Kalorian down to the ground, wiping his dagger on his trouser leg as he stood, Zaleek had waggled her eyebrows up and down before turning to fight again.

Tiern didn't have a sword like the soldiers battling around him, so he didn't dare attempt hand-to-hand with the enemy. He ran about, collecting arrows, trying not to wince at the sounds of ripping arrowheads from dead bodies. Getting lost in a sea of forward-moving fighting, Tiern grasped a branch of the nearest tree and hoisted himself up. He shot his quiver full of arrows, aiming at Kalorians who were about to take down Zorfinans, and picking them off one by one in rapid succession. One of them pointed up at him, and another turned to shoot. Tiern hunkered down and the arrow stuck directly into the branch beneath him. He quickly took down that Kalorian before he could aim at him again.

From his vantage point he could see a horde of Lochlan soldiers battling the three monsters in front of the west commons. Roaring and snarling ripped through the air, but the sheer number of Lochlans attacking were enough to overpower the creatures. A surge of excitement burned through Tiern.

After another half hour of fighting alongside the Zorfinans, the enemy was cleared out of the market area, so the allies moved forward, toward the castle. The ships had truly saved them, taking out hundreds of Kalorians and distracting them while the Zorfinans stormed the southern gates to attack from behind.

When Lochlan and Ascomannian vessels docked and soldiers came flooding out, it didn't take much longer to overcome the Kalorians. Together, the Lochlans, Ascomannians, and Zorfinans raised a cheer that seemed to go on forever. All that was left was the castle, which appeared strangely unguarded, no archers or soldiers anywhere in sight. It made no sense to Tiern. They should have been heavily guarding their prince.

As military leaders began shouting orders, their remaining troops spread out around the castle. Those who had shields held them up against possible assailants from within. Tiern watched as the elite soldiers and the Zandalee moved up the front steps, opened the doors, and rushed inside with war cries. He held his breath, waiting for an onslaught. He peered up at the balcony and parapet walkway, then the rooftop, all empty. What in the lands of Eurona was going on?

After ten minutes, Zandora came to the doorway and shook her head, looking vexed. He climbed the steps to her.

"It is empty," she said.

"But how?" he asked. "Surely someone would have seen them come out."

"Do you know the location of the underground shelter you spoke of?"

He nodded. "Follow me."

He'd not been there himself, but he'd heard the others talk about it. He, Zandora, and five other Zandalee readied their bows and pulled the bowstrings taut as they took the steps down to the cellar. When they came to the back pantry room and it was empty, he motioned toward the chest. Still holding his bow, he slowly lifted the lid with his boot and flung it upward. Seven bows pointed down the empty shaft.

Tiern climbed down first, with Zandora behind him. They both unsheathed their daggers and kicked the panel door open to see a long, dim, empty room. They walked inside through the beds and disarray. The other Zandalee joined them. And then Tiern's eyes landed on an open chest at the end of the room. He ran to it.

Once again the seven of them pointed their bows down into a shaft with a ladder. Tiern looked at Zandora.

"I didn't know about this one. There must be tunnels out of the castle."

Zandora exhaled and shook her head. "He has escaped. We must send warning."

"If it's not already too late," Tiern said.

Paxton could feel the prince's power, that zing of heat along his skin. If he could feel the prince, he was certain the man could feel him too. Paxton couldn't believe his luck that he might find the Kalorian leader without his guards. This would be his one and only chance to kill the man.

Nearby burning houses sent shadows leaping and falling along the ground and trees and smaller cottages on the outskirts of town. He held his bowstring taut and tried to steady his ragged breathing while he searched. As he neared a cottage, the feel of Lashed power became even stronger.

He's hidden within, Paxton thought. He wondered what makeshift weapon the devious man might have crafted for himself. He thought of the last house, and how the prince had escaped through the window. Paxton snuck around to the back of the cottage and found a window the same size as the other had been. He nodded to himself and went back to the front.

He felt at his waist for the black powder smoke bomb Harrison had given him. He backed away from the house, lit the wick between his fingers, watched it burn halfway down, then launched the thing straight through the front window's shutter.

Paxton sprinted around the cottage to the back and crouched, arrow pointed. It was much darker back there without the firelight. Within seconds the window was being pried open by thin hands and the prince's coughing face was peering out. Paxton waited with his heart in his throat. His instinct was to shoot, but he needed to find out where the young prince was being held.

When Prince Vito's feet hit the ground, Paxton stood and rushed forward. The prince spun, as if suddenly sensing Paxton's presence, and he backed against the wall, brandishing a glinting dagger that could imbed itself in Paxton's chest with a flick of the man's wrist.

Vito snarled. "You!"

"Aye. Me."

Apparently feeling more confident, the prince pushed away from the wall and grinned. "Why not come a little closer and we can battle like true Lashed men?"

Paxton pulled the bowstring taut. "I'm a hunter of beasts. I do not use my magic to kill for sport."

"How many men have you killed?" Prince Vito asked.

"You will be my first."

The prince chuckled. "Silly commoner. I am the prince of Kalor. This is *not* how I will die."

Paxton knew there was no way this man would give him information about Prince Donubhan. Their only hope was to kill him and capture his lackeys for information.

Sounds of battle were close. Paxton wanted to look over his shoulder, but didn't dare take his eyes off Prince Vito. He weighed his chances; the prince had excellent reflexes. If he shot his arrow, Vito'd likely throw his dagger at the same time. But to have the man dead would be worth his own life.

"You are a waste of Lashed blood, peasant. I should keep you alive, cage you in my room, and let you have the pleasure of watching me with your queen—"

Paxton shot, diving to the side as prince Vito threw his weapon. Both men shouted in pain. The dagger had sliced Paxton's shoulder, while his arrow planted firmly in the prince's thigh. Vito was now weaponless. Paxton snagged another arrow and nocked it. The prince was breathing raggedly, leaning back against the cottage wall. He let out a groaning snarl.

"You will pay for that! I will shoot arrows at you in your cage. Then heal you when you're about to die, and do it all over again. I will bring you to the brink of death over and over until you are begging to die."

"Enjoy your last morbid dreams. You're nothing but an imposter."

Vito gritted his teeth, shaking. "I. Am. The most. Powerful. Man. *Alive*!"

Prince Vito lunged for Paxton, who let loose his arrow. It lodged straight in Vito's throat as the prince's deadly fingers grazed the front of Paxton's tunic. He jumped away.

Paxton's heart gave a great jolt as he watched Vito fall to his knees at his feet, feeling the protruding arrow with trembling hands and bulging eyes. Pax stepped back farther. It was the first time he'd ever watched a creature suffer without putting it out of its misery, but he didn't dare touch him. Paxton watched Prince Vito struggle and thrash on the ground until the man's spirit finally fled, alone, behind a cottage, with no glory. And though it gave Paxton no joy, it did provide him a moment of peace. Vito was no longer the most powerful man alive.

The carriage rumbled along at an uphill slant. A bellow of agony issued from Harrison in the front, and the cart zagged from side to side. Had he been shot?

"Hold on tight!" Aerity screamed to her sister and cousin. But the cart came to an abrupt stop without tipping over.

"Harrison!" Wyneth fumbled for the door over Vixie's lap.

"Wyn, wait—" Aerity grabbed her cousin's skirts, but Wyneth rushed downward out of her grasp and into the night.

"Stay here," Mrs. Rathbrook said. "He could be hurt. I will try to heal him."

"Be careful," Aerity begged. Mrs. Rathbrook climbed down, out of sight. Aerity shared a worried look of silence with Vixie. Several minutes passed, and Aerity felt a foreboding sense of wrongness. She reached for the door handle just as a *thwump* sounded. Something had hit the side of the carriage, and flames suddenly tore upward along the fabric lining. The sizzle and whoosh were deafening. Vixie screamed, and Aerity grabbed her, pushing her toward the door. They went tumbling out together, the cart engulfed in flames. The horse took off running. Aerity saw now that the driver's seat was empty.

Two soldiers lay dead with no sign of injury and Aerity realized Mrs. Rathbrook must have killed them with magic.

"Aerity!" Wyneth ran to them, staring at the flaming cart as the horse ran. "Are you both all right?"

"Aye. Where's Harrison?"

Wyneth pointed. At the bottom of the darkened hill Mrs. Rathbrook was leaning over him, her hands on his side. "He was hit with an arrow."

At the sounds of movement they turned their eyes up to see troops in bright Kalorian clothing cresting a hill behind them, coming from the town center.

"Run!" Aerity shouted. Harrison and Mrs. Rathbrook were pushing gingerly to their feet when the girls made it to them. With any luck, the Kalorians would focus on the cottages, and Aerity and the others could be to the copse of trees at the top of this hill before the enemy troops noticed them.

From there, they could make it down the other side and to the lake on foot. The five of them ran.

"Where is Furball?" Wyneth asked, peering back over her shoulders. And then, "Watch out!"

An arrow flew directly between her and Vixie, lodging in the dead grass. Aerity turned to see a single soldier who had spotted them.

"Keep going!" Harrison ordered them as he unsheathed his sword and charged down at a sprint toward the Kalorian who was nocking another an arrow.

"No!" Wyneth screamed.

Oh, seas. Aerity couldn't watch; Harrison wasn't going to get to him in time. From the corner of her eye she saw Vixie's bow go up. With a *twang,* the Kalorian soldier was stumbling backward. Harrison skidded to a stop and looked back, confused.

Vixie had frozen to the spot, her bow falling to her side.

"Did I kill him?" she croaked. "I . . . I did good, right?"

"You did brilliantly," Wyneth assured her in a shaking voice. "He would have shot Harrison." Vixie stared at the twitching body and began to tremble. Harrison sheathed his sword and took her by the shoulder.

"Well done, princess. You've done nothing wrong. I owe you my life."

Vixie covered her mouth.

Sounds of fighting were getting louder. In the moonlight and flickering fires, Aerity spotted stout gray horses dashing up the path and between houses with broad riders shouting a coldland war chant. Ascomannians were here! And beyond the far hill from the direction of the town square rose great shouts as Lochlan commoners ran up and over, pouring down the hill toward the Kalorians. Vixie gave a peal of laughter. A deep growl split the night as Furball rose up on his hind legs beside Lief on horseback, ready to fight.

"Furball!" Wyneth yelled. The beast, having amazing hearing, cocked his head in their direction and appeared torn between fighting and going to be with his mistress.

A stream of Kalorians poured forth from behind the houses, coming around to meet the Lochlans and Ascomannians head on. And they were directly in the path.

Harrison pointed up the hill and shouted, "Go! He'll be fine!"

"Harrison!" Wyneth called, but he shook his head regretfully. He was staying to fight too.

Wyneth reluctantly turned with moistened eyes, and the four of them ran up the hill, grasping their skirts.

When they got to the copse of trees at the top of the hill, they stopped to catch their breath in the canopy of darkness.

"Are you all right, Mrs. Rathbrook?" Aerity asked. The woman was bent, hands on her knees, taking in ragged mouthfuls of air.

"Aye . . . dear . . . don't worry about me. Leave me . . . if you must."

Before Aerity could respond, a shadow stepped out from behind a tree.

"Still a slave to the monarch, Lashed One? Pity."

Aerity's skin prickled with heat at that voice. Vixie and Wyneth stepped back. Mrs. Rathbrook stood up, eyes narrowing as Rozaria Rocato materialized, smiling.

Vixie pulled out her bow and quickly nocked an arrow. "Not another step."

Rozaria stopped, sizing up Vixie. "Ah, you again? Still trying to prove yourself?"

Vixie minutely shifted her stance, tensing.

"She has nothing to prove," Aerity said. "She has my full permission to kill you right now."

"I think we both know she doesn't have it in her."

"I just killed one of your soldiers!" Vixie's voice trembled, despite her confident stance.

"Were you looking him in the eye, as you do now with me?" Rozaria spoke softly.

Vixie didn't answer, asking instead, "Where's your friend? The one who hides and sneaks?"

Rozaria appeared amused by her tone. Aerity remembered now that there was a girl, always watching over Rozaria, often in hiding. Her eyes darted around at the trees and shadows. Wyneth turned to look behind them and her eyes grew. "Harrison!"

He crested the hill, looking worse for wear with his uniform torn, dirtied, and bloodied, but he was upright and not at all as winded as they'd been. He stopped and surveyed the scene. Aerity noticed he had no sword. He must have been disarmed in battle and ran to see them off after all. She could scarcely make out his face in the dark distance.

She wondered if he was thinking what she was: that the smart thing to do would be to order Vixie to kill Rozaria now. But Aerity didn't want to force her sister. She'd been shaken after killing the man from afar. Aerity would do it herself, and she knew Harrison would as well, but in the time it would take to get the bow from Vix, Rozaria could have her hands on one of them, or run and escape. She had to trust that Vixie wouldn't let Rozaria get away again.

"Keep the arrow aimed at her at all times," Harrison said. "Everyone else stay clear of her." Now he focused on Rozaria. "You're under arrest for conspiracy against Lochlanach. You're a prisoner of war—"

A burst of mad laughter issued from Rozaria. She laughed until a savage roar rang out, causing her to abruptly shut her mouth and peer down the hill. Aerity caught something glinting from beside a nearby tree, then the glint moved.

"Watch out!" she yelled, and the object flew straight toward Vixie. In a blur, Furball threw himself in the path of the dagger, letting out a raging snarl as the weapon pricked underneath his front leg.

Vixie released her arrow and hit the Lashed girl beneath her collarbone. The girl stumbled out and fell beside Rozaria, the arrow protruding.

"Nicola!" Rozaria moved to block the girl from the rest of them.

"That was my only arrow," Vixie whispered in a panic.

"I will heal you, Nicola," Rozaria murmured down at the writhing girl. "Be still for a moment while I finish them."

Furball growled. Rozaria lifted her gaze and stared at the creature in wonder.

"He's one of mine, isn't he?"

"Not anymore," Harrison told her.

"We'll see about that." Rozaria snapped her fingers with authority and clicked her tongue at the beast. Furball gave a pathetic whimper and went back on its haunches, as if afraid or confused.

"This . . ." Rozaria pointed at the creature. "This is that useless cub!" She laughed again. "How did you obtain him?" Then she stared at Aerity in a new way. "You . . . that was *you* at my camp. And Paxton . . . he knew all along." Aerity felt a clench of fear until remembering it made no difference now. Rozaria laughed darkly, sounding maniacal. "It matters not. You will both suffer tenfold."

She began to squat beside Nicola, careful not to turn her back to them.

"Don't touch her," Miss Rathbrook said, stepping forward. "She tried to kill the princess. You will not heal her."

"How *dare* you command me," Rozaria spat. "You are the worst kind of Lashed, a traitor of magical blood!"

The royal healer continued to move forward.

"Mrs. Rathbrook," Aerity warned.

"Move away," Mrs. Rathbrook demanded.

"I will not," Rozaria fired back.

As the women eyed each other, Furball snarled, and Harrison bent to pick up the dagger Nicola had thrown.

Mrs. Rathbrook moved closer yet, causing Rozaria to rise, facing her, but still not within reach. Wyneth took a step forward on Rozaria's other side, and pointed to Harrison.

"Move away, Rozaria, or you will have a dagger in your heart."

Wyn was standing too close. Aerity was about to tell her to move when Rozaria charged toward Wyneth, her hands outstretched. Shouts and screams split the air. In a flash, Furball was there, bumping Wyneth out of the way. He let loose his most vicious roar yet, towering over Rozaria, who was suddenly immobilized by shock. Mrs. Rathbrook took the opportunity to fall to her knees beside Nicola's feet and grasp her ankle. Nicola, in a burst of renewed energy, sat up and grasped Mrs. Rathbrook's arm. Her hood fell back, her scar shining in the moonlight, eyes gleaming with passion. Aerity screamed. At the same time, both Mrs. Rathbrook and Nicola crumpled forward.

"No!" Rozaria shrieked.

"Mrs. Rathbrook . . . ?" Vixie whimpered. Neither of them moved or breathed.

Furball growled when Rozaria stepped closer, and she turned on him. "Enough! I created you, stupid creature, and I will kill you as I should have months ago!" She dived for the beast, but before she could lay her hands on him, Furball sliced a paw through the air. His massive claws slashed her abdomen. Rozaria looked down as blood began to pour from the gashes through her dress, and she rocked back on her heels. Her eyes lifted to her creation as if searching for answers to an unfathomable mystery.

And then Rozaria Rocato fell.

Paxton heaved Prince Vito's body across the back of a Kalorian horse who'd lost its rider, and began leading it toward the clearing at the edge of town where fighting could be heard. He was shocked to see hundreds of soldiers, and a mass of Kalorian carnage. Most standing appeared to be Ascomannian and Lochlan. The Kalorians who weren't dead were being subdued, pushed to the ground as prisoners, though some seemed to prefer fighting to the death.

His eyes rose up the hill at the sound of Furball's brutal roaring. Were the girls up there?

"Oy there, Pax!"

He looked over to find Lief jogging toward him. The coldlands man, splattered with blood, looked at Prince Vito's body and stopped short, his surprised gaze going back to Paxton. Leif raised his eyebrows in question.

"Aye, it's him," Paxton said. "Dead."

"You killed him?"

Paxton nodded. A grin split Lief's face, and he grasped Paxton by the shoulder, laughing heartily and giving him a good shake.

"Well done!"

Paxton handed the reins to Lief and left him standing there as he headed up the hill to find Aerity. As he got closer he saw people standing, as well as bodies lying.

Nervousness twisted his insides as he ran the rest of the way.

"Pax!" The sound of Aerity's beautiful voice filled him with immeasurable joy.

She ran to him, and they collided in an embrace. Coconut and berries filled his senses and he held her tighter, thanking the seas.

"Come," she whispered. She took his hand and led him the rest of the way up the hill, where Wyneth and Harrison stood. Aerity's eyes lowered to the bodies, filled with dark pity.

He peered down at Vixie leaning over a very still Mrs. Rathbrook.

"Is she gone?" he asked. Vixie looked up and nodded, sniffing. His heart gave a tight squeeze.

Beside them was Nicola, who also appeared dead. Then, to his complete shock, his eyes landed on Rozaria, whose bloodied hands were splayed across her abdomen, a tremor ratcheting through her. She slowly reached a hand up to Paxton, her eyes beseeching him to heal her. His stomach knotted with the same pity he'd seen in Aerity's eyes. He knew he shouldn't feel bad for this woman who'd caused so many others to suffer, but he did. And he knew what he had to do.

Paxton looked at Harrison. "Hold down her wrists. Don't

let her fingers touch you."

Harrison, though he didn't seem thrilled, nodded and bent at Rozaria's side while Paxton moved to her head. The others watched in silence. Paxton lifted Rozaria's head to his lap and when she whimpered he said, "Sh. It's almost over." He held her face in his hands, and concentrated. Inside, her body was a jumbled mess, just as Tiern's had been the night he'd healed him. Paxton's energy searched for what he wanted, and then finally found it.

His magic seized her heart and surrounded it. He sent a simple thought to halt its beat. Rozaria's eyes widened, and she struggled to suck in a last breath. Then she went still. Paxton exhaled and slid her eyelids closed with his fingers.

"You will never hurt again," he said softly. Relief washed cleanly through his body. He looked up at Aerity, who covered her mouth and closed her eyes, nodding.

A raucous cheer rose up from the bottom of the hill. He knew it meant all the Kalorians had been either captured or killed.

"It's over," Harrison said. "We've won this battle. Let's hope we can take the castle and Prince Vito."

"He's dead." Paxton stood and faced them.

"You're certain?" Aerity asked as if afraid to hope.

"I killed him myself."

Aerity watched him a moment longer and then flew into his arms, hugging him while her cousin and sister cheered. Paxton kissed the top of her head and held her close.

"Did you find out about Donnie?" she whispered to him.

"Nay," he regretted to say. "But we will find him."

Aerity's arms tightened around him. She was safe for now. He'd done his job. He'd killed for her. For his land. And he would do whatever he had to do to find her brother. He didn't want to think about what would come after that. He didn't want to think of letting her go again. For now, he held her close.

Chapter 52

For a group who had just won a war, Princess Aerity and her companions were silent on the cold, dark journey back down to the bay. Ahead and behind them, the soldiers laughed and celebrated. Lord Alvi rode without speaking, seeming deep in thought. The deaths they had witnessed lay heavily on Aerity's heart. She knew she should tell Vixie and Wyneth that the Isle of Evie had been overtaken. She'd sworn to her sister not to keep any more secrets. She promised herself she would tell them the moment they returned to the castle and not a moment later. She would let them have these moments of peace.

They rode for hours in the chill of darkness, until the first softness of dawn began to show itself on the horizon, revealing a frost that covered every blade of grass.

Now that the war was over, it would be time to rebuild—to rule, and live without her parents—it seemed unimaginable She would be expected to marry Lief, a thought that filled her with a sullen, sickening sort of grief. Especially after all she'd shared with Paxton.

Aerity turned to look at Pax, who rode next to her, staring ahead. In his far hand he held the reins of the horse that carried the bodies of Vito and Rozaria. It was beyond strange that those lifeless, now harmless, forms had hurt and terrorized so many. Paxton met her eyes and Aerity had to swallow and look away from the heartache she saw there. She stared out instead at the river to her right as it rambled along.

Before they reached the bay she saw a pack of Ascomannian riders approaching them at a fast clip. Aerity kicked her horse lightly and leaned forward to push through the crowd. Volgan, the warrior, greeted her with a nod.

"What news?" she asked, her heart pounding.

"Royal lands are secure. The castle as well. But Prince Vito and Rozaria Rocato are nowhere to be found. We think they may have—"

"They are dead," Lord Alvi proclaimed. "At the hand of the hunter Paxton Seabolt." Lief held an arm toward Paxton. Volgan stared in disbelief. Everyone turned to him, eyeing the bodies on the horse at his side, and then a deafening roar split the air. Paxton reluctantly accepted handshakes and pats on his back. But he never seemed to share their happiness.

"Let's get the royal highnesses and Lady Wyneth back to their rightful home then, aye?" Lief called out. Another cheer and then forward movement at a faster pace as they ushered Aerity home. Vixie reached out and took Aerity's hand, offering a smile. Aerity forced one in return.

Swept up in the festive atmosphere of the soldiers, Vixie let out a whoop and galloped forward. Aerity nearly smiled when she saw her sister bring her knees up into the saddle, tucking her body, preparing to do a trick. It had been so long since she'd seen Vixie be carefree. When Vixie balanced on her hands and forearms and lifted her pointed toes straight into the air, Aerity did smile. Because under her skirts she was wearing riding trousers.

The men laughed and cheered, absolutely entertained as Vixie split her legs and arched her back gracefully, pulling herself back down to balance on the palms of her hands, legs outstretched to the sides. She dropped her bottom back into the saddle and lay back, reaching her arms out and closing her eyes with a peaceful expression. *Oh, this girl.*

Aerity suddenly jolted, consumed by raw fear at the thought of her once carefree brother in the hands of Kalorians.

Aerity shot past her sister and rode up to Volgan. The man turned to her, forehead pinched.

"Good sir, my brother has been kidnapped. Did you happen upon him anywhere in the castle? Prince Vito said they had him." Oh, seas, her entire body trembled.

"Your Majesty," Volgan said in a gruff voice, "our vessels

have been keeping watch over the Isle of Evie since your kin were brought there. We've received no word of an attack, but I will check."

"Please," she said, only partially appeased. He galloped away toward the bay and Aerity turned to the others. Vixie rode to her side.

"What's wrong?"

Aerity did not want to burden her sister, but Vixie was strong. So Aerity told her, along with Wyneth.

"Not Donnie," Vixie whispered. All traces of pink drained from her cheeks.

"Seas alive," Wyneth breathed. "The children . . ."

"I must go to the bay to see what I can learn," Aerity told her.

"I'm going with you," Vixie said. Aerity nodded, grateful.

"Same," Paxton said.

"We'll all go," Wyneth told her.

Harrison sent half the troops back to royal lands and the other half to accompany them to the bay, where King Dagur awaited with his fleet. Aerity and the others arrived just after Volgan. She slid down from her horse, grabbed her skirts, and ran as quickly as she could up the gangway to the royal Ascomannian's boat with Vixie and Wyneth behind her.

King Dagur, who'd just finished speaking with Volgan, came to her and put a hand on her shoulder. "Have no worries, Queen Aerity. Your brother and the rest of your royal family are safe on the isle."

Vixie and Wyneth let out sounds of joy.

Aerity exhaled in a shudder, pressing a hand to her stomach. "You're certain?"

"We've been keeping constant watch. Your navy is sending a vessel for their return journey this very moment."

Aerity was near tears, but held them back. "Thank you. I cannot thank you enough, Your Majesty. I don't think I can ever repay you for all you've done."

A sly grin came to his face and she had to press her hand harder into her belly. She knew he had every intention of being repaid, and promptly.

"Will you please join us at the castle to eat and rest?" she asked, trying to keep her voice strong.

"I will," he said.

Aerity curtsied, and the king bowed. She turned and hugged her sister and Wyneth quickly. Then they grasped their skirts and turned to go. When she reached the shore, she felt Paxton watching her from atop his horse, but with King Dagur's words of repayment ringing in her ears, she could not look at him. She didn't want him to see the desperation she felt at the thought of losing him. A soft snow began to fall and she was thankful for an excuse to raise her hood.

"They are safe," she said softly.

"Thank the seas."

The entire way back to royal lands, despite the beauty and peace of the snowfall, Aerity fought her emotions. This wasn't the end of the world for her. It's what all princesses and queens had to do before her father's time. And though she wanted to marry no one but Paxton, she knew her options could be much worse. After nearly being forced to wed Prince Vito, Lord Alvi was a shining gem of a prospect. She owed this to her allies and the people. But still . . . her heart wept.

She pulled her cloak tighter as winds from the seas picked up, sending snow sideways. What would Paxton do now? Would he return to his village? If she asked him to stay in the castle, and provided him with work, she knew he would probably accept. And if Lord Alvi was sure to take mistresses, could she not have Paxton as well? But wrongness and guilt filled her at the thought of carrying on a secret relationship. That was no way for them to live.

These thoughts tumbled through her mind on their journey back to royal lands where they entered through the northern gates. It gave her great joy to see her castle intact, but then she saw the piles of bodies and soldiers moving more dead to clear a path. Smoldering piles of rubbish lay beneath windows, and Aerity's blood boiled as she realized what had happened.

"What have they done?" Vixie cried. "They burned our things?"

"By the seas," Wyneth whispered. "Disgraceful."

"What matters is that we are safe," Aerity said, just as much for her own hearing. Even if the entire castle had been dismantled, they were alive.

"Has anyone seen Tiern or the Zandalee yet?" Paxton asked.

"Someone said they were inside the castle," a soldier told them.

Vixie beamed and leaned forward, her horse shooting down the path toward the castle, spraying up powdery snow.

Aerity stopped and turned to Harrison. "Have a proclamation sent to the towns at once to let them know the war is over. The Rocato woman and the imposter Prince Vito have been slain, and their bodies will be on display. Let them know we will have a coronation celebration in a week's time. And as of today the laws against Lashed magic are lifted for purposes of healing. Full details of new laws will be issued shortly. Also"—she swallowed—"details of a royal wedding will be announced very soon."

Harrison gave her a tight nod and cantered away. Aerity could look at no one. She turned toward the castle and continued on.

"Aerity," Paxton called.

She gritted her teeth and slowed her horse so he could catch up. He rode alongside her in silence for a moment before speaking low enough for only her to hear.

"I will return to Cape Creek today."

"No," she said in a rush, then scolded herself. White snowflakes covered his dark hair and she wanted to brush them away. "Please, Pax. Stay until . . . I want as much time with you as I can."

His eyes reflected her own need and anguish. "I worry that the more time we spend together, the harder it will be."

She shook her head obstinately. "Don't leave. I'm not ready." Her heart was on the brink of shattering.

He stared at her a moment longer before inclining his chin. "All right, then. I will stay until it is time."

She shut her eyes. She knew she was torturing them both by prolonging the inevitable, but everything inside her clung to him. Together, they faced forward and rode to the gardens, where they dismounted. She pressed her lips tightly at the sight of piled bodies along the hedges, a layer of snow covering them in a show of macabre beauty. There seemed to be no place on royal lands where blood had not been shed. She turned away from the sight.

Inside the castle, Aerity was appalled by the damage the Kalorians had done. It seemed every room held broken or defaced heirlooms, paintings, or furniture. And while it pained her, it also satisfied her to know they would never be able to do this to anyone else again.

Only a few maids and kitchen staff had received news of their victory and returned to the castle. She was thankful to find the baker already inside the kitchen, warming the ovens.

"I knew we'd win this, Your Majesty," he told Aerity with glad tears in his eyes. "I knew good would prevail." He cracked eggs into flour and began kneading with shaking hands. It would take a while to feel safe again.

"Bless you, chef," Aerity said, trying not to get emotional.

Vixie appeared upset when she found Aerity in the hall. "He slept in Mum and Papa's chambers. It—it doesn't smell like them anymore."

Agony tormented Aerity's heart. "The maids are gone. We'll find clean sheets in the laundry rooms and air it out ourselves."

"I'll get the sheets," Vixie said, squaring her shoulders in a show of stoicism. "And some for the rest of us as well. My chamber stinks of a filthy man."

"Thank you." Aerity stopped her sister with a hand on her arm. "I'm proud of you."

Vixie gave her a weak smile and hurried away. Aerity was standing there in the middle of the hall, staring into nothingness, when Wyneth approached and swept her tangled hair back from her shoulder.

"Will you be all right, Cousin?"

"I have to be all right, don't I?" She tried to smile.

"To the public, aye. But not to me."

Aerity's voice shook. "Then I am not all right, Wyn. Not at all."

Wyneth pulled her into a tight embrace. Neither said a word, but they gave and received each other's comfort, which was the only thing they had to offer. Aerity was grateful for it. She pulled herself together and wiped her cheeks.

"I've got to wash my face and brush my hair and change my clothes before King Dagur arrives."

"I'll dress and join you in your chambers to walk together."

They turned at the sound of footsteps jogging down the hall toward them: Harrison looking dashing and healthy. Wyneth beamed as she watched him. His eyes held hers with warmth before moving to Aerity.

"The tunnels have been searched and are secured. The exit north of royal lands has been filled and sealed. A Lochlan vessel has been sent to the Isle of Evie to bring back your family."

Wyneth clasped her hands and Aerity nodded.

"Very good. Thank you, Harrison."

"Aye, Your Majesty."

Aerity left the two of them ogling each other as she returned to her chambers. She was happy that at least the two of them would get their happy ending.

Without the help of Caitrin, Aerity didn't feel as put together as she normally did. She struggled to clasp her yellow dress in the back and to brush the tangles from her hair. She fidgeted with the emerald circlet hanging heavily on her forehead, and wiped a smudge of dirt from her cheek. She frowned at the looking glass. Her appearance would have to be good enough. Wyneth arrived and they walked arm in arm to the formal dining room where they'd meet the others. She inwardly cringed when she thought of the last time she'd been in that room with King Dagur.

Their pace slowed when they saw Lief standing outside the door, looking clean with damp hair.

"Did you bathe in cold water?" Aerity asked.

The coldlander grinned. "Naturally." He approached and took her hand, kissing the tips of her fingers.

"My queen," he said, then lowered his voice to a rumbling whisper. "I need you to do me a favor."

"Aye? And what might that be?" she whispered back.

"Pretend to be offended."

Offended? She stared into his serious eyes. "Whatever for?"

Lief did not answer. He took her hand and pulled it into the crook of his arm, leading her toward the dining room. Aerity looked over her shoulder at Wyneth, who shrugged in confusion.

King Dagur stood when they entered. He was with Volgan and two of his highest officials this time, rather than his family. Vixie was also at the table, appearing glad to see her. Harrison joined last with one other Lochlan officer, and the doors closed. Covered plates had been set on the table. Aerity wondered what the chef had been able to throw together in such a hurry. Had the chicken houses survived the damage of battle?

And speaking of damage, the formal dining room did not look at all the way she remembered it. Every tapestry had been torn down. The walls were bare. The priceless vases were shattered, though someone had swept the floors and left the shards in a corner.

King Dagur shook his head. "They left your home in ruins. I am sorry to witness it."

"I'm sorry to have guests see it in such a state."

The king waved a hand. Aerity was the first to sit, at the head of the table, and the others followed her lead. Normally a servant would lift the covers from their dishes.

"We're on our own, I suppose," Aerity said. She reached over and lifted the king's cover for him, setting it in the middle. He stared at her and began to chuckle, a sound that turned to a deep laugh, and his men all joined him. Aerity blushed. The king then reached over and lifted her cover for her.

"Not on our own, Your Majesty. Together."

Of all the things to nearly make her burst into tears . . .

Aerity smiled and motioned to the others at the table, who all lifted their own covers. Inside were slices of warm bread, roasted carrots and beets, and fried eggs. Without hesitation, they all fell upon the food. For five entire minutes nobody said a word. Aerity hadn't realized how hungry she was until her entire plate was cleared. They all looked around at one another. Aerity met Lief's eyes and tried to figure out why his mood was so dark. His ominous request came back to her and she squinted across the space at him, but he was lost in his thoughts.

The king pushed his plate forward enough to put his elbows on the table and nail her with a stern look.

"We must set a date for your wedding. Without delay."

Breathe. Breathe. Breathe. "I agree."

He twined his fingers, seeming partially appeased. "This winter. Two weeks from now." It sounded like a challenge, as if he expected her to argue. She wanted to push for spring, but after all he'd done, she couldn't.

"That is reasonable," she said.

He watched her before blinking and relaxing back in his chair with his hands across his belly. "Well, then. This is good."

"Your Majesty," said Lief from beside him. "If I may speak."

The king appeared amused as Lief stood to address him.

"I will not marry Queen Aerity."

Aerity's heart stopped. All delight fell from King Dagur's face. The entire room seemed to stiffen in shock. Volgan looked as if he were choking.

Pretend to be offended.

Oh, seas. She forced herself to speak. "Whatever do you mean, Lord Alvi?"

"He is jesting," King Dagur said through clenched teeth.

Lief's chest puffed out farther. "I am in earnest." And though he stood tall and proud, Aerity saw something in his eyes she'd never seen before. Fear.

King Dagur slowly pushed to his feet. His voice was a rumble. "You. Will. Marry."

"I am sorry, Uncle. But I will not."

The king smacked Lief across the face. Aerity and the other girls jumped in startled surprise. Lief remained still, his jaw clenching.

"For what reasons, boy?"

"For reasons of my own."

"If you do this . . . if you dishonor our ally in such a way, I will disown you."

Lief paused, as if struggling. "I understand," he said in a scratchy whisper.

Aerity could not believe her ears. This was too much. Lief's honor to his homeland, it was an integral part of him.

The king clenched his fists, appearing ready to fight. "You will never again be allowed on Ascomanni lands, boy. Do you understand that? An outcast of the coldlands! Banished!"

Lief's large Adam's apple bobbed. "I understand."

She was elated at the thought of what this could mean for her, but riddled with guilt.

"Lief," Aerity whispered, forcing the words. "Reconsider." His home . . . his family.

"This is pure selfishness," King Dagur shouted at him. "You were not raised this way! How dare you put yourself above your kingdom?"

The king was trembling in fury as he turned his face to Aerity. "I did not know his intentions, Your Majesty. I would have attempted to talk sense into him."

She tried to put on a stern face. As much as she didn't want to make things worse for Lief, she had to do exactly what he said—pretend to be at least slightly offended. She would risk further damage to her relationship and trust with Ascomanni if she appeared to be glad not to have their union.

"I am taken aback as well," she said. "And my people will be sorely disappointed." She looked at Lief, who remained still. What would happen to him if he couldn't go back to the coldlands? She couldn't let him live a life of disgrace.

"You have brought me shame this day." The king spat at Lief's feet, and Aerity felt her heart whither in sadness. "You are no nephew of mine."

Lief shut his eyes, the weight of what he'd done crashing down. Aerity's mind whirled, searching for a way to right this.

"I feel as if I must give my people something," she said. "Regardless of his choice today, the citizens of Lochlanach esteem Lief as a hero."

"You owe him nothing after this," the king assured her.

"Oh, but I do. He killed the beast, Your Majesty. And he has gone above and beyond to free us from the enemy every step of the way since that hunt. He has been a friend of Lochlanach, and therefore I wish to honor him, husband or not. My southern lands are currently without a duke. It is a lesser title, but he should be glad to wear any title at all after refusing to be our prince consort." She looked at Lief. "As of today, you are Duke Lief Alvi of southern Lochlanach."

He lowered his chin stiffly in response.

"Gather your belongings and leave us," Aerity said. She motioned to Harrison. "See him out, Lieutenant." They exited together, and Aerity caught the gaping faces of Wyneth and Vixie. She had to cough lightly into her hand.

"You show him far too much grace," King Dagur said.

Aerity turned to him, a tremor running through her. "It

is done. You may remain in my home as long as you desire."

"I can see you are upset, Your Majesty. I assure you, I would never wish to slight you."

"I told you this morning that I owe you a great debt for your help in this war, and I meant it. Whether or not I am wed to your nephew does not change that. I hold you and your people in the highest regard and I hope for a future of shared prosperity with Ascomanni."

He exhaled and bowed his head to her. "I thank you."

She curtsied and then they took hands to say good-bye. His face was still strained with distress when he left them, followed by his officers. Aerity motioned for her guards to leave them. The moment the door closed, Wyneth and Vixie flew out of their seats and ran, plowing into her. Together, the three of them held tight, murmuring as quietly as possible.

"Did that really happen?" Aerity whispered. Her skin felt ready to explode from the inside.

"Aye, that Lief," Wyneth said with a shake of her head. "I think our Lochlan ways may have rubbed off on him after all."

"I worry for him," Aerity murmured.

"He is in pain," Wyneth said. "But I don't believe this was a spontaneous decision. In time he will thrive here. He is already revered."

Vixie took her hand. "Be at peace, Aer. Think of what this means for you."

Queen Aerity felt a heady rush of jubilance. "I've got to tell Paxton!"

"Go, go!" Vixie shoved her, and clasped her hands beneath her chin. Wyneth beamed beside her.

Aerity sprinted to the door and then stopped to calm herself. She ran a hand over her hair and down her gown, then put on a serious face and opened the door.

Nothing had the potential to make Vixie cry torrents more than joy. She knew it was not going to be pretty, so she slipped into the nearest quiet room she could find, the library. Vixie flounced into an oversized chair and let the wailing commence. Not all was happy and well—her parents would never be back and so many had died—but her sister was going to have true love now. It was so beautiful, it hurt.

She was not at all fit for company when she felt a hand on her shoulder. Vixie jumped to her feet and sniffled loudly, wiping her nose with the back of her hand, and then her eyes. Tiern stood there.

"I'm sorry," he said. "I didn't want to disturb you, but I came to check on you and found you crying. I couldn't not say something."

His rambling was adorable, but her cheeks still flamed with embarrassment.

"It's all right. I'm actually happy."

He tilted his head. "You were sobbing uncontrollably because you're happy?"

She sighed. "Well, aye, you see, because—"

"I present," said a booming voice from the library entrance, "Prince Hanriil of—"

"She knows who I am." Prince Hanriil grinned at her, flanked by a handful of soldiers as he swept into the room. His smile fell. "Have you been crying, Princess?"

Oh, for the love of the seas!

"Nay. I mean, aye, but I am fine. I promise. Just overwhelmed, I suppose."

The prince looked at Tiern now, with a touch of annoyance in his features. "Please leave us. I wish to speak to the princess alone."

Vixie and Tiern both went still. And then Tiern nodded his head.

"Aye, Your Highness."

Tiern then turned to Vixie and quickly leaned down, pressing his lips to hers in a chaste, albeit intimate way. Then he gave her a quick grin and turned, bowing to the stunned prince before leaving them. Her heart swelled to bursting.

"Do you always allow commoners to *kiss* you?" The prince sounded appalled.

"Nay," Vixie said. "Only that one."

"Is he courting you?"

"Aye." *He is now.*

The prince paused. "Are you open to being courted by others?"

"Not at this time, Your Highness."

He paused again, as if baffled by the entire scenario. "Well, all right. I came to say my good-byes. We return to Toresta today."

Vixie lowered into a deep curtsy. "Thank you, Prince Hanriil. You are brave and worthy. May the seas be with you."

He bowed. "And the winds with you."

Aerity walked with her chin up toward the guest quarters. Thankfully the guards and soldiers were all so busy with cleanup that they hadn't yet taken to watching her like a hawk. When she saw Harrison and Lief walking together, the strife between them seeming to have vanished, she cocked her head toward the portico at the end of the hall. They followed her into the opening, and she turned on Lief.

"What were you thinking? Your homeland!"

He shrugged lightly. "I was going to live here anyway, wasn't I?"

She stared at him. The fear and nervousness he'd displayed in front of the king were gone. "But . . . your *honor.* I never meant for you to do this, I swear it."

He cupped her cheek, as he'd done on so many kind moments before. "I know. You would have never asked or expected it, and for that I respect you."

"Then why?" she asked.

He got a sort of capricious look on his face as he released her. "I suppose I wanted to know what it'd feel like . . . to sacrifice something big for one deserving person."

"I fear you will regret it," she whispered.

"Your Majesty!" called a voice from down the hall. Aerity popped her head out and saw Caitrin with six other maids.

She waved, so glad to see them. The maids rushed down the hall and Caitrin took her hands. The girls all had red eyes as if they'd been crying, but they were all smiles now.

"Oh, Your Majesty! We came as soon as we heard! The seas have blessed our kingdom! We're so happy you're safe."

Aerity smiled. "Indeed, we are so very blessed."

"I'm sorry to have interrupted you, my queen," Caitrin said, her eyes darting up to Lief. She released her hands and curtsied. The other girls did the same. When they stood they smiled at her, and then their eyes all seemed to flitter up to Duke Alvi before they turned and dashed away. Down the hall Aerity heard several of them giggle. She turned and caught a grin on Lief's face.

"No," he said. "I won't regret it."

"Oh, you!" Aerity smacked his arm and Harrison laughed, shaking his head.

"Thank you, though," Lief said to Aerity. "For the lands. That is more than generous."

She hugged him around the waist and he hugged her back. He would make a good addition to Lochlanach. "Just don't break too many of my maidens' hearts."

He chuckled, making no promises. She pulled away and looked at the two of them.

"Have you seen Paxton?"

Harrison nodded. "He and Tiern are in the third guest chambers."

"Tell him I said *you're welcome*!" Lief called as she turned and ran.

She smiled widely, despite the heat that filled her cheeks. She felt strangely nervous as she stopped in front of the third door and knocked, then adjusted the gem in her circlet. Tiern opened the door and bowed when he saw her.

"Congratulations on your victory, Your Majesty," he said.

She gave a small nod. "The victory is all of ours. Thank you, Tiern."

"I've just come from the library. Your sister was crying, apparently happy tears?"

Aerity smiled. "She tends to do that."

She was about to inquire about Paxton, when he peeked out from behind the door and saw her. He was shirtless, drying his wet hair with a towel. He pushed the door open and came forward, nearly shoving Tiern out of the way.

"What's wrong?"

"Nothing." *Oh, seas.* All she could do was stare at this man, her tongue seeming to have stopped working. She was almost afraid to say the words, afraid that it would all be snatched away.

Tiern grasped the back of his neck. "Erm, I'll just be going, then." He ducked out the doorway to leave them.

Aerity peeked behind her. One of her guards was watching, but she knew he would not stop her or gossip. She slipped into the chamber and shut the door. As Paxton stared at her expectantly, a sudden giggle erupted out of her throat and she covered her mouth. His brow scrunched.

"What has happened?"

Aerity leaned back against the door to steady herself.

Paxton looked at her as if she'd lost her mind. He tossed the towel onto a chair and faced her.

"You're beginning to make me nervous, Aer."

In a rush, she spouted, "He refused to marry me."

His brow furrowed even tighter. "Pardon? Wait . . . *Lief*? Refused?"

Her head bobbed up and down and the giggle returned. "Aye!" Then she straightened and lost her smile. "He's been banished from the coldlands for it. I've given him the southern lands. You should have seen King Dagur—"

"Wait." Paxton's heavy, dark eyes were locked on her. "You're not to be married?"

The severity of his heated stare made her suck in a breath. "Nay." She took his hands, looking down at his strong, capable, magical fingers. "Not to him."

In a rush, Paxton lifted her off her feet, making her laugh as he buried his face into her neck and spun her.

"Deep seas!" he said. The vivacity in his own laughter was the most joyous sound she'd ever heard. They were free. Free of their enemies. Free of promised sacrifices. Free to be together. And though life was certain to bring obstacles anew each day, they would face them together.

She wrapped her arms tightly about his neck and murmured in his ear. "You're my prince, Pax. My only prince."

Epilogue

Aerity stepped out of the grand castle doors as they swung wide, and into the mild warmth of a spring breeze. Buds of white and pink shone from trees against the vivid blue sky. Tulips of varying bright colors lined the pathway, slightly overshadowed by soldiers at attention in full regalia on each side.

Queen Aerity peered down at her dapper brother, who stood tall and proud at the bottom of the steps. Beside him sat Furball with a giant blue bow tied around his neck—the ribbon in direct, ironic contrast to his brutish size and appearance. The kind beast rose up on his hind legs to watch as she made her way down to Donnie and slipped a satin-gloved hand through his arm. She smiled at the moisture in his hair where he'd apparently tried to tame the curls.

"Thank you for escorting me, Donubhan," she said.

"Thank you for allowing me, sister. My queen."

She looked at the beast who towered over her and smiled. "Good boy."

Together, they took a step forward, and music poured forth. Bagpipes and flutes played a traditional Lochlan wedding march. It sent a thrill of delight and disbelief through Aerity to hear it, knowing it was for her and her love. She'd wanted nothing more than to marry immediately in the winter, but she knew the lands required healing, and the castle needed much work before it could house guests again.

She and Donnie took the cobbled path toward the west commons with Furball bounding along beside them. Young Merity and Caileen giggled and ran ahead through the rows of soldiers, throwing tulip petals and lavender flowers high into the air. A procession of guards marched closely behind them.

As they turned the corner, cheers rang out from the thousands of people allowed into the royal lands to celebrate with them that day, even more than had come to her coronation in the winter. The people appeared well and happy. It had brought her great joy that week to receive word that nearly double the number of children had been born throughout the lands late winter and early spring as had been born the year before. In a kingdom whose population had been drastically declining, that was wonderful news of burgeoning prosperity.

They came to the gates, covered in twining vines of flowers, and the guards swung them open. A trail of flowers made a path forward. Aerity couldn't help but beam an uncontrollable smile at the sight of Wyneth and Vixie standing on one side of a vine-covered archway, with Harrison and Tiern on the other. And straight ahead . . . her feet faltered at the handsome sight of Paxton in a dress tunic and pressed trousers, his hair carefully tapered by a leather strap at the back of his neck. A slow grin came to his face.

Donnie gave her a gentle tug forward again. Her eyes moved to the sides, where familiar faces stared back apprais-ingly: King and Queen Vikani of Ascomanni, King and Queen Cliftonia of Toresta with their two sons, and King and Queen Zandbur of Zorfina. Zandora and her two sisters, along with their strapping, tall husbands. Her cousins, uncles, and aunts, with tears in their eyes. Lief sitting with her fam-ily. The Seabolt parents. Everyone dressed in their finest. All to celebrate this moment that Aerity never believed would come. But those trials made this moment all the sweeter.

To Lief Alvi's apparent bemused chagrin, Furball plopped himself right at his feet, laying with his massive head on his paws. Lief stared at the creature's ridiculous bow and, with a chuckle, gave Furball a scratch on top of his head.

The only kingdom not represented was Kalor, but they were busy trying to reestablish their monarch. King Kalieno's only living heir, a second cousin, had come out of hiding to claim his rightful place on the throne, and Lochlanach was keeping a close eye on their proceedings. But for now, Queen Aerity wanted nothing more than to put all politics from her mind.

When Aerity and Donnie came to a stop in front of Pax-ton, her brother gently brought her hand up and placed it in Pax's waiting palm. A dizzying sensation swept through her as she looked into her betrothed's deep, dark eyes. Aer-ity kissed Donubhan's cheek and he stepped aside. Aerity and Paxton faced the priest of the sea. Her hand shook inside of his, and he twined his fingers with hers, holding tight.

"Paxton Seabolt, hunter and warrior, do you give your undying allegiance, love, and loyalty to your queen, and would-be wife, Aerity Lochson?"

Aerity stood still. In a Lochlan wedding, the vow question was posed, and the couple was open to respond from the heart.

"Aye. I give my queen my allegiance, my love, my loyalty, my name if she will have it, and more." He turned his head from the priest to her, searching her face and penetrating her eyes. "I give you all that I have, Aerity, which is not much. So I offer everything I am. My life. My actions. My adoration and support. It is all for you. For our family. Our people."

Her heart squeezed, air fluttering into her lungs. They turned to face forward again, and Aerity caught Vix and Wyn wiping their eyes. She couldn't look at them for fear she'd cry as well. Her heart already felt overwhelmed.

"And do you, Aerity Lochson, queen of all this land, give your undying allegiance, love, and loyalty to this man, Paxton Seabolt?"

"Aye, good father, I do." She wet her lips and turned to Pax. "My love, I give you my honor and respect." She took a deep breath and let it out slowly. "I give you my heart, which I know you willingly share with our kingdom, and I thank you for that. Seas willing, I will give you children, and our family will grow." *Oh, seas.* Paxton swallowed, his eyes filling with moisture as she spoke. "I give you forever."

They held tight to each other's hands, and they both smiled. Aerity was first to let out a laugh of joy, and then Paxton. He released one of her hands and turned, reaching out to touch the green vine covering the archway. Aerity watched in amazement as a tiny, tight bud raised its head, grew, and blossomed wide into a fragrant fuchsia flower. As he held the vine and concentrated, a string of buds grew and bloomed, one after another. He moved his hand to another vine and did the same, this time bringing to life dark purple blossoms, then lavender and yellow. The crowd gasped in awe and cheered as the entire archway filled to bursting with bright color in minutes. A glorious representation of his power.

"It's stunning," she whispered.

"It doesn't hold a flame to you," he whispered back, taking both her hands again.

Not everyone in the kingdom had embraced the new Lashed laws, and many were unhappy about their queen taking a magical prince consort. But progress was a layered process. Aerity had faith that, in time, equality would bloom into prosperity for both Lashed and Unlashed.

Paxton and Aerity moved in closer as the priest spoke.

"Paxton Seabolt, I pronounce you prince consort of Lochlanach and husband of Queen Aerity Lochson, who furthermore shall be called Queen Aerity Seabolt. May the seas bless your union, and this kingdom, all of your many days."

"Here, here!" shouted the crowd in unison. Flowers flew high into the air, sailing down on the breeze, covering the grounds and drifting onto people's heads.

Without waiting to be told, Paxton released her hands and took her face in his palms, placing a kiss upon her waiting lips. She went up on her toes, savoring every grain of that blissful touch. A warm wind swept through the commons, bringing scents of the sea and new life. A new start for all.

Acknowledgments

I must begin by thanking my two primary readers and fellow authors, Kelley Vitollo/Nyrae Dawn and Jamie Shaw. Your feedback and enthusiasm have been vital to this process, and I adore you both to the seas!

Elizabeth May, Kyla Linde, Victoria Scott, Damaris Cardinali, and Cora Carmack, your kind words about this story world meant more to me than coffee, and coffee is everything. (Also, Tori, you're awesome for humoring my drive-by emails all these years.)

To my editor, Alyson Day, just . . . thank you. It seems so small, and I would sing it to you if I could, and dance (though my daughter urges me otherwise). It's been a wonderful journey, hasn't it? Thanks for riding with me over every bump and into every valley.

To my copy editors, Jon and Martha, you are geniuses. Rachel Abrams, Tessa Meischeid, Abbe Goldberg, Stephanie Hoover, Julie Yeater, and all my staff at HarperTeen, I curtsy to you in humble gratitude.

Major love to my dear, dear friend Ann Kulakowski, who was my word-count cheerleader, even though she had a million other important things to take care of—she checked in with me every single day to make sure I was on the ball. I have the best friends a girl could ask for. From my high school DG to my FOFs and writing friends, I am so lucky.

Hugs and kisses to Nathan, Autumn, and Cayden, my joys.

And to my readers (this is the part where I get choked up) . . . what do I even say? Every author thinks their readers are the best, and it's because that's how you guys make us feel. I am living my dream because of you. You allow me to work in my pajamas and daydream for a career. You spend your hard-earned money on my words, and take time to write me with kindness. I LOVE YOU. Jeez, thanks a lot for making me cry, guys! *sniffles* Till our next grand adventure . . .

My inspirational quote for this book: "May there be peace within your walls and security within your citadels" (Psalm 122:7).